BURNED

BLACK CIPHER FILES #3

LISA HUGHEY

SALTY KISSES PRESS LLC

October 2014

Lisa Hughey

ISBN: 978-0-9903793-3-1

Print ISBN: 978-1-950359-09-7

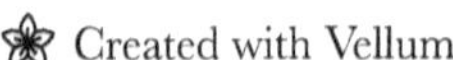 Created with Vellum

To geeks everywhere. This one's for you.

ps. While this is the conclusion of the Black Cipher Files trilogy, there are a few characters who really need their happy ever afters, so you'll see Barb and Kat again sometime in the future.

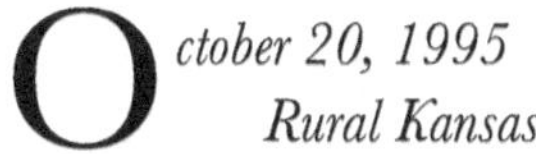

October 20, 1995
Rural Kansas

HE WAS YELLING. Again.

I stared out the window from the attic of our old farmhouse and tried to block out the shouting. A full, bright orange moon hung low in the dark blue night, lighting up the sky like it was daytime. Rain, rain, and more rain, that's all we had lately. 'Cept tonight was clear.

Squeezing my eyes shut, I squished up my face and wished on the moon.

Tomorrow was my birthday. I was going to be seven whole years old and I wanted a pair of roller blades so bad. With Grammy and Grampy coming, I might just get them. They were coming 'specially to celebrate my birthday. And he was angry.

I hid in the curtain of my long hair, the color of midnight Grampy always said, as if I could disappear behind the strands and *he* couldn't see me. I clutched my

Lunette doll from the Big Comfy Couch to my chest, snuffling the soft strands of her hair along my cheek, comforted by the familiar smells from before, when daddy was alive. Before he moved in.

Boom-boom, boom-boom.

My heart thumped, ringing in my ears, drowning out the sound of Mama pleading, sobbing.

"Claire is too old for dolls," he shouted. "We need to get rid of her." But he wasn't looking at Lunette when he said that, he was glaring at me with his angry face.

But Mama defended me, letting me hold on to the only toy left from Daddy.

She was paying for it now.

The screen door slapped shut and he pounded down the wooden stairs and stomped toward the barn. His hands were clenched tight and his shoulders shook. The leaves rattled in the trees and swirled in a mini-whirlwind through the yard.

The rumble of Grammy and Grampy's shiny new car, a Caddie-lack, struck my ears at the same time the moonlight glinted off the silver bumper as they ambled up the drive and alongside the raging creek.

Relief swept through me. I loved my Grammy and Grampy. When they visited, everything was okay.

I felt loved and protected and safe.

A crack of thunder shook the house, except...the sky was clear. A movement from the door of the barn drew my gaze. The long barrel of my stepfather's rifle, the one he used for shooing foxes when they came 'round the chicken coop, disappeared into the open doorway.

I saw the tire pop. Heard a loud screech. The car rolled like a somersault over and over until it disappeared over the edge of the road and into the creek.

Boom. Upside down, the car bounced and bobbed. The water in the creek roared. Their car rushed away from me, away from us. He stepped into the shadow of the doorway. I watched him turn, and I could feel him staring at the attic window. Right where I was sitting. He lifted the rifle barrel toward the window and pointed it straight at me. Then he shook his head sharply, and pivoted toward the creek.

I could hear myself screaming, throat raw, hurting as I ran down the stairs. Wanting only the comfort of Grammy's arms.

I ran into the kitchen, and saw the stark terror on Mama's face, the horror. Suddenly another boom sounded.

"He did it. He did it," I screamed, unable to say anything else, as I threw myself at Mama.

"Hush." Mama clamped a hand over my mouth so tight. It hurt.

Mama never hurt me. Not like him.

With her other hand, she grabbed our coats off the hook in the mud room. "You've got to hush."

The car had gotten trapped on a tree root, bright yellow flames licked at the sky. Fire. How could the car be on fire in the water?

We watched from the window. Tears ran silently down Mama's face, her eyes puffy, her nose running. He went over to the burning wreckage and looked down, still holding the rifle. Then, Mama tugged me toward the back door, toward the garage and our only car.

Mama pushed the car out of the garage, and said a quick prayer of thanks for being on top of the hill. She hopped in the driver's seat, and let the car coast down the hill.

His shout echoed furiously when he discovered we were

leaving. Mama twisted the key and the car started with a cough.

"He's coming," I whispered, clutching Lunette tightly.

He sprinted toward the car. "I won't let you go," he screamed. "You can't escape. I will never let you go."

Mama jammed her foot down and the car leapt forward. "Buckle up, baby."

And we ran.

CHAPTER 1

O*ctober 20*
2:30 am
Cambria, California

Active Measures (ak-tiv mehz-ers) n. Political warfare conducted to influence the course of events.

Zeke Hawthorne paddled out into angry waves of the Pacific Ocean, staring morosely at the black froth and the opaque, shiny rippled surface. He let the swells and wake rock him.

Five thirty in the morning East Coast time and he'd been awake almost twenty-four hours. By all rights he should be sound asleep. But he couldn't settle.

He'd been in California for all of twelve hours. And his thoughts were dominated by the mess he'd left behind in D.C.

A red badge.

He should be getting ready for the office right now, Crypto City, the National Security Agency's ultra-secure complex in Maryland. He should be thinking about his day, mentally arranging his files and getting ready to analyze data, maybe playing with bumping up the security on his encryption program, searching for patterns, searching for a traitor.

Except, even if he were there instead of in California, he couldn't actually go anywhere in the office except the commissary, cafeteria, and the gym.

He'd been under watch after he confessed that he'd been kidnapped and lost a period of time. He'd been told to keep clean and stay out of trouble while they investigated the circumstances and the intelligence fallout from his kidnapping.

But instead of staying out of trouble, he had helped one of the few friends he had. And Zeke had placed himself clearly in the sphere of one of the most wanted people in the United States. Even if he hadn't known it at the time.

Staci Grant was practically public enemy number one with her name and face being splashed all over the news a few days ago. Instead of staying squeaky clean while they investigated his background and recent movements, he'd had contact with her. Dammit. To remove himself from any more possible infractions and rule breaking, he'd hopped a plane for California because of a half-assed request to come watch over some hippy-dippy granola girl who, if she did have any problems, he wouldn't be able to save anyway.

Nice. He was throwing his own personal pity party.

With that totally depressing thought, the greasy In-N-Out burger and animal fries he'd inhaled from San Luis up to Cambria congealed in his stomach. A hot ball of emotion nearly choked him as he stared at the empty beach, ringed by a strand of eucalyptus trees and highlighted by the moon rippling over the black waves of the ocean.

The beach was closed.

In theory.

But he'd snuck onto enough beaches as a surly teenager that the skill had come right back. So here he was paddling through the angry surf with a board borrowed from the motel he was shacking up in. Surfing at night was crazy.

Surfing at night on a deserted beach with no swim buddy or spotter was downright insane.

That was him. One step over the cray-cray line.

He watched, holding back, analyzing the wave pattern, calculating the surge and swell of the ocean as he waited impatiently for the perfect wave. The ripples aligned. Further out the swells grew larger and larger, preparing for their journey to shore.

He positioned the board, aiming for the beach, and eyed the waves smashing against the sand. Seagulls squawked from above. By their concentrated dipping and whirling, he figured they'd found a late night snack.

The frigid cold of the water seared him, making him acknowledge the stupidity of not wearing a wetsuit. He knew better. He'd grown up on the West Coast. Already his feet and legs were numb from the glacial, hypothermia-inducing water.

He tried to concentrate on the waves instead of the sick worry about his situation.

He'd been red-badged.

Unlike Stephen Crane's Red Badge of Courage, a red badge at the National Security Agency meant disgrace. Shut out from accessing any critical information until they could determine if national security had been breached.

Red-badged. The kiss of death for an NSA employee.

Restricted access and a giant red rectangle hanging around your neck like a big fat scarlet A, so that everyone in the complex knew...and stared...and whispered behind their doors, in the bathrooms, in the gym.

Had he been talking to a person of dubious background? Had he had internet contact with a questionable source? What had he done to get his clearance yanked? And would he ever get it back?

How the hell had he come to this?

The background check on his security breach could take weeks and he was already going crazy with the inactivity. Not to mention, it was always there at the back of his mind, hovering...what if he never got his clearance back?

What if the chemicals he'd been injected with, a DNA-altering drug and its antidote, had messed him up in some definable way and his career at the NSA was over?

He loved his job. Loved the importance of it, the true value of it. Sure, maybe he had started under a cloud, but once he'd been there, the excitement, the true thrill of working for the NSA had seduced him.

And then when his career was threatened, he'd panicked, not wanting to admit to anyone that he'd been compromised. He had just never really thought beyond his own simple desires.

For a genius, sometimes he could be pretty damn stupid.

He'd arrogantly assumed that because he had an immunity to Sodium Pentothal that his kidnappers wouldn't have been able to extract any information from him.

The evidence proved otherwise.

According to the information the NSA had now, he had given away his encryption program. He'd given classified, extremely sensitive information to radicals. And he didn't remember doing it.

Zeke let the power of the water, the surging, swelling, sheer force of the tide, grab hold of the board.

The bitch was angry tonight. The mood of the ocean was a complete mirror of his own. As if all the turbulence and turmoil swirling inside him manifested in the ferocious magnetic pull of the current, determined to drag him under, to make him pay for his foolishness, for his mistakes, for his arrogance.

The thunderous force built below him, alongside him, as the seawater gathered might and speed. With a quick jump, his feet found purchase on the board, and he crouched, arms out, knees bent, balance uneasy.

The fine mist of frigid water on his face, the salty brine in his nose, the muted roar of the wave as it started to crest all thundered through him. His heart pumped, triumph hurtling through his veins, as he mastered the physics of beating nature.

He kept his balance on the board, the fiberglass solid beneath his feet, the power of the water challenging his muscles, he rode the freaking cold water like a penguin on an iceberg.

The gulls still dipped and squawked, seeming to move closer to the beach, as if following something. One came particularly close to his head, and instinctively he ducked.

Dumb.

His Grandpop would have smacked him upside the head for that one.

As he straightened his body, lifted his head up, he saw a silhouette on the beach. A woman, her face in shadow, her body limned by moonlight, she stood sentinel.

But the sudden movement had thrown off his balance, and his arms tipped, one up, one down to maintain his position on the board. The adjustment was too late.

His left hand swooped up, connected with the wave over his head, sucking him into the swell of water. His feet lost purchase on the board, and he began a tumbling free fall into the drag of the water. He tucked his body, and covered his head, hoping to minimize the bruises and beating he would take from wiping out.

He couldn't see anything, lost in the froth and dark black water, until suddenly the wave dropped him with a thump.

Pain, sharp and brutal, arrowed through his head.

And then...nothing.

CHAPTER 2

October 20
2:40 am
Cambria, California

I WANDERED along the sandy beach, careful to stay far away from the angry waves punishing the shore. A trail of seagulls followed me, diving and fighting over the crusts of bread I tossed.

The full moon hung high in the clear night sky, provoking the memory of another full moon as I tried not to recall the nightmare from thirteen years ago.

When life had changed irrevocably.

I wasn't even sure why I was here. The anniversary of my grandparents' murder loomed ever present in my mind.

The deliverer, my stepfather, was a demon in my memories, and water the method that killed them. And yet, like the temptation of a siren, the pull of the ocean beckoned to me. A terrible, terrifying lure.

Steely fog rolled in, misting my face and soaking my

cream cable knit sweater. The lace hem of my brown skirt, damp from the sand, brushed at my ankles, while I curled my toes into the cold, wet sand and stared out at my lifetime nemesis.

The ocean moved like a slithering serpent, curling toward me then drawing away, taunting, scaring me with allure. The frigid chill of the receding tide was a promise or a curse or a portent—I was never sure which.

Would I ever be able to break the fear?

A deep unease spread through me and involuntarily I retreated from the water still some sixty feet away. The sense of impending doom had been growing for the last few days. A low frequency of turmoil that disturbed me at some hidden level and disrupted the inherent calm I had fought diligently for, upsetting the balance I struggled to maintain.

And I didn't know why.

Nothing had changed. Mama and I had been settled in Cambria for nine years without any sign of discovery, without any hint of danger. Yet suddenly I felt as if danger was as close as the surf on the shore. I had safeguards in place, electronic alarms if my stepfather ever traced Mama, and human warning systems, the good old-fashioned gossip alerts from living in a small beach community. If any stranger in town asked about either of us, I would know by the time they left the shop where they made the inquiry.

A towel lay in the sand near the receding waves. The tide was moving out. Some tourist had left their belongings behind again. Except...the towel was dry. If the tide had come and gone, the towel should be soaking wet. A pile of clothing, t-shirt, sweatshirt, and running shoes lay discarded on the chilly sand. Next to the towel was a brick of wax. Surfboard wax.

Surely no one was crazy enough to surf on a cold Fall

night like tonight?

That couldn't be it. Must be teenagers, a secret tryst perhaps. A vagrant with no other place to sleep. Maybe. Except where were they?

I searched the beach cautiously. I had taken enough self-defense classes that unless I was faced with a gun or my worst nightmare, water, I was confident I could defend myself.

But I didn't see anyone.

As insane as it seemed, I searched the waves. The moonlight glimmered on the black water, reflecting off the ripples that were nearly blinding in their brightness against the pitch of the sky.

And there I saw him, like an ancient Hawaiian God, balanced on the board, his body bathed with moonlight, a spectacular muscular display of man and nature as the wave rolled in and the water curled over his head.

My heart pounded furiously. It pushed, *boom-boom, boom-boom*, against my breastbone as I watched him battle the swell of the wave. My blood pulsed so hard I could feel the strength of it in my throat. My breath caught, terrified and fascinated, until disaster struck, and he faltered.

I saw the precise moment when his balance failed, watched with horror as the surf battered and rolled his body, until the water dumped him on his head like a giant dropping my old, beloved Lunette to the earth.

"Oh no, no, no," I whispered into the heavy night air.

I waited for him to get up.

I would watch, make sure he was safe, and then I would flee.

The tide pulled him back out into the scruff of broken shells and kelp.

And he didn't move.

The tide rolled back in, sweeping the body closer into shore.

And he didn't move.

"Get up, get up." The thunderous beat of my heart echoed in my ears, *thump-thump thump-thump*. I couldn't move, couldn't hear anything else but my own terror as I waited.

The gulls swooped closer to him.

I imagined they were squawking to each other but nothing penetrated the terrified, panicked rush of my blood.

Completely still, he lay in the shallow bit of water, on his back thankfully, so he wasn't drowning as I watched.

Not again.

I couldn't watch someone die again.

Not this day for Goddess's sake. The universe couldn't be that cruel, could it?

The tide pulled his body out toward the waves. Water shush-shushed softly as it lapped at the shoreline and then rode back out to sea.

And still he didn't move.

"Are you okay?" I shouted, hoping the noise would bring him to consciousness. Hoping he would pop up from his prone position and laugh crazily as I'd seen surfers do, and say something nuts like, "man what a rush," and then go back out again.

But nothing.

I could see his chest rise and fall slowly, so he was breathing. But his body would shimmy on the inhale as if the cold was already seeping into his bones and muscles.

"Hey dude!" I tried again.

Just in case he was lying there catching his breath after that magnificent wipeout.

But he didn't give any sign of consciousness.

A particularly strong wave rushed in, turned his body

sideways, and pushed him further up on shore. As the next swell crested I knew that if he didn't get up soon he would end up swept out to sea.

I was going to have to go get him.

Longingly, I looked back toward the parking lot.

The *empty* parking lot. There wasn't time to go get help.

My cell was in my pocket and I pulled it out but I only had five percent of my battery left and no service. Half the time the stupid thing didn't work out here. I was the only rescue in town. Goddess help him.

I edged closer to the shoreline and his body.

The moonlight rippled on the water making the ocean appear as if the giant black hole would swallow me up. My breath seized in my chest.

I tried to breathe in, but only tiny sips of air made it past my constricted lungs.

"Huh, huh, huh," my breath wheezed. No, no, no. The chant pounded in my head, as my breath grew shorter and shorter, my vision went whiter and whiter.

At this rate, I would pass out and he would die. I could not let that happen.

I stopped. Shut my eyes. Put my hands together in prayer position, mouth closed, I breathed in slowly through my nose, imagining myself on a magnificent, spiritual mountaintop and ignoring the susurrous of the water against the sand.

Slowly, slowly I let the breath out, chanting softly, "You can do this, you can do this."

I took one step for every word, controlling my breath, reassured by the fact that I had a paper bag tucked in my skirt pocket if I began to truly hyperventilate.

He lay maybe ten feet away.

A smaller wave rolled in, coming perilously close to my

toes. I danced backward, even as my feet sunk further into the saturated sand.

"Wake up," I yelled.

I concentrated on him instead of the steadily encroaching water. I had to get to him now before another large swell dragged him back out to sea.

He didn't seem to be regaining consciousness.

I glanced up, supplicant to the moon, my namesake, the one I hadn't been able to acknowledge in thirteen long years.

And I begged.

"Please let me do this. Please."

With a deep breath, I watched and waited until the water was as far away as possible and then I ran, pleading the entire way. "Please, please."

I squatted down and hooked my hands under his armpits, scooping until his shoulders were in the crook of my elbows. Then I inhaled and yanked.

He barely moved.

"Come on, you big, you big...lug."

I yanked again.

Panicked, I looked up. The water was coming.

I watched mesmerized, terrified, while my heart pounded, my blood thickened and I wondered if this was how it would end.

Here and now.

Sucked in by the beast. Consumed by its power. Destroyed by the terror.

I refused to let my fear win.

As soon as the water hit his body, I used the motion of the tide as it rolled in to pull him further inland.

As the water rushed back out, I held on with a death grip, my fingers cramped against the bare skin of his shoulders. The sea sucked at his feet, trying to take him from me.

I waited, unable to close my eyes, gaze locked on the water rolling back in. As soon as it hit I had to pull him backwards again.

A large wave broke near the shore. And I knew this was the chance I needed. I couldn't think about the water rushing toward me, I had to concentrate on the physics, using the force of the water to pull him backwards, and not think about the black death coming for us, hovering, greedily waiting to suck us both out to sea.

The wave rushed toward me and lifted his body up. I scrambled backward, with great crab-like steps, his body heavy against mine, his head lolled against my breast.

That last little push before the wave retreated toppled me over and I fell into the cold wet sand. The damp soaked through my skirt and the bottom of my sweater. I held onto him, my arms curled around his muscled shoulders, my heels dug into the saturated sand as the tide tried to take us both back out into the abyss.

My blood thundered in my ears.

I panted with the effort. He was heavy.

His body lay limply between my thighs, his muscled legs stretched out along the sand, kelp wrapped around one ankle, arms flopped to the outside of my thighs, effectively trapping me on the ground.

Shivering, I watched another wave roll toward us, praying this one wouldn't breach our spot. My arms ached with the strain of holding him up and keeping him from being pulled out to sea. To death. To...peace. I didn't know if I had anything left.

The water sluiced onto the shore creeping inexorably closer.

I clenched him tightly, barely registering the slick feel of his cold skin, the sleek bulk of his muscles.

In the end, the wave didn't even reach his toes.

We were safe.

For a single moment I rested my cheek against the top of his head. His wet corkscrew curls were damp against my skin, soaking through my sweater and bra, chilling me with salty water.

His body shook with the force of his involuntary shivers.

I had to get him awake and warm. Somehow.

There was no way I would ever be able to get him up to my car on my own.

"Wake up, please," I whispered. "Please, please."

Warm tears rolled down my face as reaction set in. Tremors of relief shimmied through me. I had braved the monster and survived.

His dead weight held me against the sand and I couldn't move. I flopped back on the towel, slid my legs out straight, arms out at my sides, palms up and his head dropped into the concave hollow of my stomach. I stared up at the moonlight, the bright silver rays mocking me as I tried to find some measure of calm.

What now?

I needed to check for injuries. A thousand thoughts flitted through my mind but only one took root, the interesting, amazing weight of him on top of me. Sort of.

The inferno of heat from his torso burned through my clothes warming my thighs, making me feel things I hadn't felt...ever.

Suddenly, he exploded into motion, flipping over, straddling me, and pinning my arms to the ground, his face fierce, his body battle tense and primed for violence.

"What the hell?"

CHAPTER 3

Zeke didn't remember getting here.

He stared down at the woman beneath him. Didn't remember her.

His body met hers at the juncture of her thighs. His groin in exact alignment with hers as she stared up at him wide-eyed.

The slant of the moonlight and the position of his body cast her face in shadow, defining her features in shades and angles, like a scene from the old black and white movies he used to watch with his Grandpop.

Her breath was coming in short, soft pants and drew his gaze from the shadowed planes of her face to her chest. Her sweater was damp, her nipples beaded in the chill night air clearly visible.

Her hair was the color of midnight, woven together in a loose braid as thick as his wrist and resting on the curve of one very fine breast.

Totally inappropriate of him to notice, and dwell on.

They had this *From Here To Eternity* thing going on that was fuzzing his brain and making it difficult to concentrate.

The moonlight bathed her face in a silvery light, her gray eyes shone with some undefined emotion. The crisp scent of cucumber and the ocean rose from her body. She was like his own personal siren, drawing him to her and pulling him from the clutches of the sea.

Yeah, he'd figured out that one. His last memory was of tumbling into the cauldron of the surf.

As he absorbed the impression of her body beneath his and the soft shush of the surf behind them, he wished he was better with women. Wished that the men in his family weren't cursed. Wished that he knew what romantic words to whisper in her ear so they could stay here all night alone in the darkness, moonlight shining down on them and the ocean surrounding them, just man, woman, and nature.

He traced the delicate features of her face with his gaze, her deep shadowed eyes, her slightly upturned nose, and the sheer perfection of her mouth.

Oh, what he could do with her mouth, to her mouth.

His cock had risen with the nature of his thoughts. But unfortunately he had more pressing problems, not to mention he was probably scaring the crap out of her.

His head pounded like a son of a bitch. The last time he felt this badly he'd woken up from being drugged and had lost about five hours of his life. Then lost everything.

Suspicion kicked in. What the fuck?

Then his brain revved back into gear. "Hanlon's razor," he murmured under his breath. Never attribute to malice that which can be adequately explained by stupidity.

Namely his.

No one knew he was going to be here, on this beach, surfing in the dark. Not even him until about thirty minutes ago.

He thought he noticed an instant of surprise before her

perfectly arched brows crinkled into her forehead. The surf rolled and broke behind him. He could hear the water approaching when she exploded into action.

"Get off me." She panted, and dug her heels into the sand, trying to buck him off.

"Yeah, sorry. I won't hurt you." He let go of her wrists.

"It's coming."

Zeke twisted around looking for the threat, needing no confirmation that her terror was real. "What's coming?"

"The...the...the...."

Her feet scrabbled against the sand.

He looked around again and didn't see any threat. But her motion underneath him had re-awakened his body. *Hell-o.* A wave broke and headed toward them.

"Wa-ter."

He realized then she was not just wet but soaked and trapped beneath him. Great...he'd been living out his teen fantasies while the girl froze to death. That's why the men in his family were cursed.

"Yeah." He tried to get up but she wiggled and squirmed so much that every time he attempted to shift off her, she bucked him in a different direction.

"Get off. It's coming."

"Hold still, dammit."

The water curled against their toes and she shrieked.

"Jesus." Zeke rose to his knees as she scrabbled out from under him. "Are you nuts?"

She rolled backwards, kneeing him in the balls and then she jumped to her feet.

"Who's the one who went surfing at night, genius?" she sneered.

She had a point.

Zeke rubbed at the bump on the back of his head.

While he might agree in theory, he didn't take kindly to being yelled at.

"Look...." He glanced up at her from his spot on his knees.

The moon picked that moment to shift higher in the pitch black sky, shining down upon her face, bathing her features in starlight, shimmering off the radiance of her skin. Something about her looked familiar.

Shit.

Of all the beaches in all the towns, why'd she have to walk onto this one? Yeah, he was stealing from *Casablanca*.

No one in this Nowheresville, California town should look familiar to him. Except her.

The boondoggle. The fool's errand to keep him busy. The sole reason he was here.

Terrific. He'd been rescued by his surveillance subject.

CHAPTER 4

The guy rubbed his hands over his face. I tried, really tried, not to notice that his biceps bulged and flexed with each movement of his hands.

What the heck was wrong with me?

I never noticed stuff like that. Maybe it was all the years alone with my mother, maybe it was the sheer absence of men in my life, but physical features weren't something I usually fixated on. Muscles, testosterone didn't even register on my personal Richter scale. Yet here I was ogling this guy.

This stranger.

I had a natural wariness of people, thanks to my stepfather, thanks to hiding for the last thirteen years. An innate sense of caution that was difficult to overcome. For years, every stranger held potential danger. Trust was a difficult commodity to come by.

Weirdly enough, I didn't feel threatened at all.

Maybe because *I'd* saved *him*.

And maybe I was completely delusional. Because it seemed as if when he'd knelt at my feet, his head tilted while he stared at me, there'd been a spark of recognition.

A trigger, a random thought, an "oh, there you are."

Then the spark flew away on a gust of wind, and he looked at me with total disgust.

Which was not a response I was accustomed to either.

People tended to look on me with amusement, with a sort of veiled sense of superiority. They thought because my life revolved around moon cycles and essential oils that I was somehow less intelligent.

I let them think that because it enhanced the illusion my mother and I had succeeded in creating. So different from the real me that even if the monster somehow heard of me, he would dismiss the information as irrelevant.

Claire had been a math prodigy, had already been recruited by Caltech as a seven-year-old.

Sunshine Smith concocted herbal potions and aromatherapy remedies for tourists.

The odds of anyone connecting the two very different people were astronomical. Sunshine had a new birthday and even though every year my mother made a big show of celebrating on the new day, in my heart, I always had my own bittersweet private celebration to mark another year's passing and to remember my grandparents. To never forget them. To never forget him.

And to remind myself that I would never be a victim again.

We'd run from my stepfather, but it hadn't ended there. He'd found us, time and again. But finally after three different states, and three different identities, we'd discovered how to disappear. And for the last nine years our cover had held.

Our life had certain restrictions, but at least we were alive. Mama was safe. And I...I was, surviving.

I was always restless around the anniversary of my

grandparents' murder and our desperate flight, but this year my discontent, my melancholy was worse than ever.

I was pretty sure I knew what was wrong. I was young. I wanted to be out exploring the world, not cloistered in this little town far away from any action. I'd had a taste by dropping in at the local community college and auditing a few classes at Cal Poly. I couldn't outright enroll there on the off chance that he was checking college admissions.

But an audited class in physics or mathematics or biology here and there was fine. I'd almost blown it when I'd challenged a professor on the newer fifth law of thermodynamics.

"Are you okay?" He stumbled to his feet awkwardly, took one hesitant step forward before grimacing. Bet his balls ached. It was small of me, but seeing his expression of total disgust when he looked at me had hurt.

"F-f-fine." My teeth clattered as the cold set in. My gaze shifted to the waves behind him and he finally got that something about the water disturbed me.

"Thanks for...rescuing me." His expression had morphed to one of uncertainty.

My shoulders shook with the force of my shivers, rocking me as I edged back, away from the black water. I needed to bolt.

My sense of panic had receded into slightly frantic distress, but a low level buzz of discomfort still zipped through my system. The stress competed with a sense of loss that had nothing to do with my inability to attend college and stretch my brain, and more to do with an aching unrelenting emptiness in my arms now that he was out of them. How could I miss something I'd only had for the briefest of moments?

I wanted his attention off me. I was pretty sure he was

harmless but what if I was wrong? The rush of the surf behind him gave me the distraction I needed and I gestured with a shaking hand. "Your board...."

"Not mine. Borrowed." As if he didn't want me to think the slick surface with a nearly naked hula girl sporting large breasts on the fiberglass bottom was his.

"....is floating away."

He looked at me, then turned to sight the board, his body tense, as if he were trapped between two opposing forces.

"Shit." He ran toward the water, and made a grab for the borrowed board. He called over his shoulder, "Don't leave."

ZEKE REALIZED he probably looked like a total idiot racing toward the surf. Way to impress her. Except, he shouldn't be trying to impress her, he was supposed to be surveilling her. Watching out for her. Not impressing her. Not interacting with her. Just keeping an eye on her.

The wash of surf against his legs was frigid, wicked cold. "What the hell was I thinking?"

After a few aborted attempts to capture the wax-slick board, Zeke finally got ahold of the lead and pulled it onto the beach.

He dragged the board to his stuff, but she was gone.

Zeke stared at the wet hotel towel. She'd been afraid of the water. Seen a potential threat in the harmless little wave that had teased the cotton edge.

Nothing in the file on Sunshine Smith about thalassophobia...even though she clearly had a massive fear of the ocean. But the file had been pretty damn light. Just a name, address, and a grainy picture that captured the arrangement of her features but not her essence.

He stood staring dumbly after her as she scurried along the shadowed path to the parking lot, and he wished things were different. Wished he wasn't under suspicion of supplying encryption programs to wackos, wished he was here on vacation—of course what dumbass goes surfing in the middle of the night?—instead of secretly tasked with watching over her. Wished that he had the normal experiences of a normal twenty something guy and could talk to a woman he found attractive.

His first response to her departure was a frantic, "No!" He didn't want her to leave. He wanted another minute, or five, in her presence while he was conscious rather than un.

Shit. He should be happy she hustled off the beach since he wasn't supposed to have contact with her. Instead he had feeling of loss so profound it shook him to his core.

Zeke tugged his sweatshirt over his head, slung the towel around his neck, hefted the board under one arm, and trudged toward his rental SUV.

And suppressed the urge to run after her.

ctober 20
8:00 am
Seattle, Washington

OLIVER KRYCHEF WAITED in the customs and immigration line at SeaTac, in the state of Washington. Snippets of different languages, Russian, French, Italian, Cantonese, Vietnamese, eddied around him as passengers weary from transpacific flights waited to be welcomed into the United States.

This was the most dangerous leg of his return to the U.S.

He inhaled slowly, carefully, drawing in the scents and sounds of international travel. The aromas of green tea, burnt coffee, cigar smoke, heavy pungent odor of curry, and even possibly borscht, all masked by generous spritzes of floral perfume and stale body odor.

Officially he was entering from Vancouver.

He'd packed very carefully for this mission, making sure

that nothing in his bag would draw the attention of the U.S. customs agents. Clothing, some toiletries, all Canadian of course, and a bottle of duty free Lucky Lager.

In truth, failing his superiors was far more dangerous than entering the United States. This gauntlet might stop him from entering the country if his paperwork and fake passport didn't stand up to the new homeland security protocols. Which would be a disaster. His credentials should be above reproach since his superiors were as invested in him achieving his objective as he was.

Oliver Krychef was on the U.S. State Department's watch list. He'd been kicked out of the country a little over a year ago and he was still angry about it. Fortunately his forged passport identified him as Lars Andersen, and he'd altered his appearance slightly. A little nose job and padding in his cheeks and chin. This particular airport didn't have advanced facial recognition technology according to the man who facilitated his entry back into the country.

But if his contact was wrong, Oliver was *trakhal*.

Blood pumped faster through his veins, and he could literally feel his blood pressure rising with the sheer fury he felt toward that bitch. She had ruined his career. Both here in the U.S. and in his native Russia. His superiors were not happy with him. And when they were not happy, bad things happened.

Ten years of work destroyed because she couldn't handle it when she found out that he'd injected their daughter with the DNA-altering drug. Their child, Liliya, was incredibly intelligent. Of course, that was inevitable with their combined IQ. The formula had been designed to work on confidence centers, enhancing traits and making the individual stronger. He'd only thought to both augment his daughter and test the drug. All scientists knew you could not obtain accurate results on yourself so he had bestowed the honor on Liliya.

But Susan clearly wasn't as dedicated to the science as he was. She'd been unbelievably angry, most especially when they discovered the drug had some unfortunate side effects. In addition to enhancing confidence it magnified weaknesses.

He tried to tamp down his fury at her inability to see the benefits of human testing, knowing that the anger would cause his face to burn bright red. Oliver cursed his fair coloring as he approached the customs counter.

He handed over his customs declaration sheet pleased to see that his pale-skinned hand was steady.

"How long will you be staying, Mr. Andersen?"

He wasn't going back to Russia until he had the formula. Until he'd retrieved his work and taken care of Susan Chen. "Two weeks." Maybe even less. If he could find Susan, get the research, and get back to Russia sooner, he would get out of this damned country once and for all.

"What is the purpose of your visit?"

"Just a little pleasure. Las Vegas." Oliver blinked once, his heavy lids dropping over his ice blue eyes, blond lashes brushing the puffy bags under his cheeks, before he stretched his mouth into what he hoped passed for a smile as he contemplated gutting his former lover.

"I'm feeling lucky."

CHAPTER 6

October 20
        8:45 am
Cambria, California

WHAT WAS WRONG WITH ME?

Everything seemed out of place, out of whack, out of sync.

I plowed through rote tasks without really paying attention, my thoughts scattered like the strands of kelp on the sand last night.

When I flipped on the display lights over the gleaming glass bottles of hand-blended oils and scented salt scrubs, the clear light hit the rippled glass and reminded me of the moonlight on the water and the man tumbling through the surf.

I put the opening till money in the cash register, laying out the bills in sequence, and then realized I'd forgotten to count them.

Did it really matter? I shrugged and slid the drawer shut.

I wandered through the store, ostensibly to check for anything that needed to be re-stocked, and my fingertips brushed lightly over the jars and pots. The pleasing fragrance of geranium and lavender emanated from the sample brazier filled with my signature potpourri. The light touch of my fingertips along the shelf reminded me of the smooth feel of the surfer's skin beneath my hands. Reminded me too of the tensile strength in his shoulders and the little shivers of sensation that followed me still. I shook my head, and tried to shake out the tactile memory of his skin, so unbelievably warm despite the frigid water.

Gazing out the front window, I noted the pyramid of Fall candles had shifted, the balance somewhat precarious, probably after those twins were in the store with their mother yesterday.

I wandered to the display and adjusted the base square into a more solid foundation, my actions mechanical as I stared into the street without really seeing anything.

Hanlon's razor, he'd whispered. He couldn't really have referenced the obscure law, could he? Don't assume a situation is motivated by evil if it can easily attributed to stupidity.

What are the odds that he would even know that law? And why would he think he might be the subject of malice?

A particularly loud scrape from upstairs startled me out of my thoughts. Mama was moving around, her tread heavy.

Heavier than usual. I frowned.

Mama had gotten home late from the business association meeting last night. I knew because when I snuck out for the beach she still hadn't come home from the meeting. Of course, our local commerce bureau gatherings were more of a social event than a true business meeting.

They discussed town advertising and promotion ideas, any theft problems they'd been having, and general issues that plagued the local merchants for a few minutes, and then commenced to the more social aspect of their tight knit group.

The monthly meeting was more of a casual get-together at the bar in the middle of town, tucked away between art galleries and clothing boutiques, than a serious meeting. Blue's Bar and Surf Shop had been here practically before the town existed and had managed, in a town that made its living off of tourists, to stay mostly local. Not that there was anything wrong with the tourist bars.

I'd snuck back home last night, more concerned with getting in and past Mama's bedroom without waking her up. Luckily her door had been closed. I knew she was worried about me. She didn't like the fact that I'd been wandering the beach at night, the only time I could go to the ocean and attempt to tame my fears. During the day, the beaches were too full for me to test my dread of the water. And exposing my weakness to anyone was a level of trust I couldn't reach.

I was twenty freaking years old. I should not be afraid of the water.

Mama didn't understand.

I tried hard to keep my restlessness, my recent lack of excitement and joy in my life from her. Guilt was a companion neither of us wanted. We'd made our choices long ago and I would do anything to protect her from that monster.

I turned the sign that hung from an iron scrollwork hook on the front door from Closed to Open.

"Time for business," I called out, infusing a peppiness that I really didn't feel into my voice.

The door leading from the back storage room swung

open with a creak. We really needed to oil the hinges, I thought absently.

"Morning sleepy heh—" I stopped dead. Gulped. "—ad."

Blue Harrison grinned sheepishly at me. "Morning." His deep, gruff voice rumbled from behind his bushy beard, his flannel shirt rumpled and his feet bare.

"Oh, uh, Sunny," Mama stammered. "What are you doing up so early? It's...it's my day to open."

Mama completely disregarded the fact that there was a man with her. A big, unkempt, burly man's man who'd clearly not just come over to fix a squeaky hinge.

I blinked. Blinked again. A *man*.

Blue rubbed a big, masculine hand through his brown, shoulder length strands. "I think she's a little surprised, honey."

Honey? Had he just called my mother *honey*? I swallowed and tried to wrap my brain around the sight in front of me.

The last time I'd seen my mother with a man had been thirteen years ago. To the day. "Mama?"

Mama brushed past Blue to come stand in front of me. Her hands were clasped together in front of her. She was wearing a pink cotton sweater I particularly loved on her. The color gave a delicate blush to her cheeks and a sparkle to her brown eyes.

Or maybe it was the man.

She hunched her shoulders up to her ears, twisting her hands in front of her chest. "I have something to talk to you about."

I snorted. "I'd guess." Involuntarily, I moved my hand to my forehead. My heart began to pound. The lights in the store suddenly seemed inordinately bright.

"Well, I was waiting for the right moment."

Too late. "For what?"

"Blue," she faltered, her eyebrows crinkled into a little frown as she obviously searched for the right words. "Blue and I...."

Blue and I. As if they were a couple. As if they were together. Which could not possibly be correct. It was Mama and me against the world, against the monster.

My head throbbed, a deep pain at the base of my skull made me feel as if I were the one who'd gotten dumped off a surfboard and into the waves.

"It's fine." I patted her shoulder. They'd hooked up. She didn't need to say it out loud. I'd seen enough television to know, to understand what a hook up was. There was no need to embarrass anyone further.

Mama glanced back at Blue, her shoulders slumped helplessly. Then she straightened, lifted her chin. "I don't think you understand."

"Boy, that association meeting must have gotten really crazy, huh?" I smiled and pretended I wasn't completely freaked by the situation. "Blue, next time go easy on the tequila. Mom's a lightweight."

"Sunshine." Blue moved closer to me until they were both practically surrounding me. "This has nothing to do with tequila."

Of course it did. That was the only logical explanation. Although Mama sure didn't look hung over. Her body was strung tight and she radiated tension, but she was practically glowing.

"Sunny," Mama reached out, took my hand in hers, and when I looked at our clasped hands, a ring with a beautiful oval moonstone surrounded by silver filigree on her left hand shone back at me.

"We're getting married."

CHAPTER 7

R outine and discipline were the cornerstones to any
fitness regimen. And Zeke religiously exercised to
keep his body and mind in top shape. Exercise also helped
to keep his OCD from overtaking his conscious thoughts,
physical activity calmed his brain, and helped him
concentrate. Most days he loved it. The problem was, today
he didn't feel like working out.

Zeke finished his crunches and started on his pushups.

One, two, three, he counted to ten, then rested for a beat
of ten. He tried to let his mind wander as he levered up and
down, completing his daily reps, but his thoughts kept
returning to last night.

To the way the moonlight rippled over Sunshine's shiny
black braid just like it rippled over the waves. To the
shadowed fear in her eyes. Not fear of him. Fear of the
water. To the attraction that he thought flashed between
them.

Zeke tugged on his running shoes. Ugh. He'd rather be
swimming but he needed a wet suit—no duh, he'd been
crazy to get in that water last night—and none of the

swim/surf shops were open yet. He'd pick one up later today but for now he'd take a quick jog around town, get the lay of the land, scope out the logistics.

And he was abso-freaking-lutely lying to himself.

He was going to look for a certain midnight-haired sea nymph who had enchanted him. And who he should stay far, far away from.

Even if she was a puzzle. And he loved to solve puzzles.

Patterns existed everywhere, you just needed to find the repeat and suddenly everything would make sense.

He'd lain in bed long after he'd gotten back to the hotel thinking about the mystery of Sunshine Smith. Who goes walking on a beach in the dead of night when they're clearly scared of the water?

Yeah, she'd definitely been afraid. Terrified really.

Details he'd overlooked in the heat of wanting to kiss her clarified when he'd reviewed the night's events. Her skirt had been soaked, her sweater too.

Who went into the surf to rescue a boneheaded idiot when they weren't just afraid, but flat out petrified, of the water?

Yeah, he'd thanked her last night.

But the more he'd gone over every detail of their encounter, the more the reality of what she had done for him sunk in. And the more he wanted, no needed, to seek her out and thank her again.

Zeke tied his old-fashioned room key to his shoelace and headed out. Fog, thick and soupy, shrouded the street, but the reflection was bright and white, not gray. The air was crisp, clean. When the fog burned off, it was going to be an ideal day.

Zeke took off for the only drag in town. Main Street.

He knew Sunshine Smith lived in the town proper above

a store. Running up and down the main thoroughfare looking for a certain woman was about as stupid as searching New York City for one, but it had worked for his friend Jordan, and Cambria was a lot smaller than NYC. So...what the hell.

His hotel was one block off the central road, tucked behind a grove of eucalyptus and adjacent to a total dive bar. He wasn't much of a drinker but something about the place reminded him of his grandfather and he thought maybe later he'd go in and raise a pint in his honor.

His grandfather. Yesterday had been the anniversary of his death. His grandfather's murder, he now knew.

As Zeke took off down the street, it occurred to him that today was the anniversary of Sunshine's grandparents' deaths.

Her situation was a little different. Her grandparents had died in a car accident. Their tire had blown out and their car had rolled into a raging creek and they'd drowned. Based on the fact that it had been labeled an accident and she'd only been a little girl, she probably didn't even remember or register this day in her mind. But she had a right to know that their deaths were not an accident. A right to closure.

Knowing now that his grandfather's death was, in fact, murder helped some, but the man he'd loved was still gone. The man who'd taught him so much was still missing from his life. The loss left an empty ache in his heart.

For years, Zeke had been pissed at his grandfather because he'd thought that he hadn't followed his own basic safety rules for climbing, the meticulous habits that he'd ingrained in Zeke from his first climb. Those OCD tendencies that were obsessive but truly meant to be cautious. When he believed his grandfather had ignored his own rules it had changed how Zeke thought of his Grandpop and he'd been mad at him for dying.

Now that he knew his grandfather's death was not an accident as initially reported, that his Grandpop hadn't been negligent, he mourned all over again for the man who'd taught him how to be a man. And he grieved for the fact that for the past thirteen years he'd been pissed at him as if that were somehow a betrayal of his Grandpop's teachings. He was also pissed at himself for not recognizing that there was no way that his grandfather would have ever gone climbing with unchecked, faulty equipment. Zeke should have realized sooner that something had been wrong.

Thirteen years ago, someone in the NSA had chosen to activate sleepers and eliminate a group of people. The decision may have been analytical but the results were extremely personal for Zeke.

And he was determined to find out why those sleepers had been activated.

There were layers to any decision that the government chose to make. And Zeke knew the overt reasons why those hits had been ordered. But with the sense that the pattern was incomplete, Zeke had begun to unravel all the threads that made up the decision. After he'd been given a DNA-enhancing drug that ramped up his OCD and highlighted those dangling reasons, he'd realized that he couldn't just let those deaths lie.

There was more to the sleepers being activated than just political expediency. Somehow, some way, this entire situation felt very, very personal. Not necessarily personal to Zeke's family but as if there were some very personal motivation for someone to give the information about the potential threat to the U.S. foreign relations and ask the Senate Select Committee on Intelligence to make the decision to activate those sleepers. After all, in theory, the U.S. government didn't assassinate people.

But after the last month, he also knew that wasn't exactly true.

His grandfather had been murdered. Why did someone feel it necessary to eliminate a group of people within twenty hours on roughly the same day? What connection did they all share that caused their deaths? And who was the bastard who had engineered the killings?

He had pieces of information but Zeke was convinced he still didn't have the person responsible for making it all happen.

The actual assassin who murdered his Grandpop was long gone. But Zeke would stake his career, his life on the fact that the person who'd called for the deaths of those people was alive and well and…possibly still maneuvering situations to his or her own benefit.

Rage bubbled inside him. He wanted five minutes alone with whoever had destroyed his childhood.

That was the single most defining moment of his life. His grandfather had been everything. His father had always been cold, disconnected from Zeke. It was no wonder his mother had taken off. So when Grandpop died, Zeke had disappeared into the cyber world. Yeah, in the end it had all worked out, but Grandpop had always been suspicious of the government, and he'd passed that suspicion on to Zeke. So, as Zeke grew and learned, he'd felt the need to poke at the government, that was when he'd begun his hacking in earnest.

Zeke loped down the uneven sidewalk taking note of what was happening in the little town. A French coffee shop, whose patrons spilled out onto the sidewalk, a gas station, and the local market were the only businesses open.

Otherwise the streets were fairly deserted. It was too early for the retail stores to have customers.

Outside a collectibles shop, a guy in his forties swept the sidewalk with a brush broom, another woman in her sixties watered flowers in a cut off wine barrel, and further down the quaint little street, two terriers were tethered to a wrought iron fence surrounding an outdoor sales space with paintings propped on easels.

Everyone he passed had a smile and a wave.

His tension wound tighter. His muscles stiffened up rather than loosened as he settled into a rhythm. This town seemed picture perfect. Almost old-fashioned in its demeanor.

Why that set him on edge, he didn't know.

He slowed his pace to check out the stores and wondered what Sunshine Smith did for a living. That had not been in the 5491 file. In fact the file had been supremely light on details, the emphasis of the content had been on the other members who were involved in the espionage community.

As he jogged by an older stucco building that looked like it belonged in Switzerland or some Alps town, he glanced inside.

Crystals hung in the window, twisting and catching the light and refracting the light beam into a myriad of different colors and lengths until they were absorbed by a fall of long black hair. Sunshine.

Zeke slowed his pace. His heart leapt in his chest. Something about her posture screamed distress.

How he could tell he had no idea, since her back was to him and he couldn't see anything or anyone else inside the store's shadowed recesses. All he knew was he had to get to her. *Now.*

Zeke swerved across the street, thankful there were no cars to get in his way, and ran up to the store. He yanked open the door and took two steps inside, cataloguing details as he moved.

Three people, a big bear of an older man with bed head and arms the size of anchors, an older woman impeccably dressed, and Sunshine, tension in the arch of her neck and the set of her shoulders, stood inside the store. She turned toward the entrance, her mouth curved in a totally fake smile.

"Welcome to...." she trailed off. *Scents of the Sea.*

"Are you okay?" he demanded. Zeke had enough training to realize that just because the two older people looked harmless didn't mean they were, especially since the woman had her hand on Sunshine's upper arm. And the man was awfully close to both of them. Coercion could be accomplished through many methods.

Sunshine shot a furtive glance at the woman, then returned her gaze to Zeke, eyebrows raised, alarm on her face, suspicion in her voice. "What are you doing here?"

"Do you need help?" He wanted clarification that she was fine and not being pressured or intimidated in any way. His body primed, muscles hardened, he readied for violence. He would protect her, he would defend her. "Are you being harassed?"

"What?!"

"Excuse me." The older woman in the pale pink sweater stepped in front of Sunshine, placing her out of Zeke's reach. As she stared at him hard, Zeke took in other details, the woman's dirty blonde hair cut in a short pageboy, her slender build, and the familiar shape of her eyes. "And who are you?"

Great. If he wasn't mistaken he'd just accused Sunshine

Smith's mother of trying to harm her. *Way to stay in the background, way to be a shadow, a ghost, Hawthorne.*

He ran his hands through the curls of his hair, pulled them out in front of his face and then let them spring back into place.

"It's fine." Sunshine's hands fluttered, then she placed a hand on her mother's shoulder. "I'll help him."

Zeke nodded to the older people who both still stared at him suspiciously.

Sunshine floated around her mother, a long slate blue skirt with some sort of lace nearly brushed the ground and a paler blue sweater hung down almost over her hips and fell off one bare shoulder, revealing her delicate collarbone and the fact that she wasn't wearing a bra.

As she leaned closer to him, the heat from her body and her perfume surrounded him. The scents of the ocean, the beach, the sand, the eucalyptus, and the cool foggy air flooded his body, awakening his hormones, and he reacted to her nearness. A flush of desire spiraled from his head to his groin, hitting his organs, brain, lungs, heart, sex in rapid succession as he pictured them together like they had been last night. Him between her thighs. Except this time they were naked.

"What are you doing here?" she whispered with an unmistakable bite in her tone.

So much for his hormones. He'd been fantasizing about taking her and she was taking him to task. Awkward.

He took a moment to compose his thoughts, compose his answer. Because he'd messed up a minute ago by rushing in, by assuming that he would come in and defend her like the hero in the old black and white movies he'd watched with his Grandpop. He needed to formulate an appropriate answer for the level of intimacy they had right now—which was zero.

Fuck it. There was no appropriate answer.

"I thought you were in trouble."

"Trouble," she said flatly. She looked very aware of the fact that her mother and the guy were still in the store near the back. And she stepped in closer to him. Her shoulder was nearly brushing the exposed skin of his bicep. "Why would you care?"

Her look said she could take care of herself.

"Maybe I was just trying to return the favor and rescue *you*." He wanted to trail a finger down the side of her neck, where her pulse flickered with frenetic urgency. "I didn't have a chance to properly thank you."

She ignored that. "How did you find me?"

"It's not that difficult, the whole town is what, a mile long?"

He'd like to think she was leaning in closer because she found him irresistible but the truth was pretty obvious. She didn't want her mother to hear what they were talking about. Great. He was the only one affected by this incredible pull of attraction.

Subtly he inhaled her scent...which had changed in the last minute. A more heated, intense aroma now perfumed the air, as if their pheromones were mixing and blending while they stood together. The scent was enticing and enervating and wrapped around his senses like he wanted to wrap around her. Maybe he *wasn't* the only one affected.

She licked her lips, her pink tongue swirling before disappearing inside her mouth. "Consider me thanked."

"Why were you on the beach in the middle of the night?"

"None of your damn business."

But he wanted it to be. Somehow she'd shifted even closer, the threads of her sweater brushed against his bare arm, her mouth mere inches from his. She was so far inside his personal space, half a step and their bodies would be touching. And he was pretty sure she was unaware of their proximity.

"What do you want from me?" she asked.

What did he want? One taste. One taste of her mouth. One taste of paradise. He knew with certainty that it would be the most incredible kiss of his life.

Jesus, she was bewitching him. Like the magnetic pull of the moon to the tide, he couldn't seem to resist her.

"One." He leaned in closer, tilted his head, careful to give her time to move away. This was such a monumentally bad idea. On a completely un-scientific scale of one to ten this was a negative eleven thousand.

"One what?" Her breath was minty, as her lashes fluttered downward before she glanced back up at him.

"This." He lowered his mouth to hers, brushed against the softness of her lips with tender, deliberate slowness, and let his eyes drift closed, so he could experience the sensations of their kiss.

Her lips were warm, flavored with a subtle honey, and he wanted to lap her up, and draw every bit of her essence into him. Make her part of him.

His hands slid up the tactile warmth of her sweater, stopping at her elbows, resting there even as her strong fingers traced up the corded tendons of his forearms. Every single hair on his body stood at attention, his nerve endings tingled from the pads of her fingers trailing up his arms, until she stopped at his fiercely tensed biceps.

He leaned back against the entryway doorframe, tugging her gently against his body, and as she softened against him, he cupped her jaw in his hands and sipped at her lips. He wanted to go deeper, wanted to move harder, but the purity and intensity of this first kiss was so amazing, he didn't want to ruin the moment, so he played with her mouth, exploring her lips but not delving past the entrance to her hot, wet heat.

"Sunny?" A voice broke through his intense concentration, way too close to where they were entwined.

Sunshine broke away from him and whirled around. He noted the wide panic in her gray eyes and guessed she hadn't gotten caught making out before.

"Introduce me to your friend," her mother said firmly.

Sunshine whipped her head back around to stare at him in mute horror as the reality that she'd kissed a stranger blossomed in her gaze.

Because he realized...she didn't know his name.

CHAPTER 8

O*h. My. Goddess.*
What had I just done? I didn't even know his name! Thirteen years of caution blown away in a single moment. I could have jeopardized my mother and myself and everything we'd sweated blood and sacrificed for by...by....

"Zeke Thorn." Surfer dude extended his right hand toward my mother as his left arm curled around my shoulder. The heat of his body warmed me, his bare arm burned through the cotton of my sweater. He was practically naked next to me in miniscule running shorts and a tight runner's bro tank. Didn't he ever wear clothes?

"Nice to meet you, Mrs. Smith."

Oh, it was worse than I thought. I stiffened, prepping my body, going over possible defensive moves, calculating the angle of his body next to, and slightly behind, mine, analyzing how to protect my mother. If I needed to. Maybe his knowledge of our names was nothing to be scared about. Then again, maybe it was.

Shit, shit, shit.

Had we been found? Would we have to leave this town, the life we'd built here?

Waiting for his next move, I stood mutely while he charmed the suspicion out of my mother. My body primed, and vibrating with tension.

Suddenly Blue was there. Right next to Mama.

"Blue Harrison." His deep voice rumbled in his chest. Blue didn't seem as charmed as my mother.

Big, scary, former-Marine Blue, owner of a bar and apparently my mother's *fiancé*, was sizing up Zeke. I was used to dealing with things alone, but in this instance I'd take his help. Blue would back me up and things would be fine.

Blue shook Zeke's hand, his own large, strong hand fully engulfing Zeke's long slender fingers. Blue was a giant bull.

Zeke on the other hand was built like a wrestler. Wide shoulders tapered to a small waist, his arms were corded with muscle, veins prominent, and his long fingers were filled with strength. I remembered the resilient, smooth skin of his naked shoulders in the moonlight.

Blue let go of Zeke's hand. "How do you and Sunshine know each other?"

Another gauntlet. "It's a little embarrassing." Zeke straightened and looked like he was going to call Blue sir.

And I knew, without a doubt he was going to tell them the truth, that I'd been on the beach in the middle of the night. That I'd pulled him from the surf after his ill-fated wipeout. I absolutely did not want that 411 to come out.

I needed to get him out of our store, make sure he wasn't dangerous to my mother or me, and then send him on his way.

"Cal Poly," I blurted out.

Surfer dude—Zeke, I repeated to myself, *Zeke*—canted

his head and raised a brow. A tiny smile played around his mouth. His mouth. His lips were a little red, and we'd hardly even kissed. It had been chaste and romantic and—

"Are you a student?" My mother asked politely but I could see speculation in her gaze.

"Teacher's assistant." Desperately I tried, my brain going at about a hundred miles an hour, terminal velocity as I accelerated toward an absolutely catastrophic crash, to come up with something believable and get him the heck out of our store. Last night he'd referenced Hanlon's razor, so hopefully he'd know something about physics. "Remember that physics class I audited last year?"

My Goddess I wanted to get out of here. I wanted this stranger away from my mother. Away from our shop. I had to protect her, protect us.

"How is that embarrassing?" Blue asked. His gaze moved between me and my supposedly former ISA, arms crossed over his chest, his appearance bigger and bulkier than it had been a minute ago. My mother put her hand, the one with the *engagement ring*, on Blue's forearm.

"Hey, are you the Blue from Blue's Bar?" Zeke asked. I assumed he was trying to deflect Blue's attention. I couldn't figure out if that would work in my favor or against me. I was off balance from Zeke's appearance and his kiss. Why had he done that?

"Yeah."

"Looks like a great place."

"It serves its purpose." Blue's tone made it clear he didn't want to let the question go. "Embarrassing?"

"How about if I explain later," I said desperately, and knew I'd have to come up with something plausible. "Zeke," I hesitated over his name, "has to go."

"I'd like to get that cup of tea with you like you

promised, Sunshine." Zeke smiled easily, glanced at the fancy techno watch on his wrist, then back at my mother. "If that's okay with you."

"It's my morning to open." I lied, hoping that I didn't sound as desperate as I felt.

Blue looked like he was going to protest. My mother squeezed Blue's arm, and they gazed at each other with silent communication and...love transmitting between the two of them.

In that instant, I was lost.

What about me? I wanted to shout like a little kid forgotten in the backseat of the car.

"Enjoy your morning. I'll open." Mama turned back to us, the intimate glimpse of them gone. "Do you live around here, Zeke?"

"Just visiting. I...had some time off and thought I'd spend a few days surfing."

"Time off in October?" Blue asked.

"I'm in the private sector now," Zeke replied. "Hoped Sunshine could join me at the beach for a day."

"Sunny doesn't go to the beach," Mama blurted out.

I laughed as if I didn't have a care in the world. "No time."

But he'd picked up on my mother's statement. I didn't go to the beach, as far as anyone knew.

"Really?" Zeke Thorn, whoever the hell he was, gave me a speculative look.

I had to get him out of here now.

"Sunny should have you to dinner while you're in town." *Over my dead body.* "Sure."

My face was stiff with displeasure and worry and a totally fake smile that seemed to be permanently curving my cheeks and hurt like heck. I, we, needed to get out of there before the situation deteriorated any further. "Be back in a bit."

I grabbed his bicep, his skin hot against my palm, and tugged him out of the store. The heat rising from his body was immense.

For a minute, we walked along the sidewalk in silence. His step was jaunty and a little too enthusiastic. After all, he'd gotten what he wanted.

I should just ditch him but I needed information from Zeke Thorn before I sent him on his way.

As soon as we were far enough from the shop that my mom and Blue couldn't see my animosity, I asked abruptly, "How did you know my mother's name?"

"I asked about you and someone told me your last name."

Which sounded good, except he was lying. If he'd asked about either of us, the gossip network in our small, close-knit town would have kicked in and someone would have called to tell us a stranger was asking around. "Really?"

"It's been my experience," he shot me an inscrutable look, "that lying about a situation tends to backfire on you. After I was a T.A. in physics at Cal Poly, of course."

"Okay. Fine. I'm a liar." But so was he.

"Why'd you pick physics?"

"Because I audited a physics class there."

He gave me a long silent look. An indecipherable question in eyes the same blue as the pictures I'd seen of the ocean surrounding the Hawaiian islands.

What the hell.... "And in my experience most surfers have at the very most a rudimentary understanding of physics. It seemed like a good fit."

"You lie well under pressure."

"Yippee. Something to be *super* proud of." I decided

beating around the bush was pointless. And I purposefully chose an incendiary word to raise his defenses. "Why are you stalking me?"

"I'm not trying to stalk you," he said with exasperation. "I wanted to thank you one more time. Properly." He sounded sincere and he kept his body language relaxed, leaning slightly toward me, which usually meant sincerity. But I could sense, at the very least, he was not telling the whole truth.

I needed to find out why he was coming after me. It couldn't be as simple as a thank you, could it? "Really?" I injected as much cynicism into that one word as I possibly could.

He looked chagrined, but didn't answer, instead he countered with a question of his own. "Why didn't you want them to know you were on the beach?"

"None of your business."

"Why'd you go to the beach in the middle of the night?" he rephrased the question.

I should be protesting, asking him why he wouldn't let my behavior go. But instead I was drawn to the mysterious depths of his ocean blue eyes. I'd left the store with him to get him away from Mama and Blue. With that accomplished, I should walk away.

Instead I was dizzy with temptation. If I let myself go I could fall into the warmth and compassion of his gaze and he would save me like I'd saved him last night.

But that wasn't going to happen. It was a false sense of hope, a false sense of connection, so I brought up last night to push him away. "Why'd you go surfing in the middle of the night?"

"Stupidity."

If he was embarrassed, he hid it well.

And his honesty made me want to smile. No sugarcoating it.

"Well, you're welcome." I cracked my lips up in a parody of a smile. "Nice meeting you." And I forced myself to turn around to head back to Scents of the Sea even though I wanted to stay so badly.

I didn't even take one step before his fingers curled around my forearm, his hand hot through my cotton sweater. "Hey. Please don't go."

I tugged discreetly at my arm. I didn't want to cause a scene. Didn't want to do anything that would draw attention to him, us.

"Please," he said again softly. The sincerity in that please had me turning around. Wishing that we'd met under different circumstances, and wishing for just a few moments that I was a 'normal' woman.

"I'd really like to have tea with you." He was just the slightest bit earnest, and he seemed to be almost as ill at ease as I was.

"Okay." And really, I still wasn't convinced that he hadn't somehow selected Mama and I. Maybe he wasn't stalking me, but something else?

We waited in line at the English Tea Shop. I smiled at Ernie. He and his partner, Joe, owned the little shop and were the happiest couple I knew. Mama frequently went to tradeshows with Ernie looking for little tchotchkes to stock the retail section of our store and Joe would be my backup while she was gone. "Thanks, Ernie."

"No problem, doll." Ernie eyed Zeke speculatively but didn't say anything that would embarrass me in front of him. But I could tell he was dying to quiz me. I predicted a nosy phone call in my future. And when Zeke turned around to head outside, Ernie rounded his mouth and bugged his eyes, then gave me a thumbs up.

I flushed. This was going nowhere. It couldn't go anywhere.

We took our ceramic mugs to a small bistro table outside on the brick patio. A wooden pergola, with wisteria twining around the thick posts and over the slats, blocked afternoon heat on sunny days, but this morning's fog still lingered in the cool Fall air.

Once we sat down, I couldn't let it rest as I analyzed his insistence and my own out of character reaction to what was in essence a mini-date. Because I didn't date. Ever. "Why are you really here?"

"That could be answered so many different ways." He prevaricated. "Why am I here, as in, on the planet? Existential theory. Or why am I in California? Or why am I having tea with you?"

"Two and three."

"Two. Vacation." But I watched him and knew he was lying again. This wasn't a guy who took vacations. He worked constantly and when he wasn't working, if his lean fit body was any indication, he exercised. If he was on vacation, Cambria wouldn't be his first pick, and so it probably wasn't his choice.

"And three?"

"I have no damn idea why." The truth rang in his words. I supposed I should be hurt by the fact that he wasn't overcome with lust or dying to go out with me. But I was more relieved that he didn't seem to have a subversive agenda. He stared down at his hands, shook his head, his blond curls bouncing with the movement. He whispered, "It's a really bad idea, and I seem to be full of them these days."

"What do you do for a living?"

"Right now, nothing," he said glumly.

I crossed my arms over my chest and waited. My body language was defensive and I didn't care.

He sighed. "Computer programmer."

I narrowed my gaze, catalogued his corded muscles and broad chest. "You don't look like a programmer."

"Is that a compliment or a criticism?"

"Compliment." I guess. I didn't have a lot of experience with programming. I loved the idea of puzzles, but beyond a little bit of hacking research, mostly to protect my mother and me, didn't have any practical knowledge. What I did know is that it required serious brain power.

"I'm really just a hacker. I design encryption programs and test them for vulnerabilities. I also test other systems for ways to break in."

"Is it fun?" I couldn't conceal the wistful tenor of my question.

"Uh, *yeah.*"

I was supposed to be interrogating him. The vibe coming off of Zeke Thorn was rueful and not at all threatening. But I needed to know for sure. "Are you here to harm us?"

"What?" Zeke shoved back from the little bistro table with a screech. "No!"

And I believed him. His reaction was seriously horrified.

Before I could apologize, his cell phone rang. Zeke glanced at the screen and blanched. "I'm sorry. I…have to go." He jumped up from the table and ran. So, after practically begging me to have tea with him, he abandoned me almost immediately.

Well. I guess that was that. As I watched him take off, I wondered at the peculiar sense of loss from his rejection.

For a few moments I'd felt like a regular person. Not closed off, secretive, protective of my privacy, or constantly searching for nefarious ulterior motives. Just a girl on a date. But clearly I wasn't meant for every day interaction with the opposite sex. So, I shoved that sense of melancholy down into the box where I corralled all the things I couldn't do, couldn't have.

I needed to forget about him. Because, odds were, I'd never see Zeke Thorn again.

CHAPTER 9

S hit. Shit. Shit.

Zeke stared at the display. Jamie Hunt was calling him. Zeke was thankful he'd bolted from Sunshine. For some reason, he felt very protective of her and he didn't want Sunshine on Jamie's radar any more than necessary. Zeke pressed the answer button on his phone. "Yo."

"We didn't find her." Jamie didn't bother with hellos or any other pleasantries.

And then he realized Jamie said we. "You're with Lucas?"

Lucas Goodman was Jamie Hunt's new boyfriend—who had seen that coming? Certainly not Zeke who'd had a massive crush on Jamie for a while. She'd never dated anyone at the office, anyone ever, as far as Zeke knew. He'd tried several times to get her to go out with him. But a few weeks ago she'd hooked up with Lucas Goodman while she'd been undercover, searching for the people responsible for kidnapping agents and experimenting on them. Ever since then Jamie and Lucas had pretty much been inseparable.

"You missed the point. We've got squat."

Jamie and Lucas had gone looking for Susan Chen, the escaped scientist who had conducted the illegal experiments on unsuspecting espionage targets, in the most logical destination: Seattle. They believed she'd head to the Pacific Northwest to see her young daughter.

Zeke wondered about the implications of Chen not going where they expected. He didn't think they had any other avenues to pursue at this point. "What's next?"

"Dammit. I don't know."

Which did nothing for Zeke.

Susan Chen was also the perpetrator of the plot that had put Zeke in the position of being suspended. The reason he was red-badged. The reason he'd been banished to Cambria to keep an eye, from afar—yep, he'd failed that directive—on Sunshine Smith.

Susan Chen was his only hope at clearing his name. He needed to find out how she had gotten his encryption program, *and* if he had revealed any other top secret information to her and her accomplice while he'd been drugged. He hadn't believed that he was susceptible to Sodium Pentothal.

So that fact that Susan Chen's files on the illegal, unethical experiment had been encrypted with Zeke's classified NSA program had fucked him.

A program he'd developed, and the only way to access the programming code was through his brain or NSA computers, which pretty much meant that he must have given up information when he'd been abducted.

But how much information, and exactly what had he revealed? He didn't remember.

When they'd had Susan Chen in custody, the scientist

hadn't talked. Hadn't said a word. Nothing to defend herself. And definitely nothing that would clear Zeke.

After they'd grilled Chen in a maximum security prison and gotten nowhere, they'd tried multiple techniques to get Zeke's brain to cough up what he'd told the kidnappers. They'd even tried hypnosis, but whatever he'd done under the influence of the Sodium Pentothal was lost in his grey matter somewhere. The idea that he couldn't access it was pretty fucking freaky.

The NSA needed to know what else he'd done. *He* needed to know what else he'd done. Zeke had been banned from going after Susan Chen. He couldn't be alone with her without compromising the evidence chain. So right now he was relying on Jamie to find Susan Chen.

But last anyone knew Susan Chen was in the wind. She'd escaped from a prison she should have never been able to breakout of and vanished.

"The daughter made the most sense." Jamie huffed.

Zeke knew that Jamie had spent years protecting her little sister. So naturally her first thought would have been that Chen would protect her daughter. Except maybe Chen was protecting her by staying away, just like Jamie had done.

"Where is Chen's little girl?"

"Safe and sound with the sister- and brother-in-law, who claim they haven't seen Susan." Jamie sighed. "I believe them. They're terrified of the kid being taken away."

"Susan Chen knows we wouldn't hurt her daughter," Zeke rebutted, thinking through the series of events that lead to this point. He didn't bring up Jamie's sister, Bella. But by her silence, he thought she was probably thinking the same thing.

"Likely," Jamie said. "But it was the only lead we had."

"Anything else?" Zeke rubbed a hand through his hair,

his gaze unfocused as he processed the information. "Did her in-laws have any ideas about where she might be?"

"No, they were only concerned with protecting the kid. She…doesn't go outside."

Zeke went quiet. They both knew that Susan Chen's daughter had been injected with the same experimental DNA-altering drug that had been used on the espionage agents and the results had been debilitating.

All was quiet as Jamie thought through possibilities. Zeke waited her out. "I've been investigating her background," she finally said. "Her ex-husband worked on the project too."

"Oliver Krychef. Russian national. Here on an H1B visa." Zeke recited the husband's credentials.

"Oliver Krychef is actually the one who'd injected the daughter."

Zeke asked, "Where is he?"

"Deported back to Russia after the government determined he was trying to steal biotechnology and nanotechnology for Putin."

"So she wouldn't be trying to hook up with him somehow?" Zeke asked. "Maybe find a way out of the country?"

"Doubtful. She divorced his ass after he left." Jamie took a deep breath. "But that's not what gave me an idea."

Jamie Hunt was a brilliant field agent. *Brilliant.* So if she came up with something, it likely held merit. But the way she hesitated caused his stomach to cramp.

"And?" Zeke braced. Somehow he knew he wasn't going to like what came next.

"Chen went to Caltech. Both undergrad and grad."

California Institute of Technology in Pasadena. One of the most challenging math, engineering, and technology schools in the country. Everyone had heard of MIT but Caltech as a research institute was actually more difficult to get into and the programs there were cutting edge.

"She was a grad assistant. She worked on modeling genetic and biomechanical networks."

Which also made sense based on the high level genetic research she'd been doing by producing and administering the drug that had messed with all their lives.

"And?" Zeke asked impatiently. Jamie wasn't one to beat around the bush, so he couldn't for the life of him figure out why she was drawing out whatever she needed to tell him.

"You remember in that hotel room? Her main concern was making sure the antidote worked."

Jesus, Jamie was being evasive. And he was sick of it. "Are you ever going to come out and tell me what you're getting at?"

Chen had been frantic for the antidote to work so she could administer it to her daughter. He could tell her a few things about the drug and the resulting reaction to the antidote. Because he'd had both. And while he wasn't about to tell anyone else, especially his superiors at the NSA, that he had residual effects from the drugs, he might be willing to share with Susan Chen, if they could find her.

He considered that offering to share his reactions might be a way to get her to talk. An exchange of information. If she was as desperate as she seemed to get the antidote right, she might be willing to finally tell the NSA what happened when he'd been kidnapped. But they still had to catch her first.

"There's a possibility she may head to Cal Poly."

In San Luis Obispo, just a few miles from Cambria. "Why Cal Poly?"

"Her mentor, a Professor Zignar, is doing genetic

modeling research with a combined grant between Cal Poly and Caltech. They're using Cal Poly facilities in the joint project."

"So I'll see you soon?"

"We're going to stay here one more day. We got the warrant to monitor the in-laws cell phones and there has been some unusual activity here even if Chen hasn't shown up yet. Plus there's been some CommInt chatter regarding Krychef."

"You think he's coming here?"

"No," Jamie replied. "He's on the DHS Watch List as high priority No Fly designation. But he may try to contact either Chen or her relatives. I have a hunch we're going to get a break."

So who was going to San Luis? Before he could ask, she said, "You're the closest."

Oh, shit, no.

"I can't. You know the rules." He was forbidden because of the abduction. Which Jamie knew. However she didn't always play by the rules.

What Jamie didn't know was that if Zeke broke the rules again, he was done. Gone. Finished. Freedom over. That was the deal he'd made years ago, at the age of sixteen, after he'd hacked into government computers one too many times.

"She could already be there," Jamie said firmly. "I just need you to keep an eye out for her. Don't approach if you find her. Call me and Carson."

And he was stuck.

Susan Chen was the reason for his suspension. She was the only one who could clear him unequivocally. But because of her status as a national fugitive and known perpetrator of crimes against U.S. espionage agents, he shouldn't get anywhere near her. If it was discovered he had contact with her outside official channels, he would be screwed.

"You don't understand what happens if I have contact with her."

Sunshine Smith was one thing. Contact with Sunshine was inadvisable but not career threatening. A stupid move but not one that could destroy his life.

Susan Chen was another situation completely. She was directly linked to an ongoing investigation. One that he was freaking right in the middle of and under suspicion for participating in. He couldn't have contact with her. It was career suicide. It was *life* suicide.

"You don't have to have contact with her. Just watch out for her. We need to know who is behind this entire operation," Jamie said firmly, quietly. "There's no way Chen and her dead partner had the authority to engineer everything on their own. They had to have help at the highest level."

Zeke knew that. Knew Jamie was right. He had a vested interest in discovering the traitor who had let Chen and her partner experiment on espionage agents, but he had to tread with extreme caution.

Because if David Armbruster, the Assistant Director of the NSA, found out he'd been anywhere near Susan Chen he was fucked.

"I realize that, but—"

"What's going on at your end?" Jamie asked suspiciously.

Besides the fact that he was an idiot and unbelievably attracted to his surveillance subject? Besides the fact that he'd broken a cardinal rule of surveillance and actually had extended contact with his subject? Besides the fact that he'd kissed his surveillance subject and, frankly if he had the chance, he'd probably kiss her again?

"Nothing." The only threat that he could see to Sunshine Smith was himself. "It's quiet."

"What if sending you there wasn't just a hunch?" Jamie asked. "San Luis is extremely close to Cambria. She'd have access to a lab, and maybe to a test subject. After all the first round of subjects who'd been given the drug were part of Department 5491."

Zeke's heart froze. Chen's original experiments had not been a success. For all they knew she *could* be looking for new subjects. And for some reason they didn't understand, her test subjects were all from the same genetic pool.

"She could be after Sunshine." Jamie's words speared worry through his heart. Logically it didn't make sense that Susan Chen would go after Sunshine, assuming she could even find her. Sunshine had been off the grid in a major way. However Chen had access to all sorts of information and resources that she shouldn't have had. So what if Jamie were right?

"Shit, do you think so?" But as he examined the idea, he thought it was possible. They only knew about the agents that had been injected. What if she was looking for a new batch of test subjects?

Patterns. Patterns everywhere. The pattern was there, even if he couldn't see it right now. Zeke said fiercely, "She can't hurt Sunshine."

"Why does that upset you so much?" Jamie's voice was soft in his ear.

Jamie couldn't possibly have figured out he was a little obsessed with his surveillance subject, could she?

He stayed silent and Jamie continued, "The only people given the original drug and antidote are in the 5491 file.

Chen could be going after the others who hadn't been given the drug. Sunshine, Bella, and ADA, whoever that is."

"But the original experiment subjects were...agents," he argued. "People with secrets. People with security clearance."

But if Zeke thought about it, Sunshine clearly had secrets too or she wouldn't have stayed hidden for the last thirteen years.

"Who's to say Chen hasn't gotten ready to start up again with new subjects? She is frantic to make an effective antidote. And to test the antidote you have to have the drug first."

Exposing herself to capture did not seem like a smart or even viable plan to lay low, which surely should be Susan Chen's course of action. Especially if she wasn't going after her daughter. Zeke couldn't see it. Sunshine didn't fit the pattern.

But what if Jamie was right and Chen was planning on using Sunshine and others as new test subjects?

Over his dead body. Susan Chen was not getting her hands on Sunshine. She was not continuing her experiments and fucking up that woman's life. No effing way.

Suddenly everything clicked, as if his whole life he'd been fractured, a little off. The reason for his inability to connect with people, the reason he saw patterns in random facts and numbers. He refused to let anyone become a threat to Sunshine.

So if that meant finding Susan Chen and making sure she didn't get anywhere near Sunshine, he would do it. "Fine. I'll do it."

"Yeah. I knew you would. Just find her, call us, then follow her until we can get someone there to apprehend her." He could practically see Jamie's smirk through the cellular frequencies. "But dude, remember to go incognito. Remember the lessons."

Yeah, whatever. "Got to go."

Zeke nearly sprinted through Cambria's quaint downtown. The sound of the surf shushed in the distance, and crisp, piney eucalyptus and the weighty smell of fog scented the air.

He'd head over to Cal Poly, he'd stake out Susan Chen's former professor, and he'd make sure nothing happened to mess up Sunshine Smith's already complicated life. He'd seen the shadows in her gray eyes, and he was determined not to add to her burdens.

CHAPTER 10

I sat at the little bistro table and watched the morning fog swirl around the old wine barrels potted with flowers, the briny breeze off the ocean ruffled the lacy edges of an asparagus fern and drew out the sweet scent of alyssum.

I considered the empty wrought iron chair across from me then glanced down the sidewalk towards the other end of town. Zeke Thorn was striding away, gesturing restrainedly while he talked into his cell. With an odd sense of melancholy, I watched the most interesting guy I'd met in a long time, possibly ever, rush away.

Which was certainly ironic because I was usually the one running away. I'd been running since I was seven years old. Both physically and metaphorically.

He sure flowed hot and cold.

Of course, so did I. I didn't need a guy in my life. Couldn't *have* a guy in my life. That was my reality. But the overwhelming emotion tightening my throat and causing the tremble in my fingers as I picked up my teacup was regret. My throat convulsed and that last sip of tea stuck in the hollow as I watched him go. I wished I could call him back.

I could pretend for a short hour we were friends, lovers even, sharing a cozy little date with scones and tea.

A small, private birthday celebration.

I was going to be twenty years old tomorrow. I'd never had a real boyfriend, never been intimate, never had a true friend, always too worried about being discovered to let anyone get close. Always worried about having to move again.

Wistfully I watched as his silhouette got smaller and smaller, shrinking like the little kernel of hope that had swelled in me after that amazing, haunting kiss.

Ruthlessly I shoved the hope aside, and crushed the futile emotion like I pulverized the dried herbs in my mortar and pestle. I sighed, took a final sip of my tea. Time to get back to the shop. Back to reality. Back to my life.

Of course, now I had to come up with a plausible explanation for how I knew Zeke, because sure as sugar, Mama was going to ask more questions.

I didn't date. Ever. I certainly didn't kiss men in front of my mother. My introduction to the dysfunctional side of relationships came too early and with too high a price tag.

Men were pleasant enough in small doses, in public and never to be trusted to get too close. I had to protect myself and I had to protect my mother. That's the way it had always been. We took care of each other.

Except now Mama had Blue.

My cell rang. Mama wouldn't be interrupting me and that's about the only person who ever called me on the damn thing anyway.

I glanced at the display, noted it was the French pastry shop on the other end of town.

"Hello?"

"*Bonjour*, Sunny," Madame Broussard greeted me.

"*Bonjour, Madame,*" I replied automatically, wondering why she was calling. For my birthday? Then I realized tomorrow wasn't the official day of Sunshine Smith's birth. Sunshine Smith's birthday was in April.

"Just wanted to let you know zere was *un homme* asking about you and *vôtre mére.*"

Zeke. I glanced down the street, where he was all but invisible.

"He found me."

"Already?" Madame sputtered. "*Mais*...he was just here a second ago."

Madame's speech always degenerated into a mix of English with a smattering of French when she was upset or had had a little too much wine.

Alarm skittered across my neck. What if it hadn't been Zeke? "What did he look like?"

"Older, in his fifties, under six feet tall, almost bald, a broken nose, and *les yeux* a pale, ice blue." Madame always noticed the eyes, I thought with amusement.

Except her words kicked in. My heart started thumping in my chest. The eyes were the clincher. Appearances could change but the monster had extremely light blue eyes. She hadn't described Zeke. Zeke was close to my age with curly blond hair. And his eyes were the color of the ocean. Murky and deep. I should not be thinking about Zeke Thorn's eyes right now. *Focus, Sunny.*

"When was he in the patisserie?"

"He just left," Madame responded smartly. "I told you that."

"Car or on foot?"

"Weeelll, I sink on foot, but I could be wrong, we are very busy for an October *matin.*"

I shoved back the wrought iron chair and ran for the store.

I didn't like this. Two people in one day, two *strangers* in one day asking about us. What were the odds?

Not good. Dammit. Not good.

"*Merci, Madame,*" I huffed into the phone as I ran.

Had I been wrong about Zeke Thorn? Had he been some sort of advance scout for *him*?

I slammed into the store. Blue appeared to be gone and Mama was dusting the shelves. I flipped the "Be Back in 5 Minutes" sign onto the Dutch door, closed the top half, and bolted the locks.

My breath came in great gasps, and my heart thundered in my chest, but my mind was calm, almost preternaturally so as I assessed our options and figured out which escape plan we needed to put into play.

Mama whirled, her eyes wide with alarm. "What are you doin'?"

"Code Red, Mama."

She took a step back, away from me. "Now Sunny, I'm sure you're mistaken." But her arm trembled as she lay down the duster.

"At Madame's." I repeated the details as I shoved the minimal cash from the register into a Go Bag stashed beneath the sales desk. There wasn't much, but I also had more stockpiled inside the bag and it would get us out of town fast.

"We need to go, now."

As I moved around the store, I ticked off the seconds in my head.

"I...I'll call Blue," she said calmly.

"From the road."

"Sunny, wait."

I stopped at her sharp tone and gave her my full attention.

Mama stood in the doorway to the stockroom, twisting her hands, and her big moonstone ring sparkled when it caught the ray of the display light. "I think we should split up."

"What?" I stopped moving. Stopped breathing. Splitting up was *never* one of the plans. We stuck together. Always.

"Call your friend Zeke and go with him. Zeke can protect you. I'm sure of it. And I'll go with Blue." Mama firmed her lips. "He wants me, we both know that. You need to stop running and get a life."

Mama's words stabbed at me with a near physical pain, as if she'd broken off a piece of glass display shelf and jammed it in my heart. "I have a life."

"Half a life," Mama said, her eyes sad, resigned. "All because of him. You deserve more. *I* deserve more. We need to end this."

We didn't have time to hash this out now. "Can we discuss this while we're on the road?"

Mama shook her head and yelled, "Blue!"

Blue thundered down the stairs and burst into the public area of the shop.

"It's happened." Was all Mama said.

"Shit," he whispered.

Another spear of pain. She'd told Blue. We weren't supposed to tell anyone. Ever.

"The plan?" Blue asked.

"I think we should split up. You can protect me." Mama straightened her shoulders and looked me straight in the eye. "He doesn't want Sunshine."

I watched as Blue grasped Mama's hand gently. Her

fingers appeared so delicate in the clasp of his larger, protective hold.

Blue shifted his gaze to me, full of concern. "You going to be okay?"

"I'll be fine," I said softly. Not about to tell the truth. Even now I was protecting my mother.

"Let's go." Blue herded Mama toward the back door.

"Love you, Sunny." Mama's eyes crinkled with concern and maybe a touch of guilt. And she hesitated, as if maybe she was going to change her mind. It had always been me and Mama. But then Blue tugged on her arm. She gave me one last look. "Use our separation protocol and let me know where you are."

"Go." I shooed them away, even as inside my heart was breaking. "I'll be fine."

I lugged my escape bag to the store room in the back. "Love you too, Mama," I whispered to the empty store. I inhaled slowly, taking in the familiar smells, the fragrant aroma of lavender, the comforting perfume of vanilla and lemon, and the crisp fresh scent of the ocean.

As I looked around the place that had been my home for the last nine years, I wondered if I would ever be back.

Hell yes, I vowed. I refused to let the bastard win.

I ignored our cute little Bug, and cranked the engine on our getaway car. An ancient blue Volvo, parked in the garage behind the store. We started it once a month and had it serviced once a year in another town. The car was registered to an old lady up in San Francisco. The floppy sun hat I'd tugged on slanted over my face. It wasn't much of a disguise but it would work to get out of town.

I turned away from our home and toward Highway One. I'd head down to San Luis Obispo and enact our plan. Part of me, the woman who'd managed to disappear in plain sight and build a life and livelihood with my mother, wanted to confront the man who'd ruined my childhood. But the other part of me was still that scared little girl clutching her Lunette doll and running for her life.

I knew what part I wanted to triumph.

In the last few years, I'd let myself relax, convinced after all this time he couldn't still be looking for us. Even though we stuck to the plan, I'd believed that he'd finally given up.

He shouldn't still be looking. It had been thirteen damn years.

And yet he was.

Obsession, or something else? As I pressed on the accelerator I wondered why he'd kept searching all this time. And even more importantly, how did he find us? Why now?

I would need to trace everything, trace him, track our movements and figure out how the hell he found us after all this time hiding in California, laying low. We'd completely submerged our identities, hidden away, hidden our assets, hidden our very existence behind a corporate shell in another state. Besides the legal precautions, I'd hidden myself, denied myself the education I'd always wanted, to keep us safe. So how the hell had he found us?

CHAPTER 11

Zeke slipped his phone into the zippered pocket in the lower back of his compression tank top and jogged down the center of town. Traffic had picked up in the last hour. More people wandered the picturesque sidewalks, meandering in and out of stores, and stopping indiscriminately to peer in shop windows. A lot of couples held hands, and snuggled together against the crisp October morning.

Up ahead, an older model Ford F150 with a Semper Fidelis sticker in the back window turned down the street toward his hotel and Blue's bar. Sunshine's mother was visible in the passenger seat.

That was a little surprising.

Zeke continued to jog, picking up his pace as possibilities and patterns filtered through his brain, and his mind searched for a reasonable explanation for why her mother wouldn't be at the store.

He realized that Sunshine had never really explained why she'd been upset when he'd burst into the shop. They'd gotten sidetracked by the kiss.

That amazing, shouldn't happen again, kiss.

Zeke followed the truck to the front of the bar where Blue normally parked. He'd noted the cars in the lot when he'd arrived yesterday. Except Blue didn't park in his regular spot in front, he drove around to the back which butted up to a steep hill sprinkled liberally with towering eucalyptus trees.

Zeke jogged closer, and heard the slam of the screen door leading to the delivery entrance in the back of the bar. The only other things in back were the dumpster and a little alcove where the hardcore smokers went to light up.

Blue's behavior triggered an alert, as if Zeke's packet sniffer program, which looked for incursions into a secure system, had been activated.

Something was going on. He'd already met them, interacted with them, so what could it hurt to get closer and see if he could figure out what the problem was.

They were going to tell him it was none of his business, he told himself even as he drew nearer.

Blue's odd behavior likely had nothing to do with him or Susan Chen. Unless Sunshine was somehow in danger from Chen already. But how would Blue even know that? Zeke crept closer, trying to figure out a way to snoop without getting caught.

Sunshine's mother sat in the front seat of the truck, her face set in stiff, stressed lines. As if she'd gotten really bad news and was trying to hold it together.

He wondered what was wrong. Suddenly he was overwhelmed with the urge to check on Sunshine. Blue shoved out the back door, an army green duffel in one meaty fist. He tossed the duffel into the back of the truck then swung into the driver's seat. Blue gunned the engine, the loud revving disturbed the quiet morning air.

Zeke crossed the street and headed toward his motel, more convinced than ever that something was really wrong. He couldn't help but glance back as he heard the truck screech to a stop behind him. Shit, hopefully they hadn't seen him lurking.

The passenger window whirred down and Sunshine's mother stuck her head out. "Did Sunny call you?"

Everything within Zeke slowed, sounds and scents became clearer. A breeze swept through the little side street, the scuttle of leaves was unnaturally loud, and the rumble of the truck's engine seemed to vibrate through his chest, even as the scent of exhaust filled his nose and roiled his stomach.

Sunshine would have no reason to contact him. "Uh, I don't know," he lied. Because of course his phone would have beeped if he'd had another call while he had been talking to Jamie. "I've been on my phone," he finished lamely.

"Blue!" Sunshine's mother cried. "She's so damn independent."

Blue Harrison aimed a hard look at him. "What's your true connection to Sunshine?"

Time stopped. Zeke's heartbeat thundered, blood rushed through his ears, which should have dimmed his hearing but instead his senses seemed unnaturally heightened.

He thought about the threat Jamie had articulated. He would not let anything happen to Sunshine. Impossibly she had become important. More important than his cover.

His muscles hardened, he clenched his jaw, knowing that his next sentence was critical. Something was wrong. Sunshine's mother was hoping that she had contacted him. If they knew he'd just met Sunshine last night, his game was up. And he would have no way to help her.

"I won't let anything happen to her," Zeke said fiercely. "I want to help her."

Blue and Stella exchanged a loaded look as if they knew something he didn't. But then Blue turned back to Zeke and nodded. "Good. She needs your help."

He didn't care about the look as long as they told him where she was. "Is she at the store?"

"She should be gone by now."

Gone? Fear stabbed his chest, his pulse picked up. "Where?"

"I know what our plan was...." Her mother trailed off. "But we've broken the original plan."

She looked at Blue again, anguish in her gaze. "Maybe I should have gone with her. I should have never left her alone."

"I can take care of you better," Blue said firmly, emphatically. "But Sunshine could use some extra protection."

Protection?

"Where is she?" Zeke struggled to keep his voice even. He couldn't let them see, couldn't give away his worry, fear.

"San Luis," her mother said quickly. "She's on her way to San Luis Obispo."

"Where in San Luis?"

"Don't know yet," her mother replied. "Our first step is to get rid of our existing cells and activate new ones in case he's tracking us somehow through GPS. Then, once we arrive we arrange to meet."

He, who? Shit. Another threat. "How do you know where to meet?"

"You need to call this number, 555-2703." Then she rattled off the access password code. "It's an answering service. If we're separated, whoever gets to a rendezvous point first is supposed to call and let the other know where they are."

Zeke thought about protocol. About the fact that he wasn't supposed to have contact with Sunshine. But he wanted to protect her. "Are *you* going to San Luis?"

An overwhelming need to make sure Sunshine was okay multiplied like a virus through a compromised, vulnerable system.

Blue placed his large hand over Stella Smith's. "No."

No? But—

"The less you know, the better off everyone is," Blue said.

"Will you help Sunny?" Her mother pleaded, persuading him that he needed throw his caution to the wind and go now. Her anxiety for her daughter stimulated a biological imperative to protect. To shield.

Zeke looked at Mrs. Smith. She was trembling, her fear palpable in the cab of the truck. Blue appeared ready for combat, 'Always Faithful', and able to commit mayhem to protect the innocent.

Zeke contemplated the two of them, thinking about the immediate bond he'd felt with Sunshine. As if he'd known her for years instead of just a few hours.

"Poor Sunny." Her mother's eyes glittered with unshed tears. "Another birthday ruined."

"It's her birthday?" Zeke rubbed a hand through his curls.

"Tomorrow."

Zeke went under for the third time and hoped the riptide didn't kill him. But he couldn't leave Sunshine alone.

He had the training. He'd just never applied himself. It was about damn time he did, he thought grimly. "I'll look out for her."

"Thank you." Gratitude shone from Stella's gaze, lighting her whole face.

"Solid." Blue nodded his respect. "Go now."

Their truck sped away. Zeke hustled to his hotel room, changed quickly, then gathered his bag and left. As he squealed out of the parking lot in his rental Range Rover, Zeke hoped like hell he could keep her safe.

CHAPTER 12

October 20
1:00 pm
San Luis Obispo, CA

ZEKE HAULED ass and got to San Luis in about thirty minutes. The traffic on Highway One had been dense. His tension rose with each excruciating minute in the car with nothing to think about other than what kind of danger Sunshine could possibly be in.

Once in San Luis, he found an impersonal chain motel tucked behind a Safeway and strip mall and checked in so he'd have someplace to bring Sunshine when he found her.

Impatiently he checked the message center about every five minutes. While on the phone, he set up his laptop and jumped on the system. He needed to figure out who was after these women.

He'd been tasked with keeping an eye on her. However he wasn't supposed to make contact with Sunshine. He'd been sure Carson Black, his mentor, had really just found a lame reason to get him out of the way and keep him out of trouble. Zeke had been given Sunshine's current name and address. He hadn't had the time, or the interest, to delve deeper than that. Truly his attitude had been one step up from self-pity, and he'd been operating from a position of fear.

He didn't want to lose his job or his freedom.

He realized while following Sunshine to San Luis that position of fear had been replaced by another more productive emotion.

Determination.

He was done wallowing and worrying. It was time to take action.

But surprise. "No information found," the computer chirped after he'd listed Sunshine and Stella's information on a super secure, triple-encrypted government database.

Okay. That had to be damn near impossible with a last name like Smith. There should be some partial matches, something within the county. He'd found men. Singles, Pairs. Husbands and wives and kids. Husband and husband. Wife and wife. But there were no mother/daughter pairs in the census or tax records.

They owned and operated a business in Cambria. There ought to be some way to tag them. And the fact that he couldn't was mystifying.

Sunshine Smith was a complex and intriguing woman. She seemed guileless but lied like a pro. She visited the ocean in the middle of the night even though she was terrified of the water. So it stood to reason that she had even more secrets. But he still hadn't seen that search result coming. Nothing.

Unless Smith wasn't their last name.

Zeke entered some more information into the system.

And found out that neither Sunshine nor her mother existed before 1999. New identities. And nothing had come up when he'd put Sunshine's birthday, tomorrow, in the system. But it wouldn't if tomorrow was her true identity's birthday.

He dug further. Came up empty.

His Grandpop had been a paranoid bastard. Their information had been in the system but they'd moved a lot, paid cash for everything, and he worked off the grid. Grandpop had always maintained that he wasn't about to make it easy for anyone to find him.

A wave of sorrow rushed over Zeke. All those years Grandpop had thought he'd been hard to track and yet the assassin had still managed to find him and execute him once the order was given.

But that made Zeke realize that Sunshine and her mother had clearly gone to severe lengths to be almost impossible to trace.

Patterns.

Bayes theorem would suggest that their hidden configurations were just that, hidden. And that the observed signal they generated was an obfuscation of their true identities. The translation wasn't difficult. They didn't want to be found.

But nothing would make sense until he figured out *why*.

In the meantime, he had other avenues to pursue.

Finding people was like a pyramid. Start at the apex with the few known facts that he had and work down to the base. Each layer of their information he drilled down into would reveal another facet, until there was a solid foundation of information, and a recognizable pattern. Then he'd have ways to track them.

Since the personal information had mostly been a bust, the next layer down was their business.

There had to be records regarding Scents of the Sea.

What he found was the business was owned by a corporation whose officers were listed as Stella Smith, CEO, and Sunshine Smith, COO, but the address on file was a suite in Delaware. He'd bet money that the "suite" was actually just a PO Box in an anonymous box rental, strip mall storefront. And he'd bet that any mail likely went through forwarding to a box here in California. Basically they had an elaborate system in place that meant they were virtually untraceable.

He searched cable records, bank records, utility records, and came up empty-handed.

Zeke tucked his cell between his ear and shoulder while he finessed the computer searching for tax records on the business, and checked the answering service again.

Finally, there was a message. His heart stopped at Sunshine's voice. The slight tremble was only detectable because he was specifically listening for it. But he could hear the false bravado and worry beneath her simple succinct message.

"I'm at our favorite bistro."

Immediately, he yelped restaurants in San Luis and found there were several small French places that might fit. Shit. Which one could it be?

The restaurants were clustered near the Cal Poly campus, but one stood out. It was down the street from the Physics building.

Zeke had to take a chance. He pulled up the location information on Google maps and requested directions to be sent to his phone as he listened to the message again.

"I'll stay here for forty-five minutes and then I'm moving again. Hope you're okay. Check in."

No direct names, moving in intervals, this was a well-planned and well-executed escape and evade effort. But why? What threat could they both be worried about?

Zeke noted the time stamp on his computer. He had twenty minutes to get across town, hope he'd chosen the right location, and then convince her to let him help her.

Assuming she would talk to him. Assuming she wouldn't freak when she saw him.

At the last minute, he grabbed his Billabong baseball cap and jammed it over his unruly hair.

He hadn't had time to do more than glance at the records of the shop business, Scents of the Sea. The business vehicle on record was a peppy bright yellow Volkswagen Bug which totally fit her hippy-dippy image. But based on the vibes he was getting from his cursory search of Sunshine and her mother, he'd bet that they had another vehicle stashed somewhere that was not listed in their name.

Zeke kept his thoughts open and his gaze sharp as he edged toward speeding to get to *Le Bistrôt Légume* and intercept Sunshine.

He gripped the leather steering wheel, tension knotted his shoulders, his stomach churned, and acid burned in his chest with unexpected force. Zeke rubbed the blade of his hand over his breastbone, and wondered how someone he'd known less than twenty-four hours could become so important.

He had an unreasonable need to see her, touch her, reassure himself she was fine.

She'd left the message not more than ten minutes ago. But he couldn't settle, couldn't relax until he verified she wasn't in immediate danger and he saw for himself that she was safe.

He pulled into the triangle-shaped parking lot at the corner of the strip mall that housed the little French bistro.

His gaze darted around the minuscule lot, and tried to find a space while also looking for Sunshine's car. No VW bug was in the lot.

But in the corner, car backed in ready for a quick getaway, was an ancient blue Volvo. And with a certainty that was illogical, he knew that was her car. Zeke blocked the Volvo in, parking so it would be impossible for her to get out.

Relief swelled through him. Sweat sheened on his face, his pulse ticked in his throat, as he contemplated his next move. Did he attempt to confront her in the restaurant or wait until she tried to leave in her car?

His basic problem was if she realized he had gotten her location from the answering service his method of tracking her was compromised.

He didn't think he had any choice but to approach her inside the restaurant and hope she wouldn't make a scene.

Zeke got out of his Range Rover and headed for the strip mall and the bistro. He strode toward the entrance, his steps purposeful and his gaze trained on the single door.

An awning with fat green and brown stripes shaded a display window stenciled with green letters in a curlicue font on the glass. A delicate depiction of a cornucopia, with a variety of vegetables tumbling from the horn, also in flowing green lines decorated the center of the large window and gave the entire restaurant a French feel. Iron tables and chairs hovered under the awning like cows under a shady tree.

Zeke noted other details. A rack of display cones exploded with bunches of gerbera daisies, roses, gladiolus, and alstroemeria in front of the flower shop to the right. On the left, a used bookstore had a display table with markdowns and textbooks for purchase. A 'We Buy Books

Back' sign with a large dollar symbol was propped on the table.

Inside the tiny restaurant, there was a relatively long line at the counter and all the tables were occupied. Zeke took a deep breath and prepared to explain himself. He wasn't even sure what he was going to say. Women weren't his strong suit. In fact, except for a few casual rock climbing and surfing buddies, people weren't his strong suit. Someone with more experience could likely charm Sunshine. But Zeke wasn't the smoothest of talkers. In his head, he was still that dorky geek boy who had trouble talking to girls.

Zeke pushed open the glass door. Right now, he had to let his insecurities go and aim for achieving his goal. Get Sunshine Smith to listen to him. After all, he knew she and her mother were afraid, but really, how bad could the threat to them be?

CHAPTER 13

I slumped at the tiny wrought iron table, back to the wall and a clear view of the entrance. Although even if I saw the monster come in the restaurant, where could I go? The tables were crammed into the small vegetarian bistro with barely an inch between the backs of the chairs.

Suddenly I was re-thinking this location. I'd panicked and come to the first place that popped into my mind after I'd unloaded my old cell in a dumpster behind the Chevron gas station on the way out of town. Then I'd immediately programmed my Go Bag burner cell so I'd have a method of emergency communication. As soon as I arrived here, I left a message for Mama.

I'd followed the procedures that we set in place years ago. If we were separated, we used the answering service to communicate. Except when we put that system in place, there'd been no discussion of separating on purpose. So I was unsettled and jumpy.

I stretched out one leg in case I needed to bolt, and the other rested on the ball of my foot. My knee jittered up and down and my teeth clacked together although it was so loud in the minuscule eatery that no one could hear them except me.

The rat-a-tat clicked in time to the bounce of my knee. Conversation trembled and roared in the enclosed space as I surveyed the patrons in line and kept a tight watch on the door.

I didn't think Mama was going to show up with Blue. I'd made the call, just in case, left my position, in code of course, and how long I'd be here. I was a little bit jealous that Blue was taking care of Mama right now. That was *my* job.

Mama had gotten us away from that farm in Kansas. It was my job now to protect her.

There was no way, *no way*, my stepfather could trace me here.

Even if Blue let Mama get captured—very doubtful— she wouldn't give me up. Would she? My position should be secure.

But in my mind, the threat of him loomed like a menacing shadow. Taking me back to when I was seven years old, he was aiming that rifle at me, and then we were running for our lives.

A chill skittered over my spine.

My gaze darted around the restaurant, and I checked out the people waiting to order. A mother with twins in one of those giant double strollers that took up half the space for the line. An Asian woman, who looked about as tense as I felt, stood rigid and straight while her gaze systematically scoured the restaurant. She was too old to be a student. But in yoga pants and a matching zippered jacket in simple gray and black, she was dressed too casually to be a professor.

Two male art students, portfolios slung on their backs,

hair asymmetrically cut and unnaturally black, appeared as if they'd stepped straight out of their anime portfolios. A mother/daughter duo, who looked to be about the same age as Mama and me, gestured animatedly at the deli display case, clearly discussing their lunch choices. The mother laughed at something the daughter said, and the family resemblance was instantaneous, which made me suddenly wistful at their easy and carefree appearance.

I'm sure Mama and I had those moments, but I was never more aware of the fact that our relationship was haunted by fear. And now that Blue was on the scene, we'd never have the lighthearted affection that bathed those women in a happy glow. Likely, our relationship had changed forever.

The bell over the door jangled, and I cut my gaze sharply to the left. A beach bum guy in ragged board shorts, t-shirt worn thin that outlined impressive muscles, his head covered with a Billabong cap, shoved into the store.

He wasn't Mama and he was too young to be *him*.

Initially I dismissed the guy, and glanced at the time on my phone again. But something about him drew my gaze and when I looked back I knew why.

Underneath the bill of the cap, Zeke Thorn's ocean blue eyes stared at me.

I shoved up, my back scraping against the wall, my pulse pounding in my throat. I tried to swallow but I could barely breathe.

What were the odds that he would happen to be in this restaurant at this particular time? I had a better statistical chance of getting hit by lightning.

He wound through the tightly grouped tables, making his way straight toward me. I clutched my across-the-body tote bag with stitched peace signs and patchwork squares in my hand and straightened.

Somehow, some way he had tracked me here. Followed me? Although I sure hadn't noticed anyone following.

I had to get out. Get gone.

My breath solidified like sludge in my lungs, slowly cutting off my oxygen and leaving me gasping for air.

Zeke put out a placating hand as if to touch me. I had to get away. From him. Out of here. Great Goddess, had my system with Mama been compromised?

Could Zeke be working with *him*?

Maybe nothing about our last few interactions had been happenstance. Maybe he really was stalking me, maybe he was here to get me, so the monster could get Mama.

Fear shuddered through my body, working through each organ starting at my head and rippling to my toes in a wave.

"Great place." Zeke's shoulders were loose. He smiled and his body language was as non-threatening as possible.

"College hangout," I said trying to breathe normally as if I wasn't about one step away from completely hyperventilating. One step away from total breakdown.

He couldn't pretend to be nonchalant any longer, his gaze earnest and just a little bit pleading. "Sunshine, it's okay."

I glanced around frantically. "I have to go." If he had tracked me here, then anything was possible. I eased around the table, staying as far away from him as the space permitted and trying desperately to keep some object between us.

Zeke followed, advancing on me, gaining with every step. "Your mother sent me."

Oh, no, no, no. I was shaking my head, even as I picked

up the pace. Mama wouldn't send him. She wouldn't jeopardize our system with a complete stranger.

Except....Mama thought we had something going on. "Lying is never rewarded," I whispered as I edged toward frantic.

My lovely co-dependent Mama had sent me a white knight.

Except we didn't know diddly squat about this guy. Mama only thought I knew him.

Zeke reached out, trying to grab me across the table where the two art students now sat. The clink of the metal silverware on ceramic plates, the trill of laughter from behind me, the smell of the coffee that had sat a little too long on the burner, and the distinct odor of frying potatoes registered with my senses even as my vision tunneled to his very masculine hand. To his long, almost elegant fingers, with the dings and scrapes from his tumble in the ocean last night and the dusting of fine blond hair over his knuckles.

I stared as if I'd never seen a male hand before, unable to tear my gaze from his fingers or break away from the sudden and inexplicable urge I had to trust him.

To place my hand in his and let him help me.

Which was craziness. No one could help me. No one but me. I'd learned long ago only to rely on myself.

I backed away, and in my haste, bumped into the last person in line, causing a small chain reaction. Half the people turned around to see what the commotion was.

I'd inadvertently created my own escape distraction.

Zeke's attention was split for precious seconds as his focus shifted to the people in line and their annoyed stares. I scuttled toward the door praying I could get out before he realized I'd given him the slip.

Unable to help myself, knowing it was a horrible, bad, no good idea, I glanced back.

Zeke stood transfixed, staring at the Asian woman now at the counter.

The look of horror on his face was mirrored on hers.

Weird. Something very weird was going on. But I wasn't about to hang around and find out what. I had to get out of here now.

CHAPTER 14

"**S**hit," Zeke whispered. Susan Chen was in line. He'd noted the kinematics of her actions when she'd started to turn, recognized the pattern, the Euler angles of her joints, and the familiarity of her movement. All those elements had pulled his gaze toward Chen instead of staying squarely centered on Sunshine.

Everything in him slowed. The world narrowed. His heartbeat clanked in his ears drowning out all other noises. Images strobed as his attention fractured.

Ka-thunk. Susan Chen who looked as horrified as he felt.

Ka-thunk, ka-thunk. Sunshine beating a frantic exit made tracks for the damn door and away from him.

Ka-thunk. Susan Chen. National security. A sinister plot that had cost one agent his life, and two other agents had been irrevocably changed by the results of her science experiment. If she would just tell his superiors what he'd divulged when he'd been kidnapped and drugged, he would be off suspension. He hoped.

Ka-thunk. Ka-thunk. Sunshine. Whom he'd vowed to protect from Susan's evil clutches just a few hours ago.

Sunshine who was clearly frightened. Because of him? Because of the unnamed threat to her and her mother?

Ka-thunk. Susan Chen. The key to all his problems, but she could also be the downfall of everything.

Ka-thunk, ka-thunk. Sunshine, who had someone after her, was clearly terrified that Zeke had something to do with whoever, whatever, was dogging her and her mother.

Ka-thunk. Susan Chen who had the ability to clear him. But, if she didn't clear him and if his bosses found out he was anywhere near her, expressly against their directive to stay away from anyone who compromised national security, he was done for. His job was to find her, follow her discreetly, and call someone else. Chen wasn't supposed to actually see him.

While he was clicking through his two options, Susan Chen beelined for the door. Zeke couldn't let her escape.

Zeke followed desperately.

As she reached the door of the café, he curled his palm around her bicep. She whipped her head around, and her eyes were wide, frightened. The stark fear in her trembling body shocked him and he loosened his grip.

As soon as he did, Susan yanked open the door and bolted outside. She jerked her head left, then right. Zeke caught up to her again.

But then he spotted Sunshine Smith frantically turning over the engine on the old Volvo.

Shit.

Chen tugged at her arm. But this time he wasn't letting her go.

"Please," she begged. "Don't do this."

The grind of the starter pulled his gaze toward Sunshine. She was no longer looking at Zeke. Her attention was directed across the street. Sunshine was staring at an older man with a wide chest, large arms, and a nearly bald head scattered with salt and pepper hair. The sheer terror reflected on her face was so strong it made Susan Chen's expression seem like a placid lake of calm.

Sunshine had hunched over the steering wheel. Her grip on the molded plastic was so tight he could see her bones.

The condemning beat of his heart echoed in his ears. Susan Chen was tugging against his hold. She hadn't said another word since that one bout of pleading.

The guy Sunshine was afraid of glanced down the street, his gaze skimmed over Zeke and Susan and kept going. If he scoped back up the street, he would see Sunshine in the Volvo.

Ka-thunk. Ka-thunk. Sunshine who was alone in the world. Who'd saved his ass last night. The least he could do was return the favor.

Options clicked through his mind as he searched for patterns, searched for the right path. His next move. He stared at Chen. Trapped, cornered. He caught her vibe, and considered that she was as trapped as he was.

The patrons eating at the outdoor section of the café were beginning to murmur. So he needed to either apprehend Susan and get her in his Range Rover or let her go. Otherwise, he was guessing the police would be here soon. And that definitely didn't constitute laying low.

Ka-thunk. Wallet. Cards. He reached into his back pocket, observing mechanically as Susan Chen ducked.

She thought he was going for a weapon. Of course the last time she'd seen him, her partner had just had his head blown off.

Zeke flipped a card at her, hoped like hell he hadn't just fucked himself. He couldn't believe he was going to do this.

Because while Susan Chen looked trapped, Sunshine Smith had been terrified. "If you want to talk, call me."

He headed for Sunshine, walking quickly and trying not to draw the older man's attention.

Ka-thunk, ka-thunk, ka-thunk. His heart rate increased. Zeke hoped he wasn't making the biggest mistake of his life.

Oh wait, the biggest mistake of his life was hacking into the Pentagon at sixteen. The government had owned him since then. And fuck him if they hadn't wrung every drop of remorse out of him. How could they think that he would jeopardize his entire future, his freedom by giving away national secrets?

Of course leaving Susan Chen here, along with his business card, might top that cluster.

But something, he wasn't sure what, instinct, insanity, was telling him that he needed to be with Sunshine. She was his mission priority.

As soon as the older man shifted his attention down the opposite side of the street, Zeke ran toward her Volvo. Sunshine was getting ready to ram the hell out of his rental.

He stretched his stride, kicking his feet as if he were on the last twenty-five meters and headed for the finish line. His feet slid forward in the Merrill's, and he held his hands out in supplication.

Her Volvo would seriously crumple the side of the Rover, but the SUV would hold. More importantly, he needed to get her out of here before they drew any more attention.

In the back of his mind, he calculated odds, inconsistencies, and probability, factoring in all the variables as his brain whipped through possible scenarios, and came to one conclusion.

Susan Chen's appearance in that bistro was unexpected and unwelcome but he was pretty sure, random.

It also meant a shift in all of the other calculations he'd been mentally compiling. For some reason, he'd assumed that the threat against Sunshine and her mother wasn't extreme. But because of the way they'd responded, now he was re-thinking his analysis of their situation.

He should have acknowledged two facts before jumping to that conclusion. One, women who were virtually untraceable by him, a gray hat hacker, and two, a woman who was afraid of the ocean and still dragged his sorry butt out of the water, wouldn't overreact to a threat. They weren't easily scared.

Sunshine gunned the engine of her Volvo. She hunched her body, curling in on herself, as if she could will the car to lift out of the box he'd cornered her in and fly.

Thinking strategically, he wound around to the passenger side and yanked open the door. "I'm not here to hurt you."

"Did he send you?" Her foot hovered over the gas pedal. Her eyes were wild. If she pressed down while he was hanging onto the car door, he was in trouble.

Jesus, whoever *he* was, she was terrified. Zeke had to find out. He threw himself into the passenger seat and pulled the door shut. "I don't even know who he is."

OH MY GODDESS.

How had *he* found me?

The monster was here. Across the street. He'd gotten out of an old pickup truck and had clearly been scanning the sidewalks and businesses. If I didn't get out of here soon he might see me. Bile swirled in my stomach, like the angry waves from last night, and my forehead blossomed with sweat.

"Him." I jerked my head toward where my stepfather had stood. Terrified to call attention to myself. A big black Range Rover blocked the Volvo and had partially hidden me from the monster. But if I rammed the car blocking my way, my stepfather was sure to check out the commotion and see me. "Get out."

I yanked the seat belt over my body, and sent up a prayer that these old Volvos truly were built like tanks.

Zeke Thorn hadn't budged. He was scrutinizing the street. "I won't hurt you," he repeated.

"Then why the hell are you here?" I cried. "Leave me alone."

"Come with me, in my car. Whoever you're afraid of won't be able to identify it."

I shook my head so violently the strands of my hair sprang from the tight braid and curled against my cheek. "I don't even know you."

"Shit. I'm no good at this people stuff." Zeke tugged at the neckline of his O'Neill t-shirt. "This is why I stick to numbers, programs, equations. You plug in the variables and come out with an answer."

Had the monster seen me yet? I tried to peer through the windshield without lifting my head very far above the dash. Fear and rage clashed violently inside me, and I wondered how long I could keep down the scone I'd eaten for breakfast.

I needed to get the hell out of here before he could get me.

I flashed back to him staring up at me in that attic window. To the menace in his eyes before he'd turned around to make sure my grandparents were dead. To the first three times he'd found Mama and me and we'd managed to escape before he got close enough to grab my mother.

In thirteen years, this was the nearest I'd been to the man who'd murdered my grandparents and stolen my childhood. I couldn't even think about how he'd found me, us. How was that possible?

"Look, I only want to help you." Zeke sounded desperate.

Welcome to the club, asshole.

"You can't. No one can." *Just leave me alone.*

"Let's take my car. Tell me about your problem and we'll see what I can do." He spoke calmly, gently, all trace of desperation gone.

Maybe he could help. Maybe there was something he could do. Except I knew nothing about him. Nothing.

"We'll never know unless you tell me about it."

The unseasonably warm October sunshine streamed through the window. He waited, on the edge of a precipice for my decision. His focus shifted across the street. Reflexively, I slid further down in the seat.

"Was that the guy?"

"Can't you just leave me alone?" The urge to scream obstructed my throat. Which was fortunate, because I shouldn't do anything to draw attention to myself.

"I want to help you." Zeke craned his neck to peer over my head.

"Don't stare."

It had been nine years since the last time he'd tracked us down. I'd still been a kid. Now I was a full grown woman. And he still had the power to terrify me. I wasn't sure I could move if he saw us and turned that malevolent gaze on me. Which was why I had to get the hell out of here. Since I didn't know how he'd found me I had to assume everything I owned was compromised. Which I then realized meant I needed to ditch the Volvo.

"Which car is yours?"

"The Rover."

"You blocked me in?"

"I wanted to make sure you talked to me."

"You aren't some crazy stalker, are you?"

That's all I needed. Another crazy stalker.

"No!" Zeke burst out. "Come with me. I want to help you."

The monster was now out of sight. He'd headed down the street toward the flower shop and the bistro. But he'd have to come back this way to get in his nondescript old truck.

Zeke adjusted his ball cap. "I am the good guy," he snarled.

I yanked my keys from the ignition and threaded them between my fingers, making a fist with my right hand. I couldn't go anywhere in my car, which was potentially compromised anyway, and he was blocking me in. I had to get out of here before the monster came back.

"Let's go." Then I said fiercely, my throat tight, but my resolve absolute, "But if you have anything to do with him, I'm warning you. I won't give her up. Ever. And I'll make you sorry you ever came after me."

For a moment, he went boneless as if every muscle released the tension he'd been holding in a rush of relief. Zeke gripped the door handle of the Volvo. "You won't be sorry."

"I'd better not be."

I prayed I wasn't making the last mistake of my life. I'd

lost my freaking mind. But I really didn't have a choice. The monster could come back at any moment. I could ram the Rover but the commotion would draw attention I couldn't afford.

I could run from Zeke, and my stepfather, but with that powerful SUV Zeke would be able to catch me fairly quickly.

I needed a place to re-group and hide until I could figure out how my stepfather was tracking me. And I needed to let my mother know that the monster really was here. That he'd found us.

For right now, I had to trust Zeke. He was my best option for getting away from my stepfather. I still couldn't believe that Mama had given him access to our communication network.

But until I could talk to my mother and explain that I'd lied about knowing him, she might keep feeding Zeke Thorn information.

Besides that, I had this irrational urge to trust him.

The look on his face while trying to convince me had been determined but not desperate and somehow vulnerable. As if he didn't want to hurt me and he knew enough about me that he could have used other methods to get me to go with him, but hadn't.

His obvious sincerity had been what finally convinced me that he was my best option right now. I reached into the back seat and hefted a pink canvas duffel bag into my lap. "Let's go."

CHAPTER 15

Z eke started the Rover.

"You want to hunch down?"

"Yes." She crouched in the well of the passenger seat. "Get the license plate number of the old Dodge truck parked across the street."

Her demanding tone struck a chord within him. And he admired her strength. Because for all her terror, she hadn't fallen apart.

He noticed the graceful length of her neck, the fall of her hair, and the curls that escaped to drift around her resolute face, softening her, making look more vulnerable.

Ka-thunk.

"Who is after you?" Zeke needed more information if was going to be able to help her. The old truck was just that. Old. Nothing special. He needed to find out why she was so terrified of the guy. He didn't look threatening. He'd been mid to late fifties. Balding, with mostly gray hair and a paunch at the waist. He had the look of a man who'd played football in his youth but the muscle had gone to fat.

Her silver eyes were shadowed with fear. "Where is he?"

Zeke stopped at the exit of the parking lot and searched the crowded street, looking for the man who'd induced a blank terror in this amazingly strong woman.

"Don't see him."

"Turn the opposite way from the path he took."

Zeke turned right out of the parking lot and headed away from the campus. He kept glancing in his rearview mirror. And, surprise, the man was peering into the driver's window of the old Volvo.

The man straightened and his gaze zoomed in on the Rover. Zeke cursed silently, unsure, but hoping the guy hadn't made him. Zeke quickly turned right, noting in his peripheral vision that the man was headed leisurely toward the truck. However his gaze was pinned on the rear of the Range Rover. Dammit.

If he hadn't caught Zeke's plate, then he'd likely be running. But the guy was taking his time. Zeke didn't know if that meant he'd already mentally noted his number or if he didn't think that Zeke had anything to do with his search.

Zeke thought about keeping the information from Sunshine but then decided to be up front with her.

"He may have made the Rover."

Zeke rubbed the cap forward and back over his head and repressed the urge to put a comforting hand on Sunshine's shoulder.

Her face whitened but otherwise she showed no outward emotion.

Zeke had actually rubbed some dirt on the plate to obscure the numbers but the guy's attitude made him think the ruse hadn't worked.

Depending on what kind of skills he had it wouldn't take him more than a day to track down Zeke's name. Then he'd be able to trace his credit card purchases. So they had time before they would need to ditch this car. In the meantime, maybe he could find out why Sunshine was so afraid of the guy.

"What kind of skills does he have?" Zeke asked.

"Since he found me?" Sunshine rested her forehead on the leather seat next to her. "Pretty damn good ones."

That's what he thought. "Who is he?"

"Who was the woman in the café?" she asked, deliberately ignoring him. As if she were trying to distract herself from her own problems. Or she was trying to distract Zeke.

He tried to shove Susan Chen out of his mind. But as he held his breath, the roar in his ears grew louder. He didn't want Susan and Sunshine on the same radar. When Sunshine had rushed out of the bistro, Susan hadn't seemed to recognize her but another look could tip her over the edge. He didn't know how much information Susan had about the names of the people she'd used in her unauthorized science experiment but every one of those unwilling subjects had one thing in common. They were members of a very small list of people whose family was killed on either October 19th or 20th, 1995. And Sunshine, while not part of the experiment, was definitely on the infamous, at least among a select few agents, 5491 list.

Did Susan know that? She'd had access to so much. And they still had yet to figure out how. Although, oddly, no one seemed to be pursuing that part of the investigation. Everyone seemed fixated on getting Susan Chen back.

"She's part of a...situation I was involved in a few weeks ago."

"A situation?"

"She's wanted by the U.S. Government."

"Why haven't I seen her picture on the news?"

Zeke snorted. "Her situation is the kind that never makes the news."

"Right." Sunshine laughed harshly. "So now you're part of some shadowy government organization?"

She flicked a hand at him.

"The NSA is a recognized and established intelligence agency." And the more he thought about it the more he really didn't want Sunshine and Susan inhabiting the same space. "And I'm worried she could be dangerous...to you."

He could take care of himself.

"I've got much bigger problems, but I'll bite. Why me?"

"It's a long story."

"The NSA, dangerous women, convenient appearances." She mocked. "You really expect me to believe all this?"

That's when he realized that he hadn't so much as convinced her to come with him as she'd chosen him as her last viable alternative.

He knew he should be more polished, more persuasive. In theory, he knew enough about the MICE recruitment incentives when covert operatives tried to recruit foreign assets. Money, Ideology, Compromise, Ego. He'd had training in how to convince someone to become an asset. Convincing her to believe him could be achieved, but this was different. This was personal. Way too personal. And he couldn't seem to find the words to finesse her.

She was too important.

He'd just given his card to Susan Chen. If she was caught, if they found the identifier on her person, *if, if, if*— he was done.

He refused to look away from Sunshine. Refused to back down. "I want don't want you to get hurt." Then he reiterated, "I want to help you with your problems."

She stared at him for another loaded moment, her gaze searching his. Zeke felt as if she were staring into his soul, and all his uncertainties and longings were exposed to her laser perception.

"I think my problem is too big and unsolvable," she admitted in what must be a moment of total insecurity.

"Nothing is unsolvable. It just hasn't been deciphered yet," he replied, wanting her to believe him.

Moisture shimmered in her eyes. "Okay," she whispered.

Relief and satisfaction flooded him. One problem down. She'd agreed to let him help her. Now he had to take care of his other problem.

"I have to make a phone call about that woman," Zeke said glumly.

Zeke punched Jamie's cell into his phone. He'd only talked to her a few hours ago. And he could imagine her response when she picked up the phone. "Did you find her already?" Jamie would tease. "You stud."

He dreaded having to tell her he'd found Susan Chen and lost her almost immediately.

So it was petty of him but Zeke was more than happy when instead of Jamie he got her voice mail.

"Hey." Zeke confessed, "She was here. But I lost her."

He knew he needed to give Jamie as much information as he could. He rubbed a damp hand on his board shorts. "It seems almost impossible, but she was in San Luis." He thought about how Susan Chen's gaze had skipped right over Sunshine. "I don't think she's after our target."

Zeke swallowed. He hated to admit defeat. But he couldn't even promise to go after Chen again until he figured out what was going on with Sunshine.

"Let's touch base again later." Zeke tightened his mouth and pressed the end button.

"You didn't really lose her, did you?"

Sunshine's subdued voice from the other side of the car startled him out of the beginnings of another self-pity party.

"Nope."

"You came after me instead."

"Yep."

"And we got away."

But from who and why? Zeke couldn't wait to find out.

"Yep. So now that you've agreed to let me help you, tell me who that guy was."

CHAPTER 16

W hat had I just agreed to?

I had to stop thinking about my stepfather or I was going to hyperventilate. I was desperately hoping Zeke Thorn was wrong about the monster catching his license plate. And yeah, I'd agreed to let Zeke help me but I still wanted some sort of confirmation that he was who he said he was.

"Do you have some sort of government I.D.?"

Wasn't that what they always did in the movies? Ask to see identification? Except, I was in a position to know that identification could be falsified.

He flushed. A huge red wash over his entire face. "Not on me."

But his mouth had turned down and the look on his face made me wonder.

"I do have a business card. Of course, you can go anywhere and get fake cards made but...."

"But?" I prompted when he stopped and didn't continue. I thought of something else. Why did this guy

keep turning up? "Did you engineer the meet on
the beach?"

He laughed sharply and turned right again. "Uh, no.
Pretty much the story of my life though."

"Why?"

"Zeke the Geek strikes again." The bitterness in his tone
was unmistakable.

"What does that mean? What's wrong?"

"What isn't?" He avoided explaining. Instead he headed
up the ramp to Highway One, trying to put distance
between us and the monster. And that woman?

His problems had to do with the woman. "Why did she
look so surprised?"

"She's wanted by the federal government, and she
knows that my bosses are after her. She escaped from a
federal prison. My guess is she didn't think anyone would
find her in a bistro in a tiny California town. Especially not
me." Of course, he'd been one of the people to find her the
last time.

"Then why'd you let her go?"

He glanced in the rearview mirror, then shifted his
attention firmly back to the road, and shrugged. "You."

"Me?" What the hell? Was that supposed to convince
me of something? If that woman really was wanted by the
government, and he really did work for the NSA, why didn't
he grab her? That made no sense whatsoever. I was just a
victim of an obsessive stalker. One of thousands. No one
special. "Why?"

"Can I take you to my hotel room so we can talk?" he
asked tightly. His hands gripped the steering wheel so
fiercely I thought it might break apart in his fingers. "I've
tried to think of a more neutral place but I don't want you

in public and at this point I don't know where else you would be safe."

I hesitated a moment longer. But the reality was my stepfather had found me. Right now, no one except myself and Zeke knew where I would be. And he hadn't exactly abducted me.

I didn't get any kind of 'I'm going to hurt you' vibe from Zeke Thorn. Which meant for the near future I would be safe with him. Unless, of course, he worked for, or with, the monster. But I just couldn't bring myself to believe that. "Fine."

He could be playing me but somehow I didn't think so. He was far too self-deprecating and disgusted with himself over letting that woman go. The tone in his voice when he'd left the message struck a chord with me.

He kept rambling even though I'd already agreed.

"I'd take you somewhere more public but based on your reaction to that guy," he paused, as if waiting for me to fill him in on who the monster was. "I don't think hanging out in public is a smart move right now."

He'd be damn right about that.

Because the monster had found me in SLO after being in Cambria this morning asking about my mother, and I wouldn't have thought we could be traced that quickly.

So I was going to use Zeke from the NSA to find out how my stepfather had found us again after all this time. I hated the idea of having to move again. We had a decent life in Cambria. If Mama wanted to be with Blue, it was time to fight back. Even if I did want to throw up at the thought of confronting him, and getting him to back off once and for all.

"Why me?" I pressed, one more time. I really needed to understand what was happening here. Everything seemed upside down or backwards or discombobulated. And I couldn't discern any sense of it all. Entropy, the second law of thermodynamics, disorder into order was what I needed.

"You needed my help," Zeke said softly.

"You don't even know me." *So why would he want to help me?*

"I know enough." Zeke pulled off Highway One and headed to the outskirts of San Luis. "And you saved me."

I couldn't wrap my head around his response so I kept quiet.

"You're terrified of water and yet you dragged me out of the surf," Zeke replied seriously. "That takes a depth of courage that few possess. Frankly, I owe you."

His praise gave me a warm glowy feeling. I never felt brave. Most of the time I felt like a big fat coward, hiding away from the world, hiding my true self, so that my stepfather couldn't find us. With just a few words, Zeke had managed to bolster my confidence.

"You probably would have been fine." But my heart skipped a beat as I remembered the encroaching waves pulling at his unconscious body.

"Lucky for me you were on the beach." Zeke said, "Lucky for me that we met at all."

"But our meeting wasn't by chance," I countered. "You admitted that you were here for me."

"Yeah. Except we weren't supposed to meet at all." Zeke took another turn. "I was only supposed to keep an eye on you."

"So...."

"I fucked up," he said harshly. "I wasn't supposed to make contact."

"With me?"

"Yeah."

"But you did and...."

"And you're in trouble. I'm not just going to walk away."

He seemed to have an unrealistic sense of obligation that I just didn't understand. No one took care of me; I took care of myself.

"Let me help you," he said it again.

"How?"

"Who's after you?"

"You really think you can help?" I calculated odds and his sense of responsibility. Maybe, just maybe, I could find out about my stepfather and we could come up with a way to save me and my mother.

If I used Zeke Thorn's resources, I could find out where the monster was staying, maybe even his permanent address, maybe somehow I could end this need to hide, this need to constantly be vigilant, and end his reign of terror. Once and for all.

Dammit, between our mini-date this morning and my mother's sudden surprising relationship with Blue, I was lonely, and sick of running. I wanted to *live*.

Zeke interrupted my musings. "I'll do my best."

I knew he meant it. Why did I have the inexplicable urge to trust this man? Truthfully he'd done nothing to inspire that trust. My suspicious nature, cultivated from years of being on the run, was oddly dormant.

Zeke pressed his lips together. "I won't promise any more than I can deliver."

He pulled in to the parking lot of the nondescript motel behind a strip mall and a grocery store. His room was around back, hidden away from the street. Our comings and goings would be obscured by the traffic from the stores.

He parked at the end of the lot, the car nearly hidden by the dumpster. Room card in hand, he hustled toward a service door. He swiped the key card and pulled open the door. "Let's talk when we have privacy."

His gaze was constantly moving, and he had put his body between me and the outside. Protecting me or herding me toward captivity? He looked left, right, then headed down the hall. He stopped in front of a door with a Do Not Disturb sign on the handle. He swiped the key card once, twice, three times. Then tightened his mouth. As soon as the lock clicked, Zeke nudged me inside.

The room was lit with the glow of light from an open laptop and the desk lamp. The blackout curtains were drawn so that no one could see in the room.

One last thing. "Show me your card." I wasn't about to reveal anything until I'd seen some sort of proof.

Although he was right. Anyone could have fake cards printed.

Trepidation and, oddly, a budding sense of hope swirled through me.

I sat in the chair at the desk. The room was decorated in a generic beach theme, blues and greens with peach accents and lots of seashells. The design was background noise without any flash. Nothing notable about it. Most people would likely stay here and after they left, they would have no remembrance what the room looked like.

Kind of like me. I faded into the background, bland, pastel, unremarkable. I didn't make waves. I didn't show my intellect. I didn't ever show the hunger that existed inside me. That black hole that craved new knowledge like a heroin addict craved a needle. But I didn't just yearn for knowledge. I wanted new experiences.

And I was tired of hiding. I wanted to be me. I wanted to be visible. I wanted to have choices.

He pulled a card from his wallet and extended it to me

held between his pointer and middle finger. I tried not to notice the curve of his bicep straining at the cuff of the short sleeve t-shirt and the smooth tan skin of his forearm, his veins prominent in the rippling muscles. His eyes were an intense, ocean blue as I reached out slowly to take the white linen rectangle.

"Uh, wait." He jerked the card back and cocked his elbow up. "There's one thing."

Right. Here it comes. I tensed, getting ready to make a break for it. I was closer to the door, although with his physique he could probably overtake me. But I had to try.

"What?"

"My name isn't Zeke Thorn."

"Oh." Somehow Zeke had really seemed to fit him.

"It's Zeke Hawthorne."

"Oh." Boy, did I sound intelligent.

He handed me his card. The white card was simple, a government seal with a bald eagle, key clutched in it's talons and crest across his chest, Zeke's name in navy blue, and National Security Agency printed in the gold band that surrounded the eagle.

"What do you do?"

"I'm a programmer."

"So that part was true."

"Uh, yeah."

He sat, trying I was sure, to project an air of trustworthiness. He didn't know that I'd never in my life trusted anyone. Not since I was seven years old. But the temptation to believe in him was strong. "You going to trust me?"

Finally, I blurted out, "I need to find that man."

He didn't make jokes, he didn't smirk. It was almost as if he understood that this was a huge leap of faith for me.

Faith I'd lost long ago. Perhaps never had.

"Do you have a name?"

Somehow I'd expected him to ask other questions first, like why, who was he, what did he mean to me? But Zeke got right to the point.

My heart thumped in my chest. My hands trembled as adrenaline flooded through my body. I wasn't sure I could do this. My throat constricted, my mouth was dry. And I was freaking stalling.

"Of the person who you think is after you," he clarified, as if he thought I didn't know what he was talking about.

I hadn't spoken the monster's name aloud in thirteen years.

When we left, we'd looked back but we'd never, ever, *ever* said his name again. As if by uttering the words we might conjure him up.

The thought was terrifying and crazy. And I felt like I was seven years old and fleeing for my life again.

"Do you have a name?" he asked again.

I couldn't stall any longer. The terror gripping me gave way, broke over me like a wave. If he was working with my stepfather, I would know in a minute. Watching him carefully for any sign of recognition, I quietly spoke the name of the devil. My devil.

"John Stanley."

CHAPTER 17

J ohn Stanley.

Sunshine had said his name as if waiting for Zeke to recognize the guy.

There was an expectant pause in her body language, and he knew he needed to tread carefully over the next few minutes. She was so damn skittish that he thought if he showed even a slightly overt interest she would bolt.

"Okay." To begin, he touched the top, the exact center of the left edge, the exact center of the right edge, and the bottom of his laptop keyboard. "That's the guy we just saw?"

She pressed her lips together tightly, swallowed, then nodded.

"Let's start with the license plate."

He'd memorized the full plate number. First Zeke accessed the California DMV database. But when he pulled up the information on that plate number it was for a late model Lexus. Not an old Ford truck. The Lexus had been reported stolen two days ago.

Zeke sighed. "That was a dead end."

She slumped. "Do you think he got your plate number?"

"Even if he did it will take a while to track down the rental information and then my credit card information. You're safe." *For now.*

Sunshine stiffened her shoulders. "So that's it?"

"Of course not. It just means this will be a little more difficult."

So Zeke tried some basic internet search stuff.

It was a pretty uncommon name but several names came up ranging all over the country. "Do you have any idea where he lives?"

Her face was white, her gray eyes large granite pools in her face. "Ah, he used to...live in Kansas."

Zeke scrolled through the names, clicking on page after page, but no one with his general characteristics popped in Kansas. "Can I ask for more information?"

She licked her lips. "Like what?"

"What are you willing to give me on him?"

She sat there as if paralyzed. She was truly terrified by this guy.

Finally he couldn't stand her fear any more. Zeke asked gently, "What did he do?"

If Sunshine was this terrified, the threat was real.

She shook her head. A strand of her black hair escaped her loose braid and curled along her neck, momentarily distracting Zeke from his questions.

Couldn't tell him? Or wouldn't?

"I need more information." Or he needed to contact someone else to get the information. "Or I've got to use a contact within the NSA to dig deeper."

Which would expose him and the fact that he'd made contact with Sunshine. At this point, he should probably call Carson, and come clean. About Sunshine and Susan.

Zeke thought that Carson would keep his secret. But he couldn't be sure. Dammit.

Of course yesterday he'd suggested Carson assist Jordan and Staci with a sting. He hadn't heard from his pal today, but that wasn't surprising. Especially if Jordan was still with Staci. He knew that Zeke needed to stay far away from the fugitive.

He would need to call Carson at home. Away from the office.

"No! Don't call anyone else."

"Why are you looking for him?"

"He...killed my grandparents."

Zeke reared back. She knew the name of her grandparents' assassin? On the heels of that thought, he connected the pieces into a pattern that had him salivating for more information. What he wouldn't give to talk to this guy. "Is he out of prison?"

She laughed bitterly. "Who said he went to prison?"

So he'd killed her grandparents and gotten away with it. And then suddenly he realized what that meant. This guy was a sleeper sent specifically to murder her grandparents.

Just like his Grandpop had been murdered.

And there too the murderer had gotten away with it. But Zeke had no idea who had murdered his grandfather. Then another connection fused. "Honey, if he killed your grandparents, you're safe." He had no idea how he was going to explain it all to her but he'd have to try. She wasn't in any danger. The subtle tension that had gripped Zeke when he thought about her being in jeopardy eased its constriction around his lungs. All of the sleeper assassins had killed their targets, sometimes with collateral damage, but no one had come back for the descendants years' later.

Sunshine threaded her fingers together in her lap and

worried at the chipped lavender polish on her index finger. Her head was bent at such an angle that he couldn't see her face, couldn't see her eyes.

A tear dripped on her clenched hands.

He wanted, no needed to reassure her, but based on the level of her terror, she wasn't going to be easy to calm down. Although he knew she was safe, she didn't have any reason to believe him. "You don't need to worry about him anymore."

She whipped her head up. "You're wrong."

"How did he kill them?" he asked gently. The report indicated that they had drowned after their tire blew out.

"He shot their tire. The car went into the creek. We'd had unprecedented rain that year. The creek was angry, swollen almost to the banks, and they were swept away." She wrapped her arms around her middle and rubbed her biceps briskly as if trying to get warm. The anxious move brought his attention to the slender strength in her arms. And his brain kept trying to make the connection between this fragile woman and his muscled bulk.

He shifted gears, thinking about last night. "How the hell did you ever get me out of the water?"

She shrugged. "Physics."

"Thank God for science nerds," he murmured.

She snorted, her silver eyes brightened for a second. Then fear dampened their glow and a guilty expression crossed her face. She was thinking about her grandparents again.

"At least you had closure." He couldn't help but think that she was lucky. She knew her grandparents were murdered. After all, until a few weeks ago, he'd believed his grandfather had died in a climbing accident.

"God should not allow monsters to live and angels to die," Sunshine said bitterly.

"God didn't have anything to do with your grandparents' death." Zeke countered, trying to keep the snap out his words. "They were murdered."

But how did she know exactly what happened when, according to the info he had, the coroner had ruled it an accident? "Are you sure about what happened?"

"I saw him do it."

Shock, sharp and unexpected, surged through his body. His vision blurred and a chill rippled down his spine. "You saw him?"

She nodded.

Jesus.

But even so...she should be safe. The assassin had completed his task.

Except, she'd seen him. And she knew what he'd done. Was that why he was after Sunshine and her mother? Although it didn't explain how she knew his name. Or why, years later, he would still be after her and her mother?

"It was thirteen years ago." Zeke pondered, "Why is he still after you?"

She surged up from her perch on the generic bedspread, then fluidly reached into her long hippie bag, pulled out a small SigSauer P229, and cocked the trigger with the barrel pointed straight at his sternum.

"How do you know how long ago it was?"

"I ASSUME you know how to use that?" Zeke nodded his head toward the Sig, not moving anything else.

Not even twitching.

He was motionless. He wasn't sweating and he wasn't screaming. What the hell that meant, I had absolutely no idea, but he wasn't reacting the way I'd anticipated. Usually people were afraid of guns. *I* was afraid of guns and I was holding the damn thing.

"Answer the question." I held the cold, black, anodized metal steady using both hands. I might be shaking like a palm tree in gale force winds on the inside, but my hands were rock solid and sure on the outside.

After his initial blink of surprise at the gun, he hadn't looked at it since. He kept his gaze squarely on my face. But he still hadn't answered my question.

I couldn't decide if I was impressed or pissed. Pissed won.

"Aren't you afraid I'll shoot you?" I wanted him cringing in fear, cowering before the might of my weapon. His uncanny calm only made me more angry.

"You know, yesterday I probably would have said go for it. But today I have new reason to survive."

He didn't say live.

I wondered if he even realized the distinction. I sure did. For too long, I'd been surviving rather than living. And I was tired of it.

"You still haven't explained how you knew about my grandparents."

Zeke sighed, rubbed a hand across his neck. "It's complicated."

"I live for complicated."

"Ah, can you lower the weapon first?"

I kept the Sig Sauer pointed at him. But the reality of pointing a gun at a real person, a human being, especially a guy like Zeke with his broad chest and ripped abs, strong biceps and lean forearms, generated a roiling mess in my stomach.

"Please?" He cocked his head to one side, his unruly blond curls brushed one shoulder and drew my attention right back to his body. The deep ocean blue of his eyes and the serious set of his mouth told me he understood how close to the edge I stood and how much I was teetering.

"Explain."

"I knew about your grandparents because thirteen years ago yesterday, my grandfather died in a climbing accident," he responded evenly.

"What does that have to do with my grandparents?"

"Their deaths are connected."

"Connected," I said flatly. "How?"

"I can't tell you."

"Excuse me?"

"It's a matter of national security and you don't have clearance."

I snorted. "You have got to be kidding me." My shoulders slumped. Why had I come with him? Given in to him? Clearly he was crazy.

National security? Clearance? My stepfather had been a farmer in Kansas.

"Goddess," I whispered. I'd let my longing for a connection with a man override thirteen years of caution and borderline paranoid isolation.

On the other hand, the good news was Zeke couldn't possibly have anything to do with John Stanley. I wanted to relax into a puddle of relief. Zeke wasn't after me or Mama.

Mama.

My brain was still examining, calculating, processing. And that's when I realized that I still couldn't relax.

We weren't safe. The monster had found me in San Luis. Which should have been impossible.

And I was right back to where I'd started. My stepfather was still after us. And I was on my own again.

Zeke clearly didn't know who John was. There had not been an ounce of recognition, no flinch, no flicker of an eyelid, in his response to John's name. He'd just written the name down and then started looking for John Stanley on his computer.

I really was on my own. Zeke was crazy so he clearly couldn't help me with him. Mama was safe with Blue. And I had the overwhelming urge to just let loose and cry. Sob until my grief was gone, and I was empty of all the wants and needs I'd had to suppress for thirteen long years. Worries I was unable to reveal, and hopes I was forbidden to indulge, chained to my psyche and dragged me down. But I was afraid if I let go, I might not be able to pull myself back from that edge. He'd given me hope and then snatched it away. The sense of loss was startling.

So my crying jag would have to wait. I had to go. Had to find out why my former stepfather had been in Cambria this morning and how he had found us. We'd been safe for nine years, so why now?

I carefully stored the gun back in the pocket I'd sewn into my patchwork purse.

I didn't look at Zeke. Couldn't really. He'd been a wisp of an idea. A longing to connect. A wish for something ephemeral that was just that. A silly childish wish. I would never be free until he, *John Stanley*, was dead.

Neither would Mama.

"Thank you for your time," I said formally. My gaze shifted around the impersonal hotel room, mentally collecting my belongings and packing up my life. Again.

"Wait, what?" Zeke jumped up, blocked my path.

He'd stepped closer. So close in fact I could see the striations of aqua and navy in his blue gaze. He'd invaded my personal space. As close as he'd been when he'd kissed me. Given me a gift. There had been tenderness and desire in our brief contact this morning.

Now that I knew what they felt like, I resolved to experience those sensations again. I just had to take care of my problems first. And then, I vowed, I was going to chase that feeling again.

"I need to leave."

The heat from his body was intense as he curled his fingers around my bicep. "You can't." Zeke edged closer. His warmth surrounded me like a comforting hug.

"Sure I can." I tugged at my arm.

"I can help you. But you need to tell me why you think this John Stanley would come after you." Zeke tilted his head, his brows scrunched in an adorable frown. "And how you know his name."

It shouldn't matter if I told him. Since he didn't know who John was. I purposely swallowed down my fear and tried to keep my voice even, calm, unemotional. "I know his name because he is, was, my stepfather."

CHAPTER 18

Zeke opened his mouth. Closed it. The assassin was her stepfather? That was a sleeper who was way too close to his intended targets. He couldn't wrap his brain around that kind of illicit intimacy.

"He married the daughter of his target," he spoke the words aloud as if trying to make sense of what she was telling him. The act held a level of evil that was hard to comprehend. What exactly had happened?

"Target?"

And Zeke knew he was going to explain to her. Even if it was a breach of national security. She deserved to know.

"He was a sleeper." He forced the words out of stiff lips. If he didn't share something, she was never going to believe him.

She snorted. "A sleeper cell? A person or persons who are inactive for years until suddenly tasked with killing or initiating the murder of a target? You really believe a sleeper was responsible for my grandparents' deaths?"

"Yes." Zeke hesitated. Fuck, could he really tell her about this? Then he thought about the last few hours and wondered if could he really afford not to tell her about this. Would she feel violated from the truth that her stepfather was an assassin who specifically targeted her grandparents and in some weird twist of improper conduct married her mother? Or would she be relieved that now she had a reason for why he had killed her grandparents?

"On October nineteenth and twentieth, 1995, a group of sleeper cells eliminated twelve targets around the world."

"John? Sleeper cell? My grandfather was an insurance salesman and my grandmother was a homemaker." She stepped back, away from him, so slowly and carefully that he knew she was trying hard to be as nonthreatening as possible. "Why would they even have an assassin after them?"

He didn't answer. How could he? Did he really want to get into the whole World War II history of the targets and the ultra-secret joint committee, TICOM, that had captured, interrogated, and then released German code breakers? Could he? He was already breaking the rules as it was.

"So see." She tried to tug away from him, her scorn evident as she denied what he knew to be fact. "You are clearly mistaken."

Zeke was silent while he ran through scenarios, thought about the other people whose families had been killed by sleepers, and the many secrets of the past.

"It's Occam's Razor," she said impatiently.

"Yeah, in normal random circumstances, I would agree." Zeke ran his fingers through his unruly curls. "When two explanations are offered for a phenomenon, the simplest full explanation is preferable."

And if her grandparents hadn't been part of a very exclusive group of targets who were all killed within a twenty-four hour period, around the world, Zeke might have agreed with her. But, no way in hell were their deaths on that day and within that time frame only the result of an murderous son-in-law. Their deaths were not just a coincidence.

However he wasn't authorized to share the circumstances behind the order given to eliminate twelve specific targets thirteen years ago.

And without that information, she would continue to believe that John Stanley was just her stepfather. But that still didn't refute the fact that both Sunshine and her mother had been living in relative obscurity for years and out of the blue John Stanley was after them again.

"Why do you think he's suddenly coming after you?" It didn't make any sense. The whole point of a sleeper was a random anonymous killer that waited never knowing if they'd be called on to follow through with their orders. However, once they completed their job, they were supposed to fade into the background and disappear.

The sleepers who killed the targets thirteen years ago had literally been in place for years.

So why would John Stanley come after Sunshine and her mother after he completed the assassination? Especially now.

"I don't know how he found us after all this time. We've been invisible and hidden for nine years." Sunshine huffed out a frustrated breath. "This is pointless."

No. It wasn't. "Humor me."

"He's obsessed," she whispered.

Obsession.

"With?" Zeke swallowed, suddenly aware of the ways in which her statement could be construed, and prayed that he was wrong.

"My mother."

Thank God.

Sunshine crossed her arms over her stomach and squeezed. The move accented her breasts and the top of her plump mounds spilled over the loose scoop neckline. Zeke cursed his hormones for even noticing even as his palms itched to touch.

So, her stepfather was obsessed with her mother.

"He killed them. And we ran," she said defiantly.

"If you saw him do it why did you run?"

If Zeke had seen his grandfather's killer he would have made sure the man or woman paid.

"He'd just killed my grandparents." Sunshine stared at the pastel watercolor of an indistinct harbor scene, the watery faded colors merely shadows and lines without any substance. "Besides the fact that I was only seven years old? I did what my mother told me. And I was terrified of him."

"Okay. I see your point." He'd been thinking about it like the adult he was now rather than through the filter of a frightened child.

So they ran. And had been running this whole time?

"He kept finding us. Kept coming." She seemed like she was a million miles away. "We couldn't get away from him. In the first four years, he found us three times. But we've been safe for the last nine years."

"What did you do nine years ago?"

"My uncle helped us." Sunshine blinked, her gray eyes went blurry, then lasered in on Zeke. "We incorporated. Everything goes through the corporation now. Laid a false trail. And changed our names without telling anyone our new identities."

"No one?"

"Except Uncle Carson. But even he didn't know where we lived."

Uncle Carson? Carson Black, deputy director at the NSA, and Zeke's mentor.

"He isn't really my uncle."

No shit. But her relationship with Carson was a discussion for another time. They'd have to return to the subject of Carson later. He needed her to concentrate on Stanley. "And now Stanley is back?"

"I shouldn't be talking about this with you."

She stood, ready to bolt. Zeke couldn't allow her to leave, but he needed to convince her gently. He certainly couldn't hold her here against her will.

"Let me help you."

Her silver eyes were wounded. Like the morning clouds over a stormy ocean before the marine layer burned off, bruised by the events of the last few hours. Zeke could tell an adrenaline let down was going to hit her soon.

"Let me help you," he said again, trying to make his body language as reassuring and nonviolent as possible.

She shook her head. "You believe he's a sleeper assassin, not just my crazy, abusive ex-stepfather."

"What if he's both?" Zeke asked desperately. And if he was both, how did Zeke keep her safe? Because, in his mind, her safety was paramount.

If Stanley wasn't just an obsessed husband but more, if he were also the sleeper, then Zeke couldn't let Sunshine go. Stanley would have a level of training that she would be completely unprepared to defend against. That kind of expertise combined with his obsessive behavior made John Stanley way beyond dangerous.

"I want to help you."

She scoffed. "Really?" He could practically hear the

skepticism in her voice and wondered. Hadn't she ever had help?

"Let me dig into John Stanley." Zeke tried to sweeten the offer. "You can stay here. Out of sight and off radar. Lie low until we figure out where he is and what he wants."

"You think you can find out where he is?" A tentative hope shone in her eyes, lighting her up like the full moon lit the night sky and making her glow with anticipation.

"Yeah." Zeke could find John Stanley. He could find anyone. And screw it, if for some reason he couldn't find him, he would ask Jamie. Anything to keep that eager look on her face and the excitement in her eyes.

Another thought occurred to him. John Stanley was a link to what happened to the people killed thirteen years ago.

What if Stanley could tell Zeke who originally gave him the contract to kill Sunshine's grandparents? If Zeke knew that maybe, even more importantly, he could determine who engineered the terminate order? Because someone, somewhere, initiated the sequence of events that resulted in twelve families being ripped apart. And Zeke would really, really like to know who was the mastermind.

When he'd tried to hack into that information at the NSA, there hadn't been any kind of record. The sleeper information had been buried somewhere not associated with 5491. Zeke hadn't even found a reference to the fact that there were sleepers. The only reason he knew was because Jamie Hunt and Staci Grant had uncovered the conspiracy.

Stanley was a new avenue to explore. And although he could find Stanley without Sunshine, but he didn't want her out there if she was in danger. He knew it was irrational but ever since he'd awoken on the beach last night, he had this insane urge to protect her. And that internal mandate had only grown stronger with every moment spent in her presence.

On the flip side, Zeke analyzed the data he had right now. Stanley was after Sunshine and Stella. He had been in Cambria this morning, which made Zeke consider some options. If John Stanley came after Sunshine, and Zeke could capture him, he might be able to gather serious intel. He wished he'd known who Stanley was earlier when they'd been within fifty feet of each other.

A sudden sense of guilt assailed him. Sunshine Smith was terrified of this guy. Zeke shouldn't be thinking about bringing him anywhere near her stratosphere. But he'd just met her and while the biological urge to shield her was strong, his need for vengeance was even stronger.

Patterns. There was a pattern here he couldn't discern yet.

But information from John Stanley could possibly be the piece of the puzzle he was missing.

He gestured to the bland room behind him. "There are two beds."

An unguarded disappointment flashed in her somber gray eyes before her gaze flickered to the beds then back to him.

Smooth, Hawthorne.

Suddenly his mind went back to last night, as he lay between her thighs, the heat of her body, the subtle welcome as her hips relaxed and cradled his, and the soft vulnerability in her eyes. And how much he'd wanted to find surcease in her arms for a few moments.

Their attraction, the inalienable magnetic power, positive to negative, that he'd suppressed, and buried in his subconscious while he reasoned out the puzzle of John Stanley, boomeranged to the forefront of his brain.

Sunshine blushed, a deep pink that traveled up her cheeks and brightened her eyes. "Oh, um…." She shifted her gaze away from him. A charming, entrancing innocence shone in her eyes. He was no horn dog but he was pretty sure he had far more experience than she did. Which was damn crazy since he had inherited the Hawthorne family curse. The men in his family had no luck with women.

Heat poured off her body and the air grew heavy with the scent of cucumber and the sea. Suddenly the large hotel room shrunk to encompass just the two of them, cocooned in a cloud of lust. If he was reading the atmosphere correctly, she was as interested in him as he was in her. And the temptation to move closer, to explore the unexpected shot of desire overriding his thought processes and rendering him stupid, was like a unexpected line of new code in a tired old program.

But he didn't want her to feel threatened by him. Of course that was probably stupid. No one ever felt threatened by Zeke.

He was Zeke the Geek. A genius idiot. Genius in the office, idiot with women.

Shaped by his family. Shaped by his childhood. Shaped by his upbringing.

She shifted just slightly, her shoulder angled so that her body was more closed off. Zeke recognized that she was shutting down, shutting him out. But even that was okay, as long as she stayed her where he could keep her safe.

And if that sharp feeling in his gut was a stab of disappointment he'd get over it. He always did. He wasn't important. Sunshine's safety was paramount. He'd do almost anything to keep her safe.

"I need to use your cell phone," she said abruptly.

"Sure." Without hesitation, he handed her his iPhone.

She punched in the numbers with her thumbs, her head bent. Little wispy curls had escaped from her braid and straggled against the tender curve of her neck. Zeke turned his back to give her privacy, but he could hear the answering service message on the other end of the line. The same one that he'd called earlier where he'd listened to the information about where she was.

"Sunny. I'm safe. Blue's got me."

Zeke moved a little further away.

"You stay with your friend, be safe. We'll touch base tomorrow."

Unlike Sunshine's earlier message, Stella Smith didn't tell Sunshine where she was. She offered no information on her location, only reassurance that she was secure and with Blue.

Basically leaving Sunshine to twist in the wind.

Dammit.

Zeke turned around to reiterate his offer. To convince her that he could help her, but Sunshine's shoulders were slumped and the pure dejection in her posture was so heartbreaking Zeke couldn't help but put his palm on her shoulder to offer her comfort.

Shit, she was freezing.

Sunshine jerked as if she'd forgotten he was there. "Stay here with me, Sunshine."

Zeke was so tempted to pull her into his arms. To pull her against his body and curl himself around her to keep her safe, to protect her not just from the physical threat but the emotional rollercoaster she was on.

But he'd been rejected enough that he kept his arms loose, down by his sides. He'd learned his lessons well. His comfort would not be well received.

She shrugged, straightened her shoulders and lifted her

head. She jutted her chin out with determination, and her body screamed resolve. She was sending a very clear message to back off. She was alone. Didn't need his comfort or his solace. She took care of herself.

"Only if you let me help look for him."

Since that meshed with his needs, he agreed. "Sure."

As if she could tell that he was only humoring her, Sunshine said fiercely, "This needs to end."

Shit, he'd promise her the moon if she'd agree to stay with him. There was no way in hell she should be looking for a sleeper assassin and obsessive stepfather.

But unfortunately, there was no way in hell he could not look for John Stanley.

CHAPTER 19

I watched Zeke Thorn, Hawthorne, I corrected, carefully. Even though I was pretty sure he wasn't working with the monster, he was still spouting some crazy ass theories.

Before I called the answering service, while he'd had his back turned, I'd surreptitiously scrolled through the list of calls received on his phone. The call he'd gotten this morning when we'd been having our tea, the one that caused his hasty exit from our 'date' was from a restricted number.

Same with the phone call he'd made in the car after we'd left San Luis.

No contact information displayed. It was extraordinarily uncommon, and most people had no idea how to block their own numbers. And it made me wonder who had been on the end of that line. Because Zeke Hawthorne had some seriously nut job ideas.

He believed the monster was a sleeper? I couldn't wrap my mind around it.

I reminded myself that people who were crazy believed their crazy. But….he didn't seem crazy.

He seemed earnest and sweet and totally geeky.

But not crazy.

On the other hand, maybe that was my girl parts talking. I'd just discovered that I am a sucker for a geeky guy. He was smart. Nearly as smart as I was, it seemed, which was unusual in itself. And shockingly that was a huge turn on. His outdoorsy air and sun-tanned, hot body certainly didn't hurt either. I'd never been so aware of another person's skin, their movements, or even the heat from their body as I was of Zeke's.

This itchy, crawling out of my skin feeling was new. But I'd read enough to realize that I was horny. Making decisions based on physical attraction was never a good idea. But I really, really wanted to believe him.

When he'd mentioned the beds, I'd been back on the beach last night, with him solid and hard and male between my thighs.

I wanted to feel that quickening of my pulse, the tingle in my belly, and the elevated boom of my heart again. Before the water had scared me. *Stupid Sunshine.* One more thing to blame my stepfather for. I used to love the water but now I lived in a beach town and couldn't tolerate the ocean.

I could potentially write off the remembrance of last night as sheer fiction. But this morning when he'd kissed me, I'd gotten lost in the sensations he'd evoked. Gotten lost in front of my mother and Blue no less.

Mama and Blue. A pang of despair hit me. Mama was choosing Blue. I knew that was irrational and not really true. She was trying to protect me. But all my life, I'd protected my mother. Since I was seven, it had been the two of us against the world, against *him*, and now suddenly that changed. I was adrift in a sea of confusing and conflicting emotions. I wanted her to be happy. Of course I did. But how could she be happy without me?

What did I do now?

I knew. I needed to protect Mama from *him.*

I didn't need Zeke's help. I really didn't. I could do this on my own. But I wanted to let him help. Did that make me weak? I didn't know.

"Hey," Zeke said. "You okay in there?"

I had been staring blindly at the plain, pastel blue bedspread while I worked through the problem in my head. I could solve complex quadratic equations in minutes but I couldn't figure out my own conflicted emotions and come up with a plan without zoning out.

Zeke had bent his knees so that our gazes were level. He repeated, "Everything okay in there?"

I flushed again, this time from pure embarrassment, but didn't answer.

"Don't sweat it. I get lost in my head all the time." He grinned, his smile wide and open in his tanned face.

He got me. How weird was that?

"I'm...okay."

"Brilliant," Zeke replied.

"But you have to promise to show me everything you find about...." I swallowed.

"Yes, I'll show you. We can work together."

Zeke understood. Better than I would have thought.

"His name only has power if you let it."

A profound rage rose up in me, but I shoved it down. Rage was fuel but it would cloud reason. And I needed reason. I was smart, smarter than the man who'd ruined my childhood, stolen my life. I had better start acting like it.

I needed to find John Stanley and put an end to this once and for all. "So is he wanted by the NSA?"

That must be why Zeke knew about the sleeper aspect. Knew when my grandparents were killed exactly. The NSA must want to find John Stanley too.

"What?"

I gritted his name out through clenched teeth determined to get over the crippling fear his name invoked. I wasn't seven years old anymore. "John Stanley."

Zeke blinked. Anger swirled in his blue eyes, a tempest of emotions ebbed and flowed, before he finally answered, "I certainly would like a few minutes in an interrogation room with him."

And the cute, geeky Zeke was gone. The man in his place was hard, unforgiving, vengeful, and looked like he could do some damage. He was primed, the veins in his arms had popped, and his face was cast in intense angles. A tremor of fear worked its way through me. He reminded me of how John had looked when he was angry.

But then Zeke shook his head as if shaking off his fury. Something flashed in his gaze, too quickly for me to interpret.

Before we could get started, I needed to take care of one more task. "I need to leave a message for my mother."

Zeke gestured to his phone. "Have at it."

I quickly punched in the answering service numbers again. "Mama. It's me. I'm fine but I needed to let you know that he was here. In San Luis, so we were right to evacuate. I have help." I was hesitant to mention Zeke on the line. "I don't know how he found us, me. But I promise you, I will figure it out and end this once and for all."

I hit the end button on his phone and stared at the keyboard for a few moments.

"Come on." The affable, dorky guy was back. "Let's see what else we can find out about this guy."

He pulled the desk toward the bed and situated the chair for me so we would both be able to see the screen.

He took a moment to position the laptop just so. Then he folded and unfolded the screen and angled it at precisely ninety degrees. I watched him touch each edge of the keyboard, top, left, right, bottom, before typing in his password. Which was some ridiculously long sequence. Clearly no one would be hacking him any time soon.

I'd spent my whole life, or at least what felt like it, running from John Stanley. And suddenly I was mad as hell. I refused to let him steal anything else from me. He'd stolen my childhood, and my teen years. I was only twenty. I had my whole life in front of me. Or at least I would when he was taken care of.

But I would be foolish to take Zeke Hawthorne at face value. He'd said he wasn't supposed to make contact with me. What did that mean? If what he told me was true, then he had known about John killing my grandparents, just hadn't known John's name.

I thought back to when I'd revealed John's name. I'd watched him carefully. There had been no recognition in his response, or rather non-response. He had no idea who John was. But then why would Zeke be watching me? What possible reason could he have for being here in California and watching me if he didn't have anything to do with John?

"Do you know if he has a middle initial?" Zeke typed some information into the search program and waited.

I licked my lips. Hesitated. I hadn't spoken about what happened in a very long time. The urge to run was strong. My heart thudded against my breastbone, and my breath went short. My fingers were clenched so hard in my blue cotton skirt that my hands hurt. "I…don't know."

"Sunshine." Zeke placed his hand over mine and gently uncurled my fingers. He stared down at my hand in his.

His hand was callused, warm where I was smooth, cold, like alabaster. My vocal chords were as frozen as my body.

"I won't let him hurt you."

He pressed my palm flat against his and threaded our fingers together until I was squeezing his hand instead of the thin cotton.

"Why?" I whispered. "Why do you give a damn?"

No one had before.

I'd been alone for so long. Lonely for so long. His shoulder brushed against mine. Both the touch of his hand and shoulder were innocuous. But the simple contact ignited an instant raw response as if I was awakened from a lifetime slumber by the groundswell of lust.

"Because I can."

My growing arousal was shattered by his words.

I blinked. What kind of answer was that? From a guy who quoted scientific laws and was a computer programmer and self-proclaimed geek, shouldn't his answer make more sense? Be more grounded in fact?

"That's it?" I asked skeptically.

Because I can?

"Do you really want me to say that I'm inexplicably drawn to you? That I feel a connection that is impossible after knowing you less than twenty-four hours?"

It was as if he were in my head, spouting the same nonsense that I kept feeling. The same strange and wondrous emotions, terrifying because of their intensity, that were not logical.

"Because if I told you something like that, it would

probably make you freak the fuck out," Zeke gutted out harshly. "And take off running."

I trembled violently. My entire body flooded with adrenaline, fear, and most importantly longing. As if I teetered on a cliff about to dive into treacherous waters, I stood on an emotional precipice. Poised, yet not moving either forward or backward. Afraid. Wasn't this what I wanted? To live. To be afraid of something other than being discovered. Because the end result of conquering fear was joy.

I wanted that. I wanted to admit to him that I was feeling the same. If he knew me at all he would know that truth by the simple fact that I was here in this hotel room with him. That was already a huge leap for me.

But the words constricted in my throat, which tightened until I could barely swallow let alone force the confession out. As if I was glued to the chair, I couldn't move. Stuck on the wish to change, but the fear of it too. And the fear of what that change would bring.

I was comfortable in my rut and I realized that I might wish for change but I was frozen by the actuality of it.

Zeke jumped up from his perch on the bed. "Sorry." He turned his back to me, then he bent his head and rubbed the back of his neck, while muttering, "Fucking curse. That was exactly what I was talking about."

I opened my mouth to confess, but it was too late.

He whirled around and crouched down next to me. "Don't run." Zeke reached his palm toward me then curled his fingers and dropped his arm.

"I'm not running." My words grated along my throat. And while I couldn't bring myself to take that step. To actually say aloud the words that would admit I had the same feelings, at least I could reassure him that I wasn't going anywhere.

I reached out tentatively and touched his shoulder. No more than a flutter of my fingers against the worn cotton t-shirt. His muscles bunched and released beneath my light touch. His body was full of power. Full of strength.

I repeated the words again more firmly. "I'm not running." Not anymore.

He lifted his gaze to mine. The shadows in his blue eyes were tinged with hope. "So, I didn't completely freak you out?"

I had to be honest. This was the new me. The beginning of my life. "Not *completely*," I said.

Zeke grinned, his mouth split in a wide smile that tipped up at the corners and crinkled the tan skin around his eyes. "Cool."

And before I could chicken out, I smiled back. My fingers had flit against his hard muscles, but now I curved my palm over the ball of his shoulder and let it rest, heavy and somehow meaningful, against him. His skin was an inferno. Heat poured off his body and traveled up my arm, through me. Warming me, heating up places that had been frozen forever.

His gaze dropped to my mouth.

My lips parted on a quick indrawn breath as I realized how close we were. I sat on the chair while Zeke was on his knees on the floor. Less than a foot separated our bodies, and he knelt between my spread legs, which had widened further to accommodate his broad chest. He was tall enough that our mouths aligned with seamless ease.

Fine blond hair dusted his forearms, thick veins, and sinewy muscle corded as he lifted his palm to cup my cheek. His thumb brushed over my cheek. My cheek! And my heart thudded harder beneath my breastbone, and my mouth buzzed.

Arousal spread, like the thick local honey I used in my body scrubs, through me and I wanted to melt into the capable shelter of his arms.

Zeke leaned closer, his chest pushed my legs further apart as he tilted his head and gently eased me against him. His lips brushed my top lip, a mere second of contact and yet the effect was startling. My heart beat a hard tattoo against my ribcage, and my nipples tightened. My entire awareness had tunneled to the places we touched: his palm against my cheek, his lips against mine, his rib cage against my knees.

I swiped my tongue over my ultra-sensitive lips, aware that he hovered almost protectively waiting for my move. Waiting for my acquiescence rather than just taking. Which I appreciated since so much had already been taken from me, but I didn't know what to do. My body tilted toward his, leaning ever so slightly into his embrace. His lids drooped, and he pressed another kiss against one corner of my mouth and then the other. His lips were firm, and yet, so soft.

How was that possible? He'd seemed so hard, so primed just a minute ago.

With a gentle, persuasive stroke his tongue traced the seam of my lips and then sucked my bottom lip into his mouth. I parted mine, hoping he would recognize my subtle surrender and take the contact further.

With one long, lazy lick, his tongue stroked mine, the sensual invasion caused me to shiver, the tingling zipped up my spine. I sank to the floor on my knees, our bodies in alignment. Zeke wrapped one arm around my waist and held me carefully, as if I were a precious abalone shell, and he continued to sip at my mouth with sensual nips and increasingly intense forays.

I felt like I was floating, lighter than air as I swayed against him. His hold was gentle, easy, and I thought that he was merely kissing me because I'd somehow transmitted my desires. But then his erection brushed against my thin cotton skirt and burned my belly through the material. He was thick and long against my stomach. He might not be moving with urgency but his body was on fire.

Everywhere I softened, he hardened. My sex clenched and relaxed as if preparing to welcome him inside. My breasts swelled and seemed to plump against his hard, firm pectorals even as my nipples tightened painfully. My bones felt as if I was liquefying.

He trailed a chain of kisses along my jaw until he reached my earlobe then he suckled the sensitive skin behind my ear.

The soft moan in the quiet room shocked me.

That had been me. What was I doing? Kneeling on the floor of a hotel room with a man I'd just met? I never trusted anyone, let alone a guy who lied to me before he told me the truth. Assuming he'd even told the truth. Because Zeke had spouted some seriously strange ideas about what had happened thirteen years ago.

It was like I'd fallen under a sexual spell. A total cliché, the inexperienced ingénue falls for the older, more sophisticated man. I stiffened in his arms, rejecting the powerful attraction that blanketed me and snuffed out all my defense mechanisms. I couldn't trust him. So I certainly couldn't trust him with my body.

What in the holy heck was I doing?

Before I had a chance to push him away, Zeke had

released me and executed an athletic hop to his feet like he was jumping on his surfboard to catch a wave.

He rubbed his hand through his curls, and I thought he might be about to apologize. So I waited.

He held out his hand, the strength in his callused fingers, belied the subtle way he tried to put me at ease. "I just want to help you up."

I hesitated for one more moment, his gesture seemingly innocuous but somehow, I had the feeling that if I took his hand things would change forever. Irrevocably. And I would never be the same.

His face flushed. And his fingers started to curl. The awkward embarrassment at my unintentional rejection shot a protective bolt through me. I didn't want to hurt his feelings which was crazy. Weird.

So I placed my hand in his and hoped I wasn't making a huge mistake.

CHAPTER 20

O*ctober 20*
5:00 pm
San Luis Obispo, CA

ZEKE WASN'T sure what had just happened.

Dammit, he was so much better at code and patterns than he was with people. Women. He shouldn't even attempt to make a connection. He'd just mess it up.

Zeke paced around the hotel room that seemed to be shrinking exponentially with every second they spent in close confines. He needed to figure out what to do next. But the thing that kept coming back to haunt him was the fact that John Stanley had *married* Sunshine's mother.

Shouldn't someone, somewhere have been keeping track of the sleepers and known that he was breaching protocol?

He glanced over at the bed. Sunshine was sitting cross-legged on the bed, eyes closed, hands rested on her knees, palms up and thumbs and index fingers touching. Her chest rose and fell in measured breaths. The difference between their reactions to stress was almost comical.

Her face was the picture of serenity. He noted the graceful arch of her midnight eyebrows and the delicate line of her collarbone as her sweater slipped off one shoulder. One bare shoulder. No bra strap showing, reminding him she was naked beneath that sweater.

Zeke swallowed. He had to stop obsessing about Sunshine and his physical reaction to her. But he'd never responded to another woman the way he did to her and that fact had his brain returning again and again to their physical interaction.

He pulled his cell phone from his pocket.

He needed more information. How could he protect her against the threat of Stanley if all he knew was that he'd married a woman named Stella Smith, which wasn't even her original last name?

Before he could give himself time to think about whether this was a good idea or not, Zeke punched in Carson Black's cell number.

Carson wasn't his boss. They were in completely different divisions of the NSA but he'd been Zeke's contact after his grandfather died. Carson had taken care of his family and become Zeke's mentor both personally and at the NSA. He'd become more of a father than Zeke's biological father ever had been.

He glanced at the time on his phone. It was 8 pm in D.C., which meant there was a fifty/fifty chance that Carson was still at the office. If that was the case, Carson wouldn't be able to answer his phone since cell phones were strictly forbidden inside the NSA headquarters.

But at the very least, Zeke could leave a message.

Zeke quietly stepped outside into the empty hallway to gain privacy for his call.

The phone rang once, twice. "Black."

"Carson?" Zeke couldn't keep the surprise out of his voice.

"You were expecting someone else to answer my phone?" There was a touch of amusement lacing his words and Zeke could almost see Carson's bald head gleaming in the lights as his mouth quirked up in a very small smile.

Even though it had only been a few days since he'd last chatted with him, Zeke felt disconnected and out of touch.

"How did last night go?" Zeke had recommended that Jordan and Staci involve Carson in a sting against a U.S. Senator.

"For the most part, excellent. We were able to get to the bottom of the mess with Staci and get her name cleared. Did you see the press conference?"

Press conference? "Um, no."

"Staci Grant has been cleared of all wrongdoing."

Which could only be good news for Zeke since it would eliminate one of the counts of impropriety lodged against him. "That's great."

"Yes," Carson agreed. "Unfortunately Jordan suffered a gunshot wound."

"What?"

"But he's expected to make a full recovery."

"And Staci?" Zeke didn't know much about Staci Grant but he had nothing but respect for Jordan Ramirez. And he hoped everything worked out for them.

"She's fine." Carson's voice softened. "David Armbruster has been handling the logistics and sensitive details of the press conference and personally looking out for Staci."

"Good. That's good news."

Armbruster was a champion of the field operatives. Zeke didn't have much call to interact with him since he was primarily involved with Vulnerability Discovery and not active in the field. But Zeke knew that Armbruster took the safety and necessity of maintaining covers for their agents very seriously.

The fact that Armbruster was such a supporter of field agents actually worked in Zeke's favor. Armbruster wouldn't condemn what happened with Zeke out of hand but would make sure he researched all the nuances of his kidnapping and subsequent actions before a verdict was handed down. It was the one piece of this whole clusterfuck that gave Zeke the most comfort.

Armbruster protected his people.

Zeke took a deep breath and gathered his scattered thoughts. "I have a situation."

All amusement erased, Carson snapped, "What's going on?"

"If a sleeper were to marry a member of the target's family, wouldn't that be a breach of proper conduct?"

"Jesus," Carson blurted out. Not much surprised the man, but this clearly had. "Are you saying—"

"John Stanley, Sunshine Smith's stepfather, killed her grandparents." As Zeke imparted the information, he realized one important fact. Carson had not known that Stanley was the assassin.

A rush of sadness hit him. For Sunshine, for him. His Grandpop's death thirteen years ago hit him all over again.

"How are you doing?" Carson didn't respond to Zeke's flat statement, clearly also remembering the date and the significance for Zeke.

Once again, Zeke pledged to find out who had

masterminded the attacks on those twelve families. His Grandpop would be avenged.

"Fine," Zeke said shortly and went right back to his revelation. "How did that fact slip through the cracks?"

"It shouldn't have." Carson was silent. "Why didn't Stella tell me?"

Zeke hesitated. "So this is a problem."

"Yes." Carson waited knowing that Zeke wasn't done with whatever was on his mind.

"He's stalked them for years."

"That I knew." Carson replied somberly, "That's why they dropped off the grid nine years ago."

Uncle Carson. "You helped."

"Yes. When Stella asked me for help, he hadn't done anything illegal. I should clarify, he hadn't done anything illegal that I knew of. It's very difficult to enforce a restraining order until a crime has been committed. Dammit."

"Even if you had known that Stanley was the assassin could you have done anything?" Zeke asked.

"It would have been very tricky." Carson mulled over the implications. The federal government had paid John Stanley to assassinate Sunshine's grandparents. That could not have come out.

Zeke thought about the entire situation. "Have you known where they were this whole time?"

"No. We purposely set it up so that I wouldn't know their exact whereabouts. However I could get a message to them if I ever needed to." Carson confirmed. "Until two days ago, I hadn't had any contact with Stella since their last move. And they've been safe."

Two days ago? "Well they aren't safe anymore."

"He found them?"

"He got to Cambria. They split up but he found Sunshine in San Luis Obispo this afternoon."

"That is not good news."

"What if he can lead us to who gave the orders?" Zeke asked quietly, and hoped that Sunshine was still on the bed meditating and not attempting to listen to his conversation.

"We already know that I gave them."

"But don't you think he has to be connected in some way if he was able to marry Sunshine's mother and still be in place as the sleeper?"

"It's definitely against protocol."

"Sunshine says he's obsessed with her mother," Zeke said.

"'Sunshine says'?"

Shit. "You wanted me to keep an eye on her."

"I didn't expect you to actually interact with her."

"Yeah, well, sometimes plans go sideways."

There was silence on the other end of the line while Carson digested Zeke's revelation. "She okay?"

Zeke heard the concern and the affection in Carson's question.

"Right now, she's dealing," Zeke answered. "But she's been in hiding and on the run for years. She's worn down."

Zeke might not have been on the run but the threat of prison had been hanging over him for a long time. Always there hovering in the back of his mind that if he screwed up, his life could be taken away from him. Sunshine's life had been taken away. And she hadn't even done anything wrong. He wondered how she had managed to deal with that stress and without the outlet of a job she loved.

Zeke thought about how her face lit up when she talked scientific laws. She'd mentioned Cal Poly but Zeke hadn't found any evidence that she'd actually been enrolled in college. What a waste.

"So why are you calling me?" Carson interrupted his musings.

Trust Carson to bottom line it. "Can you get me information on him? Whereabouts? Cell tracking? Anything? She and her mother have split up to keep him off balance. But I'm wondering if we're going to have to bait traps to keep him from Stella."

"I'll get you the information as soon as possible."

"I'd appreciate it."

"Keep Sunshine safe," Carson commanded.

"That's my plan." Zeke hesitated, wondering if he should tell Carson about his other discovery.

Carson sighed. "Spit it out."

"I may have run into Susan Chen."

"What?!"

Zeke jerked his head back from the phone. He'd never heard Carson raise his voice.

"I had to make a choice." Zeke refused to be defensive but he also wanted to explain. "Her or Sunshine. And at that moment, Sunshine was in more danger than Chen. Stanley found Sunshine."

He mentally kicked himself, he should have called Carson right away. Obviously it had only been a few hours ago, but if he'd been thinking, he should have alerted Carson to Chen's presence in SLO. Crap. "I guess Jamie didn't call you."

His emphasis had been on getting Sunshine to safety, and after he'd made the call to Jamie, he'd shoved the other woman from his mind.

"We need to find her." Carson grumbled. "She escaped

from a maximum security facility. She's got answers
we need."

"She's in California somewhere."

"You need to stay away from her until we can capture
her and interrogate her," Carson said grimly.

Zeke was well aware that if Susan Chen were captured
with his card on her, it wouldn't look good for him. He
debated whether to reveal what he'd done or keep it to
himself, but in the end he figured he'd better come clean.

"Yeah, about that."

"Jesus, Hawthorne, what now?"

"I may have given her my card."

Zeke could practically see Carson drop his head into his
free hand.

"Okay. Okay. It's good that you told me," Carson said.
"Full disclosure. But you need to know that I may not be
able to protect you if we apprehend her with evidence that
you've been in contact and shit hits the fan."

Zeke flinched. He really hadn't thought his actions
through. He'd been too anxious to get to Sunshine. He was
a programmer, looking for patterns, searching for answers.
He didn't automatically think like a covert agent. Which
might just be his fucking downfall. And he definitely hadn't
been thinking like a covert agent when he'd made contact
with Sunshine and then followed her to SLO. He'd been
thinking like a guy.

"Did she say anything?"

"No. She was terrified of me." Zeke frowned. If only
he'd had the time to talk to her, get some information from
her. Just a little before he'd had to go after Sunshine. But it
was too late now. And he wasn't sorry he'd made the choice
he had.

"Okay." Carson said, "I'll see what I can dig up on John Stanley and get back to you."

"I appreciate it."

"Just keep our girl safe."

Our girl. If only.

Zeke clicked the off button and turned to see Sunshine standing in the doorway to the hotel room. He hadn't heard the door open. Hadn't heard her at all. Jeez, he sucked at the covert stuff.

There were so many ways this conversation could go bad.

And then she asked, "What did Susan Chen do?"

CHAPTER 21

I watched Zeke mouth the word, "shit," and then tuck his phone into his Hawaiian hibiscus board shorts pocket. I had to wonder if he was going to lie to me.

Probably.

He closed his eyes, and tilted his head back. Then he squared his shoulders, shifted his head so that he looked straight at me with bleak resignation. "I can't tell you."

Well, it wasn't quite a lie but it certainly wasn't an answer either.

I probably should have asked more questions earlier but between my freak out and his tension and I'd reacted instead of analyzed.

"Time for me to go." I blurted without thinking, reacting again. More secrets. More lies. I couldn't take it. My stress level rose and the last twenty minutes of meditation went out the window.

He looked so discouraged, I almost backed down. But then I thought about my life. If I was truly going to take charge, I needed to actually 'take charge'.

The truth was, I didn't want to leave, I wanted him to give me a reason to stay.

His entire body vibrated with intensity, with unspoken need, some unspoken tension. "Go inside." Zeke waved his arm at the interior of the hotel room. "Fuck it."

Okay. Finally. I went back into the hotel room. Zeke followed closely behind me.

The door swung closed with an ominous thunk.

Zeke gestured to the bed. "Have a seat."

And he proceeded to tell me a crazy tale of abduction, experimental DNA-enhancing drugs, antidotes, suspensions, and prison escape.

I wanted to get it right. And let's face it, the story he just shared was so fantastical that I had to clarify. "So you were illegally injected with some sort of genetic enhancement drug, abducted, had your encryption program stolen, and illegally injected again with an antidote. All by this Susan Chen?"

"Yep." Zeke nodded. "And an accomplice."

"When she was caught, you were suspended because you 'gave' her the encryption program, and then she escaped from a highly secure federal prison."

"Yep."

"Except you don't remember giving her the program."

"Yep."

"And that was the Asian woman in *Le Bistrôt Légume* earlier."

"Yep."

"But you didn't apprehend her…you came after me."

That was the part I really didn't get. This woman held the key to clearing his name. Because only she could corroborate that he hadn't colluded with the bad guys and that his sharing of his program was because he was under the influence of Sodium Pentothal.

"Yep."

I remembered what he said earlier, but really I had to ask another time. After all, insane weird attraction was no reason not to save himself. "Why?"

He just looked steadily at me. "You really want me to say it again?"

My heart thudded painfully in my chest as the implications of what he was saying, or really what he wasn't saying, penetrated. I was smart, a genius really. He didn't actually think I would buy what he wasn't saying.

Because of *me*, because I was in imminent danger from my stepfather, he hadn't chased after the woman who had the power to clear him. A woman who is supposedly a fugitive from the federal government and who is the subject of a huge, *quiet* manhunt by the NSA.

"Really?" I resisted the urge to roll my eyes but it was close.

How dumb did he think I was? Like most people, he catalogued my ultra-feminine skirt, the loosely crocheted sweater, and the new age potions and concoctions in Scents of the Sea, and assumed I was some free-spirited flower child chasing moonbeams and butterflies without a concrete, intelligent thought in my head. I'd thought someone that smart would be able to see beneath the surface to me.

"Believe what you want." Zeke shrugged as if he didn't care, but an odd vulnerability flashed over his face as he cut his gaze to the bland watercolor over the Formica desk. "But for inexplicable reasons, I seem to be compelled to help you whether you want it or not. And you were terrified of John Stanley."

A feeling of warmth, of sweetness, spread through me. I wanted to believe him, I really did. But I'd been cynical and distrustful since my seventh birthday because of my stepfather. And truly, because of his obsession with my mother, he was the poster child for unhealthy attraction. Fortunately, Zeke wasn't giving off a creepy stalker vibe. But thirteen years of abject cynicism couldn't be eradicated in one simple day.

"Besides, I have my orders," Zeke said.

"Orders?" I'd believe that over some completely illogical and badly-timed attraction.

He sidestepped my true question quite neatly. "Your mother asked me to look out for you."

And that quickly my animosity deflated. Mama would have thought I needed someone to look after me. She'd needed someone her whole life, even if she didn't really recognize that I had been taking care of her for years. I didn't need someone to take care of me. And he may have blithely ignored the question but I knew he wasn't talking about my mother's request.

"I don't understand why you would have orders to keep me safe." I shook my head trying to reason out why anyone in the NSA would care about a pair of women with no ties to anything illegal or even of national security. The idea was preposterous.

Zeke pressed his lips together. And didn't say a word.

"You aren't going to tell me," I said flatly. Unfortunately I couldn't seem to keep the disappointment out of my voice and I could feel my heartbeat slow as I understood he was done sharing. There had to be more to this situation than my mother and I and a crazy ex-stepfather. Zeke worked for the NSA for Goddess's sake.

National Security Agency.

There was no way that the NSA would concern

themselves with our little dysfunctional, violent triangle. And I couldn't figure out why it had taken me so long to clue in to that fact.

What were the odds that Susan Chen was here, in San Luis Obispo where Zeke was, where I was, where John Stanley was? When I thought about that I was even more bewildered.

How was it all connected? And why?

It was a puzzle that needed brain power and more information. But before I could delve into an analysis of the seemingly disconnected items and events, he interrupted.

"So what's it going to be?" Zeke raised an eyebrow. He was attempting to be casual, but I could feel his tension even from across the room. He really did want me to stay.

He was giving me the power. The decision. Giving me the choice. Rather than telling me what to do. I wanted to say I was leaving. Getting the heck out, but the reality was, I didn't want to go too far from home until I reconnected with my mother and Blue. And I could use a decent nights' sleep.

At the end of the day, I needed a place to stay and he was offering. So I crossed my arms over my chest, and gave him the most vacuous smile I could while I calculated the best odds for staying ahead of my killer stepfather.

Because no matter what Zeke Hawthorne said, John Stanley was the threat to me, to my mother. But he shouldn't be able to track us from Zeke's license plate that quickly, which meant I would be safe for tonight.

"I'll stay."

His relief was unmistakable.

I eyed him as he rubbed his palms over his board shorts. "What would you have done if I'd said I was leaving?" My curiosity got the better of me.

"I'd have followed you to make sure you were safe," Zeke replied emphatically.

A strange warmth settled in my belly. I was so used to taking care of myself that it had never occurred to me that anyone else would do the honors.

"Oh." I smiled, it was tentative, hesitant, a peace offering and an invitation all at once. I couldn't help my soft reply. "Thanks."

"My pleasure."

Pleasure. And just like that the elephant was back in the room. I thought about those kisses. I thought about him lying between my legs. Solid and masculine. Not even twenty-four hours ago. Was it only last night?

Then I thought about how much I'd missed out on in my life.

I was tired of missing out.

I remembered last night on the beach, before the terror, after I'd pulled him from the sea like my own personal watery treasure. He was my spoils and I was going to seize this moment like a true pirate.

Zeke Hawthorne wasn't going to know what hit him.

CHAPTER 22

"Whatever you're thinking is not a good idea," he said almost desperately. But I was pretty sure the same thoughts had crossed his mind too.

I wasn't about to let him stop this. Stop me.

"How would you know?" I crossed my arms, compelled to use defensive posture even though I knew it was a bad signal. The move plumped my breasts until the small mounds were lush and full and nearly spilling out the loose neckline. And what do you know, his gaze seemed drawn to my breasts. His words stalled, as he stared intently at my body. My defensive gesture had oddly worked in my favor.

I tossed my head, the movement shifted my loose braid and the tip came to rest right over my left breast, pointing down like an arrow to the tight hard bud of my nipple. I ached. I wanted his hands on me. On my body, cupping my breasts and pinching my nipples.

He still hadn't lifted his gaze from my breasts. Which was beyond thrilling, but I wanted him to move. To touch me. To take me. I prowled to the end of the bed.

The flush on his face, combined with the obvious bulge

in his board shorts, told me all I needed to know. My hard nipples and short breath hopefully told him all he needed to know.

Zeke took a step back. He was going the wrong way. I wanted him to barrel forward, haul me into his arms, and press his mouth against mine.

I knew he wanted me. It was kinda hard to deny. But as soon as he opened his mouth, I realized he was going to try and stop this. *No. Way.*

"Sunshine. I can't let you do this. Making this kind of decision in the midst of the turmoil—"

Oh, he did not just say that. "Every single big decision of my life has been made in turmoil." I dismissed that argument, and prepped for another.

He rubbed his hands through his unruly hair. "I want you more than I want my next breath."

"Then take me."

I wanted him. Bad. Even though I'd had a weirdly sheltered upbringing, it wasn't like I lived in a convent. I'd had some sexual experiences, but no boy had ever tempted me to throw away all caution and share my body. No *man* had ever made me feel the way he did when he'd been between my thighs, mostly-clothed, last night. And he hadn't even been trying.

My pulse thudded and my nipples tingled just from his gaze on my body.

I wanted it all. I wanted the experience. I wanted the rush of sexual arousal. I wanted his body, thick and hard and over mine. I wanted his cock inside me, and he'd barely even touched me.

Something about our chemistry, as if he were vinegar to my baking soda, the two of us together caused an immediate, explosive result. I nearly combusted at his caresses.

"I don't want you to regret anything."

"Right now, there's nothing to regret," I snarked, impatient with his delay tactics. I wanted him, now.

And in the middle of my life-altering, taking back my power decision, Zeke laughed. He threw his head back, and I found myself salivating over the corded muscles of his neck and the tight bunch of his pectorals beneath the thin t-shirt.

"My stepfather stole my childhood and my teen years from me. I'll be damned if I let him continue to fuck up my life. I want this. I want you, Zeke Hawthorne. And I'm going to have you." I let everything I was feeling, heat, desire, yearning show. So he could see all the emotion and longing that boiled inside me.

He wasn't laughing any longer.

I knelt on the side of the bed, arms at my sides. Waiting. I'd just laid it all on the line for him. I needed Zeke to make the next move. And if he didn't I'd just quietly die of embarrassment.

Then, he burst into action. Zeke strode to the side of the bed, and cupped my face. The small hotel room was redolent with the scents of the ocean, sand, salt, fresh air, and cucumber as if my warm, aroused body had diffused my essence into the air and wrapped us in a sensual haze.

Zeke burrowed his fingers in the hair at my nape. His thumbs brushed my cheeks, and I lit up like a lightning strike.

"You're sure?" Zeke asked one more time.

I rested my palms at his waist. Desire rose between us thick and viscous, as I pressed my body against the straining proof that he wanted me right back. I glanced down, my gaze fixed on the large bulge of his erection beneath his shorts, and my breath caught.

Goddess, he was big. I knew that a woman's body was meant to yield to the intrusion of cock, but a band tightened around my chest as I contemplated how he was going to fit.

Still, I nodded yes and licked my lips.

Zeke let out a silent groan, and searched my gaze. I tried, hard, to send the right message, 'please, please have sex with me, show me that there's even more to what I've been feeling.'

"Have you done this before?"

My heart nearly stopped. Oh hell no, I was not confessing my virginal status. I didn't want any reason for him to stop.

So I went for distraction. "Would you shut up and kiss me, please?" I curled my fingers around the waist of his shorts and pulled him against me. His hard chest pressed into my softer breasts and his firm biceps curled around my back. His cock, thick and long, rubbed against my softer giving belly and my body clenched as if already trying to pull him into me. He surrounded me, overwhelmed me.

Then finally, finally his mouth was on mine.

Zeke wasn't stupid.

She hadn't answered his question. But at her urging he tilted his head and slanted his mouth over hers, as she clutched his waist. Her nerves were apparent in the tight set of her shoulders.

He knew what it was like to want something so badly that your entire body vibrated with hope. Adrenaline and pheromones flooded his body. He understood her wariness and her impatience. The contradictions drew him as much as her plump lips and lush curves. He needed to handle her with care even as he strained to dive into her sweet, eager body.

Zeke didn't want her nervous. He wanted her turned on and anticipating the entwining of their bodies. So he set about making that happen.

Her mouth was soft and enthusiastic beneath his as he kissed her top lip, then each corner, left then right, and finally her bottom lip.

He thought he'd known, thought he'd understood the power of sexual need, but ever since he'd lain between her thighs last night, an urgent, overwhelming lust had throbbed below the surface. Under the layer of his conscious mind, need for her pulsed steady and unrelenting.

It was crazy, insane, completely unexpected.

And he could no more stop the feeling than he could stop kissing her. Because he wanted her with an unprecedented fierceness, he knew he needed to take extra care.

Zeke pressed kisses along her jaw, swirling his tongue against her skin in a subtle caress until he reached the tender spot behind her earlobe. "Any time you feel uncomfortable, just say stop." He sucked at her soft skin as she tilted her head back, and granted him better access.

Zeke was suddenly struck by her unconscious beauty. The graceful curve of her slender neck, the haughty arch of her cheekbones, and with her eyes closed, the dark fringe of her eyelashes against her milky white skin. Arousal flushed her cheeks and reddened her lips.

Her response was to nuzzle the same spot under his ear and then she dragged her tongue down the cord of his neck until she reached the curve between his neck and shoulder and bit him gently.

Jesus. His cock surged at the light nip.

The need to plunder, to invade, pounded in his blood. But he knew he had to proceed slowly. She couldn't have much experience. Zeke pressed small kisses along her jaw, tracing his former path until he got to her chin, then he pressed three open mouthed kisses on her lips, with each kiss his tongue slid a little further inside her honeyed mouth. Then Zeke traced his lips along the other side of her face, giving her right side the exact same treatment he'd given her left.

Sunshine's fingers burrowed under his thin t-shirt and explored the muscles in his back. The hard points of her nipples stabbed into his pecs as he continued with his lazy journey, pressing kisses along her neck and then the curve of her bare shoulder. Her sweater slid off her left shoulder and exposed the delicate line of her collarbone. He was trying to savor each step. Trying to treat her with care. And tenderness.

Underneath the slow, gentle journey, his blood pulsed with an urgent demand to take.

Sunshine grabbed his hand and pressed his palm against her breast. Zeke groaned into her mouth and brushed his thumb over her distended nipple.

She melted, her body going soft, pliant against his. She sank back onto the bed, pulling him with her. Zeke pressed his knee between her spread thighs and leaned over Sunshine as she lay back on the pastel bedspread.

His hand trembled as he brushed a curl from her cheek. He opened his mouth to ask one more time if she was sure.

Sunshine grabbed his shorts and tugged. With the element of the unexpected, he tumbled on top of her. The heat from her sex was like an inferno, and he rubbed his cock against the concave curve of her stomach.

Sunshine moaned and wrapped her legs around his waist, her bare heels dug into the back of his thighs and made him aware of all the ways he was a hard man and she was a soft, welcoming sexual woman.

He wanted her. Bad. He'd wanted her since he'd regained consciousness in this same position yesterday. Zeke wrapped his arms around her, unable to halt the spiral into frenzied desire, as if drawn by a rare earth magnet.

But just like that extra strong magnet, without a protective coating she would be brittle and susceptible to crumbling under the force of his hunger.

The same unexpected and forbidden feelings were rushing through him and he realized he was equally susceptible to crumbling.

He stared into her intense gray gaze looking for answers to all the questions in the Universe. And saw what he needed to see. No hesitation, no fear, only anticipation and arousal. And dammit he wanted to partake of her offering.

With reluctant restraint, he held back. Her sensual pull was nearly overwhelming, but Zeke knew that he needed to handle her with care. And he needed to approach with caution.

So he dove into the joy of discovery.

Zeke scraped her loose sweater up over her ribcage, his callused fingers explored her soft skin as he bent and dragged his tongue along the sensitive bow of her belly. Her stomach contracted in response. But Zeke gave no quarter and kissed his way up her ribcage. He wanted to roar in triumph as she responded to his sensual touch.

He pushed her sweater up and bared her breasts, perfect handfuls, to his avid gaze.

"You're flawless," he breathed as he bent to the distended coral bud.

"Actually, I'm a little small proportionately," she said breathlessly as a flush spread across her chest.

"Flawless." Zeke licked her nipple into his mouth and suckled on the erect tip. He swirled his tongue around her tight bud, while he squeezed and plumped her other breast in his palm and pinched the nipple until she was arching beneath him, nearly bucking him off her.

She was so sensitive.

All Zeke's blood thundered to his cock, until he was harder than the volcanic rock he'd climbed as a kid. He rolled her nipple on his tongue and then pressed hard, flattening his tongue against the roof of his mouth, and drawing with intense pulls.

Her soft moans filled the hotel room.

Sunshine clawed her short fingernails against the muscles of his back and then scraped along the edge of his waistband and pushed his shirt up until his bare skin rubbed hers. He wanted to go slow, show her through his actions that he respected her, treasured her. But as her hands moved restlessly, her strokes sure and confident as if she was trying to imprint the tactile feel of him, his vow to go slowly was sorely tested.

The scent of the sea and the sharp bite of cucumber rose from her heated skin as Zeke nuzzled the underside of her breast. He was harder than he'd ever been in his life, and he hadn't even gotten her undressed yet. Only the flat plane of her stomach and the pale rounded globes of her breasts were bare.

Zeke's practical experience was limited. Of course, he'd had sex before but he'd never been in a relationship. The Hawthorne curse had preceded him.

He'd actually never really wanted a relationship. He'd been in college at fifteen, a total nerd, and years younger than his classmates. He was jailbait. And no college girl was going for a pimple faced teenager when she could have an older, experienced guy. Kind of like his clumsy pursuit of Jamie. She'd chosen Lucas. Not that he could blame her. If he was a girl, he'd have chosen Lucas too.

So his sexual experiences consisted of drunken one night stands and random hook ups until he'd started working for the NSA. Then he realized that because of his work and his security clearance and the fact that he was a total nerd, he was a prime espionage target for female agents willing to use their body and sex to get secrets. So every time a woman came on to him, in the back of his mind, he wondered if there was something else going on. Some other reason why she wanted to have sex with him.

Crazy as it seemed, Sunshine's reluctance and worry that he had an underlying motive actually freed him from those concerns. He had gone after her. Not the other way around.

That relief that she wanted him for him was immense.

And because he loved that she wanted him for him, he was determined to show his appreciation in a measured physical way. If he didn't slow things down, take time to learn her body's secrets, take time to learn what made her gasp and what made her sigh, this would be over in a nanosecond.

But she seemed to want nothing to do with slow and easy.

Her legs moved restlessly beneath his larger, heavier body as she explored his skin. His cock was hard and insistent against the V of her legs. He couldn't wait to be inside her.

Sunshine lay beneath him, one foot on the bed, knee propped up, the other leg flat, spreading her open for him. Zeke groaned into her neck, and circled her ankle with his thumb and forefinger. Then he sensuously slid his fingers along the back of her leg, skimming her soft flesh and pulling her skirt up slowly. He bared her legs to the cool early evening air with questing fingertips until he reached the elastic of her panties.

She was so freaking soft. She had muscles but they were sleek and smooth, banded to her feminine frame and infused with an innate sensuality. Her hips were rounded, and her ass would be a handful.

He slid his hand beneath the waist of her simple cotton briefs, and caressed the dimple in her lower back before he circled around to her front, his fingertips brushed along her skin delicately. He feared if he pressed too hard, she would skitter away. Her stomach contracted and a soft moan whooshed from her mouth.

He eased his fingers into her wiry curls and teased her plump flesh. He slid his fingers along the outside of her sex; she was already slick with arousal. Her body had primed for him with impressive speed. And fuck him but he couldn't wait to slide inside her and plunder her spoils like a conquering hero. But with a previously dormant sense of perception, Zeke forced himself to go slowly after he noted her slight tensing.

Zeke rolled off Sunshine and to his side, pulling her with him, until they lay on the bed facing each other. He pressed a calming kiss in the hollow of her neck. With a gentle glide, he eased her loose sweater over her head and bared her upper body.

He could see her instinctive need to cover her exposed breasts when her arms twitched. "Don't."

She'd averted her gaze, her lashes lowered to hide her shyness from him.

He couldn't help but stare at her beautiful form. Her breasts were high and tight and round, not overly large, but they fit her. Her coral areolae were the size of silver dollars and her nipples had puckered when exposed to the cool hotel air. She was beautiful.

And for right now, she was his.

CHAPTER 23

Oh my Goddess.

So many different sensations. His fingertips were rough as he reverently caressed my skin. The skim of his pointer finger along my ribs elicited a tingle in my sex. The pinch of his fingers on my nipple send a sharp zing through me. He seemed determined to test and measure each section of my body with almost scientific precision.

Which might have amused me, except with every new touch amazing sensations grew inside me. Each light stroke, each pleasurable cup of his palm and firm embrace, and my body blossomed under his attention like the marriage of two scents into a perfume. His exploration caused my body to expand and contract. My breasts plumped while my nipples tightened. My sex softened even as my womb clenched. The two contrasting forces created a subtle tension as the tingle grew into a buzz that grew into a swell of lust so powerful, so crazy intense that I couldn't hold it in anymore.

I moaned.

The sensual sound startled me out of the haze of arousal

fogging my brain. I blinked, forcing my eyes open, marking the awareness of where I was and who I was with. His body was tan, he clearly spent a lot of time out in the sun. Blond hair dusted his forearms and roughened his thighs. He had smattering of hair on his knuckles, his fingers dinged up, and I had the strangest urge to buss my lips over the small cuts and calluses. The desire to express that bit of tenderness took me off guard and left me feeling over-exposed.

To protect myself, I wanted to cross my arms over my naked flesh, feeling stripped bare by the emotions Zeke was eliciting from me. But as if he sensed my reaction, he trailed his fingertips over my shoulders and skimmed them down my triceps and along my forearms until his palms were flush with mine. He lightly held my hands at my sides so that I was incapable of covering myself. "Don't," he whispered again.

My body tingled and goose bumps raised on my arms as his tactile touch activated nerve endings I didn't know I had. My nipples, wet from his mouth, peaked to an insistent hardness, and a throb centered low in my belly.

I moved my legs restlessly, aching and needy, yet unable to ask for what I wanted. What if I asked the wrong question and Zeke figured out how little experience I actually had?

I'd managed to deflect his question the last time but I wasn't sure I could do it again. I was truly afraid that if he knew I was a virgin, he'd stop. He seemed to have a core gentlemanliness. He was just a tad bit old fashioned underneath that surfer dude exterior, and that inner chivalry might force him to stop before he deflowered me.

And I really wanted to be deflowered. In the worst damn way.

He nibbled a path along my naked collarbone. I shuddered. So he did it again.

His palm was hard and thick and solid in my hand. As hard and thick and solid as his body had been between my legs. I wanted that again. The heavy weight of him on top of me, holding me down and yet burning me up.

Zeke guided my hand to his chest, placing my palm on his pectoral, right over his heart. As if asking me to guard the organ for him. Treat it and him with care.

Which was fanciful and not at all like me. Plus, he was a guy. He didn't need me to treat him carefully.

Then he took my mouth with gentle, sipping kisses following the same pattern again, top, left, right, bottom.

With his free hand, he stroked along my arm and across my waist in what should have been a seriously un-erogenous zone, but the tingling in my sex was back with a vengeance.

He skimmed his fingertips up the curve of my calf, twirling a lazy pattern along the back of my knee. The back of my knee! And my body clenched. He continued his sensual journey along my hamstring and I parted my legs again.

His palm cupped my butt, rubbed my skin, his fingers trailed along the crease of my ass, but didn't go anywhere near the part that ached for him.

I wanted him to touch me. To slide between my swollen sex and penetrate me. With every caress, his fingers crept closer but he never quite touched me where I needed it most. My hips rocked in insistent little jerks. I begged without actually begging. Until my breath stopped in my chest and expanded my lungs as I held there waiting, waiting for his intimate caress.

But he seemed content to rub his palm and fingers over my aching flesh, arousing without ever fondling my most intimate place. Every glide ratcheted my tension to another level.

Anticipation fluttered in my belly, and my body wept preparing for his penetration.

"Touch me," I finally pleaded. Needing more.

Anticipation fizzed in my blood as he slowly unbuttoned the waistband of my skirt and eased the cotton down my legs. Finally I was going to experience what felt like every other twenty year old the planet already had.

Sex. It might not be romance or love or affection. But that was fine. At least I would finally get close to a man physically. Which was more than I'd had to this point.

In the dark of night, when I couldn't sleep, perhaps I had dreamed of letting someone get close enough to share my body. But it had always been more of a fantasy because in the morning reality would return and I'd remember my circumstances, suffer the death of that hope, and tumble back into reality.

But right here, right now, Zeke Hawthorne knew my deepest darkest secret. I didn't have to guard against spilling my secrets because he already knew.

And that truth gave me the freedom to let go. The freedom to relax, allow him entrance into my other deepest darkest places.

Finally he slid his fingers beneath the elastic of my unsexy panties and against my slick wet lips.

I moaned into his mouth as the rough pad of his fingers spread that slickness against my clit. My head went dizzy and my knees went weak at the sensual caress. And in taking, I wanted to give as well.

I wanted to touch him the way he was touching me, intimately, to arouse his passion. I slid my fingers over his hard chest and rippled abs until I connected with the waist of his shorts. With fumbling fingers I untied the thick lace and then pulled. The rip of his Velcro fly as it separated was loud in the heated stillness of our hotel room. I spread the placket of his shorts open and curled my fingers around his erection.

He pulsed hot and hard, his arousal like a living breathing entity.

"Fuck." Zeke pressed his forehead into the curve of my neck. "That feels fantastic."

I really didn't know what I was doing. Of course, I'd read about this, so in theory I knew the mechanics. But the reality was so different from my imaginings that my confidence shriveled.

His skin was smooth and hot as I squeezed. He was hard, and yet, not.

"A little harder, babe," he commanded. Then he groaned when I swiped my thumb over the head of his penis.

As he gave me directions, he curled his middle finger just inside me. I held still, my body shaking, tremors rippled through me as I waited on the precipice for him to push inside all the way. But he curled his fingers, teasing my outer lips and barely penetrating me.

I was empty. Desolate. I needed more.

And yet I was afraid of more. My body had tensed, I couldn't help it. I was just hoping that he hadn't noticed. In desperation, I pushed his shorts over his hips and down his thighs. If I could just get him naked, maybe he'd come inside me then.

"Please," I whispered as he lifted his hips to help me get rid of his shorts.

Too many sensations bombarded me at once. His hairy thigh holding my legs apart, his fingers rubbing my sex, curling lightly inside but not coming all the way in, the smooth planes of his chest against my diamond hard, sensitive nipples. We shared breath through open-mouthed kisses and dueling tongues.

His cock was thick, long, and pulsed in the wrap of my fingers. I kept trying to ignore the worry of how he was going to fit inside me. Scientifically, I knew it had worked since the beginning of time, but personally, I kept wondering how? I knew that my soft would yield to his hard but it still seemed nearly impossible to imagine that we could fit together.

And that it wouldn't hurt.

Finally Zeke slid his finger all the way in. His palm cupped my swollen sex even as he did something with the finger inside that caused my whole body to jerk. Sensations bombarded me.

"Damn, you're tight," Zeke murmured against my lips.

I didn't want him to focus too much on that. If he started thinking, he might realize that I didn't have much experience. Or none.

My head was swimming. And my sex clenched. I just wanted him inside me. I curled my fingers around his cock and squeezed, not so subtly letting him know what I wanted from him.

Now.

Zeke finally acceded to my urging. He rolled over so that he hovered over top of me. His cock rubbed at my slick lips, and I arched my hips, begging for him. Then he stopped. Held still.

No. No. No. I tugged on his hips. He propped over me and looked desperately into my eyes. His blue eyes were glazed pools.

"Condom?" he gutted out.

My eyes went round. My body still throbbed and I could have cried. Of course I didn't have a condom. I shook my head mutely.

Zeke let his head drop, his curls nearly brushing my jaw. His body jerked, and his head came up. "I might have one."

He jumped up, and made a beeline for his duffel bag. His body was a study in masculine excellence. Long ropy muscles, round glutes, shoulders that could hold the world. He dug through his bag and then lifted his fist in triumph. He grinned widely. "I have one!"

His obvious pleasure convinced me that he was as into this as I was.

I lay on the cool cotton sheets, my body open and exposed. I should be embarrassed, nervous, at my vulnerability but instead an inner peace stole over me. This was right.

Zeke strode back to the bed. From the nest of blond curls at his groin, his erection jutted, long and thick with a bulbous head, blue veins pulsed. His body rippled with muscle, and my breath stopped in my lungs at how absolutely beautiful he was.

He tore the package open as he came over me. He stopped, his gaze traveled from my toes up to meet my eyes, and his sincere appreciation overlay with lust caused me to flush.

"You're perfect," he uttered as he pressed his beautiful body on top of mine. I stared into his ocean blue eyes and wanted to get lost in him. He just lightly penetrated my slit, the contact slick and bold, but he didn't come inside, he just rubbed my clit and along the wet opening, teasing me. My whole body arched, as I silently begged him to penetrate me.

My sex clutched at the head of his cock, as I thrashed

and grabbed onto his firm ass and tried to pull him inside.

Finally, he slid home. There was no barrier, nothing that made his entry difficult. The pain was minimal. He felt incredible.

Goddess, he was big. A thick intrusion, full and deep, as he pushed in to the hilt. The sensation was indescribable. As if he were splitting me in two and at the same time making me whole. My entire body shivered in response to his penetration.

But I needed something more.

He held still as if savoring the clasp of my sex around his erection. Then finally he began to move. He slid nearly all the way out, hitting spots along the way that sizzled through my entire body. I began to shake, my limbs buzzed and my head went light as he rocked in and out of me.

Sensation, overwhelming and dizzying swelled through me, then like the wave that took him out last night, thundered over me and I tumbled into orgasm. Rocked, buffeted, battered with sensation, and emotions I hadn't seen coming as I shattered into fragments of consciousness.

Zeke exploded at the same time. His body went rigid, neck arched, hips jammed against mine, as his erection pumped against my inner walls.

I hadn't expected this. This feeling of connection, of being in total sync with another person. I was euphoric, riding on a wave of endorphins so thick that I could convince myself that this wasn't a one off, that we could build something together, become something together.

My heart thudded against my breastbone. Against Zeke's thick chest as he collapsed over me. Still buried deep. His body was heavy and yet comforting, as if the world would have to go through him to get to me.

And that thought was enormously appealing.

CHAPTER 24

O*ctober 21*
        7:00 am
San Luis Obispo, CA

I WOKE NAKED.

That fact was so surprising that I lay still, absorbing, remembering. The slightly rough rub of hotel cotton sheets against my bare skin sensitized me, made me aware of my body in ways I never had been before. I ached pleasantly, my skin tingled and my hair was tangled around my head and Zeke's muscled forearm. He had his arm wrapped tightly around my waist as if anchoring me to him so I couldn't go anywhere. And I liked it.

I was snuggled up against his body, my back to his front, and his morning erection prodded my butt.

I was a virgin no longer. The thought made me smile. Big. Bigger than big.

Last night had been one of the best of my life. With only one condom, we'd had to get creative. And boy did Zeke get creative. His slightly OCD tendencies had manifested in very thorough methods of sexual exploration. I'd fulfilled about a thousand fantasies in the last twelve hours.

Happy Birthday to me.

Last night was the best present I could have ever hoped for beyond being able to live without fear of my stepfather. A warmth filled me and I realized how long it had been since I'd done something just for me.

It had been amazing. Awesome. Crazy good.

But as the light flowed through the gap in the blackout curtain, I realized that my night of indulging myself, of taking what I wanted, what I needed, was over. Time to return to reality.

And reality sucked.

A sick dread trickled through me. While last night had been fantastic, my problems had not disappeared. They were all still waiting for me. Hovering like buzzards over the carcass of a dead sea lion washed up on the shore.

But I would always have last night. Every single second of my sexy times with Zeke was imprinted on my brain. I could take the memories out and relive the sensations and feelings in the late of night when insomnia was my enemy and I had no one to turn to.

I knew what my life was and what I could have and Zeke Hawthorne was not it.

He was a going to be a memory. A cherished, surreal memory that I would hold tight to and that no one, not even John Stanley, could take away.

Up to this point, Stanley had taken everything from me. I wasn't ever going to be able to make more memories until John Stanley was one. I just had to figure out how to make that happen.

✳

ZEKE WOKE to the unexpected warmth of a body spooned with his. Sunshine's scent, ocean and cucumber, crisp and fragrant wrapped around his senses and intertwined with the musk from their night of sex. Her rounded butt cradled his morning wood. This was a most excellent way to wake up.

Her long black hair draped over his chest and wrapped around his bicep tightly like her vulnerability had wrapped around his heart.

He was painfully aware that he'd fallen into serious crush mode. He was drawn to her. It wasn't that he hadn't done this before. He had a habit of falling for women, especially the ones he slept with, but as easily as he fell in, he fell out, usually about the same time they decided they were done with him. And they were usually done with him once his geek-meter kicked in and either they didn't understand him or they thought he was weird.

Her curves were soft beneath his arm, and he savored this moment, understanding that this connection between them likely wouldn't last. His family was cursed. He knew that.

And hell yes, he knew it was illogical, but it was also true. His grandma had left his Grandpop in the fifties. In the fifties. Back when no one got divorced, and she left grandpa to raise their son, his dad. Who did that happen to?

His mom left his dad, and him, as soon as Zeke was born. And his sex life, romantic life, up until this point would be considered anemic.

He knew it was an anomaly, considering his analytical, scientific brain, but a tiny part of him really believed that the Hawthorne men were cursed. At least it felt like it.

Her ribs expanded as she breathed in deep and curled her fingers to mesh with his and she pulled his hand to rest under her cheek. His heart warmed at the unconscious intent to twine them together and the gentle, innocent gesture.

Innocent.

She'd been a virgin.

The silk of her hair slid over his body, bringing his mind back to their creative play because he'd only had one condom. Something he planned on rectifying as soon as possible so he could get inside her again.

After he'd gone down on her, to satisfied cries of pleasure, she'd returned the favor, sucking his cock and learning to give him a blow job with joyful inventiveness. Her hair had feathered against his groin and thighs.

He hardened even further, his cock ready for a repeat of the previous night. His morning erection pulsed against her butt as if saying, "notice me, notice me," and she wiggled back against him nonverbally indicating she'd be up for another round. He certainly was.

Except, no condom. Dammit.

He was still thanking the Universe that he'd had one in his bag. He wondered if she'd mind if he ran to the hotel sundry store. Even this little strip hotel should have a small shop open during the day and stocked with hangover cures and protection options for random sexual encounters.

Before he could do more than kiss the sweet curve where her neck met her shoulder, Darth Vader's theme song emitted from his phone and broke the sexual spell that wound around them.

And crap, he wanted to ignore his phone. But he couldn't. The intimate moment was over anyway.

"I need to answer that." His voice was husky, his throat raw.

She nodded and released his fingers. She curled her body into a tighter ball and buried her head under the sole pillow still on the bed.

Zeke reluctantly rolled away from Sunshine, his right arm cradled her body, and he reached with his left hand over to the nightstand to grab his phone. He pressed the answer button on his encrypted cell. "Yeah?"

"I'm sorry," Carson said.

Zeke frowned. Darth Vader was not Carson's ring tone. And this call was coming from an unrestricted number.

"For what?"

"You're going to be formally charged."

Zeke's heart stopped. The silence in the thick accusing air was absolute.

"What—" He licked his lips, tried to corral his careening thoughts, but he was having trouble making the shift from warm, sexy female and post-coital morning erection to the utter destruction of his career, his life. "With what?"

Zeke yanked his arm from underneath Sunshine and shoved out of the bed. His entire body was stiff, tight, angry as he turned his back on the absolutely wrecked bed. The pillows and bedspread were strewn across the hotel room floor like confetti after New Year's Eve, except there'd be no celebration here.

"Treason," Carson replied. "Under the Patriot Act, they can get away with quite a bit."

"Are you fucking kidding me? Sharing a computer program with scientists is hardly an act of terrorism." Zeke tried to mentally assimilate Carson's bomb. But he couldn't seem to wrap his mind around anything. Random thoughts floated in his head, unable to coalesce into a solid picture or cohesive reason why Carson's announcement was wrong. He couldn't seem to mount an argument. Couldn't force his brain to process. Only one thought penetrated the fog. Treason. This was way bigger than his prior worry that he'd go to jail for hacking. The threat that had hung over his head since he started at the NSA now seemed trivial.

"I'm fucked." He scooped a handful of hair into his fist and tugged hard. Trying to wake up and make sense of everything.

Carson didn't respond, which was in itself a response. "I'm giving you this heads up."

Zeke raised his eyebrows. His entire adult life, Carson had looked out for him. Since the accident that killed his grandfather, he'd been a figure in the background that he could turn to when he needed advice since his father had trouble dealing with life. Carson had been the one to help Zeke navigate the legal proceedings after he'd been caught hacking by the NSA.

And then luckily for Zeke, Carson had turned Zeke's innate distrust of the government around, given him a job, given him a purpose, and given him his life. But now, now he'd just told Zeke that they were going to take it all away.

"Don't lead with your chin."

Sports analogies. Never a good sign when Carson started using them. And basically Carson was telling him to stay protected.

Zeke processed Carson's unspoken message. After this phone call, Carson couldn't have any contact with him. "I'll dump my cell phone."

"I can't advise you on what to do." Carson had basically just indicated he was going to disavow Zeke. Shit. "But if it were me I'd get to a bank."

Assets would be frozen. But it was okay if his official

bank and investment accounts were inaccessible. There Zeke was in luck because his grandfather and father's distrust of the government was strong enough that he had money ferreted away in several foreign banks and the credit cards to extract that money if he ever needed it.

He also took precautions every time he traveled so he had plenty of cash in his duffel.

"Why now?" The question nagged at Zeke. He was on leave. He'd had his interviews, but usually there was more discussion, more thought before the order to relieve someone of their job. And in this case, fuck,…treason. There were usually lawyers and personnel questions, avenues of groundwork that had to be laid, questions that had to be answered, and military lawyers and miles of red tape before a person was consigned to prison. The speed and severity of this punishment was drastic.

"I don't know."

He guessed that made sense. Carson was not his direct report. But it wasn't as if Zeke could call up his boss and ask.

"Figure out how to clear your name," Carson commanded. "I'm in your corner but I need help. And I have to be discreet. You have anything I can use?"

He had nothing. If he hadn't let Susan Chen go yesterday he might have more answers.

"Since yesterday and now? No." Zeke had no idea what he was going to do next.

"I'll do what I can on this end. But Director Armbruster indicated that he'd delayed as long as he could and finally had to put the order in motion." Carson cautioned. "Be careful. And watch your back."

There would be no public outing on national television like they'd done with Staci Grant. Zeke would just be apprehended in a hotel room somewhere and disappear. No one would ever hear from him again. If he was lucky, he'd end up languishing in a federal prison in the U.S. But if he was unlucky, he'd be shipped off to Guantanamo, imprisoned in obscurity.

Zeke couldn't wrap his head around any of it. His emotions seemed as frozen as his assets. He was numb. His whole life his grandfather and father had shown him how to protect himself, insulate himself from hurt, but as he stood naked and stripped bare he realized he'd still managed to grow attached. It just hadn't been to a person, it had been to his job, the ideal of his service and his honoring of his intellect by using his brain power for good.

Yet in a nanosecond, he'd been metaphorically stripped as bare as his body. And because he'd done such a damn good job of staying remote from people, besides Jamie, Lucas, Jordan and Carson, it was likely no one would even realize he was gone.

He didn't have time to feel sorry for himself but the emotion was there, underlying the sharp edge of panic.

His heart thudded hard in his chest and he realized that he needed to get gone. About three hours ago. Carson's heads up would give him some lead time but the agency would have an idea of where he'd started based on the GPS in his government-issued cell. He quickly popped open the back of the phone, snapped out the memory card and the other identifiers, then he grabbed one of his running shoes and crushed down hard with the heel even as his brain was working on getting out of here.

Zeke was mentally packing, calculating his options and probable hideout destinations, working at hyper speed to outthink the agency. Outthink his bosses.

Ignoring his nudity, he threw his clothes into the beat up

canvas duffel, pawing through the sheets to find his shorts and t-shirt from yesterday.

Sunshine's palm against his back stopped him suddenly. "What's wrong?"

Her voice was soft, soothing, like an eye of calm in this sudden maelstrom. Her hand supple and real against his skin, the contact grounded him.

Shit. Sunshine and her problems. He'd forgotten all about her. Zeke stopped. He didn't have time to explain. Didn't have time to do more than get the hell out of here.

"I have to go." He turned to face her. She'd wrapped the sheet around her body, shielding her skin but she couldn't block the flash of hurt in her eyes at his abrupt dismissal.

She took an involuntary step back. "Oh. Okay." She turned away from him and lifted her skirt from the floor. "Thanks for the place to crash last night."

Shit. Shit. Shit.

He couldn't just leave her. He'd promised to look after her. But he'd basically just been burned. Which meant that his contacts were no longer going to be able to help her. And being with him could actually hurt her.

Zeke started, "Look—"

"No, it's all good." She'd tugged the skirt on and was now clutching the sheet against her chest barely covering the curve of her naked breasts.

"Sunshine…." Zeke trailed off, wondering at his shit luck, wondering how he could even explain what had just happened.

Worst morning after in the history of the freaking world.

She'd pulled her sweater over her head. "I'll just get out of your hair." Her voice was steady but her fingers trembled as she tried to smooth down the wild tangle of hair around her face.

Zeke wanted to stop and revel in how her hair got tangled. But they didn't have time. "I'm burned," Zeke blurted out.

She paused as if finally realizing that he really wasn't just blowing her off. "What does that mean?"

"It means that the agency has decided I'm no longer necessary." No need to freak her out by telling her that he was likely being tracked by satellites at this very moment. And in all probability, the 'shoot to kill' order was in place if he chose to resist apprehension.

Zeke edged closer to her, instinctively going into protection mode. He wouldn't let anything hurt her.

It was then that he realized she was going to have to come with him. Even though he had no idea where he was going or what he was doing, if she stayed here and they found her and connected her to him, she'd be apprehended and interrogated. So that clinched it. She'd have to come with him, at least for now.

"It means you have to come with me." Zeke zipped up his duffel, open it back up, looked inside. Then repeated the action twice more. "Get packed. We have to get out of here."

"Wait. What?" She'd stopped, her hands propped on her hips.

"We've got to get out of here."

He was burned. Burned. Fuck. What was he going to do now?

"You don't need to take me with you." She shook her head. And she didn't move.

"This isn't just about you and your stepfather." Zeke grabbed the laptop and shoved it in the carrying case.

Luckily he'd packed both a duffel and a 'go bag' inside his duffel. They'd need to secure his laptop and other identifying things at the storage unit he'd scoped out on his way here. He'd packed the cylinder lock and key in his duffel as rote, just like he packed his toothbrush and toothpaste.

Who would have thought he'd need to use the EPA, Evasion Plan of Action, that he had prepped for? The standard planning had become second nature whenever he went anywhere. His OCD tendencies hadn't let him ignore preparations. Which was a damn good thing.

"I get that," she said stubbornly.

No, she didn't. His mouth hardened and he growled, his voice low and harsh. "And I don't have time to coddle you. We need to fucking move."

Sunshine blinked, her silver gaze narrowed. But she finally seemed to understand his urgency. "You can drop me off somewhere."

"Fine." Whatever it took to get her in the damn car. And then he just wouldn't stop.

He dampened a washcloth from the bathroom and began wiping down all the finger printable surfaces, taking extra care anywhere that Sunshine might have touched. They would know he had been in this room, but he didn't want them finding proof of her presence.

Zeke took one more pass through the room after she finished packing.

The bed was wrecked, sheets and comforter and pillows littered the floor. He flashed back to their night. Of course the best night of his life had been followed by the worst morning ever. The Hawthorne curse continued to rear its ugly head. Hawthorne men didn't have good, normal relationships with women. They burned hot, then crashed hard. And the women left.

But this time, he couldn't let her leave. Not yet.

CHAPTER 25

I had no idea how I ended up here.

There didn't seem to be one single decision that landed me on the run with a man I barely knew. Rather, a series of small changes in my normal method of dealing with life put me squarely in brand new, uncharted territory.

Zeke had asked me to drive his car. And because I thought driving would give me a measure of control over the out of control that had spiraled since he answered his phone, I'd agreed.

So now I was driving a high end SUV. The Range Rover was bigger than what I was used to maneuvering and I swear I was driving like an old lady.

"You can probably pick it up a notch. Won't hurt to go a whole twenty miles an hour." I didn't want to take my eyes off the road, but I was pretty sure he was smirking.

I ignored him.

"Turn left at the next light and then pull into that self-storage facility."

I glanced in the rearview mirror, his obvious paranoia was starting to rub off on me.

"I can't go into the office of the storage company. I'm going to need you to do it for me." Zeke said, "Do you think you can?"

I was quiet. Storage facility? Burned? NSA, sleeper cells, treason? When had my boring, unassuming life become a spy novel?

"Sunshine?"

"Yeah."

"I need to secure my laptop," Zeke said softly. "There's too much sensitive information on it, even though there isn't anything classified, of course."

And geez, I wanted to bail. But instead, I turned the car into the storage company parking lot, and parked in the spot closest to the office. Zeke was slouched in the passenger seat, a Billabong cap on his head, blocking his face from view. "What do you want me to do?"

"Rent the smallest unit you can, pay in cash if possible, and rent under Sunshine Smith. They'll be looking for a rental in my name."

It all seemed a little crazy to me. "Why are you storing your laptop?"

"GPS tracker."

Zeke barely moved his mouth and my gaze zeroed in on his lips and I remembered what he'd done with his mouth last night. Wow. I needed to shut that down right away.

"I disabled it at the hotel, but I need to get rid of it. Just in case."

I pulled on the door handle.

"Wait. Here." He pulled an odd-shaped lock and key from his worn duffel bag and pressed it into my hand.

I curled my fingers around the cool metal, my fingers tingled at the fleeting, innocuous contact, and I was a little breathless as I told him, "Be back in a sec."

"To be clear. We need to get this locked up and get gone."

I was trying not to be totally annoyed. And I wondered how he had convinced me to stick with him and do this, but the truth was that his freak out while he was on the phone earlier had touched off an unexpected protectiveness in me.

I'd taken care of my mother for years. And I don't know why but I had the unshakeable belief that Zeke really needed my help. Needed *me*.

My shoulders tensed.

"Relax. Act casual."

Yes, because I was totally relaxed, on the run with a stranger, my stepfather after me and my mother, and who knows what else or who else was dogging me and Zeke.

Acting relaxed was going to be a bit of a stretch. But I would try.

I opened the glass-fronted door to the little office and smiled at the small Indian man behind the counter. His deep black eyes were kind as he waited patiently for me to get to the counter.

"Can I help you?" He smiled back, and his gaze shifted to the car in the parking lot.

"I'd like to rent a storage unit." I fluttered my hands toward the secure units behind the gated entrance and hoped that would be enough to bring his attention back to me and away from Zeke.

"Yes, okay." He pulled out a single Xeroxed form and slid the piece of paper across the Formica counter. A small television sat on the desk in the corner, the sound low as he watched what looked like an Indian soap opera. Even though I couldn't understand the words, the drama on the screen was obvious.

I quelled the urge to run and slowly, methodically filled

out the forms with a steady hand as he watched me patiently. "Do you need a lock?"

"Nope." I held up my right hand, the cylinder-shaped lock and key clutched tightly. "All set."

"Ah, so you come prepared." His words lilted in an almost lyrical manner.

I smiled tightly. "Yes. Thank you."

"Very good." He handed me the rental agreement forms.

"You mind if I give you cash for the six month rental?"

"That is very unusual." His black brows crinkled over his dark eyes. "But not a problem as long as you also give me a credit card for renewal."

I gave him my 'on the run' Visa. All my existing Sunshine Smith cards were locked away in the safe at the store. That was the plan Mama and I had put into place. Dump everything that we'd been using, and then use cash unless it was an emergency. Only use the black credit cards if there were no other options. I was thinking this qualified. "I'll probably come in and pay cash when it is time to renew."

"Very good. Unit 350 is around the corner and up the hill in the third row."

"Thank you." That was good. I wanted away from the inquisitive eyes of the manager. Although I noted that now the television screen showed security shots of a row of storage units, then the screen switched again, showing another area of the complex. I shoved the papers into my purse.

"You are very welcome." He tilted his chin down in a parody of a bow. "Do you need any further assistance?"

"No, thank you. I've got my muscle in the car." I smiled

and jerked my thumb towards the Range Rover as he peered over my shoulder into the parking lot.

"That is most excellent."

"Thank you again." I turned and headed out to the SUV, hoping it didn't look like I was running even though that's what I wanted to do. Head for safe ground. And when I realized I was thinking of Zeke Hawthorne as safe I wanted to turn and run the other direction. I trusted him, but what did I really know? I could be an accessory to some horrible crime that I didn't even know about. Destined to be on one of those true crime shows as the naïve, unwitting sidekick to a criminal mastermind. As I made tracks to the Range Rover and Zeke Hawthorne, I had a moment where I wondered just what the hell I was doing.

But an adrenaline rush fizzed through my bloodstream, and my step lightened as I swung into the driver's seat of the fancy car. Far fancier than I'd ever driven. Range Rovers were not low profile.

"I did it." The urge to giggle was strong.

I drove up the hill to unit 350. We made quick work of putting his laptop in the unit. Cobwebs and a smattering of debris littered the dark corners. Zeke pulled a smaller bag out of his duffel and placed the backpack carefully on the cement floor.

He'd wanted me to stay in the car but for reasons I couldn't name, I didn't want him doing this alone. He squatted down by the unassuming backpack, his bronzed legs spread as he rested his butt on his heels.

He opened the zipper and looked inside, closed the zipper, opened the zipper and looked inside, closed the zipper, and then did it one more time for good measure. Zeke patted the backpack and stood.

His little quirk made me smile.

"What?" He crossed his arms defensively over his chest, but my gaze was drawn to his muscled biceps and the light dusting of blond hair on his forearms. And I knew he was being defensive about the quirk, but suddenly memories from last night came rushing back to me.

The power in his body as he'd spread me wide and erotically licked my body in his signature pattern. The tenderness in his touch. The fascination and appreciation in his gaze.

My breath caught. The air in the little room was stifling. I couldn't breathe and my body was melting at the sensual memory of him between my thighs and the residual ache that I felt not only in my sex but in my heart. The swell of emotion kinda freaked me out.

Zeke stepped forward.

I stepped back, an involuntary, instinctive reaction to the predatory almost feline movement of his body as he stalked toward me. With my heart thudding in anticipation, I let myself be caught.

Zeke tunneled his fingers through my hair, his palms warm and commanding against my neck as he lowered his mouth to mine.

Anticipation hummed through me. Oh Goddess, he was going to kiss me again. Against my better judgment, I melted against him. The puff of his breath was soft on my lips as he pressed his mouth to mine in a fierce, quick kiss. He sipped at my mouth, sucked my top lip in between his, then kissed the left corner, then right corner, then nipped my bottom lip in the zig zag pattern, just like he'd explored my body last night.

His touch soothed me even as he aroused, and I calmed with his hands on me.

Then he skimmed his hand along my shoulder and traced the curve of my elbow and the length of my forearm before he threaded his fingers through mine. "We've got to go," he said against my mouth.

I nodded without speaking.

Zeke secured the lock on the storage unit, hefted his duffel over his shoulder, all without letting go of my hand. As if he intuitively sensed that I needed the contact.

We'd switched places and now Zeke was driving the rental Range Rover up Highway One keeping just at the speed limit. A cool dreary fog lingered close to the black top, and a low cloud layer enveloped us in a cocoon of gray and white. Traffic was sporadic after we bypassed my current hometown of Cambria. As if sensing our frenetic mood, the ocean waves crashed white foam against the kelp-strewn brown sand, and the bellow of the sea lions could be heard even through our closed windows.

We were traveling away from the home I'd had for the last nine years and a wave of melancholy rolled over me. I was so tired of living in fear. I just wanted a normal life. College. A boyfriend. I thought about last night. A sex life.

Instead, I was running from yet another threat. One that had nothing to do with me. So after years of hiding, years of not getting to do what I wanted, and making the decision less than a day ago to take control of my life, seize my destiny and claim my due right, and triumph over John Stanley, here I was…still running.

The earlier calm instilled by Zeke's kiss began to dissolve into an escalating panic.

Thoughts whirled furiously, mind in a state of chaos as I tried to figure out what I was doing here, with him. That nerdy, somewhat goofy guy had disappeared with one bad phone call and in his place was a harder, more confident, in charge man. But I had no doubts that this guy could keep me safe. I might have been a master at hiding mama's and my identity but as far as physical safety, I knew I was no match for John Stanley or the threat that now followed Zeke.

Zeke had never really explained what burned meant. They didn't need him anymore didn't sound that ominous. But I knew from his actions and his paranoia and urgency in getting out of that hotel and on the road that it meant more than not being needed.

I concentrated on that rather than the fact that I'd lost my virginity last night. Somehow I thought my change in status would be more climactic, or more obvious. I'd always known that the event wouldn't be romantic. I'd never had the luxury of getting close to anyone. No friends, man or woman, because of our secrets. And while the night had been lovely, satisfying, and hot, even knowing it wasn't logical, I'd hoped for something more romantic from the day after than running again.

Last night, having sex with Zeke had been beautiful and as necessary as breath, but right now I was seriously questioning my decision.

Since we'd gotten on the road, Zeke's tension level had escalated until I thought he'd snap. He hadn't said a word. And I didn't want to interrupt his intense concentration. But his silence gave me far too much time to think. And my thoughts weren't giving me warm fuzzies. My thoughts were freaking me out.

I glanced over at him. His jaw was clenched, a muscle ticked in the corner and he was tapping an unconscious rhythm on the leather steering wheel.

I had to wonder if he wasn't crazy. I'd entrusted my

welfare to him and if he was nuts I could be in danger. But he'd seemed so worried, so concerned for my safety, that I'd squashed my misgivings and gotten in his car. All those doubts came flooding back as I watched the asphalt roll by. At least Mama was safe with Blue.

I decided to press him again. "What does burned mean?"

"They decided that I am no longer employed and I am considered a threat to the organization, and to the country." Zeke's fingers gripped the steering wheel. "And if they catch me before I have a chance to clear my name, everything will be taken from me."

I could relate to that. Losing everything in one moment was terrifying and disconcerting and unsettling. It had happened to me when I was seven years old and I'd never gotten over it.

"Do you deserve it?"

Zeke opened his mouth, closed it, and frowned, then glanced in the rearview mirror. "I don't think so."

That wasn't an overwhelmingly positive response. On the other hand, he wasn't loudly proclaiming his innocence either. "How do you not know?"

Zeke pressed his lips together. "Since I was drugged when I was kidnapped, I don't remember what happened."

I thought back to his explanation of why the government was after Susan Chen. "But you were drugged."

"Yes."

I needed to think about the implications of that more but right now I wanted specifics. "What was the drug?"

"Sodium Pentothal." Zeke's blond brows arched down into a deep V. "I thought I was immune to SP and similar drugs."

Drugs, chemical interactions, were one area where I had no expertise. I was more of a math/physics girl. So I couldn't be any help there. "How does you being drugged turn into you being burned?"

"I may have associated with questionable people, whether homegrown terrorists or foreign nationals who are considered a threat to public safety and national security. I may have given away national secrets. I may have— Fuck."

He may have what? His eyes had narrowed and his mouth had tightened. I got the gist of what he could have done and I got the burned part now. I studied him. "What are you going to do next?"

"I'm working on it." Zeke huffed out a breath. "We need to ditch this car. Not just for me but in case John Stanley does have the capability to track down who rented it."

We were heading north along Moonstone Beach.

"Can you suggest a place where there would be a lot of cars?"

I thought for a moment, but there was really only one place that came to mind.

"Hearst Castle Visitor Center." Which was a few miles up ahead in San Simeon. "But once we ditch this one, where do we get a new one?"

"We're going shopping," Zeke said cryptically.

By the time we'd pulled into the parking lot, I'd figured it out.

Hearst Castle was a huge tourist draw run by the State of California. Tourists didn't drive up the hill to the massive estate once owned by the famous mogul William Randolph Hearst. They parked at the giant visitor center and gift shop then boarded buses to go up the hill to the castle. And left their cars unattended. I'd bet we were going to steal a car.

We'd hit at an unplanned yet precisely beneficial time. A

tour bus coming back from the mansion had just pulled into the depot station and people were pouring from the bus like ants crawling over a picnic. Some went into the gift/souvenir shop, while others headed straight for their cars. As that group left, a new batch of tourists arrived and lined up at the depot for the bus to head back up the hill. Zeke and I sat in the Range Rover, waiting. There were cars and people everywhere. When the bus closed its doors and headed back up the hill, Zeke pulled a small screwdriver out of pouch from his duffel bag and beelined for an older model Honda Civic that had just recently been parked.

"Keep a lookout," he demanded as he crouched down in front of the light blue battered car.

"Why this car?" I asked curiously.

"Traditionally the number one most stolen car in the country."

"Huh, really?"

"Yep."

Zeke switched license plates with the car next to the Civic, which was a Honda CRV.

One of his unruly blond curls had fallen over his forehead and fell into his vision. He shook his head then bent to finish the task of switching the license plates on the two Hondas. Then he switched plates with the rental Range Rover and another car of the same make, but a different color.

The whole process had taken all of ten minutes.

"Let's get out of here." Zeke used a Slim Jim to open the Civic's driver's door and then unlocked the rest of the car. He threw his duffel in the backseat and by working some automotive magic that completely escaped me, he hotwired the car. Within a few minutes, he had the engine running.

"Sweet music." He grinned, his teeth even and white in

his tanned face. Slight blond stubble obscured the clean line of his jaw and the scruff gave him a rakish air.

The rumble of an Army truck hit our ears at the same time.

Zeke twisted in the driver's seat, just as I swung my body into the passenger seat. A convoy truck barreled up the paved road to the Hearst Castle Visitor Center.

"Shit." Zeke shoved out of the driver's seat and quickly hopped into the back seat. He lay on the tattered fabric seat on his back so he wasn't visible unless you were staring straight into the car, and commanded me. "You drive."

"What?"

"Act casual." Zeke's muffled voice came from the backseat. "Don't speed. Don't stare overlong at the truck. Just drive like you're a tourist."

My heart boomed in my chest. "You think that truck is for you?" *Us?*

"I can't afford not to think it," Zeke replied. "Get us out of here."

I got behind the wheel and slowly exited the tourist center parking lot. The Army truck went flying by as if on a mission. "Maybe they're just getting ready to do some repairs at the Castle. After all, it is a National Landmark."

I was grasping and I knew it. But that Army truck made everything that had happened this morning real in a way that I didn't expect.

"Do you really want to stick around and find out?"

He had a point. I tooled down the winding road. At the stop sign to Highway One, I asked, "North? Or South?" We couldn't go west, that lead straight into the ocean. East lead up the hill to the castle which was only accessible by official buses.

"Camp Roberts is south and east, Fort Hunter Liggett is

north and east. Roberts is closer. North would send us near the Ventana Wilderness and towards Monterey." Zeke's voice ruminated from the backseat. I didn't freaking care I just needed to know which way to go.

"Which way?" I asked again almost desperately.

"South."

So I turned left, and we were on our way. I glanced back at the visitor center. I couldn't be sure but I thought the soldiers were clustered around the Rover that Zeke and I had abandoned. But he'd switched plates so I wasn't sure how they knew the correct one.

My palms began to sweat and I blew out a nervous breath. "I think you were right," I whispered.

"Then let's get the hell out of here." Zeke's muffled voice was stringent.

We headed south, my mind whirling at a hundred miles an hour even as I kept the car's speed just under the posted limit.

Zeke pushed up to sitting and hung his arms over the backseat to stare out the side window at the slowly receding visitor center.

Those Army guys were after him. As if he were a public enemy. And I voiced the thoughts that were swirling in my head since he'd told me his impossible tale. And given me new information about my stepfather. If he was right, and John Stanley was a sleeper, then more was going on here. "What are the odds that my stepfather and your problems are not connected?"

He didn't say anything but his dark blue gaze met mine in the rearview mirror. The older car's mirror was mottled with age, the blemishes in the mirror obscuring and revealing his features and giving him a slightly demonic cast.

"The Single Law of Chance," Emile Borel's work on

evolutionary inevitability I mused aloud, "would presume that the probability that these events are connected is so small it would never occur."

Except, that it had occurred. John Stanley had been in Cambria. Susan Chen had been in San Luis Obispo. Zeke had been burned. And the Army was in San Simeon. "Taken alone they are all on the edge of impossible. However, all of those events had happened which means, at least in my mind, that they have to be connected."

Zeke was still silent.

When he didn't say anything I thought maybe he didn't know what I was talking about. "Are you familiar with Borel?"

"Of course," Zeke snapped. "I'm just trying to wrap my head around the fact everything is tied together."

Ooookay.

"Usually I see patterns before they're patterns," he muttered. He didn't say it but I could hear the question. How did he miss it? And how was everything connected?

"You…and me."

As far as I knew there weren't any other variables that intersected us, so in theory, our problems should be mutually exclusive. "Unless there is another Venn intersection that I don't know about."

He continued to stay silent.

"You know, Venn diagrams. Circles that overlap. Some variables are unique to each circle but the variables that both have in common are in the overlapped part."

"Jesus, yes, I'm familiar with Venn Diagrams. Pretty sure everyone learns about them in third grade," Zeke said.

I could practically hear his brain churning in the backseat. He knew something. Something else that tied us together.

But the longer I waited, the more sure I became that he had no intention of sharing with me. Which totally blew. And he could tell I was waiting.

He finally said, "It's classified."

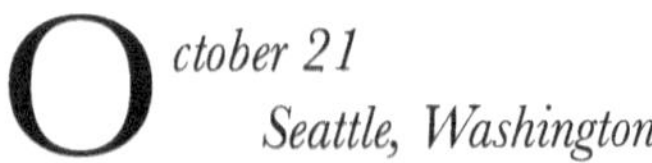

CHAPTER 26

October 21
Seattle, Washington

OLIVER STUDIED the simple tract house in the suburb of Seattle. He'd hated coming to dinner at this house. Susan's family was dry, boring, and mundane. He'd been a premier scientist and to have to share a meal with the plebian and simple tastes of her Asian sibling and Caucasian wife trying so hard to be the quintessential American family had driven him insane.

But he'd done it. He'd tolerated those dinners and backyard barbecues all for the sake of science and for the cause of mother Russia.

His rage built as he stared at the simple tri-level clapboard house with its red brick foundation and cement walkway. He hated the rounded, precisely-trimmed bushes out front and the little pots, filled with cheerful Fall flowers and trailing greenery, that flanked the cement steps and iron railing.

They had talked *ad nauseam* about their stupid flowers and their minivan and their neighbor's vacations and what universities their darling, brilliant children were going to attend.

It was so tempting to just torch the house. He spied the electrical box attached to the side of the house near the fenced backyard. He could probably even make it look like an accident. He could just zap the fuse box, engulf the house in flames, and get rid of his former in-laws permanently.

But he needed Liliya. And he needed his *wife*.

And, most importantly, he needed their research.

He'd tried contacting her through the silly method they'd set up years ago. An online chat room that was just for them. She hadn't responded. Hadn't acknowledged his attempts to get in touch with her in any way.

That seriously pissed him off. He was not to be ignored.

Of course, she had no idea he was in her country.

He wasn't about to put that onto the internet even to get a rise out of her. But he didn't know how else to make contact with her. He'd been at this house for the last two days and she hadn't come to see their daughter. The in-laws had other visitors. Official looking men in navy blue suits and white shirts, which meant he wasn't the only one looking for his absent wife. Another visitor who appeared to be a tutor came every day for several hours.

It was time for more desperate measures.

Oliver sat in a car down the street hoping that the brat would show soon. He'd thought he'd caught a glimpse of her in the window earlier but since that one quick shadow, his daughter hadn't come outside. He could concede that perhaps giving Liliya the DNA-enhancing drug was not well thought out, but at the time he'd only meant to increase her brain power while testing the drug, and help her agoraphobia, not make it worse. Unfortunately there had been unforeseen consequences to the drug's effects.

He was done waiting around for Susan to respond. He'd make it impossible for Susan to ignore him.

Oliver sat up in his seat as the tall, thin woman in a light blue Prius parked in front of the house. The tutor, he presumed. She was carrying a bulging messenger bag. She rang the doorbell and was quickly ushered into the home by Susan's sister-in-law. No sign of his daughter.

Oliver continued to wait. As he canvassed the neighborhood, he noted that there was a banged up, white service van, with some sort of logo on the side, parked at the opposite end of the street.

Something about the van and the fact that no house on the street seemed to be having any type of work done set off his radar.

Oliver tried to see if there was someone in the back of that van. It was possible he wasn't the only one waiting for his darling wife to show.

But damned if he'd let another spook take what rightfully belonged to him.

Oliver kept one eye on the house and the other on the van. But nothing changed.

Two hours later, the woman exited the house. He caught a glimpse of Liliya but no Susan. She had to be coming here, right? She was so fucking protective of the girl. But what if Susan was not in Seattle? How the hell would he find her? The United States was a big fucking country. Although she had limited mobility since it was likely that every intelligence and law enforcement agency in the country was on the lookout for her. He needed her to come to him.

As he watched the Prius drive away, he contemplated his next move.

Ring the doorbell? Grab the girl? His employers had given him two weeks to carry out his mission but he didn't want to use all the allotted time. It would be best for him to get out of the United States as quickly as possible. The longer he was here, the more chance he could be discovered.

He didn't have time to waste.

He'd been in front of this house for the last two days, and nothing. Maybe he needed to think outside the box, as the Americans liked to say.

Susan was not answering his communication efforts. But he knew one way to get her to talk to him.

Oliver watched the van but still there was no movement. He must have been mistaken about the house being under surveillance. Finally, he was ready to make his move. But he still had to make sure no one saw him.

Oliver put his rental car into gear and drove away from the house slowly. When he hit the next intersection, he turned left and then turned into the alleyway behind the house.

He parked one house down from his in-laws and pulled the syringe from his duffel. He'd hoped to avoid this solution for several reasons but the most important was he hadn't really wanted to deal with the girl's problems.

But if he didn't get the formula and notes from Susan he was dead. Self-preservation won every damn time.

He tucked the syringe in his Seattle Seahawks windbreaker pocket and exited the car. He approached the back door, holding the thick, heavy Wonder Bar jimmying tool alongside his thigh.

Oliver lifted his fist and rapped against the back door, hard enough that his knuckles stung from the force. Susan's sister-in-law peered out the back curtains. Her fearful gaze widened as she saw him. She started shaking her head and her mouth formed the word *no* even as she jammed the curtains back into place.

Yob. Fuck.

He banged again. This time even harder.

But she didn't come back to the door. Oliver shrugged. Guess he'd have to do this the hard way. He wedged the Wonder Bar between the frame and the door near the doorknob and cranked until the flimsy door cracked under the pressure. God bless the Americans and their inventions. A sledgehammer would have been so much noisier.

Oliver forced his way inside the house. In his peripheral vision, he saw the frying pan coming toward his head. Instinctively he threw up his left arm to block the blow. The impact reverberated through his entire body.

"Fuck!" He roared and swung back with the Wonder Bar, catching his sister-in-law in the temple. She dropped like a sack of flour and blood poured from her wound onto the Saltillo tile floor.

Bliad. He fought the urge to spit on the bitch.

The blinking red light from their house alarm pad indicated that she'd pressed the silent notice button for the police. He sprinted through the house looking for his daughter. He knew it would take the security company a few minutes to verify the alarm was set off on purpose. On cue, the home phone began to ring.

He pulled the syringe from his pocket and started searching for his daughter.

Susan couldn't ignore him now.

October 21
San Luis Obispo

ZEKE SWEATED in the back seat. Dammit. How did they find him so fast? He didn't have a tracking device implanted like some of the field agents. He was only a programmer who spent most of his time in the office working on code and developing unhackable encryption programs or trying to hack into other programs. There was no need to implant him.

Could they have put in some sort of nanobots when he'd gotten the original DNA-enhancing drug? That had never been mentioned by the scientists but still, they had located him pretty damn quickly.

Clearly his evasion choices were too easy to predict. He needed to step up his tactics or he'd be in prison before he could blink.

And then it occurred to him. "Which car were they around?"

"The Range Rover."

"My rental or the one I switched plates with?"

"Yours."

The rental company tracking device. Zeke wanted to slap his forehead. Dammit. He knew better than most people how many ways an individual could be tracked.

Zeke knew Sunshine was still pissed because he hadn't answered her question about how else they intersected. Her idea of a Venn Diagram was actually a good one. It might not hurt to diagram out all the different variables and see if there was anything he was missing.

"We need to lay low for a bit."

"Where are we going to do that?" He hadn't imagined the snippiness in her voice. As a matter of fact if she hadn't been driving he wasn't sure she wouldn't have just rolled out of the car at the last stoplight.

He needed to find a hole-up/hide site. To do that he needed a new phone and the internet.

He had an idea. The beach wasn't a very defensible position which was exactly why it made a lot of sense. The NSA would be searching specific locations, train, bus stations, the highway, even possibly the little airport in San Luis for avenues of escape from the area.

And they likely wouldn't think about him staying here, right in plain sight. The surfboard racks on top of the car they borrowed would be more camouflage. Even if they looked twice at the car in a beach parking lot, they'd likely assume it was owned by beach rats out to catch some waves.

They could hit the beach and he could look for a more permanent solution to his problem.

He knew Sunshine wasn't going to be keen on the idea. But they didn't have a choice. Zeke needed to find a safe place for them to hide while he figured out what the hell he was going to do next.

"I have a few ideas. But we need supplies."

They should switch license plates on the Honda again. "We need to hit a Target to get camping gear and some other supplies."

She shot him a dark look in the mirror. "Camping?"

"Yeah. Misdirection. We're not actually going to camp, but if anyone remembers us they'll remember the gear." And they'd be prepared for anything, even the possibility of sleeping outside in case they did end up camping. Hopefully it wouldn't come to that. However they both needed a change of clothes and to alter their appearance. "Can you get me to the nearest Target?"

Once they arrived, he had Sunshine park at the end of the lot. Zeke crammed his faded Billabong hat with a ragged brim over his curls and pulled the bill low over his forehead.

He studied Sunshine, wondering if she had anything in her bag to change her appearance.

"What are you looking at?" Her eyes were narrowed, the gray mere slits in her face.

He was about to have one pissed off woman on his hands. "I think you should cut your hair."

Her eyes rounded and her long graceful fingers went straight to the thick braid that hung down over shoulder. "Wha—"

"I know, I know, it's a symbol of your feminine mystique."

"Excuse me?" She propped her fists on her hips and her eyes sparkled with annoyance in the morning light. She hissed, "I wear my hair this way because it's convenient, I could give a rat's butt about my hair but I think I deserve at least an answer as to why I need to cut it."

Zeke took a step back, impressed at her wrath. And oddly turned on. "We need to change our appearances."

She snorted. "And you think that cap is going to do it for you?"

He jerked back. "What?"

"We need to buzz your hair," she countered. "Right now that curly mop is pretty damn distinctive. And if you've forgotten they're after you, not me."

As far as they knew. And dammit, she'd nailed it. "Jesus. You're right."

She nodded smugly.

"Okay so we need hair clippers, hair dye, tent, lantern, food, a new phone. Several new phones." Zeke ticked items off on his fingers as they walked toward the entrance and the giant red Target sign. He'd never done anything as mundane as shop with a woman.

He knew she wanted answers. "And before you ask, let's just get through shopping first."

"So many questions, so little information," she snarked.

"I'll tell you what I can," he finally said. "Once we're someplace less public."

"You promise?" Sunshine gave him the side eye but he could sense her feeling a little lost. "Because right now I feel like I've put my trust in a guy who isn't being completely honest. And frankly I'm more than a little freaked."

Zeke understood. He was freaked too. So he shared something as they walked into the store. "I've never done this before." He ducked his head and looked at his feet.

"Done what?" she asked softly.

"Gone shopping with a girl."

"I'm hardly a girl." The shadows in her eyes were too ancient for her to be merely a girl.

"You know what I mean." He felt stupid telling her that

but she needed something from him so that she would know that he was vulnerable too.

"Yeah. I've never done this either," she said.

Zeke balled his fist and held it for her to bump. "Let's do this."

She nodded, and if her chin trembled a little, he was going to ignore it. Because emotion was not in his wheelhouse. It wasn't even in the neighborhood of his skillset.

They walked in to the store together, Sunshine threaded her fingers through his and put her head on his shoulder. "As an act, in case anyone is watching."

"Ah, act normal."

She snorted, then blurted out, "I know nothing about normal."

"Yeah. Me either." Something they had in common. "But we're both smart. We'll figure it out."

"Good point." Sunshine's mouth lifted and her eyes brightened.

The pleasure he derived from that little sign of happiness was a surprise.

Zeke tugged Sunshine toward the sporting goods section. He thought about the weather. San Luis, West Coast, in October. It was going to be cold tonight.

Zeke picked the sleeping bag with the lowest temperature rating that Target carried, but that was still only the 3 Season bag. Hopefully he could find them a house to hole up in. But if they ended up sleeping outside, a long shot, they needed to be prepared. They were going to have to keep warm together.

As he imagined himself and Sunshine entwined inside the tight bag, other parts of him warmed up. Zeke mentally added condoms to their shopping list.

A Target employee in a red vest smiled inquisitively at them. "Need any help picking out equipment?"

Great, they would have to find the only helpful box store employee on the planet.

"We're good." Zeke smiled and leaned across the aisle to grab a high powered battery- operated lantern. "Thanks."

"Well if you need anything, let me know." The kid's gaze lingered on Sunshine. And Zeke's possessive meter rose. Not cool to be checking her out when it was clear they were together. But Zeke couldn't call him on it, they couldn't afford to draw any extra attention.

"Pretty sure we've got this." Zeke slung his arm over Sunshine's shoulder, letting the kid know that not only that they could handle their shopping, but that he and Sunshine were a couple.

She stiffened slightly. The kid smiled nervously and slunk away.

As soon as the employee was far enough away that he wouldn't hear them, Zeke said, "Time to get the clippers and the hair dye."

Sunshine raised her eyebrow. Her fingers twitched as if she wanted to grab her braid. She'd said she wasn't attached to her hair, but her fingers were curled around the braid in a very protective manner.

"We need to disguise ourselves." Of course, Zeke's baddies were more likely to see through any disguise that he used, especially if they ran his face through any facial recognition software. But it still didn't negate the fact that he needed to alter his appearance and so did she.

He was ready to do whatever it took to keep her safe and him out of federal prison. Instinctively he rubbed his palm over the hat that was hiding his curls. "I'll shave my head."

He shrugged. "But we still probably need to color your hair or cut it."

As he said it, Zeke's heart clenched. He remembered last night, her hair surrounding their bodies in a private, warm curtain, blocking out the rest of the world. "No cutting your hair," he backtracked huskily.

"Why not?"

"I changed my mind." He needed to have some visual reminder of last night.

Her eyebrows lifted in surprise. "No argument from me. Besides, they don't know we're together, right?"

Zeke contemplated her question. After entering Target, even paying in cash, chances were that if there were eyes on the store, whoever was after him would verify that he did in fact have a companion. He hated to be paranoid but he was well aware of the advances in facial recognition software. He just had to hope that the main places the NSA was staking out were transit hubs and not the local shopping centers. No need to scare her but he wouldn't lie either. "Hard to say."

She swallowed. And he knew she understood what that implied.

They finished their business in subdued fashion, power-shopping, picking out everything they needed, electronics, camping supplies, and even some new clothes and shoes, in about half an hour. No dithering over colors or even what was essential. Since it was one of those super Targets they were able to buy groceries as well. Of course, Sunshine had no idea what he had planned.

They loaded their eclectic purchases onto the checkout belt. He gripped the hair clippers, the last to go on the conveyor system, too tightly.

Zeke could feel the worry wrapping around him like a

killer wave wrapped around an unsuspecting surfer. He wouldn't let anything happen to her.

"Jeez, don't be such a baby." She teased completely misinterpreting his angst. "It's just hair."

He pretended to shudder and placed the last item on the belt.

While they'd been shopping, Zeke had been thinking about his problem. Problems.

The more he thought about it the more he was beginning to think that the only person who could save him was Susan Chen. If he could find her, bring her in, and get her to reveal her secrets, maybe just maybe he could clear his name.

But now that he was burned, he wasn't going to be able to do it alone.

Zeke decided it was necessary to get in touch with Jamie and Lucas. Of course, he couldn't call Jamie, her incoming calls might be recorded by the office. But he could call Lucas Goodman. Her boyfriend. And yes, if you'd asked him two weeks ago if Jamie would date someone long enough to have them qualify as an actual boyfriend, he'd have said not just no, but no way in hell.

Zeke had been slightly in love with Jamie. Just like he'd been slightly in love with Anna before Jamie. And now he was slightly in love with Sunshine but somehow this felt different and he didn't know why.

He needed to call Jamie and reason things out with her. She was the super-agent. He was just a computer geek. Sure he'd helped rescue Jamie's sister but he'd been tech support, and not much more.

After they exited the store, he used one of the burner phones they'd bought to dial Lucas Goodman. Luckily Zeke had an aptitude for numbers, so he had no problem remembering Lucas's cell number. Jamie would know what he needed to do. And he needed to tell her he'd been burned. He didn't want her getting in trouble because of him. Jamie had had enough trouble lately. He wasn't about to dump more on her head.

The phone rang and rang. Then finally. "Lucas Goodman's phone," Jamie answered.

Even better.

"Hey." Zeke paused.

"Oh my God. You will not believe what happened." Jamie blurted. "Major problems."

Zeke wanted to swear. More problems?

Jamie Hunt did not exaggerate. If she said there were major problems, the fucking apocalypse was near.

There was a fumbling sound, then she said, "What phone number is this?"

Zeke said, "Got burned at the beach. Lost my cell phone."

Silence. "Burned?"

Yeah. Saying it aloud didn't make it any more fun. "Yep."

"Shit." Jamie continued, "Okay, okay. Don't worry about losing—"

"Let's keep it clean." Zeke interrupted her. But at least he knew she'd gotten the message.

"Yeah, Geek boy. I've been around the block a few times." Jamie said, "Pretty sure we'll be seeing her soon anyway. Big happenings. Her ex somehow managed to enter the area, and kidnapped the kid."

Oliver Krychef was in the U.S.? And he'd kidnapped Susan Chen's daughter? Kidnapped his own daughter? Holy shit. "Wow. So you following him?"

"No," Jamie said with disgust. "He went in the back,

hurt the sister-in-law, snatched the kid. We didn't know until the paramedics got there. We lost him. But we're monitoring the situation. I'll keep you updated."

"Sounds good."

"Since he snatched the kid, we should have a line on her soon."

Which would mean Zeke had a chance at clearing his name. But first they had to catch Susan Chen. "That would be good for me. That was why I called. I need her to stop the burn."

"Yeah," Jamie said. "You're right."

The only person who could clear him was Susan Chen. He and Jamie spoke for another few minutes considering how Krychef would make contact but they couldn't afford to stay on the phone much longer.

Jamie said, "What are you doing in the meantime?"

Zeke forced his mind into a calmer state. "EPA."

"Good call," Jamie praised him. "Keep in touch. Regularly."

For obvious reasons, she couldn't call him. Because if they found out she'd been in contact with him and hadn't reported it she could get in trouble.

"Thanks," Zeke swallowed past the ball of gratitude in his throat.

"Stay safe."

"You too." Zeke pressed the end button, then opened the back of the phone. He needed to make sure the GPS signal wasn't transmitting and that there was no way to track this phone. If for some reason the NSA had tapped Lucas knowing that Jamie and Lucas were together, they might be monitoring his incoming and outgoing calls. He didn't think that was the case but he wasn't about to assume a thing.

Jamie's willingness to keep in touch with him even though his status was damaging affected him.

"Shit."

Sunshine gave him a strange look. The panic that had been lingering at the edge of his subconscious mind like the tide edging up the sand, slowly encroached on his ability to think and obliterated all rational thought.

"You okay, smart boy?" she asked.

She was right. He was smart. Smart enough to figure this out.

Zeke squared his shoulders. They had problems. Multiple. Obviously Jamie was actively tracking Susan Chen, so Zeke needed to let her keep on top of that situation. His next move had to be list each problem, break down the steps to correct it, and then in a logical, orderly manner execute the plan.

And part of the logical effort to solve problems was to use all assets at hand.

Sunshine glanced around the parking lot. "I assume we're going shopping again." A small smile quirked her peach lips and he could see her analyzing and discarding cars in the lot, trying to figure out which one they should steal to replace their ride.

That's when Zeke realized he had the biggest asset of all standing right next to him.

"Actually we just need to switch out two Honda license plates and keep the car we have." Zeke suppressed the pang of guilt that he'd left someone without their ride. He'd make it up to them by sending money to the registration address once he was out of this mess.

"Okay, here's what we're gonna do." For the first time since this whole crazy adventure started, Zeke had the confidence to see it through. That was all Sunshine.

That's when he realized he was more than just a little in love with her.

"What's wrong?"

"Nothing's wrong." Zeke lied. "I just realized I'm not using all my resources."

He gave her a steady look until understanding dawned in her gaze and a brilliant smile spread over her face like the sun rising over the horizon and bleeding onto the landscape.

And Zeke felt like he was ten feet tall.

"You'll tell me about our connections?" Sunshine asked quietly. "Despite being classified?"

"Fuck classified."

Zeke swung into the driver's seat of the Honda. His brain churning. He rubbed his palms together. "I can't wait to mine that giant brain of yours."

Jesus, could he be more of a nerd? What woman wanted to hear he was attracted to her brain?

He curled his hands around the steering wheel. Did he apologize for being a complete geek or try and gloss over? He thought about it for another minute.

Apologize.

"Um, sorry." He shot her a glance, thinking she'd be irritated but she was smiling. "Sometimes I talk before I realize how it sounds."

"Don't be sorry." She patted his bare knee. "I don't get the opportunity to use my brain as often as I'd like. Logic puzzles and coming up with new fragrances only take me so far."

Then she blushed and ducked her head as she realized she'd just confessed to doing simple logic puzzles.

Zeke's skin sizzled where her hand touched him. But his heart electrified. She understood him. He felt as if he'd found a kindred spirit. Zeke deliberately lifted one hand from the wheel and placed it over hers.

"Fellow nerds unite." He clenched her fingers and lifted their entwined hands in a fist pump.

Sunshine laughed out loud. The sound was like a waterfall, light and joyous, tumbling over his senses. He couldn't deny that he wanted more than her brain. His semi started to rise. Just being around her seemed to be some sort of aphrodisiac. At random moments, his brain would shift to last night in their hotel room. Shift to the remembrance of Sunshine sleek and naked, like a sea nymph with her long hair draped over round breasts and flat stomach tickling his chest, as she bent to kiss him.

She'd gone from tentative to confident, blossoming with each new sexual experience. After a few hours, she'd intuitively learned what did it for him and set about ramping up his arousal. She'd accepted his foibles, sometimes his OCD could make him self-conscious but she hadn't blinked.

Of course he'd had some lovers who mentioned that his attention to detail was a good thing. He'd had just as many who'd been a little freaked by his obsession with order. So it was kind of a mixed bag. He never knew what kind of response to expect.

Her other hand came up to cover her mouth. Her shadowed gray eyes widened and her gaze connected with his. The wonder there made more than his cock swell. Pride expanded his chest like propane filling the canopy of a hot air balloon and lifting him into the air. He understood that something amazing had just happened even if he didn't understand exactly what that was.

"I...don't laugh often."

"Then I'm glad that you were able to laugh now." Safety

zone. He loved that she was comfortable enough that she could let loose with him.

Zeke cruised down Highway One, thankful that in the time it took them to leave the more populated town of San Luis Obispo, she had lightened up.

After about twenty minutes, she asked, "Where are we going?"

Zeke pulled off the highway and into the small secluded parking lot. "The beach."

She swallowed and her gaze cut to the water. Sunshine took a deep breath and he tried not to notice the swell of her breasts as she inhaled. *Focus, Zeke.* And he was a total dog for thinking about sex while she was clearly wrestling with her demons.

"You'll be okay," he coaxed.

"Really?" She shifted so her back was to the ocean and her grey eyes were narrowed as she pierced him with sharp gaze. "I watched my grandparents drown."

She addressed her fear straight up. A misplaced sense of pride swelled through him.

She opened her mouth, he guessed to tell him he had no idea what he was talking about, but he interrupted her before she could speak. "Okay if you don't want to face your fears, no judgment, then you can just sit on the blanket. Nowhere near the water."

"Why the beach?" Her fingers tightened on his.

"It's temporary." He glanced at her. The color had drained from Sunshine's face and her hand went lax in his. "Every Evasion Plan of Action requires a place to hole up and hide."

"We're hiding on the beach?"

"No. I am going to find an empty rental house," Zeke said. "And we will hole up there."

"And do what?"

"Wait, plan, execute. Talk."

She sighed.

"First rule of the acronym Bliss, part of any EPA is to Blend." Zeke handed her one of the bags. "Got you a swim suit and a floppy hat. Let your hair down rather than in keep it in your signature braid."

The bikini was a simple blue cotton, macramé design. "But—"

"Camouflage, babe," he said as he pulled in to a parking space.

They were at the same beach where they first met.

So much had happened in the last few days that Zeke could hardly believe the changes. His life had completely turned around. He'd gone from thinking only about himself, to shifting his attention to Sunshine, and now thinking about them both. He realized that he wanted to clear his name *and* protect her.

So that one day they could end up on a beach for fun.

I WAS BACK at my test beach. The one I liked to visit in the middle of the night to work on my fear of water. Like some surreal Groundhog Day where I kept returning to the same place to learn my lesson. But what if I'd changed my mind? What if I didn't want to learn?

My palms were sweating. And a sick churning had taken up residence in my stomach. Which come to think of it, hadn't been fed today. Somehow Zeke Hawthorne had convinced me to come with him. And suddenly I was confronting my biggest fears.

I awkwardly changed into the skimpy swimsuit,

removing my underwear from beneath my clothes and then replacing them with the bikini. Fortunately he'd also bought an oversized sweatshirt, because the beach was going to be cold. Even with a mid-October Indian Summer, the sand and the water would be freezing. Not that I wanted to get anywhere near the water.

The need to check in with my mother was weighing heavily on me. My stepfather had found me yesterday, what if he'd found Mama too?

"I want to call the answering service."

Zeke had pulled off his threadbare t-shirt. My mouth went dry at the rippling expanse of bare skin. "Go for it. But keep it short."

I nodded mutely and turned on my phone. I called in to the service and pressed the security code to listen to the messages. There were two messages from my mother, which was odd. It hadn't been that long since the last one.

"I forgot to tell you a second ago," Mama's voice rang in my ear. A melancholy hit me, so sharp it pierced my heart and made it difficult to breathe. "Your Uncle sent a friend. Pretty sure he's with you now."

Uncle Carson sent a friend? Mama thought Zeke was Uncle Carson's friend. That's why she'd been so willing to let me go with Zeke. Her instant trust made so much more sense now.

As the message center gave me the date and time the message was left, I realized that our messages must have crossed last night.

I deleted the message then pressed the button for the next one.

"He was there?!" The distress in Mama's voice came through loud and clear. "Oh my God. Are you okay? How did you get away? Oh, I wish I could give you a hug. Leave me another message. Let me know you are okay. Be safe. And no sign of him here." Wherever here was.

I punched in the numbers so I could leave her a message. "We're fine." Which wasn't precisely true but at least she had escaped from her stepfather. No need to worry her mother with all the other craziness going on. "Let's check in twice daily. Love you."

I finally realized that this whole situation was nuts. The threat of John Stanley had to be eliminated once and for all. But I wasn't sure how to go about making that happen.

"Ready?" Zeke asked.

I stared through the stand of eucalyptus trees at the rippling waves of the ocean. The fog still lingered, and the sun played peek a boo with the clouds, flickering in and out. A ray broke through the cloud and shone on the gentle waves of the protected cove.

So pretty. Like a postcard. But the effect was anything but calming. My stomach churned and my limbs filled with a paralyzing fear. Was I ready? No. "Yes."

I squared my shoulders.

"You're going to be okay."

I sure hoped so.

We walked to the beach together. Zeke had his new phone in his palm, while I carried the thin blanket we'd purchased for inside the tent.

I shuddered. We better not be camping. It would remind me too much of those early days on the run from my stepfather.

Zeke grabbed my free hand and swung my arm back and forth like a little kid. "Cover." His palm was warm, comforting, a lifeline as we neared the encroaching waves. The salty scent of brine spread through my senses. A brisk breeze whipped my hair around my face and I tugged the floppy hat low over my brow.

"What are the odds you'll see someone you know here?" Zeke asked.

"Small." My footsteps faltered and stuttered as I stepped closer to the ocean. "My friends are all shopkeepers."

Except they weren't really my friends. Our only connection was that we ran shops in town. They didn't know that I loved math or science. They thought I worshipped the moon and concocted homeopathic scents and scrubs for tourists. Not that they weren't lovely people but I had nothing in common with them.

That fact made me sad all over again.

I shook out the blanket with a sharp snap, then let the light Mylar square float to the ground. The shush of the waves was soothing. As long as we stayed away from the water.

Zeke plopped onto the blanket and began messing with his phone.

This was a smaller beach. No lifeguard tower, no lifeguard stand and mostly deserted at this time of year. The water was awfully cold unless you had a wetsuit—I gave Zeke a side eyed glance as I recalled his surfing adventure from the other night—Or you were crazy.

"We need a defensible position, multiple exits, safe from the sky, and unexpected," he muttered as he thumbed through rental listings on his phone.

He did some more searching on his phone and I thought about my fears. About the fact that thirteen years later, my stepfather still had a stranglehold on my life and I was sick of it.

I shoved to standing.

"You okay?" Zeke glanced up from his intense concentration of the screen.

I squared my shoulders. "I will be." I took one large, determined stride toward the surf.

Zeke considered that big step. "You need me, I'm here."

Gratitude and another more subtle emotion flowed through me. I could do this. I would do this. I took another step. The sand was cool and wet, squishing between my toes and rubbing along the ball of my foot as I took another stride forward.

My heart banged against my ribcage as I drew nearer to the receding water. Fear tingled in the tips of my fingers and toes as I decided I had to meet the incoming tide not wait until it came to me.

I shivered in the chilly mid-morning air. The fog parted and occasionally the sun glimmered through the gray. A few hearty tourists lay on beach towels and a pair of small children, a boy and a girl, frolicked in the shallow surf.

Kids could do this.

I could do this. I took another step, the fear was dizzying. Then I realized my chest hurt because I needed to breathe. "Inhale deeply," I muttered.

The squawking seagulls was nearly drowned out by the rush of terror in my ears. Frigid water seared my toes as I took my first voluntary step into the ocean in thirteen years. I forced myself to stand in several inches of water, hypnotically watching the roll of the tide and the sparkle of the sun on the waves. My heart still thundered in my chest and the tingling in my body didn't abate, but I forced myself to endure.

I was going to beat this fear if it killed me. The sharp cold burned and I danced backwards a few feet. But I did it!

I whirled around to tell Zeke.

And there was my second greatest nemesis. My stepfather.

I fell a step back into the surf. My vocal chords were so tight, I couldn't even utter a squeak. I hadn't been this close to him in years.

Years that had not been kind to him.

My heart beat so hard I was afraid I might pass out. My entire body shook on the inside as fear shot through me.

John Stanley loomed in front of me. Oddly not as large as I remembered. His chest was still broad but he had a belly, that old muscle had gone to fat. His lined face was marred by spider veins and the red cheeks of a man who drank too much. His nose looked as if he'd broken it and his hair, what was left of it, was more salt than pepper. Unlike the devil black it used to be.

"Hello, Claire."

"That's not my name anymore," I said evenly, refusing to show him fear. I'd been forced to forget my name, forget my identity when I was seven years old.

"How did you find us?" My voice cracked. From fear. From frustration. From sheer rage.

"It wasn't a stretch," he said derisively. "You've loved the water since you were a baby."

He mistook my meaning. I didn't mean here at the beach. I meant Mama and me in Cambria.

But as his words registered, I jerked away from him.

"Not since that night, you bastard." My thoughts caught in an emotional vortex. "I hate the water."

I wouldn't give him the knowledge that I was terrified.

The tide rolled in, hitting my heels. Damn him.

He had taken that away from me. I had loved the water. Any kind of water and I would usually kick my feet through it or paddle around in it. I'd forgotten how much I loved the water when I was a kid.

Since I was a baby, he'd said. Did that mean that he'd known of me before he met my mother when I was five? Which implied that he'd been watching us for far longer than I'd, or Mama had, ever realized.

The thought cramped my stomach. Reflexively I clutched my hands over my belly and felt the hard outline of my cell phone in the front pocket of the sweatshirt.

My new cell.

That had to be it. Somehow he'd been tracking me through my cell.

I'd activated that cell immediately after dumping my old one. Could he have a way to check for new activations? I would have to ask Zeke.

"Where's your mother, *Claire*?"

Claire was dead. Then I realized what his question implied. He hadn't found Mama. Thank Goddess.

He hadn't found her and he wouldn't. Not through me anyway. "I don't know." I smirked. He could do whatever he wanted to me but the reality was…"I have absolutely no idea."

A particular mean-spirited pleasure bubbled through me and I laughed with spite. Hard.

His dark eyebrows lowered over his rage-filled gaze. He clenched his fists, and his body bulked, his shoulders seemed bigger. But as I stood there I realized that John Stanley wasn't that much larger than me now.

I stood about five foot nine in my bare feet. Stanley was maybe five ten or five eleven.

"It's time for you to go away, *John*." I used his name derisively. "We're done with you."

He took a menacing step toward me but I refused to back away. "But I'm not done with you."

My tunnel focus widened as I took in the beach around me. I could hear the kids still splashing in the surf a few yards behind me. I saw the other adults with their wide eyed stares as he bunched his fists and advanced on me.

I was trapped between my stepfather and the water, the two driving fears in my life. And then a larger wave rolled in and splashed high on my calves.

I yelped and jumped. I couldn't help it.

"What the hell?"

He jerked as if shot. Beyond him I saw Zeke. Zeke who was coming to save me. I'd been so wrapped up in the confrontation that I completely forgot about Zeke. But Stanley must not have realized I was with someone or he never would have turned his back on Zeke.

John whirled around at Zeke's tap on his shoulder, fists clenched and up near his face like a boxer.

I heard the sirens in the background.

We were out of time. I pressed my thumb into a spot between Stanley's neck and shoulder, in a move I'd practiced in self-defense class over and over again but never actually completely executed. Stanley dropped onto the sand with a thud. "It worked."

"Nice move." Zeke said, "But it's time to go."

I looked at Stanley unconscious on the sand. Nothing had really be resolved. This was not how I wanted this confrontation to end. But we couldn't afford to stick around.

"Cops will be here soon."

CHAPTER 29

Time to get the hell out of Dodge.

Zeke had managed to get into the local real estate website and look up available rental properties. Then he'd picked the best one for both location and defensible position.

Sunshine seemed to be reeling from the confrontation with her stepfather. Zeke cursed the fact that he hadn't had a chance to ask John Stanley any questions. But Sunshine had definitely been in danger. And right now they had no options.

Zeke couldn't be anywhere near the authorities, so they couldn't afford to wait for the cops to arrive. Currently, John Stanley had only *asked about* Stella Smith. Which was not a crime. Even if Sunshine could file a restraining order against him, since he technically hadn't done anything, it was doubtful the police could or would be able to do anything.

"We're going to have to hide the car." Zeke talked aloud as he turned over the engine.

"Why?"

"With the way he's tracking you he's got some training. He likely memorized every make, model, and license plate in this parking lot." Not to mention if any of the tourists were watching them leave the parking lot and reported the plate to the cops. One of them must have called the police.

She was shaking. Delayed reaction.

"So he can track us?" She was grabbing the front of her sweatshirt. "Track. Track. Dammit. Somehow, that's how he did it."

She pressed the button to roll down the window. The cool air rushed into the car and swirled the junk in the backseat. Sunshine held a cell phone in her fist, looked around to make sure no one was following them, and no one could see her, then she threw it out the car window as they cruised down Highway One.

"I think he had my new cell number." Sunshine said fiercely, "That's how the bastard found me in San Luis and again on the beach. He came to both places where I used my phone. I hadn't used it since yesterday at the café until I turned it on this morning to call the answering service."

"It's new?" he asked.

"Yeah. How could he have figured it out?"

"He may have monitored any new activations within a certain radius."

"What about Mama?"

"She could be using Blue's phone." In which case Stanley would have no idea and no way to track him.

That made the most logical sense. But if they caught up with Stanley again they could ask him. Zeke mulled that over while he drove them toward their new digs. He kept watch in the rearview mirror to make sure they weren't being followed while Sunshine tugged her skirt back on.

Zeke parked two houses down, also available as a weekly rental. "Stay here."

"A house?"

"I told you." Zeke grinned. "We're going to play tourist."

"What are you going to do?"

"Need to tinker with the garage door so we can park inside."

She didn't even blink at his proclamation that they were going to break in. She moved right on to the next concern. "So we really didn't need that camping gear."

"Backup plan." Zeke said, "It served a dual purpose. Misdirection and backup. Always need a backup plan. Act casual."

"Let me be clear, I'm not very comfortable with squatting," she called out as he slammed the car door.

"Noted." Zeke cautioned her. "If you see Stanley, take off."

Zeke easily broke in to the two car garage. There was an old Toyota stored in one of the bays. Excellent. New wheels when it was time to leave since the Honda was likely compromised.

It only took him a few minutes, then he gestured to Sunshine. "Start 'er up and pull right in to the garage."

After Sunshine drove the Honda into the garage, they secured the garage door. Zeke popped the trunk. They unloaded only the bags they needed, the perishable groceries, the extra cell phones, and the hair products. Everything else stayed in the trunk. "Let's get these inside."

They walked inside. As an example of architecture the house was stunning. Floor to ceiling windows in a wall across the entire front of the house showcased unrestricted views of the ocean and Moonstone Beach. Knotted wood paneling graced the interior walls of the two story cathedral ceiling living room, complete with exposed wood beams and tile flooring. The other walls were decorated with beach-themed paintings.

This section of Moonstone Beach was still mostly deserted, similar to the beach they'd just left. The wind blew across the sand, the beach unprotected by any vegetation. The temp of the ocean, a frigid fifty degrees this time of year, would keep most people away even with the sun out. Which worked well for his EPA.

Sunshine paused, her gaze mesmerized by the wall of windows and the view. Zeke noticed that she was staring at the beach. Her longing was an almost physical presence in the room as she observed the tide roll up the sand and then draw back out to sea.

Her yearning was painful to witness.

While he'd been looking for a place to hole up, he'd kept one eye on her as she tested her fear of the water and one on his phone as he searched for a place for them to hide. He'd been damn proud of her for boldly walking into that water. Damn John Stanley for interrupting her forward progress.

Zeke wished they could go out to the beach so she could try again.

But they needed to stay hidden.

As a place to stay out of sight, the house left quite a bit to be desired, but he'd chosen a property that also had empty houses on each side.

"We'll have to stay out of view of the windows," he said carefully. "But we can see the ocean from the loft." Zeke gestured to a set of stairs tucked into the back corner. At the top was a small loft with a bed and a spectacular view.

The house was split in to several sections. The

downstairs garage served as the foundation, with a back stairway that lead to the second floor of the structure, but the first floor of the interior. On one side was the kitchen and a bathroom. Fortunately it was older construction so there was only a small doorway that lead to the exposed open living room. They might be able to spend time in the living room at night once the sun went down, with lights off so no one could see them.

But they couldn't afford for anyone to catch sight of them inside the house, so during the day, they had to avoid the living room at all costs. Off the kitchen was an extension of the stairway from the garage that lead up to the third story and featured two bedrooms and one Jack and Jill bath.

They were going to have to share a bedroom. Zeke didn't want to presume, but he also needed to be as close to Sunshine as possible in case there was any trouble.

But he'd bring that up later.

They took the bags into the kitchen and he breathed a small sigh of relief. For right now anyway, they were safe. He thought she'd want to talk about Stanley but when she spoke it had nothing to do with her abusive stepfather.

"You want lunch?" she asked. "You can explain everything while I cook."

"Wait." He thought she'd want to hash out what had just happened on the beach but her expression was closed. She wasn't ready.

Then her words registered. Zeke rubbed his hand down his chest. A strange pleasure rolled through him. "You're going to cook for me?"

"Unless you want to make your own lunch." She looked uncertain. She held still, her expression indecipherable.

"Ah, no. It would be great."

"You want to fill me in on why you're acting so weird?"

He felt stupid but answered anyway. "It's just that…no one has ever cooked for me before."

"Oh." Her tone was skeptical.

But Zeke was precise with his speech. He knew what he meant to say and what he meant was *no one*.

As if she clued in to that fact, her eyes widened. The silvery gray reminded him of the moonlight on the ocean waves.

"No one?"

"No." Zeke unloaded the groceries and put them in the refrigerator avoiding the question in her gaze. Thinking he should have just kept his mouth shut.

"But, what about your mom?"

"Left when I was a baby."

She let out a soft, sympathetic sigh. "Dad?"

"Not much of a chef." Zeke understated but figured he might as well go all the way so she'd know how much of a freak he really was. "We ate chili and soup out of cans and canned vegetables and fruits. Dad showed me how to use a can opener."

"Um, you mentioned your grandfather."

"Where do you think my dad learned how to open a can?"

"They didn't cook, ever?"

Zeke thought back to his childhood. No. The men who raised him didn't cook. Things changed after Grandpop died. He eventually learned how to cook, basic stuff, by surfing the net. Or what comprised surfing the net back then. Because he had been a scrawny kid, he'd wanted more bulk and to be healthier. Until the day his father died, Dad had lived out in the desert and ate out of cans.

"Uh, no."

She dug through the bags. "We don't have much to work with, but I'll see what I can whip up."

"You don't need to go to any trouble."

She shot him a steady look. "We need to eat. It's no trouble."

"All right then." That's when he figured out she needed something to do.

She began pulling items out of the plastic bags. Eggs, butter, bacon, peppers, onion, tomato, cheese. "You were hungry?" she teased.

"Omelets are easy if you're camping, and yeah, I'm hungry," he said sheepishly. "I've developed a real taste for fine dining but I work too much to spend a lot of time cooking."

She pulled one more box out of the bag, a deep flush spread over her face and she jammed the box behind her back.

Zeke craned his neck to see what she was holding. "What's wrong?"

She giggled nervously. "Nothing's wrong."

And then he figured out what she had in her hands. The box of condoms he'd thrown in their supplies with a sense of hope, and a determination to be prepared if she were interested.

She whipped around, dragged open the drawer near the stovetop, and shoved the box inside.

Zeke dropped his head. He shouldn't have assumed, but then he thought about her reaction. She hadn't thrown the box at him in disgust. She'd tucked it behind her. And blushed.

A sign that perhaps she didn't hate the idea.

For as good as he was at reading patterns and discerning

connections that others missed, Zeke didn't have much luck at reading women.

After she'd hidden the condoms, Sunshine removed an apron from the drawer. It had a pale aqua band at the top, with a square neckline, and the body of the apron was white fabric with little aqua, yellow, and pink flowers, another band of aqua at the waist extended to long ties. She tied the wide swath of cotton around her back in a bow. The hem hit at the top of her thighs. The cheerful fabric emphasized her tucked in waist and the flare of her hips. The design was straight out of a fifties sitcom.

For a moment he imagined what she would look like wearing only the apron, her breasts minimally covered by the square and that full bow perched above her bare rounded butt when she turned around.

Great, she was starring in his own little X-rated *Leave It To Beaver* fantasy. One he didn't even know he had until she'd put that apron on.

"Well I'm no gourmet but I started out on a farm, and my mama is one hell of a cook. She taught me everything I know," she chattered nervously as she lay the items out on the granite island.

The tension that gripped him since the phone call from Carson slowly ebbed from his body. "How can I help?"

"I think better, absorb better, when I'm moving. Kinesthetic learner. Drove my mother crazy. Teachers even crazier." She efficiently cracked eggs into a plastic bowl. "Just talk to me."

"You want to dive right in and figure this out?" He was still trying to gauge her mood.

"Could we…" Sunshine brushed a lock of her hair from her cheek with the back of her hand, the move innately elegant and so feminine it took his breath away. "…just talk while I make lunch. Like normal people?"

She glanced around the fancy kitchen, white cabinets, white granite with swirls of pale teal and gray, and stainless steel appliances. Sunlight from the transom above the kitchen doorway and the mostly closed blinds over the sink let in enough ambient light to allow them to see without turning on the kitchen lights, and created a surreal atmosphere, as if their surroundings were filtered by a diffusion lens, bathing everything in watery lines and intriguing shadows. "We're safe here. Right?"

The breath he hadn't even realized he was holding spewed from his lungs. "Yeah. I think we can spare an hour to reset."

He wasn't even aware he'd needed it either. But the more he thought about it, the more he thought it was a great idea.

He'd been turning over all the facts in his head until there was no recognizable pattern, it was one giant pile of mush, as if multiple cans of paint had spilled and mixed together, making each color indistinct and resulting in a giant puddle of pinkish brown so muddy nothing was clear.

"That's actually a great idea."

"You don't think they can track us?"

Zeke shook his head. "Car model doesn't have any kind of GPS locator in it. I disabled the GPS in the phone that I used to call Lucas. You threw your phone out the window. We should be safe. For now."

They wouldn't be able to hide forever. But he wouldn't bring that up. "So what do you want to talk about?"

Sunshine pulled out a large chef's knife and a cutting board. With efficiency, she chopped off the head of the onion, sliced it in half and then started a quick dice. The girl was good with a knife.

Her gaze shifted to the mostly closed blinds. The weak Fall sun shimmered on the waves and the light reflected into the kitchen. She was like a moth to a flame. He'd noticed her longing, that look of pure hunger as she stared at the waves rolling up the brown sand.

"Hit me."

"Why do you like the ocean so much?" Sunshine asked.

He knew the question wasn't casual. Her yearning was like a physical presence in the room and he wanted her to discover the same love of the ocean that he had.

"I grew up in the desert." He shared. "I didn't see the ocean until I was about five."

"Desert, like Las Vegas?" Sunshine dug around in the cabinets searching for something until she pulled out a sauté pan in triumph. She set the pan down carefully on the burner, turned the knob. The tick, tick, tick of the gas starter was loud, like a time bomb, while he hesitated to reveal how crazy his family had been. As if eating out of cans wasn't enough.

"Desert, like rural So Cal, between Barstow and New Jack City, lots of rock climbing and not much else."

"Oh."

"Yeah. My Grandpop and father were survivalists."

"So were you part of a commune or community?"

"Hell no." Zeke played with the fringe on the sunny yellow placemats that decorated the round oak table. "They were paranoid bastards who trusted no one."

Which was sort of ironic if he thought about it. Since he was in this predicament now. They were right to be paranoid. Tension stole over his shoulders again.

Sunshine dropped a bit of butter in the pan, waited for

it to sizzle, then scraped the onions off the cutting board and into the pan. With quick efficient movements, she chopped off the head of the pepper and started eviscerating the veins and seeds inside.

She stayed silent as she absorbed his meaning. The onions simmered in the butter and the savory aroma filled the kitchen. "And then when I was about five, for some reason we relocated to a beach for a while."

That was where he'd gotten his first taste of the ocean.

"It's so fucking vast." He touched each side of the rectangular placemat. The top, the left, the right, the bottom. "I remember standing in the surf and a giant wave sucked me in as if the ocean were calling me home."

He ducked his head. It sounded stupid when he said it aloud but that memory was absolutely vivid. The sensation of being swept into a universe larger than himself.

"You could have died." Sunshine shuddered. "Weren't you afraid?"

"I was pissed when my Grandpop pulled me from the water." Zeke closed his eyes and pictured that day. The sun had been shining in typical Southern California fashion. The sunlight on the waves had been glaring, nearly blinding. And he'd been hypnotized by the undulating ripples on the surface of the water.

She snorted. "I thought you were smart."

"That moment wasn't about intelligence. It was about emotion." Zeke confided, "I felt connected to something so much larger than myself for the first time."

Sunshine sliced the peppers into slivers with quick rocking motion of her arm. "You were only five," she said, as if trying to discount his feelings, clearly uncomfortable with his admission.

"True." Zeke thought back to that long ago experience.

"But when I sink under the water, being surrounded, embraced in every pore, it still gives me comfort and...acceptance."

Sunshine sighed as he ended his soft confession.

"You know what I think of when I think of bodies of water?" She dumped the peppers into the pan with a sharp swipe. "All that water, pulling me down, suffocating me." Her voice tightened with the last few words.

"It will buoy you up, give you an indescribable high."

"Wouldn't that be nice?" she whispered.

He wanted to give that feeling to her. To give her a love of water. He wasn't sure how he was going to do that but Zeke swore that if he could, he would make that happen. He realized that little bit of crush love he'd acknowledged earlier had changed. She was warm, compassionate, funny, beyond smart, and real. He was starting to like this girl, really like her.

CHAPTER 30

An aqua and white striped ceramic pitcher to the left of the cooktop held cooking utensils. I grabbed a wooden spoon so I could stir the vegetables while they sautéed, and gave Zeke a minute to compose himself.

I could tell he was a little bit embarrassed. But I wasn't sure why. I loved that he'd shared something so intimate with me. Attraction simmered in the air between us. With the muted shadows and the rippling waves of sunlight coming through the partially closed blinds, the air was laden with intensity and anything we said would be cloaked in anonymity.

Even though he sat plain as day across the island from me, I felt like I could say anything, confess anything and he would accept me. Welcome me. Embrace me.

And phew, wasn't that just a little fanciful?

I was becoming the hippy-dippy girl that everyone assumed me to be. Which wouldn't do at all. That girl was naive, inexperienced, and vulnerable.

I had to shed that persona, stop hiding behind the illusion, and be the woman I was meant to be.

In that moment, I understood, even if he didn't, the ocean was his hug from his mother.

"To feel connected, that must be…." I didn't finish. I wasn't even sure what I wanted to say. That I had felt disconnected my whole life. That without my mother this last day that disconnection had intensified, until I was adrift on a lonely sea.

Except I wasn't completely alone. Zeke was here.

"That must be nice." Such a tepid word for the sheer longing inside me. And maybe I knew what he was talking about because last night in the shadowed, darkened hotel room, as I'd learned his body and he'd explored mine, I'd felt those moments of connection as if we were tied together by some invisible string. Unbreakable string.

But then the morning had come and his first thought was to get rid of me. His instinctive reaction had hurt on a mammoth scale. I still wasn't sure why. Perhaps because he had seemed so sincere when he'd been convincing me to lay low and keep out of John Stanley's sight.

Zeke startled me out of my melancholy. "Best memory. Go."

I grabbed the whisk from the ceramic pitcher and began beating the eggs with fervor, ignoring his challenge.

"C'mon. Play along." Zeke touched the placemat again in that particular way of his.

Fine. I whipped the eggs even harder, my shoulder and arm beginning to ache. "I grew up without men around. Of course, there were men, in the store, at the mechanics, even at the business association meetings, there were men. But, after the age of seven, I had no constant father figure."

The exact opposite of Zeke. He had father figures, no mother.

"I barely remember my Papa. He was a big robust man

and he had a huge laugh. But I do have one memory of him holding me in his lap and laughing at something I said, or showed him, and his whole body shaking with it. That rumble would vibrate through him and into me. And I'd feel this, this well of happiness rise up in me."

I beat at the eggs in the bowl, my arm moving faster and faster as I realized how much I'd lost when I'd lost my father. I hadn't thought about his presence in my life for so long.

"Then he died. And after time, the well just dried up, disappeared. I haven't felt it since."

I wiped my hands down the purloined apron. And realized I should have stopped after telling him about Papa's laugh and the well of happiness. I'd gotten too intimate. But that's why I rarely laughed. And why it was such a surprise earlier when he'd made me burst into laughter.

I missed my father. Horribly.

I continued, as if by admitting my lack of joy, I'd opened some secret fountain inside me and everything came flowing out. "When we first went on the run, I remember thinking, if Papa would just come back…things would be okay. We could go back to normal."

I couldn't seem to stop. "What a laugh that was. We were never going back to normal. I'd already been accepted to Caltech because of my ridiculous IQ but I still foolishly wanted my Papa back."

I threw the whisk into the bowl full of frothy eggs. "What the hell was I ever thinking?"

"Hey." Zeke rose from the table and came around the island. I kept my back to him, not wanting him to see the tears shimmering in my eyes. Pretending nothing was wrong, I concentrated intently on dumping the onions and peppers onto a clean plate, then I poured the egg mixture into the sauté pan.

Zeke rested his chin on my shoulder and soothed his palms down my biceps and forearms, before he draped his arms around my waist and hugged me tight. He nuzzled his nose behind my ear. He was literally wrapped around me like a boa constrictor, but for some reason my internal personal space meter wasn't going crazy, and the embrace was comforting rather than constraining.

His chest was pressed up against me, the bulk of his body a welcome presence behind me as if he'd have my back. As if he could absorb my pain into him and melt it away.

I grabbed a spatula and lifted the edges of the solidifying egg mixture to let the uncooked liquid seep underneath the already puffing eggs. "Sorry. Sorry."

This certainly wasn't what he'd signed up for. Hello, my name is Sunshine and I'm neurotic, emotional mess. My fingers were white from how tightly I clutched the spatula. Zeke peeled my fingers and gently took the utensil from my hand. Then he turned me until we were face to face.

"The eggs."

"This is more important." He speared his fingers through my hair and tilted my head back until I was looking into his ocean blue eyes, murky with some unnamed emotion. "We make our own normal. And screw everyone else."

He stroked my tears away with his thumbs. The gesture was unbearably tender. We both suddenly realized we were standing very close. My breath caught. The inhale lifted my breasts and I brushed against his chest. His fingers tilted my head just so.

His heat pressed against me intimately. As if my body recognized his, the resultant chemical reaction was intense. My core softened, my nipples hardened, and my heart picked up its rhythm. The ba-boom, ba-boom echoed in my ears as he slowly bent his head toward me.

He was so close I could see his pale blond lashes and the variations of blue in his irises. The darker ocean color was really a tumbled mix of pale blue, darker blue, turquoise, and a hint of thundercloud gray. I could see the burgeoning blond stubble that dusted his strong jawline and upper lip. I remembered what that bit of coarse hair felt like against my softer skin.

The light in the room dimmed.

At first I thought it was just his head, blocking out the light, but then I realized that the sky outside had gone dark. Before I could register anything else, his lips brushed mine. The slight rasp of his stubble was a delicious abrasion, as he rubbed our mouths together in the gentlest of caresses. He captured my bottom lip between his and sucked erotically. Then in his customary pattern, he licked my top lip, his tongue touched mine lightly, before he licked at the left corner, right corner and then my bottom lip.

"You're okay, Sunshine Smith."

Instead of deepening the kiss, he eased away from me and turned me around to face the stove. The entire incident only took a few seconds, so the eggs were fine. "You want me to finish?" Zeke asked.

"I've got it." I sprinkled the onions and peppers over half the eggs, snagged the package of sharp cheddar cheese, and drizzled some on top of the veggies.

Zeke grabbed glasses from the cupboards and filled them with ice and water. Then he set them at the table as I waited for the cheese to melt. The scene was scarily domestic and normal. Something I never thought I would experience. And I couldn't ever remember being happier.

I plated the omelets and set them on the table.

"You ready to talk about those Venn Diagrams?" Zeke asked.

Yeah, normal sure hadn't lasted long.

A pang of remorse hit Zeke. He was going to reveal classified information to a civilian. A civilian with no security clearance who barely even existed in citizen databanks.

It wasn't that he cared so much about national secrets. He kept them because that meant he kept his job.

He'd started his life with an innate distrust of the federal government. His grandfather had drilled that mistrust and paranoia and suspicion of everyone into him at an early age. They'd lived out in the desert or along the ocean. Grandpop usually tried to get paid under the table, wanting to give as little money as possible back to the government. So Zeke had spent his formative years being homeschooled and basically living a hand to mouth existence. They camped, sometimes illegally, in the state parks and sometimes at the beach.

He grew up in a vintage trailer that had hooked up to an even older Ford truck. The small trailer had louvered windows, faux wood paneling, and linoleum floors. A far cry from the extravagant home they were in now.

This kitchen was a palace compared to their cramped economical trailer kitchen. It had been the size of a small bathroom, with a Formica tabletop that folded down so that he could extend the bench seat into a bed. Dad and Grandpop slept in the bunk beds. They had emptied their own septic tank and carried their cooking heat which they never used.

He'd spent the majority of time either outside or, as he got older, in libraries.

His dad and Grandpop had taught him about math and science and how to survive in the wilderness. They'd been a little light on reading the classics or learning anything that didn't have a serious practical application.

His upbringing had been unconventional at best, downright crazy at worst. And at fourteen, when he'd decided that he wanted to take standardized testing and go to college, his father had been against it but Zeke had earned his own money and set up the testing without his dad's knowledge.

They'd never had an actual internet account. They'd tapped into satellites and cable internet or used the computers in the libraries they'd frequented. Zeke had cut his teeth on anonymous hacking before he'd gotten caught and corralled into working for the NSA.

His Grandpop would be horrified that he worked for the government and brought home a regular paycheck. Even if he had tried to honor his grandfather's teachings by continuing to be somewhat of a rebel, he'd never done anything that would get him fired.

He loved his job too much.

But now he'd been burned. The NSA had basically disavowed him and his life's work.

Which meant he needed to take extreme measures to try

and fix it.

As he saw it they had three main problems. One: He'd been burned. Which meant he had to stay one step ahead of the people looking for him. Two: Figure out how/why he gave Susan Chen his encryption program so he could clear his name. Three: John Stanley was after Sunshine and her mother. He needed to be neutralized.

Zeke's goals were to keep Sunshine safe, and figure out if John Stanley had any intel about who really ordered those hits. So if they found Stanley again, Zeke might finally be able to solve the mystery of who originally ordered the hit that killed his grandfather. But to get to that point, he needed to clear his name. So finding Susan Chen had to come first. Luckily he had Jamie working on Chen's whereabouts too. Hopefully she and Lucas would get a bead on Chen now that Oliver Krychef had abducted their daughter.

Sunshine sat at the table next to him, waiting patiently. She'd distributed the omelet between them, cut into one-third and two-thirds, and given him the larger piece. "Venn Diagrams?"

"Uh, yeah." Zeke grabbed a piece of paper and a pen from the small desk tucked into the corner of the kitchen. He drew two large circles that overlapped significantly. He labeled the circle on the left "Sunshine" and the circle on the right "Zeke."

It was still damn hard to push the words out of his mouth. The secretive and cloistered culture he'd lived and breathed over the last six years had become ingrained.

The most obvious intersection of Zeke and Sunshine's lives was Department 5491. And so he wrote, "5491", inside the intersecting circles.

"What is 5491?" She sliced her omelet wedge down the

middle and the cheese oozed out the cut.

"5491 designates a department at the NSA."

She let the cheese drip off her fork. "Which has nothing to do with me as far as I know."

"You get monthly payments from that department."

Her gray eyes widened, mouth open, fork halfway to her mouth. "My mother does receive monthly payments. They're direct deposited into our corporate account. Whenever I asked, she told me it was insurance money."

"No. The money is recompense from the NSA for the deaths of your grandparents."

She frowned. "You're talking about the supposed sleeper thing again. But I told you before, my grandfather was an insurance salesman and my grandmother was a homemaker. She's the one who taught me and mama to make soaps and scrubs. Girly stuff. The basis for our store."

She still wasn't getting the big picture. "He had a secret life before your mother was born. He was part of a group of German code breakers."

"You really believe this. But to me it seems so fantastical." Sunshine stared at the glass jar filled with sea shells set in the middle of the table, her gaze far away as she tried to come to grips with the idea that her grandfather had been someone, something else. She shook her head as if shaking loose her thoughts.

Zeke very precisely angled his plate and cut his portion into two equal triangles, then he aligned the points with the top of the placemat and carefully cut into the point.

"Okay. What else?" she asked.

"You don't want to know more specifics?"

"I want the big picture before you get into the smaller details and I try to put it all together." Sunshine shoveled another random bite of omelet into her mouth.

"Okay." Zeke said, "So there are twelve people on the 5491 list."

"There's a list?"

"Yep."

Outside their intersecting field, he wrote, "Injected with DNA-altering drug," in his section of the circle.

Inside the intersecting field, he wrote, "Grandparents killed by sleepers."

In Sunshine's circle, he wrote, "Sleeper: John Stanley."

In his circle, he wrote, "Sleeper: Unknown."

In the middle of their intersecting fields he wrote, "Off the charts genius."

Sunshine interjected, peering over his bicep, "Which makes sense if our ancestors were code breakers. We should have an aptitude for math."

Zeke paused, pen poised over the paper as he ran through details, trying to find any other way they intersected. But as far as he could see it all lead back to 5491.

"Okay, so if this is really the only thing we have in common, then how did you end up following me?" When he looked at the diagram he realized she was right. Their only obvious point of intersection was 5491. But, circumstantially, they had many more threads in common.

Zeke took his time, cutting off a piece of omelet from the left side of the triangle. "Because everyone on the 5491 list who was also in the espionage community was injected with Susan Chen's DNA-altering drug. The three exceptions are you, Bella Holden, and one other person listed only with the initials ADA. I was sent to keep an eye on you after Susan escaped."

Sunshine shoved her chair away from the table. "You think she was coming after me?"

"Personally, no." Zeke chewed his bite slowly, counting ten times before swallowing. "I think I was sent here on a boondoggle to get me out of the way."

"But then you saw Susan Chen in San Luis."

Zeke segued into the next connection. "Which leads me to Susan Chen."

And the only person who could tell them how she and her partner had chosen the test subjects was the scientist herself. They needed to find her and then somehow to convince her to give up the information.

Sunshine was an asset and he'd be stupid not to use her intelligence. Her unfamiliarity with the whole situation would mean she'd approach everything with a different perspective.

"Okay."

"Chen's test subjects were all from the 5491 list. And I gave my encryption program to Susan Chen."

Zeke crinkled his brow. Dammit. How could he have given her the damn encryption program?

"Do you know how Susan Chen got those names?"

"No. She wouldn't give any answers after she was apprehended." Zeke huffed out a frustrated breath.

"What about her partner?"

"Liam? He's dead."

"But he's still a piece of the puzzle. Why not do more research on her partner?" She continued to stare at those sea shells.

The idea had merit.

"How did he die?"

"That would be another mystery." Zeke chewed another bite of omelet. "We had him cornered in a hotel suite, but before we could arrest him, someone shot him."

"So wouldn't it stand to reason that whoever shot him is

the key?"

Zeke had been so caught up in the other things that had happened in the last few weeks that he realized that the identity of Liam's shooter was a loose thread. He couldn't ask Carson about it but maybe Jamie could.

"Even if you don't know who shot him, you could still investigate the partner. There has to be a connection somewhere. Right?"

Zeke pressed his lips together as he rolled the idea around in his brain. "It's a possibility."

He wrote Liam on the bottom of the paper.

"Everyone receives payments." He wrote that inside the circle even though it went along with 5491, he wanted to get as specific as possible.

"How many people?"

"There were twelve people on the original list," Zeke said.

"Were?"

"One person is dead."

Sunshine's gray eyes rounded. "Do you know all of the people?"

"I know some. Besides you, Bella, and the unknown ADA, everyone else works in the espionage community." Zeke precisely cut another piece of omelet.

"Bella?"

"She's a college student and not affiliated with the espionage community in any way."

Sunshine mulled that over for a few minutes. "Okay. Then what about this ADA?"

"I don't know anything about that person."

"And you haven't figured out who that is?"

"No." The patterns were beginning to take shape in his mind.

"Could anyone else on the list have given Susan Chen the encryption program?"

"No one except me." Zeke shook his head, his curls brushed his cheek. They'd have to go soon.

"What about the mysterious ADA?"

He raised an eyebrow. "I can't discount them."

Sunshine had been a single name with no identifiers. The only other person on the list who wasn't identified was ADA. So if the intersection was the 5491 list, the person who was orchestrating this whole fiasco likely had to be someone in power who actually knew who all twelve of the people were.

Obviously, the second intersection was smaller. The abducted all had relatives killed thirteen years ago, they all were receiving payments, and then a smaller subset of that list were intelligence agents who had been injected with a DNA-altering drug.

"So the only true intersection we have is 5491." Sunshine stated as they both stared at the rough Venn Diagram between them.

"Yeah." And that surprised him. When he purposely lost his focal point, let his mind go blurry not concentrating on one single detail, and tried to look at the situation like a big indeterminate blob, there were more connections shimmering just out of reach. "I feel like there's a veil over my face and if I could just...rip it away, the picture would be in front of me, clear as a cloudless sky."

It didn't seem right. He couldn't make a concrete connection to link them together any other way. They had several avenues of investigation. Liam, ADA, John Stanley, Susan Chen.

Maybe the connections lay in the unknowns that haunted him.

CHAPTER 32

The urge to immerse in Zeke's problems was overpowering.

I could feel my brain stretching, uncurling like a small shoot of the herbs I grew to scent the soaps and scrubs Mama and I sold. Like those starter seedlings reaching for the warmth and growing power of the sun, I could feel my cells transforming. The opportunity to use my brain to actually solve a problem other than how to maximize our store profits or dream up new combinations of massage oils and bath salts was like an addiction. While I loved the creativity and chemistry of concocting new scents, I wanted it to be a hobby, not my life's work.

And here he was with a puzzle that included me. The stakes were high. Which ramped up the appeal about a thousand percent. I almost started rubbing my hands together with glee. But that would probably be inappropriate since his career was on the line.

I subdued the visceral thrill that tunneled through me. If we were going to work together, I needed the entire picture down to the last pixel.

"So right now you have no job, and you are at risk of losing your freedom."

"I'm at risk of never begin seen again," Zeke quipped.

I didn't think he was kidding.

With his knife, he pushed the last of his omelet to the edge of the plate staring at the small yellow triangle as if it held the secrets of the Universe. "My job is all I have."

"Explain again why you're burned."

"Because under the influence of Sodium Pentothal I supposedly gave up my encryption program."

Under the influence. "I guess that makes sense." I tapped my index finger against my lips.

"No, it doesn't." He shoved his plate away. "I thought I was immune to the drug. It normally doesn't affect me."

I quirked a brow at him. "What makes you so sure?"

"Let's just leave it at training." Zeke propped his elbow on the table and pressed his forehead into his palm, his posture one of abject misery.

"Okay you can't answer that question." I rubbed my finger over the fringe on the cheery placemat, putting his problem through my own filter.

"Arrogance," he muttered. "I assumed that I hadn't given away anything, even after I'd been kidnapped."

"But if you gave away the program under duress how can they hold it against you?"

"They're the Federal Government. They can do anything they damn well please."

I thought about his words. Knew they were true. Mama and I had managed to stay off the radar in many ways, sifting everything through our corporation.

"Jesus, my Grandpop is probably rolling over in his grave at the fact that I worked for the government. And I had to give them the figurative middle finger whenever I could. That is going to fucking count against me."

"Could it have been deciphered by someone?" I interrupted his worries. "Schneier's Law: Any person can invent a security system so clever that she or he can't think of how to break it."

"Yeah. Maybe I'm not as smart as I think I am." Zeke grimaced. "But I had my fellow hackers test it."

I said, "Maybe they just aren't as good as you are."

"And my…compulsions dictated that I checked and re-checked on a regular basis for weaknesses in the code or structure of the program."

"Okay."

Zeke kept explaining. "I worked on the basis of Kerchoff's Law."

I knew this one. "A cryptosystem should be secure even if everything about the system, except the key, is public knowledge." I stated just to make sure I was right. Even though I knew I was.

"Yep." Zeke's raised eyebrow told me he was surprised.

I had read about Auguste Kerckhoff as a teen. Because when I wasn't reading young adult romance, I'd studied science heroes and heroines.

"So I don't see any other reality." Zeke was glum all over again.

"Like I said before. Let's go back to Susan Chen's partner."

Zeke was silent. He tilted his head just slightly to the right, a sure sign he was analyzing the idea and searching for flaws, running it through his brain to see if it held merit.

And I knew this was meant to happen. Yesterday I'd been living the same boring existence feeling stagnant, static, and trapped. In the span of thirty-six hours, my entire life had been turned upside down. A strange exhilaration gripped me. I could do this. I could help him.

Happiness bubbled up as I thought about the possibilities, pushing through my body with effervescence almost like the fizz of a fine champagne.

The chance to use my brain.

"Please." I put my palm on his forearm. The contact sizzled through me. This wasn't like when I touched his skin this morning when he'd still been wrapped around me and I'd felt so connected that I'd threaded my fingers with his. This was different. Sexually charged and darkly erotic. "I can help you."

Zeke's attention dropped to the spot where my fingers touched his bare skin, his blond lashes pale against his tan face, hiding his thoughts.

"I don't want you to get hurt." He lifted his gaze to mine and I saw something else lingering in his eyes. Some other worry that I couldn't place. "I'd rather you were safe."

"I've been trying to be safe my whole life," I said fiercely. "I'm tired of playing safe."

"I can definitely use your brain power to collaborate with."

It was as if he reached inside, found my deepest desire, and acknowledged that I was capable. More than capable, exceptional.

And I thought my heart would burst right out of my chest.

"But Sunshine…it will be dangerous."

As if I hadn't already figured that out when the Army had been zooming by us looking for his Range Rover.

Which reminded me. "We need to buzz your hair."

Zeke grimaced but didn't argue.

We quickly cleaned up from our meal, rinsing the plates

and putting the dishes in the dishwasher. The scent of butter and simmering onions lingered in the air.

"Where do you want me to do this?" I stepped closer to Zeke.

"You don't have to—"

I ran my hand through his hair, the curls were a silky mass and tangled in my fingers. I gloried in the tactile sensation of his hair sliding against my skin. "I may want to cut the longer strands with scissors, and then shave your head."

Zeke shuddered. And I realized I was absently massaging his scalp and somehow I was closer than I meant to be.

His heat slammed into me as he circled his arms around my waist and pulled me snug against his hard body.

The rounded lip of the granite countertop dug in to my lower spine. I spread my legs to accommodate him, and he edged between my thighs, his hips pressed against mine, trapping me.

My softer curves yielded to his possessive embrace without thought. He wrapped his arms round me in a tight hold as if he were afraid I would break free. Before I could say a word, he'd slanted his head and possessed my mouth.

This was no easy, tentative seduction. He devoured my mouth with far more passion and messy intensity than the omelet he'd precisely parsed into small bites.

The stubble from his unshaven jaw rasped against my tender skin. He slid his palm up the center of my back, his touch firm against each vertebrae. The contact over my sweater sizzled through me and I ached for him to slide his rougher hand against my smoother softer skin. His other hand cupped my butt and urged me into his erection.

The intimate touch was thrilling. My head went light

and my legs went weak. I gripped his waist tightly and held on. Zeke spun me around and lifted me onto the kitchen island. The granite was cool beneath my legs, chilling me even through the barrier of my skirt. His biceps bulged beneath my palms as I clung to his arms.

The urgency in his movements exhilarated me, and my heart thudded as he scraped his palms up my legs pushing my skirt until the material bunched in my lap. His thumbs rubbed at the crease between my thigh and hip along the edge of the bikini bottom and I nearly shot up to the ceiling.

I was already trying to rip his t-shirt over his head. "Don't want to get hair on this," I murmured against his lips.

He snickered and lifted his arms so that I could get it off. Zeke leaned against the island, his erection rubbed against my damp panties. I curled into the contact, so hard against my soft.

Zeke was tugging my sweater over my head and took the biking top with it. I pressed open-mouthed kisses over his pectorals, hungry for the taste of his skin.

He rubbed his palms against my ribcage and cupped my breasts in his hands before he pinched the nipples. The zing from the pleasure/pain sizzled through my body like electricity through water, and all my thoughts shorted out.

He dragged his tongue down my neck and I tilted my head back to give him greater access. The wet heat of his mouth sent tingles across my skin.

He nipped his way across my collarbone, then bent his head to suck my nipple into his mouth. I wanted to reciprocate, I wanted so many things but I didn't know how to tell him. Still unsure of myself.

I wanted him inside me. I wanted the long, slow invasion

of his cock and the sensual glide of his skin against mine. But I already knew this wasn't going to be like last night.

My heart triple-timed at his carnal intent as he pressed me down until my bare back lay on the chilly granite. Then he bent his head and consumed me. His mouth, his hands were everywhere. He trapped my arms against my sides so I couldn't touch him. In desperation, I shifted my hips rocking my damp sex against his erection, still covered by his board shorts, desperate for him to take me again.

"Please," I whimpered. So caught up in the sensations rocketing through my body I was nearly insensate.

He lifted my hips, his palms skimmed along my inner thighs, and then he bent his head to taste me. His mouth was hot, wet, wicked. Finally I was able to move my arms, I fisted my fingers into his curls, pulling him closer, as he rubbed his stubble against my swollen sex. He lifted his head to smile at me a flash of white teeth against his lips, red from our frantic kisses, and his chin slick with my juices.

Suddenly I felt overly exposed, my bare breasts pointing toward the ceiling, my skirt bunched around my waist like a wanton, and my legs spread wide open as I sprawled on the kitchen countertop. This wasn't me. I didn't do this kind of thing.

But his laser concentration didn't even see my sudden vulnerability as he stripped his shorts to the floor. He pushed me further back so that the counter's edge hit at my knees and then he climbed between my legs and lay over me, his pecs flattening my breasts, and his erection hot and thick against my belly. He yanked open the drawer behind my head and pulled out the box of condoms. He did a one armed pushup off my body and ripped the box open with his teeth.

His urgency calmed my insecurities, as he dropped a

condom square onto my sternum. I grabbed the package and tore it open as he tossed the box onto the counter next to us.

Once I got it open, Zeke smoothly rolled the condom down his erection.

As if he couldn't wait any longer, the bulbous head of his cock nudged my opening.

I couldn't help it, I tensed. Last night the pain had been fleeting but he was definitely big and my body definitely had needed time to adjust to his size. He rubbed against my clit, stimulating me, little sparks sizzled through my body. And then suddenly he was rocking against me, into me, with each foray of his hips he eased a little further inside. I tried to relax, but I was still tight.

A belated concern entered his gaze. His sudden realization of where we were and what we were doing was palpable in the dappled light of the kitchen. Oh no, we were not talking about that now. In desperation, I lifted my head and went straight for the flat disk of his nipple. I licked the tight button and unexpected pleasure flowed through me when he groaned.

My womb clenched, arousal dripped, slicking the way for his invasion. "I want you." I needed him inside me. I curled my fingers around his muscled ass and tugged, silently begging him when he continued to move slowly.

The granite was cold and hard beneath me, the ceiling fan turned lazily above. Zeke was propped up on his elbows, his expression fierce, and as I stared into his face, light speared through the slits in the blinds, and created a halo around his blond curls, darkened his eyes. His concentration was intense as he tunneled his fingers through my hair, and held my head.

"Wrap your legs around my hips," he murmured against my mouth.

I lifted my hips and finally he slid all the way inside.

He was buried as far as he could go, and I felt his thick length from my cervix to my clit. He filled me, completed me as if he were the other half of my soul. That thought was so profound, I couldn't breathe.

His cock pulsed against my g-spot and each beat of his blood caused an answering throb deep in my sex.

"You okay?" he asked huskily.

I nodded. Everything about the moment embedded in my brain and I knew I would take it out and relive it. Over and over again.

Then he started to move.

His knees between mine, he spread me wide and plundered.

The hair from his thighs rubbed against my softer inner thigh, the root of his cock pounded against my clit, and lightly fuzzed hair of his chest teased my nipples. His thumbs brushed against my cheeks as he devoured my mouth.

Each thrust pushed me to a new dimension. Sensations bombarded me. The swell of something, more than physical but I refused to name, built like a tidal wave until with one final thrust he jetted his come into the condom, the force of his orgasm triggered mine. And I soared off the cliff, freefalling into pleasure so intense that my vision went white.

My orgasm steamrolled through me, and everything arrowed down to where we joined. Love and endorphins swallowed up my body and I was made of pure light.

I convulsed around him holding on tightly. His hands in my hair, his body slick with sweat, we were connected from our knees to our heads.

Zeke bowed over me, his forehead against mine. His breath puffed against my neck, with each soft huff shivers raced down my spine. My heart pumped against his chest as I soothed my hands over the strong muscles of his back.

He lay atop me in what should have felt crushing, but instead I felt cherished, as if anyone would have to go through him to get to me. I could rest, secure in the knowledge that he would be there to protect me.

I clung to that feeling, knowing it couldn't last, that nothing that good ever did. I wrapped my arms tight around his back and held on, wanting to prolong this moment for as long as possible.

Temporarily, endorphins had clouded my brain and I'd believed that I was destined for something new, something good. But as our heartbeats slowed, the hard uncompromising granite at my back and the bulk of him between my legs transformed into a prison of hope. Because even though I wanted that happiness, wanted that closeness with another person, that was not my lot in life.

CHAPTER 33

P*ing. Ping.*
My tablet alarm sounded from inside my purse, reminding me it was time to call the message center to check on my mother. For a short while I'd forgotten my problems, mired in the complex labyrinth of Zeke Hawthorne's life and how we intersected. The amazing sex, the sense of connecting with him on a plane so ephemeral that it seemed like an illusion, had let me forget. But all that was a mirage. A wish for a different life.

With that innocuous ping, all my problems came rushing back. Mama, Blue, the threat of John finding us. Again.

Because even with Zeke's issues, my primary worry was John Stanley. And oh my Goddess, what had I just done? Besides the obvious sex on the kitchen island, we both had much bigger problems than satisfying our physical urges.

"I need to check in," I said almost desperately.

Zeke pulled from my body, and my sex clenched resisting letting him go, trying to hold him inside. He brushed his hand over my hair gently. The caress was affectionate, charming.

He hopped down from the island and sauntered naked toward the little bathroom off the kitchen clearly unselfconscious about his nudity. Whereas I wanted to cover up as soon as possible. I rolled off the island and quickly snatched up my sweater. Then scrabbled around looking for the bikini bottom.

By the time he came out of the bathroom, I was dressed and had grabbed a new burner phone from the Target bags.

I activated the phone, dialed the answering service, and entered the numeric code to get access to the messages.

My mother's voice, calm and…happy, reverberated in my ear as I listened to her message. She and Blue were on the move and hadn't seen John. Which of course I knew since he'd been on the beach with me a little while ago.

They were headed north to San Francisco. Although she didn't come out and say that's where they were going, she referenced a coffee shop that we had visited last year, and a confusing mix of emotions tumbled through me. I was thrilled she was okay. But did she have to sound so happy without me?

In what felt like the blink of an eye, my entire world had shifted. My mother didn't need me anymore. My previous joy for helping Zeke was overshadowed by the fact that I was superfluous now. Which was a little crazy. I should be pleased, thrilled. I'd been wishing for freedom for forever.

Hadn't I just been thinking about how much I wanted independence? About how trapped I'd felt? Finally I had the chance to do something with my brain. To do something that I wanted. I wasn't going to be constrained by my crazy stepfather anymore, I'd found my new beginning.

But after hearing her message, hearing the happiness in her voice, I was lost again.

Goddess, I was such a mess.

"How's your mom?" Zeke asked quietly as if sensing my mood.

I was thankful we'd been able to skip all the post-sex awkwardness because we'd been interrupted. Again.

"Peachy," I replied, tempering the sarcasm with an overlay of cheer. "They're going north."

"How far?"

"Sounds like San Francisco." I smoothed a hand over my wrinkled skirt. The only good in that message was the fact that when my stepfather had asked on the beach, I hadn't had any idea where my mother was. "Far away from John."

She didn't need me. Wasn't that really what I wanted? A chance to be me. A chance to take control of my life and do what I wanted?

"Good thing she doesn't need you because I do. Badly." How had he narrowed in on what I was thinking? Was I that transparent?

Zeke began to backtrack. "Uh, for your brain. You know."

I should be happy for my mother. I wasn't about to sacrifice her happiness for my own crazy mixed up need to be needed. So if Mama was happy I wanted her to stay that way. And I would do whatever it took. She'd been my responsibility for so long. I couldn't let go. And the only way to keep her happy and safe was to find a way to get rid of John Stanley for good.

As if he reached into my thoughts, Zeke said, "You know, since you're helping me with my problem. I want to help you with yours."

How did he even know my problem? I didn't even know my problem, I was so messed up in the head from everything swirling around.

"How so?" I scrunched up my face.

"I need to find Susan Chen and get her to clear my name."

"Not sure how that helps me, Zeke," I snarked.

"What if, after we find Chen, we go after Stanley?" Zeke threw the idea out. "We control the time, the place, everything, we just set it up so that he thinks he's found you again when in reality we've lead him right where we want him."

My heart quickened, my pulse thudded in my ears, part anticipation, part fear. Mostly fear. I'd held my own in the altercation on the beach. But to actually go after the man who'd kept me prisoner, and really take control of my life. Seize my future.

Could I do it?

I didn't know. But the desire to confront him was like a physical taste on my tongue. I could erase that bitterness he'd forced on me and replace it with the sweet ability to do what I wanted, go after my dreams. Find my true place.

Goddess, the temptation.

"I can see you like the idea," Zeke teased.

I was practically vibrating with the need to do it now.

"How?" I paced around the kitchen, my mother forgotten as I tried to picture the confrontation and couldn't see past the result. I stopped cold. And went back to his original statement. "What about your problems?"

"We'll take care of my problem with Chen first. But it's possible Stanley can help me too." Zeke said seriously, "I can question him about who hired him. That person had to know that he married your mother, which would seem to be a serious breach of sleeper protocol."

Was going after John Stanley the right move? But if I didn't, I would never be free of him.

Zeke said, "Let's jump."

I threaded my fingers through his. "Together?"

We were both doing something scary, something that had the power to change the course of our lives.

"Together," he said emphatically.

ZEKE LOOKED at the trust shining from her and hoped he wasn't leading her down the wrong path.

His suggestion wasn't just about helping her. He needed to help himself too. And trusting anyone was difficult. He finally figured out that he wasn't going to be able to do this alone. He was going to need help. He was forcing himself to slough off his aloneness so he could save his career, and his life.

Now that Sunshine was on board, he needed to call Jamie and Lucas. He needed to proceed carefully so that Jamie didn't have any blowback from helping him. And he wanted to confirm that if anything happened to him, Jamie would look out for Sunshine.

He definitely wouldn't let Sunshine suffer because she'd helped him. He had to guarantee her safety. He refused to put her in additional jeopardy.

Zeke curved his arms around her waist. The same move that had led to the amazingly hot sex on the kitchen island.

He couldn't help the little smirk that lifted his mouth.

"This is hardly a laughing matter." But she smiled at him. "Geek Boy."

He pressed a line of kisses along her jaw, happy that she was comfortable enough to tease him. He licked her upper lip, then pressed chaste kisses against the left, then right corner of her mouth. But instead of merely brushing her bottom lip, he sucked her lip into his mouth and nipped the plump flesh.

"I'll never look at granite the same again, Granola Girl."

A flush spread from the scoop neckline of her sweater past her collarbone and into her smiling cheeks.

Sunshine ducked her head. "Um, yeah."

"I think we have some hair to cut."

She whipped out the scissors far too quickly for his peace of mind.

Sunshine laughed at whatever was on his face. "Worried?"

"Should I be?"

"I'm wicked good with scissors," she replied.

"Where do you want me?"

He realized the loaded nature of that question after it came out of his mouth.

She just grinned. "Bathroom. In the tub," she commanded.

Sunshine grabbed some trash bags and cut them down the sides until they were spread open on the floor of the tub.

"You ready?" She held the scissors in her right hand. The hair clipper was on the vanity counter ready to go.

Trust. With a leap of faith, Zeke closed his eyes, and gave her a piece of his soul. "Do it."

Thirty minutes later, his hair was gone. The mess had been wrapped up in the garbage bags and put in the kitchen trash.

Zeke rubbed the half inch of fuzz that covered his head. The air from the ceiling fan was cool against his nearly bald scalp. He rubbed the back of his neck with one hand. It felt...weird.

His head was oddly light.

Sunshine stroked her palm over the top of his fuzzy

head like he was a little kid. This reminded him of his childhood when his hair had either been a long, tangled, stiff with seawater mess, or he was bald as a cue ball because his dad or Grandpop would randomly decide to shave his head. The suddenness of the act had always been a disconnect with no time for him to get used to the idea of shaving off his hair.

"I should probably take a shower to get rid of all the bits of hair," Zeke said. His mind immediately went to Sunshine naked. Water sluicing over her body and down her small breasts, her convex tummy, and her thatch of dark curls at the entrance to paradise.

Sunshine stretched, her sweater falling off one bare shoulder. "I would love to change clothes."

"There's a drought here." He smiled slyly.

Sunshine flushed, quick to catch on. "Water conservation is always a concern in our little beach town."

"I like to do my part for the environment."

She giggled. The sound music to his ears. He knew from their earlier conversation that Sunshine had little joy in her life.

And he wished he could make it his life's mission to make her laugh.

CHAPTER 34

After their shower, Zeke got down to business with a smile on his face. Sunshine had grabbed a condom from the box before he could even presume and they'd gone for round two in the shower.

"We need to lay low." Zeke had put on a Curious George t-shirt, and a pair of khaki shorts that he'd picked up at Target. "Which means we'll have time to research."

But they should stay out of sight.

"We can use my tablet," she said.

Hopefully the house had wireless service. But if not, he could probably piggy back on another house's internet service if needed.

No one should be able to trace the tablet back to them. Just to be safe, he would log on to a site that could divert their IP address so it bounced all over. Since they were doing simple research it was probably overkill but it never hurt to be extra cautious.

"Let's go up to the loft." From there they should be able to see the ocean.

The little room wasn't much bigger than the king size

bed that dominated the space. Sunshine flushed and Zeke pretended that he wasn't thinking about other things when he sat on the side of the bed and plugged in the tablet.

He shoved the pillows against the far wall and rested against them. The position gave them a wonderful view of Moonstone Beach. The owners had installed a wrought iron railing instead of a half wall and the vista was magnificent. From the shadowed interior of the tiny loft no one should be able to see them from the road.

The morning fog had completely burned off. The thick pea soup had given way to a misty Fall sunshine. Sunlight bathed the loft in blurry rays and filled the room with a hazy, dream-like filter.

Wow he was certainly waxing rhapsodic, but with Sunshine snuggled next to him so they could both see the screen, they had settled into an easy camaraderie.

The end of Sunshine's braid tickled his bicep as she bent her head to peer at the screen. He discreetly inhaled the scent of her shampoo, somewhere between sweet and sultry, with hints of plumeria and patchouli. And damn if his body didn't react.

He'd cracked one of the windows in the back of the house. The sound of the ocean soothed him.

Sunshine's gaze was increasingly drawn to the crash of the waves against shoreline. He could see her longing in every sideways glance and tiny frown between her dark eyebrows.

He said, "Maybe later—"

She pulled back, shoving her spine against their cushions and nearly knocking her head on the wall behind them. "Uh, no."

Damn, it seemed like all the progress she made before John Stanley accosted her on the beach had disappeared.

It was becoming more and more important for him to give her the love of the ocean.

"You're tough." Zeke derailed her argument before she could blast him. "You can overcome your fear."

No babying her. She *was* tough.

And she needed to believe it.

"Let's just keep the emphasis on your problems," she deflected.

Sunshine had melted into his side, but now she straightened away and he missed the warmth of her body.

Zeke turned on the tablet, absently went through his pre-work ritual. And they spent the next few hours researching Susan Chen's partner, Liam.

But after several hours, they weren't any closer to figuring out a connection between Liam and someone at the NSA. Liam had grown up all over the globe. Searching backwards to before he'd struck out on his own and conducted illegal experiments, he'd been at the CDC, The Johns Hopkins Hospital and med school, Oxford undergrad, and boarding school in England.

"This is pointless. We've gone all the way back to The American School in London." He'd had a long and illustrious career until he decided to throw it away on experimental research that could have destroyed the lives of everyone they tested.

"Fortunately everyone who is still alive was given an antidote." Zeke rubbed his palms over his bare head, still trying to get used to the lack of hair. "But there's nothing that connects him to the intelligence community. It's like looking for an extra 1 in an entire program of binary code."

They'd made no headway in the search for Liam's well-connected accomplice. They'd have to focus on another aspect of Liam's life.

Sunshine was on the same page. "So where did Susan and Liam meet?"

"She was in grad school and he did a guest professor stint at Caltech." He huffed. "None of this is getting us any closer to solving my problems."

Sunshine tried to soothe him. "Every piece of information fits into a pattern somewhere."

"Susan Chen is still my best bet for clearing my name." He quelled the urge to toss the tablet over the railing. "I hate waiting. But that's all I can do. Until we find her and she corroborates that I didn't give her the damn program."

"What if we did an experiment?" She had clasped her hands together and was twisting her fingers back and forth. Her anxiety was a physical presence in the tiny loft. "I have an idea."

He was fresh out of options. "Go for it."

"One of my professors at Cal Poly—"

"Thought you weren't enrolled?"

"I couldn't register and take classes in the system." Sunshine glanced through the metal railing, her gaze faraway. "But I managed to audit some upper level classes and I…may have been an unofficial research assistant on some studies."

Even now with him, she wasn't committing to anything.

If her professors were willing to break the rules to have her assist in high level projects, she must be brilliant. "How smart are you?"

"Um, I don't know?"

"You've never been tested?" Zeke asked.

"Not since I was seven."

But he had a feeling she was lying. "Ballpark it. Or give me some other bit of data."

"Well, back then my testing IQ was around 180."

Sunshine ducked her head. "And I may have been asked to attend Caltech as soon as I was old enough."

"You…." Caltech was even harder to get into than MIT. They didn't ask seven year olds to come to their school, kids literally worked their entire lives for the chance to attend.

Holy shit. "What are you doing making bath salts and massage oils?"

"Hiding," she said flatly.

He finally understood how much John Stanley had stolen from her. "We are going to eliminate this problem." She ought to have the life that she wanted. "You *deserve* it," he said fiercely.

The silence in the house was fraught with her gratitude and a heavy expectation.

"Thank you." Sunshine skimmed her hand over his forearm and squeezed his wrist lightly, the contact zipping through him like a lightning strike. *She* was comforting *him*.

Zeke swallowed the sudden lump in his throat. "Tell me about the experiment."

"You're familiar with monitoring brain wave patterns in the hippocampus?"

Zeke nodded. He could tell already that this was going to be complex.

"So this experiment analyzes brain wave recordings using pattern recognition methods, like multiple discriminant analysis, and collapses the data into smaller dimensions."

Complex didn't even begin to cover what she was talking about.

"Then using hierarchical clustering analysis—"

"Distill it down for me," Zeke interrupted.

"Okay, so basically when a brain is monitored while being put through the same event over and over there is a repeated brain wave pattern, neural cliques, that are like a memory code. Take that data and simplify it even further into binary code, using only 1 for active state and 0 for inactive state. Each series of actions is a pattern in a pyramid structure, with the most basic repeated event at the bottom, your foundation, as the base. Then each succeeding event has a pattern, and the tip of the pyramid indicates the most specific action."

Zeke watched her eyes light up, glowing almost silver in the shadows. She'd been using her hands to mark each level as she mimed a pyramid. Her cheeks, which had been pale earlier when he'd asked about her smarts, were now flushed with excitement.

He basically understood. But he wasn't sure how this experiment would help him. "So what do you propose?"

"Typically the analysis is used to compare patterns from one brain to another, but what if we do a control experiment with you? While under the influence of Sodium Pentothal, you start up a laptop and do some other tasks to get a baseline."

Zeke could feel his cheeks redden. Clearly his OCD routine had been noticed.

"And then we do another experiment with you giving up the key and the details of your encryption program. Then compare the two binary code structures."

"What will that tell us?"

"You're convinced you didn't give away the program, right?"

"I don't see how. I've never revealed anything under the influence of Sodium Pentothal before." Zeke squeezed his eyes shut trying to pull the information from his brain. "But I just don't remember."

"So what if we do the experiment and the brain wave

patterns show that you didn't give it up?" Sunshine said excitedly. "It would be evidence to support your claim."

Maybe his odd, repetitive tendencies could help him in this case.

Sunshine said, "Except, we'd need a place to conduct the experiment."

A place where they wouldn't get caught. As far as he knew there was no sort of official warrant or APB out for him. Zeke assumed the government would want to quietly apprehend him rather than make a big splash. Media attention, which could mean that certain details of this supposed security breach would become public, was something they'd want to avoid at all costs. After the fiasco with Staci Grant, they really couldn't afford another big hoopla in the press so soon.

"I need to make a phone call."

Zeke turned on one of the burner phones they'd bought at Target. He'd missed four calls. Shit. All from Lucas Goodman. He hit redial immediately.

"Goodman."

"Saw you called. What's up?" He was careful not give any identifiers.

"Sec." Zeke heard the rustling.

"Hey." Jamie's familiar voice calmed him. She was the best field agent he knew. With her help, they could do anything.

"Any luck finding our friend since I lost her?"

"We finally struck pay dirt by tapping in to the ex-husband's online activity."

"And?"

"I need you to take a look at the site."

Zeke poised his fingers. "Hit me."

Jamie rattled off a secured chat site and gave him the log on. "It's in code. I could only figure out part of it."

Zeke stared at the messages. Sunshine peered over his shoulder.

She pointed to the string of numbers. They'd used GPS coordinates, but then they'd separated the GPS coordinates with seemingly random key words and children's riddles.

"They've set up a meet. For tomorrow."

"Got that." Jamie said, "But I'm not sure where. The riddles in between negate the actual GPS coordinates in the message."

Zeke assessed the coordinates and the phrases that were almost like nursery rhymes. "Looks like Ocean Beach in San Francisco."

"She's supposed to bring everything, all the data she has on the project," Jamie said.

Which sounded great except that Zeke was pretty sure that the government had seized all of Susan Chen's experiments and her data.

"So he doesn't know we confiscated her work?"

"Or she had a hidden copy that we never found," Jamie posited.

Which might make sense. Susan Chen had continued to conduct experiments on unsuspecting agents in order to find an antidote for her daughter.

Shit. He'd love to get his hands on that information. But even more he'd love to get his hands on Susan Chen. She was the only one who could confirm his innocence. And yeah, right now he was banking all his hope on a woman wanted by the Feds.

"Damn, I need to get her."

Jamie said, "No! You need to stay far away from this."

"But—"

"It's going to have to wait. We don't know enough about the husband to know how this is going to go." Jamie shut him down.

"What do you know about him?"

"Not much. He's Russian. He's a scientist. And clearly has sociopathic tendencies since he injected his own daughter with an untested drug."

"Any idea how he got back into the country?" Oliver Krychef had been on the Homeland Security Watch List.

Jamie said, "His threat level was dropped and he is no longer on the No Fly List. He wasn't even listed as a Selectee. Otherwise he would have been detained at the border."

"But who did it? And who has the authority?" Zeke rolled his shoulders in disgust. "One more damn puzzle we need to solve."

"Yeah." Jamie didn't sound happy. "Back to our other problem. So now, instead of kicking her ass, I have to save it."

Jamie had no love for the scientist after Chen and her partner had kidnapped Jamie's sister to use as leverage against Jamie.

"Okay, so in other news, we need a lab. A safe lab and a tech to administer something a little on the unusual side."

Zeke glanced at Sunshine sitting on the bed next to him, her loose hair a slightly damp fall of silk down her back. He smiled at her, and after a moment she returned the smile, her lips curved sweetly. And in that moment, he was ridiculously happy even with everything unraveling around him.

Silence on the other end.

"You still there?"

"*We?*"

Zeke broke eye contact. "Uh, yeah, about that."

"Oh my God, you didn't."

"Look."

"Let me put this in language you understand. Dude, are you crazy?" Jamie practically yelled. "Seriously. You weren't supposed to make contact."

"There were some extenuating circumstances."

"How extenuating…was your dick extenuating?"

Zeke could hear Lucas in the background laughing. But his temper was starting to rise. "Her sleeper was after her and her mother."

That shut Jamie up.

"How could she possibly know that?" she demanded. Jamie's family had died in a car bomb blast, everyone except for her and her sister.

"He married her mother."

More silence as she processed what he was telling her. "And he's after Sunshine?"

Zeke exhaled. "Yeah."

"Wow." Jamie hesitated. "Where's the mom?"

"With her fiancé."

"Okay. Okay. If we can prove that you didn't give Chen the damn program, this will be small potatoes anyway."

Jamie's immediate attempt to placate him caused a burn of something uncomfortably like affection in his chest. "Thanks, Jamie."

"Yeah well, we still have to prove it."

And with that acerbic comment she pretty much shut him down again.

Sunshine eased off the bed and headed down the stairs to give him some privacy. "So the showdown between Oliver and Susan—"

"Ocean Beach, tomorrow afternoon," Jamie bit out.

"Okay."

She reiterated. "I don't want you anywhere near that meet."

"I'm a big boy," Zeke replied.

"Yeah, who doesn't always listen."

Zeke was silent. "I just need some control." She must have hear the quiet desperation in his voice.

"You cannot be there, Zeke." And there it was, pure affection beneath the worry.

"I know." Zeke had to wonder. "Why'd Oliver choose San Francisco?"

Jamie speculated. "No clear idea. Chen is from Seattle. Take her out of her comfort zone? Or maybe the Russian has contacts in the area." Definitely possible. San Francisco had a healthy Russian mafia population.

They needed to move on. And it wouldn't do to be on the phone for too long. "Any chance they're tracking Lucas's phone?"

"Doubtful," Jamie said. She tended to turn her paperwork in as late as possible. They shouldn't have too much on Lucas. As far as he knew the only people who knew about Lucas and Jamie were Zeke, Jordan Ramirez, Staci Grant, and Carson. And Jamie's sister, Bella.

"So, any ideas on the favor?" What he'd started with before she got off track.

"Why a lab?"

"Sunshine has an idea." Zeke knew she was right. At the very least the analysis would be another piece of evidence to refute that he gave his program to Susan Chen and her partner. "But we need a lab with an EEG machine."

Jamie started laughing. "Well, I supposed Barb might be able to help you out."

Zeke had no idea who Barb was or why that was so funny.

"Where is she located?"

"Outside of San Francisco." Jamie whispered something unintelligible to Lucas.

Patterns. Zeke kept seeing patterns that created bigger pictures. And every thread was leading them toward San Francisco. And he couldn't help but think that everything and everyone was converging in San Francisco for a reason.

Sunshine's experiment was a worth a shot.

"Give me her number?"

"I'll let Lucas do the honors." Jamie inhaled, let it out slowly. "Be safe."

Again that hidden bit of affection was there.

"You know it."

"We need to keep our conversations to a minimum," Jamie said quietly.

Zeke agreed. "I don't want any blowback on you."

"It's not that. But it wouldn't surprise me if they are tracking my movements again."

"How?" They'd eliminated all of Jamie's tracking devices when she was on the run from Susan Chen and her partner.

"Cell likely." Jamie said sneakily, "It's a good thing I'm right where I said I would be."

"Any word from Carson?" Zeke couldn't help it. He was feeling a little abandoned by his former mentor.

"He's on his way out."

"Out here?"

"Yeah. He wants to question Oliver. Because…how the hell did he get back in the country?"

Zeke would like to know too.

"We're keeping this extremely on the DL." Jamie

confessed. "There are too many hanging threads and outstanding questions that don't form a cohesive picture about this entire situation."

"I didn't do it." Zeke wanted to make sure she knew that. That she heard it from his own mouth.

Jamie didn't even hesitate. "I know that."

"How?"

"You don't have the subterfuge gene," Jamie replied. "And I mean that in a good way. You risked your career to help me when the evidence pointed another way. I want to return the favor."

A lump grew in his throat. "Thanks."

"Yeah. Enough mushy shit." Jamie handed the phone to Lucas and he gave Zeke the phone number for his friend Barb and instructions on how to introduce himself. Then they signed off quickly.

Zeke pressed end on the burner. It was time to get rid of this number. With efficient movements, he popped the SIM card and any other identifying pieces of the phone.

Then he headed downstairs, checked the path through to the kitchen, making sure there was no one on the beach before he scooted across the exposed area and into the laundry room. He found a tool box with the requisite hammer and smashed the phone, and the SIM card, into bits. Then he scooped up the pieces and dumped them into a baggie and put it in the trash.

"What's going on?" Sunshine stood hesitantly behind him, clearly intuiting his mood.

He and Sunshine needed a nap. Because later on they were hitting the road.

"We're on the move tonight." Zeke crossed his arms over his chest. "A little after midnight."

"Where are we going?"

"San Francisco."

"But that's where my mother is."

"It's where everything is." Zeke still couldn't see the pattern but he knew it existed. He clenched his fists in annoyance. If he still had the drug coursing through him he could see the pattern and the answer.

CHAPTER 35

I hated the idea of going anywhere near my mother.

The ceiling fan was still, and the air in the kitchen was stifling. A stray beam of light speared through the dust motes and cast his face in sinister shadows.

The veins in his tanned forearms had popped when he crossed his arms over his chest. Something about that light altered his normal happy-go-lucky expression into a discontent mask. As if he'd hit the wall and was done being a nice guy.

His cheekbones were harsh angles, and his hooded eyes were dark with secrets. A visceral thrill shimmied over my spine at his intensity.

"We can't leave now?"

"Under cover of darkness we'll leave."

"I…guess we should get some rest." My breath caught. I didn't want to rest. I wanted all that intense awareness on me.

"We should." He stalked toward me, his chin lowered as he gobbled me up with his stare. The powerful regard was like a physical caress. "But we aren't going to."

The air simmered with unspoken promise.

"What are we going to do?" I didn't even sound like myself. My voice was breathy and demanding, as I waited for him to tell me what I wanted to hear.

He yanked open the drawer and grabbed the box of condoms. Then Zeke seized my hand. His rougher, callused fingertips slid along my palm and threaded our fingers together. Without a word he tugged me toward the loft.

Hours later, I lay naked, entwined his muscular arms and surrounded by his heat. The embrace should have been pleasing, but the way he curved around me felt more like possession than comfort.

His erection prodded my butt, and I wondered how he could possibly be ready to go again. The hard length of him was like a brand against my skin. He cupped my breast with his palm and squeezed gently. That little bite of pain pulsed low in my belly. And even though I was sore, I was game.

I tried to roll over, but he wouldn't let me. "Not this time," he growled against the shell of my ear. The puff of breath tingled through me. And my heartbeat quickened when he wouldn't let me move.

Zeke slung his leg over my thighs, pinning me in place as he pressed wet open-mouthed kisses down my spine. The combination of his burning skin and the cool suction of his mouth was an interesting dichotomy that ramped up my arousal. That and being held in place as he rolled me on to my stomach.

In one fist he gripped my hair and turned my head for his kiss as his other hand slid down the center of my body and his fingers found the nest of curls guarding my sex. I tried to lift my hips but he held me in place while his middle finger rubbed my clit in little circles, playing with me, before he plunged his finger inside.

He groaned against my mouth. "So fucking wet."

His cock throbbed against my hip even as I tried in vain to move. The combination of his hand moving inside me, rubbing against my slit, pressing into me, while his tongue thrust in my mouth was dizzying.

He broke away from our kiss. "How sore are you?"

"Not that sore."

And oh my Goddess he did something with his fingers, pinching my clit as he rubbed and thrust. "Let me move."

"After." He nipped my shoulder, then sucked the spot hard.

My hands were under my head so I was basically helpless against his explorations. I wanted to touch him. But he refused to let me up.

My sex wept with arousal as he continued to slide his fingers in and out, each time he curled them and tapped while he held me captive.

My orgasm was building, each thrust, tap, kiss pushing me to a new high. I trembled with an excess of energy and no way to release it. If I could just move. The sensation of being trapped should have made me panic but I trusted him. Trusted him to take care of me. Trusted him to not hurt me. Just…trusted him.

I trusted him. In a moment of pure physical sensation, I tumbled over that edge. I began to convulse around his fingers, but he pulled them from me and quickly rolled on a condom. I cried out, bereft at the loss of him, the sound shocking in the quiet stillness of the loft.

I convulsed around nothing. Empty and unfulfilled.

In an athletic move, he lifted my hips and slid his cock all the way to the hilt. My fingers were bunched around the sheets at my head. As he knelt between my spread thighs, Zeke paused, held himself still. His thick hard rod filled me, the sensations on the edge of uncomfortable. But then other impressions registered. His balls swollen and snug against my sex, his palms spreading me wide, and the hair of his thighs brushing against my softer inner thighs. He grabbed my hips with his hands, the gesture primitive and demanding.

And then he started to move.

His movements slow, he rocked back and forth. And all the sensations from my overstimulated body began to build again.

On all fours, I began to push back against his thrusts. Hard. Every time he pounded into me he rolled over that spot, tension escalated as we hammered against each other.

His fingers tightened on my hips digging in so fiercely, I'd likely have bruises. And I didn't care. I slammed back against him, reaching, reaching for another high. With each thrust he hit my cervix, rubbed his head against my g-spot, pulled out until the head of his cock caressed my clit. He was pushing and prodding every one of my erogenous zones and my head was swimming and my body began to shake. The sensations, the bombardment was too much for my system.

I could feel him inside me, swelling impossibly larger. "Fuck, Sunshine."

He was going to come.

"Not without you," he gutted out.

Zeke reached around with one hand and lightly tapped on my clit. It was as if he'd hooked up a live wire to my sex and my orgasm hit like a supernova. Sparks, eruptions, explosions tore my body apart from the inside as I milked him so hard, I saw stars.

My blood gathered in my belly, and drained every other

sense from me, as we continued to pound against
each other.

I could feel the force of his ejaculation against my inner
walls, sheathing him tight as he came, and came, and came.

Zeke brushed the hair from the back of my neck and
gave me a hard kiss. Shivers cascaded through me as I
floated down from the sexual high.

Zeke curled his arm around my tummy, the hair from
his forearm brushed against me, and another burst of
adrenaline shimmied over my skin.

He was still buried deep inside me, his belly snugged up
against my ass, his arms curled around my waist. A sense of
safety and peace flowed over me. Which was crazy since we
were about to embark on the most dangerous journey of
my life.

OCTOBER 22
5:00 am
Livermore, CA

HOURS later we pulled into a parking lot in Livermore, a
suburb outside of San Francisco. We'd taken the Toyota
Camry parked in the garage after we found a set of keys in
the kitchen pantry. We left our stolen Honda, with some
cash for the owner's trouble, at a Best Western, one in a
string of hotels along Moonstone Beach.

Instead of taking the highway to head north, we'd
meandered through back roads, up and down mountain
roads, through valleys, and along the ocean. At one point we

hadn't seen a car in three hours, because no one was driving at that time of the night.

Now we were positioned at the end of a deserted row in the parking lot as far from the security lights, but as close to the door, as possible.

We were supposed to meet Zeke's friend's friend at an Urgent Care clinic location. Only one other car, a bright red Tesla, was parked near the door.

"Are you sure about this?" I was nervous about meeting this woman. We didn't know anything about her.

Zeke rubbed his palm over the fuzz on his head. "Jamie vouched for her."

I was beginning to hate this Jamie chick. What made him trust her so easily? "And who exactly is Jamie?"

Zeke replied, "A friend. A good friend."

"How good a friend?"

Zeke smiled and lifted my fist to his lips. "Not as good as you."

Okay, then. We sat in silence in the stolen Toyota and studied the single door to the clinic.

"You told her what to bring?" Nervous energy coursed through me.

Zeke had set up the meeting, told Barb what they needed to do a rough approximation of the experiment. Supposedly she had somehow gotten access to the equipment at the closed clinic. And the Sodium Pentothal.

While we waited, Zeke seemed almost as reluctant as I felt, and the atmosphere in the small car thickened. Finally Zeke pressed the car keys into my hand. "If something goes wrong, get the hell out." He curled my fingers over the sharp edge of the keys.

"What?" I tried to shove the keys back at him but Zeke refused to take them.

"Keep them." He yanked open his car door.

"You want me to just leave." It wasn't a question.

Zeke blinked, his pale lashes crescents against his tan cheeks, then deliberately glanced away. "Yes. Find your mom and Blue."

"Abandon you."

"Sweetheart, I'm in some really deep shit here." He propped his fists on his hips. "And I don't want you caught in the crossfire if it all goes to hell."

I knew he was trying to protect me but I was still mad. "I'm not running again," I declared.

A light flashed on in the back window of the clinic. "We've got to go."

"Fine." I stomped toward the clinic door. The hiking shoes were unfamiliar and clunky on my feet. I usually wore loose flowing skirts and sweaters and no bra. The khaki shorts, long-sleeved gray Henley, heavy hiking boots, and my pretty pink bra took me out of my regular habits and the effect was somewhat startling. I thought I looked pretty good but I still felt a little weird and bundled up.

Zeke strode toward the clinic, subtly placing his body in front of mine.

"You think there's something to be worried about?"

"No." He shook his head. "But I won't let anything happen to you."

His words beat like a drum inside my brain, the message pounding against my skull. He was protecting me. Before I could really process what his actions meant, the most gorgeous woman I'd ever seen opened the door and gestured us inside. "Hurry."

I was literally struck dumb at her beauty. She was a light skinned African-American woman with black hair in a pixie cut, aristocratic cheekbones, and a lush set of lips. My inexperience with men and my general feelings of inferiority when dealing with the opposite sex hit my confidence hard. I waited for Zeke to be equally as bowled over. But he just thrust out his hand.

"Barb. I've heard great things." He wasn't really looking at her but instead was checking out the surroundings and peering into the interior of the building, in no way acknowledging her stunning looks.

Even with her figure hidden beneath a shapeless white lab coat, she exuded sophistication and a subtle sexuality.

She smiled as if she had a delicious secret and tugged him inside, gesturing for me to follow. Then she locked the door.

"Zeke, nice to meet you." Barb eyed me with a gorgeous chocolate brown, and slightly suspicious, gaze. "And you are?"

"Not important," Zeke dismissed me. So, I only thought that he hadn't noticed how gorgeous she was. His utter rejection stabbed into me like a hot poker. The pain so fierce, I couldn't draw a breath.

"Relax, sweetie." Barb patted my shoulder. "He just wants me to have deniability."

For my gigantic brain, I sure was stupid sometimes. I nodded, still unable to push any words past my constricted throat.

"Lucas owes me. Again," she muttered. "Come on back."

We followed her into an exam room at the back of the building.

"I'm actually familiar with this study," Barb said as we entered the small room. The EEG machine was already set up to record the electrical impulses and patterns in Zeke's brain. A syringe of what I assumed was Sodium Pentothal sat on the little metal rolling tray table. And she'd brought a laptop. Because we didn't think the tablet was the correct test material for the experiment. "But it's somewhat obscure. How did *you* know about it?"

She directed her questions at Zeke. I stayed silent, but he wasn't about to let me be modest. He jerked his thumb toward me.

Barb turned and raised one perfectly-arched ebony eyebrow. The interest in her gaze went up about one hundred percent. "Excellent." She smiled, her white teeth gleaming in the low light of the office. "You can help."

Zeke sat on the exam table and Barb began applying the electrodes to various areas of his forehead and at the base of his head. Then she rubbed her palm over his fuzz. "Gonna have to shave some spots."

"Fine," Zeke said.

I sat on the chair next to the exam table, held the laptop, and waited until she was done applying the leads and wires.

"Two things." She stepped back so she had us both in her sights. "First, the original study did not use Sodium Pentothal. I'm assuming there's a reason you chose to administer the drug."

Zeke nodded.

"Second, you realize that what we're attempting will likely not be permissible evidence in a court of law?" Barb cautioned.

"It's just a piece of evidence," Zeke said. I wondered how much Barb knew. He wasn't wanted in the general sense but if he were caught things would be…
uncomfortable for all of us. He neglected to mention that he'd be tried in a potentially secret, military tribunal. And imprisoned in a highly secure federal penitentiary if convicted.

Yeah, he may not have come out and told me that but I could connect the dots.

"Ready?" Barb asked.

He took a deep breath. I held mine. I hoped this worked.

Barb pushed up his shirt sleeve. He'd changed into a plaid short-sleeved shirt and khaki cargo shorts he'd bought yesterday at Target, very different from his usual board shorts and t-shirts.

Barb wiped his skin with rubbing alcohol. Then she efficiently uncapped the syringe and injected the Sodium Pentothal into his arm.

"We've got a few minutes until that starts working. We'll do two separate readings as he does one rote thing, and then does the thing that he's accused of doing." Barb told me, since Zeke's eyes were glazing as we stood there.

"This won't work," he said glumly. "I'm immune."

The odor of the rubbing alcohol burned my nose. My eyes watered, because of the smell, not the defeat in his voice. At least that's what I told myself.

After the drug had time to enter his system, I handed Zeke the laptop. He very precisely aligned the edge of the laptop with the edge of the counter. Then he performed the same routine he always did before he used the laptop. He touched the top edge, the left, the right and finally the bottom of the keyboard before he powered it on.

As Zeke went through his motions, Barb input notes along the time stamp so they could analyze his responses to stimulus.

"You think that's enough data?" I was watching the EEG machine register the spikes in his brain waves. "Should we have him surf the web?"

Zeke nodded and began typing on the laptop.

"It gives us a baseline." Barb cautioned worriedly, "Again, this won't hold up—"

"Doesn't matter," Zeke said. "I'm pretty much screwed."

I thought about asking him a question that he normally wouldn't answer. "What did you hack into that got you in trouble when you were sixteen?"

But he just pressed his lips together and shook his head. "Nope."

"Come on, we need the baseline of you giving up a secret," I cajoled.

He stared at me. I could see his brain working. Finally, he said, "Not gonna answer out loud." However he leaned over and whispered the answer in Barb's ear and I squirmed with a spike of jealousy. Jeez, I needed to get a grip.

The EEG continued to register the spikes and drops in his brainwaves. "Power down the laptop," I said impulsively.

Zeke did what I asked. And we had our baseline.

Barb ended the first test. She input Zeke's name, and the words "Under the influence of SP and Baseline for brain patterns when doing rote tasks, plus subject imparted classified information." She saved the results to a USB drive. Then she reset the machine.

"Let's do the second test." I patted Zeke's hand.

Barb said, "Okay. So after you power on the machine this time, do whatever it was that got you into trouble."

Zeke performed the same series of touches and motions that he always did when he set up and turned on his laptop. The EEG machine registered his brain waves. There was a jagged spike first, then the lines went nearly flat.

And he just sat there. He pressed his palms flat against the top of his thighs and didn't move.

"Zeke Hawthorne." I said sternly, "Share your encryption program."

Zeke opened up a new file and looked at the cursor on the blank page. He typed out a bunch of data slowly. His fingers moved slower and slower as the machine results continued to spike and dip. I couldn't be sure without analyzing the results but it definitely looked different from the first pattern.

Finally he stopped, his fingers resting on the keys, not moving as he stared at the screen.

"What did you write?" I asked.

"I wrote out the program," he said smugly.

I recalled our conversation from yesterday. Kerchoff's Law. "But did you give us the key?" Because without the key the program was worthless.

Zeke stared at the screen. Saved the document. "I can't do it."

"But we need to see—"

"I may be accused of giving up national secrets, but as far as *I* know, as of right now I've given none. And I'm not about to start." He reached for the leads.

"Wait," Barb said frantically.

I wished there was something we could ask that would either confirm or deny his resistance to the drug since he was so convinced that he was immune. Even running this experiment there wasn't necessarily a way to confirm his resistance to the drug because he needed to do certain things to get the reading. "Can you think of a casual test?" I asked Barb.

Barb bent down and got right in Zeke's face. So close she could probably kiss him with one slight move. Jealousy reared again. "What's her name?"

But Zeke just stared into her deep, dark chocolate eyes and said, "No."

"Come on," she said enticingly and ran a single finger

down his arm. I wanted to punch her. "You can tell me. I'm a friend of Lucas's. A good friend." Her voice was sultry, seductive.

"No." Zeke shook his head, frowned, and lifted his hand to tug at his hair and grasped nothing. Then his brows lifted as if he'd remembered he'd cut it. "Not gonna happen."

Barb straightened. "Pretty good verbal resistance."

He powered down the laptop. All without looking at either Barb or me. When the laptop was off, and closed he turned to us.

"I'll finish the experiment the exact same way we did the other one." She completed the same steps, and labeled this file, "Zeke, Under the influence of SP and Attempt to divulge secrets, but didn't give up the secrets."

We waited while Barb saved the second test to the USB drive, then powered everything down and handed the drive to me. Zeke was still kind of out of it.

Zeke had grabbed my fingers and twisted our hands together. Barb stared down at our entwined fingers. "Um, you guys have a place to stay?"

"Aiding and abetting." Zeke brushed his lips over my knuckles. "Not a good idea."

"Where else are you going to go to analyze the data?"

She had a good point. We needed someplace to lay low until we heard back from Jamie and Lucas. Wasn't gonna lie, I didn't like the fact that we were dependent on so many other people. As a matter of fact, the reliance on others gave me the willies.

Barb took off the shapeless white lab coat. Underneath the generic covering, she wore black wide leg pants and a black and white hound's-tooth crop jacket and simple black patent pumps. She reached into a matching black leather bag with black patent accents.

"Go back to my place." She retrieved a single key on a Tufts University lanyard from the purse. "He's going to need a few hours to recover from the drug. Even if he didn't reveal any state secrets, Sodium Pentothal still packs a punch in dimming awareness and slowing reaction time."

I studied Zeke for a minute watching the slow track of his vision. She was right. He was not at one hundred percent. I could use her computer to analyze the data we'd accumulated and see if there were any conclusions or if this morning had been a waste of time and a potential breach of Zeke's safety.

I curled my fingers around the woven cotton. "Directions?"

Barb quickly rattled off instructions on how to get to her house. The sky was beginning to lighten and I knew I needed to get him out of there.

Zeke was borderline docile as we all walked together to the car. His lack of awareness was beginning to worry me.

"Good luck," she called out.

"What about your key?"

"Just leave it in the entry." Barb slid into the 'in your face' red car. "I'm headed out of town for a conference."

I didn't know what to say. "Thank you."

She paused, one foot touching the ground. Barb gripped the door handle and glanced between Zeke and me, her gaze wistful. "Be careful."

I nodded and started our stolen car. I drove quickly but didn't dare go over the speed limit. Within fifteen minutes, I was pulling into the driveway of a very elegant French-style chateau with rear windows that overlooked a working vineyard. Barb had given me the code to her garage and I quickly entered it on the numeric pad installed on the frame. I drove inside as soon as the door went up.

I turned off the engine and jerked the key out. With economy of movement, I pressed the button for the garage door and breathed a sigh of relief after the door was down and all the light was eliminated and we were in the semi-darkness.

I peered in the car at Zeke. His head lolled against the passenger window and he was sound asleep. With his buzz cut, random patches of bald skin all over his skull, and his face slack he looked like a little kid worn out after a long day at the park.

My heart clenched at the thought of disturbing him. But he'd be more comfortable inside. I bent down and pressed one knee on the driver's seat as I leaned awkwardly over the console to wake him up. I didn't want to open the passenger door because he might accidently fall out of the car.

"Zeke," I whispered.

But he didn't stir. He snored softly and I huffed out a breath. "Zeke," I tried again a little more loudly.

But he still didn't wake.

So I caressed his shoulder, his muscles hard beneath my tentative touch. With that small contact, he jerked awake. His blue eyes, oddly so much darker in his tan face without the shadow of his curly hair, cleared within seconds of awareness. His palm cupped my cheek and he nuzzled his lips against my neck. The contact was sweet and affectionate.

"Sunshine." He skimmed his lips along my jaw and pressed a tender kiss to my top lip, then repeated at the left corner, right corner, and then he sucked my bottom lip into his mouth. He pulled me off balance until I tumbled into his lap.

"Where are we?"

"Barb's house."

Zeke sat up straight and glanced around all teasing gone. "I was that out of it?"

"You still didn't give anything away." I could sense his unease.

He huffed out a breath in disgust. "We don't know that for sure."

"We do at least for today," I said. "You refused to divulge your program, or any other secrets. You wouldn't even tell Barb my name."

"Information that didn't matter." He closed his eyes and thunked his skull against the headrest. Except he had refused to reveal my name to Barb. He had protected me even when he was out of it.

"So let's go analyze the data."

We let ourselves into Barb's house. The chateau-style house was as refined and put together as she was, not an item out of place, no dust lingered on the wood surfaces, no dirty dishes stacked in the sink, no clean laundry piled on the sofa. Until I peered into her bedroom. Clothes littered the floor around what appeared to be a dirty laundry hamper as if she'd shot them like basketballs and missed.

That little inconsistency made me like her more. I peered into what I assumed was the guest bedroom. "You want to lie down?"

Zeke frowned. "No. Let's see if we can find anything of significance."

We worked on the data in a comfortable silence. Zeke was able to use an online website for translating statistical data into binary code of ones and zeroes. The memory coding for the experiment was set into binary code with one representing an active state and zero representing an inactive state.

Using a mathematical treatment called matrix inversion

to compare patterns from one brain to another was the object of the original study. For our purposes, we were going to compare Zeke's results against Zeke's results. Once we did that, we would be able to assess the baseline where he set up the laptop and then verbally gave away information, and compare it to the second set of data, when we tried to get him to reveal secrets, both at the computer which he would have done if he'd given Susan Chen his program and verbally, and he had refused.

I stared at the graphs from the two sets of data. One thing was glaringly obvious. The end of the second set of data was vastly different from the first which meant that he hadn't followed the same pattern.

In all of the standard tasks that Zeke had performed, the base coding through to the end of the task, the binary results were the same, even the one where he told Barb what he'd hacked at seventeen.

But the two instances where he'd refused to answer, giving away the key and revealing my name, had produced vastly different results. Which meant that he'd refused to give up his encryption program. The binary code was different.

We turned to each other. A sense of glee zinged through me. "According my analysis of this," I couldn't even finish I was so excited.

"I didn't give Susan Chen the program."

I threw my arms around his shoulders, and rubbed my cheek against his stubble. He wrapped his arms around me. The sense of coming home burst within me like a water balloon popping. Relief swelled.

My euphoria faded, and Zeke stiffened in my embrace as we both realized something crucial at the same time.

"If I didn't give her the program, then who did?"

CHAPTER 36

Zeke's pleasure faded almost immediately as flaws in their data and results became clear. It really didn't *prove* that he hadn't given up classified information. It also didn't disprove his theory. There were holes no matter how he looked at it.

His head spun with discouraging thoughts and absolute despair. "I'll never know what really happened."

Sunshine jumped up. His normally calm, laid back girl was agitated and waving her hands around. "There is a way."

"Look, Sunshine. This was a great idea. Really thinking outside the box. But we didn't necessarily move forward."

She paced back and forth staring at the cream Berber carpeting as if it could help them out of this mess. "We need to ask Susan Chen. Tell her these results and demand her corroboration or denial once and for all."

That might be the only option left.

The connections fired in his brain. If they could intercept Chen before her meeting with Krychef, Zeke could ask her what really happened. How did she get his program?

Make it personal. When they'd interrogated her before, they hadn't told her anything about the consequences of her having that program.

Hadn't this been what he'd wanted since the moment they had captured her the first time? To have her tell him, tell the NSA, definitively that he either had or hadn't given her and Liam his encryption program?

Except, he'd promised Jamie that he'd stay far away from the Chen/Krychef meet. Maybe he could ask Jamie to ask Susan. But when he dialed Lucas's phone with his new burner, there was no answer. He clicked End without leaving a message.

"We know when and where she's going to be."

But he'd given his word.

As if she read his mind, she said, "I know you promised. But this is your *life*."

She was right.

They did know where Susan Chen was going to be.

Zeke logged on and went to the chat room where Oliver had sent the details of his meeting with Susan Chen.

Clear as day, once you figured out the code, Oliver stated that he would give Chen her daughter if she handed over her research.

But some of the details had changed. He'd switched the meeting place. Zeke needed to let Jamie know. But if he talked to her, she might figure out that Zeke had something planned. So he texted Lucas on his new burner phone, identifying himself in code, and letting Jamie and Lucas know the new details of the meet. But Zeke tweaked the time, telling Jamie and Lucas that the meeting would take place ten minutes after the correct start time.

Zeke glanced at the clock on the wall. They had a few hours to get some shuteye. If they were going to intercept

Chen before she met with Krychef, they had to get there early, find a defensible, well-hidden position and wait until she arrived.

He couldn't help but verbalize his concern. "This is probably a bad idea." On so many levels.

"Go on the premise that you didn't give them your program." Sunshine urged. "That someone else, much higher up, did."

Zeke realized that was true of every single piece in this puzzle. Someone higher up gave Susan Chen the encryption program. Someone higher up had to let Oliver Krychef sneak back in to the country. Someone higher up had orchestrated the experimentation on the espionage agents. Someone higher up had to know that John Stanley married Stella. Someone higher up had engineered the original kill order.

But who?

That's what they needed Stanley for. So after they cornered Susan Chen, they had to go after John Stanley.

But Chen first. They were going to need a disguise. Because Jamie and Lucas's objective was to capture both Chen and Krychef. And he had no idea if they planned to bring along reinforcements.

Zeke definitely didn't want to make it a trifecta by giving them the opportunity to capture him too.

He might have to bolt out of there fast, but luckily both Chen and Krychef were higher value targets. At least, he hoped they were.

After all, Susan Chen escaped from the federal prison, and Oliver Krychef had managed to sneak back into the States even though he should have been on the DHS No Fly List.

Except, Zeke was wanted for treason. Shit. He might have to bolt.

Four hours later they were on their way to San Francisco. They planned to record Susan Chen confirming or denying that Zeke had given them his encryption program. Proof, again not admissible in court, but that was okay. The confession just needed to be enough to get Armbruster to back down on the charge of treason and Zeke's arrest.

They still had over two hours until Susan Chen was supposed to meet her ex and trade her research for her daughter.

The more odd twist, the girl was Krychef's daughter too.

"What kind of sick fuck uses his own kid?" Zeke wondered as they slowed down for construction on the road.

Sunshine shrugged. "Parents, grandparents, they all make choices that are a mystery to me." Her voice was tinged with sadness.

Impulsively he reached for hand and squeezed. "You okay?" The contact soothed him, an unexpected mirror, since he was trying to soothe her.

"Yeah," she said softly.

"You thinking about your mother?"

"We were so close."

"Why don't you check in with her?"

"After we deal with this."

He figured she didn't want anyone or anything to track her movements or find a way to draw her mother out.

"If you change your mind, you can use my phone."

Sunshine scooted as close as she could and brushed a kiss across his cheek. "You're so sweet."

Zeke winced.

"What's wrong?"

"Uh, no guy wants to be called sweet. It ranks right up there with *nice*."

"I have news for you." She tapped his shoulder. "Some girls want sweet. And nice."

Not in his experience. He thought about Jamie with Lucas, who was a badass. And Staci Grant with Jordan, who personified badass. He laughed sardonically. "Next you'll be telling me they like geeks too."

"This girl does."

That shut him up. Because he thought her brain was sexy. So why couldn't she think his was sexy too? And why had he never figured that out?

Zeke glanced at Sunshine. When they'd been at Target, she'd picked up different clothes than what she normally wore as well. So she was dressed in hiking boots, khaki shorts, a gray Henley that cupped her bound breasts, the first time he'd seen her in a bra, and her hair was piled on top of her head in a fun bun rather than in her signature braid.

But he thought the look suited her smarts.

Zeke navigated the congested streets of San Francisco, as he headed toward the Bay and the San Francisco Zoo, Krychef's new meeting point.

They had two options. They could park at the zoo or on the street. Zoo parking would have easy access to the car if they needed a fast getaway but the street would be less obtrusive if they needed to be stealth rather than fast.

"Parking lot." Sunshine chose. "Getting away needs to be our number one priority."

After parking nose out, and as close to the exit as possible, Zeke and Sunshine made their way into the zoo and headed for the reptile room.

Cinnamon and sugar dusted chalupas and roasted hot dogs competed with the briny sea breeze to scent the air.

Sunshine shuddered as they held hands and pretended a leisurely interest in the various animals while they made their way to Komodo Alley. Even on a weekday, the zoo was jam packed with kids and parents running amok along the cement pathways that surrounded the animal pens.

Sunshine was quiet. "Poor thing."

"Who?"

"The little girl." Sunshine shuddered. "She's agoraphobic right?"

"Yeah."

"Then this," she gestured to the weekday crowds of adults and kids of every color, shape, and size laughing and pointing at the howler monkeys, "is likely going to freak her out."

"Good point." Zeke rubbed his thumb over her palm, thought about forcing someone with a severe fear of being outside into this environment. It would be nearly impossible to keep her calm. "I bet he'll drug her."

Sunshine casually swung her head from side to side. "So how do you hide a drugged kid?"

Zeke noted the family at the Chimpanzee exhibit. Two bigger boys hung on the railing, elbows cocked and chests pressed against the rail, as they peered over the edge, while their mother rocked a stroller with a little girl passed out in the seat. "Stroller. Kid will just look like she's asleep."

Sunshine nodded. "Okay, so that gives us a line on him."

Sunshine stared at the two older boys for another second, then tugged his hand to continue walking toward the reptile exhibit.

"What was that look?"

"What look?" Her face was blank.

"When you were looking at those two kids."

"Oh, that." Sunshine shrugged. "I never really thought about kids. About having them I mean."

She laughed but it wasn't happy, more filled with uncertainty.

"Until yesterday I never thought I'd get to have sex. Kids weren't even a blip on my radar. The possibility was about as likely as getting hit by lightning."

Talking about kids should have made him sweat but he was in pretty much the same boat. He'd never really thought about kids. He didn't even know anyone who had kids.

"And….?"

She glanced around at the chaos of children everywhere, running, screaming. "Probably take a while to get used to the idea. And yet, Susan Chen was so concerned about her daughter she did crazy things."

He snorted.

"She must love her daughter an awful lot." Sunshine reflected somberly.

"Yeah." Zeke agreed. She'd broken out of federal prison just to get her daughter and make her the antidote. "And?"

"It does make me want to call my mama and thank her."

"So do it."

But she shook her head. "No contact is better. Safer." She stayed silent.

"We got rid of the phone he was using to track you." Zeke reminded her.

"I know but I'm used to thinking of my stepfather as all knowing. I can't shake the idea that if I use a phone again he'll find me. Find her."

"We're close to taking care of this, and then we'll tackle

Stanley." Zeke said, "Let's get to the reptile exhibit and get this over with."

Sunshine agreed.

Once they reached Komodo Alley, they entered the darkened building. "He chose well." Zeke noted the employee exit on the other side, very discreetly marked.

Fortunately there were benches in the corners. After studying the room, he decided the bench closest to the employee exit was their best point of egress. "Any problems, we can slip out this exit."

Sunshine nodded and sat on the bench gingerly. "What are you going to do if your friend sees you?"

Zeke tugged her down onto the bench and wrapped his arm around her shoulder. As natural as breathing, Sunshine nuzzled against his neck and pressed a tender kiss to his jaw.

"Run fast?"

She pulled back from him to see if he was serious. "What if she tries to bring you in?"

"She'll give me an out." He infused confidence in his voice. "But if for some reason she doesn't, get to the car, and go back to Barb's house."

"I couldn't leave you." Sunshine's hair was piled on top of her head in a floppy bun, soft tendrils curled against her cheek only emphasized her fragile femininity.

"Promise me."

Her eyes were mysterious pools of gray, deep like the night sky, in the darkened interior. "No."

"You do not need the shit storm coming down on me if I can't get my name cleared." He couldn't even stand to think about her caught up in his mess. "Find your mom and Blue if that happens."

"We should probably lay out a plan of attack." Sunshine fiddled with the new burner phone, trying to find the record button. It wasn't a bells and whistles smart phone but it had a decent recording function.

Zeke didn't like the fact that she'd blown him off but he let her distract him for now. They could come back to the issue again. Or he'd just shove her out the door.

"Best guess, Susan will get here first." Zeke whispered into her ear, a shiver raced down her spine, "Jamie and Lucas will likely be here early too but since I pushed out the meet time a little I'm hoping I'll have a chance with Susan Chen before the others arrive."

"Good."

But as if he'd conjured them, Jamie Hunt and Lucas Goodman sauntered into the reptile house.

Shit, shit, shit.

Zeke pretended a keen interest in the actual Komodo dragon in the glass case to their right and hoped his lack of hair, they'd shaved the rest of his fuzz to eliminate the patches left by the electrodes, so now he was completely bald, and different clothes in the dark would be enough to keep them off their tail. He eased Sunshine into the curve of his arm so she hid most of his body.

"They're here." Dammit. He'd hoped that he would be able to interrogate Susan Chen first.

Zeke flashed back to the last time he'd tried to hide while following Jamie and the ease and quickness with which she'd made him. He sighed.

But Jamie didn't approach them. He had his phone on silent. He took it out to pretend to take a picture, and checked the screen for messages, but she hadn't called him. She was on her cell now, shaking her head, arms crossed over her chest. Lucas had eased down onto the bench exactly opposite them and stretched his jeans-clad legs out in front of him.

He'd tilted his head and was studying Jamie, a small smile playing over his mouth, seemingly absorbed in watching his girl. But then he raised two fingers to his brow and flicked them in a universal sign for hello.

"Did they see us?" Sunshine was staring into the glass-front of the reptile cage as if she could find the answer to all their problems in the armored scales of the Komodo dragon. He realized that she was actually watching Jamie and Lucas's reflection when she said, "Looked like he signaled."

Zeke tensed. Lucas had seen them. But he wasn't approaching. And Jamie was ignoring them.

Before he could figure out exactly what was going on, Susan Chen walked into the room. She paced inside, glanced around. Her gaze darted from corner to corner, ignoring the couples and focusing on the two families with children in the room.

But her shoulders slumped when she realized her ex and daughter weren't in the structure.

Jamie had wrapped her arms around Lucas's neck and appeared to be making out with him. He was hand signaling Zeke. He watched carefully and understood that Lucas was telling him to get to Susan while he had the chance.

"They saw us," Zeke said.

"Sure?"

"Yes, and they're giving us the chance to talk to her." Zeke squeezed her shoulders and then let his arm slide down her back. "Get the recording button ready."

Susan Chen walked jerkily around the perimeter, not even pretending to look at the various snakes and lizards. As she approached their corner, Zeke eased to standing. She still had her eyes on the entrance. So when he curled his fingers around her bicep, she whirled and sent the flat of her hand flying toward his nose.

Fortunately he'd anticipated the move and bent backwards so she literally spun and fell into him.

Zeke wrapped his arms around her and across her chest at the bicep level. Even as she struggled he said quietly into her ear, careful to keep out of range of a head butt, "I'm not here to take you in." Which was true. Jamie and Lucas were here to take her in. Not Zeke. "I just want to know how you got my encryption program."

She stilled in his grasp. "What?" Her voice was frantic as if she was so terrified she couldn't comprehend what he was asking for.

"I don't care about you or Oliver or your daughter. I just want to know how you got my encryption program."

"Seriously?" she asked shrilly, drawing the attention of the other patrons.

"Yes." He didn't explain he was in trouble. He didn't give her any leverage. "I know Oliver is coming soon. So tell me what I want to know and I'll let you go."

"Fine. No, you didn't give it to me."

That still didn't help him. "Then how did you get it?"

"Liam," she faltered as if remembering the last time she'd seen Liam, dead on the hotel room floor, the carpet and her splattered with his blood. "Some friend of his from boarding school."

"Boarding school?" Zeke had researched all the way back and still he was stunned. Liam had gone to boarding school in England. The American School.

"They went to some super special school where all the expatriates at the time sent their kids. They were besties ever since sixth grade." She snarled, "Now leave me alone."

"Do you know his name?"

"No." She shook her head so hard she knocked into Zeke's jaw but he could tell it wasn't to harm him. She was so frantic that she wasn't thinking straight. "Liam always called him Army."

"So he was in the armed services?"

"I don't know." She started to struggle. "It was his nickname."

Zeke contemplated that information.

"That's where they originally came up with the idea to modify human DNA. They used to dream about creating a super spy."

So whoever gave them his program had to either work at the NSA or had to have a very high contact. And the man had to be older, old enough to be Liam's peer and to have been in the Army.

"How did you get the names and contacts to conduct the experiment?" Now that she was talking, Zeke wanted it all.

"Same guy gave us access."

"What does he look like?" Zeke couldn't resist asking.

But she was done. She broke away from him.

"Go away," she whispered fiercely.

"One last thing I thought you'd want to know." Zeke could feel her tension, her wish for him to leave her alone. "The antidote."

She stopped, didn't breathe, didn't move.

"It mostly worked."

Tears flooded her eyes and leaked from the corners. "Really?"

"I still have a few lingering effects but I'm actually functioning better than before I had the drug in some ways."

She dropped her head to his shoulder for a second. The relief made her wobble against him.

"I'm sorry about your daughter."

She swallowed down a sob and nodded. "I need to fix it. Fix her."

"We've got what we need," Zeke said to Sunshine.

Zeke hand signaled to Lucas that they were done. Then asked if they needed help. Lucas signed back, Leave, even as Jamie stuck her arm behind her back and flipped him her middle finger.

Zeke grinned.

"What are you laughing at?" Susan Chen snarled.

"Good luck with your daughter." Zeke pulled Sunshine to her feet just as Jamie headed to Susan.

Susan whirled around and nearly ran into Jamie. "No," she whispered.

"You need to come with us." Jamie and Lucas surrounded her.

Chen shook her head violently. "My daughter."

Lucas touched his finger to his earpiece. "We've got your daughter and your ex-husband."

"No harm will come to her? And I get to see her?" Chen had pulled out a knife with a large, serrated-edge blade. It was clear she didn't want to use it. But she would if pushed.

"You'll get to see her." Lucas put his palm on her shoulder, ignoring the weapon.

Jamie gave him a look. "Really? Step away from the weapon, Goodman." She was clearly unhappy with the fact that he hadn't even flinched at the danger.

"As long as you don't mention...." Lucas jerked his head toward Zeke.

"Yes. Okay. Fine. But I want to see my daughter." She started to put the weapon away but Jamie very effectively disarmed her and tucked the knife into her pants.

Zeke stood there uncertainly.

Finally, Jamie looked at him. "Better get out of here before Carson spots you."

"Shit. Forgot about Carson."

"After what happened the first time we apprehended her," Jamie said. "He couldn't afford not to be here."

"Uncle Carson is here?" Sunshine piped up from behind him.

Jamie shook her head. "Another Uncle?"

"Mama was right." Sunshine whispered, "He did send you."

"What are you talking about?" Zeke turned to Sunshine. Then she frowned. "Carson works for the NSA?"

"Voice down," Jamie growled at Sunshine.

Zeke didn't want to actually ask her about bringing him in, but he knew she would do what she had to. "What about me?"

"Am I really known for playing by the rules?" Jamie cuffed him on the arm. "But best to avoid Carson, his compass isn't as ambiguous as mine. He'd probably have to bring you in."

"You knew I'd be here?" Zeke said.

"Hell yes." Jamie smirked. "Knew you wouldn't be able to resist trying to talk to her. Planned for contingencies."

Zeke sighed. "So you made me right away."

"Nope. Nice job hiding behind the girl." She adjusted the collar of his plaid shirt in a very uncharacteristic touchy feely gesture. Then she rubbed his mostly bald head. "You'd never be caught dead in this shirt. And the haircut completely changes the way you look."

Zeke flushed.

"Better get out of here," Jamie said.

"I didn't give away the program." Sunshine stood silent behind Zeke. He purposely placed himself between

Sunshine and Jamie, giving her a chance if she needed to run. "We taped her denial. And found out that Liam was working with a friend he knew from boarding school in England."

"I'll tell Carson, but it might not make any difference."

Zeke hesitated. Then held out his palm to Sunshine. She instinctively knew exactly what he was asking for and handed him the cell phone. "The recording is on this phone. There's more intel about Liam's contact. I'm trusting you with my future. With my life."

Zeke pressed the phone into Jamie Hunt's hand. Her look was solemn. "I'll see what I can do."

She glanced at the way he had shielded Sunshine.

"So that's how it is. Carson's on his way. Better get out now." She gave Sunshine an assessing look. "Don't hurt him."

CHAPTER 37

O *ctober 22*
      5:00 pm
Ocean Beach

WE'D DONE IT.

Between us we'd come up with a way to lure John Stanley to us and get him for good. "You think it will work?"

Since we had figured out that Stanley had found me through my old cell deactivation and new cell activation locations, we knew he likely had both my and Mama's information. So I called and left a message on Mama's old cell voice mail. I gave her the location of where we were going to be, and told her to meet us here in about half an hour. Mama wouldn't check those messages. But....

"If Stanley is as resourceful as we think, and he is monitoring your old cell numbers, then yeah, I think it will work. And in half an hour we'll nab him."

Zeke was kind of jittery. Now that Susan Chen confirmed he hadn't given away the program, he had realized that whoever did give her the program had to be much higher up the food chain at the NSA. And John Stanley might just have a name for him.

Ever since he'd connected those dots, he hadn't been still.

I stood motionless on the beach. We were plenty far from the waves but I was still nervous.

I needed to channel the way I felt yesterday, before Stanley had accosted me.

Zeke stopped pacing and stood in front of me. "How you doing?"

Did I want to confess? No, I didn't. But he probably needed to know.

I swallowed hard. "Um, not great."

"Maybe I can help." He turned me around to face the waves. They were still far enough away that I was safe. He carefully lowered my purse which held my gun for the confrontation with my stepfather to the damp sand. Then he walked me two large steps toward water. My heart rate accelerated and sweat bloomed on my face and palms.

"I'm right here with you," Zeke said in my ear. His front pressed against my back, and his arms wrapped around my waist. He was a comforting presence behind me. We stopped about five feet from where the waves were encroaching on the shore.

"Take off your shoes."

Zeke kicked off his Chuck Taylors. My hiking boots were a little harder to manage. But I finally got my boots and socks off.

"Dig your toes into the sand." He laced his fingers with mine. "You want to connect to the ground."

Now who was the one sounding hippy-dippy?

"Okay." I curled my toes in the cool, damp sand. A shiver worked its way up my body.

"Look. The ocean won't hurt you," he murmured. "Don't be afraid of it."

I watched the water slide further up the shore. The waves were still about three feet away from where we stood and I vibrated with the need to back away. But Zeke was behind me, holding me in place. And I knew I could do this. With him supporting me I could do anything.

"You're stronger than the fear."

"The only time I wasn't afraid was when you were between my legs the other night." I confessed.

"That's—"

Zeke's whole body jerked. He dropped, like Sir Thomas Newton's apple straight to the ground, and pulled me down with him. What the hell?

I rolled, in a panic, and looked up into the face of evil. It had worked. John Stanley had found us. But this wasn't how we'd planned out his capture. He was early.

"What did you do?" I cried.

He held up a stun gun. "Tased him."

"Who are you, Veronica Mars?"

"Shut up, *Claire*." He sneered.

I shifted to kneeling, legs covered with sand, feet bare and Zeke lying prostrate next to me.

Our plan had worked. Except Stanley was early, and the plan didn't include Zeke unconscious.

I could hear the waves behind me. Coming closer. But I had bigger problems than the water right now. The gun was in my purse, only about six feet away but that chasm between me and the weapon was practically the Grand Canyon right now. I sank my fingers into the damp sand and realized I had another weapon at my disposal. I curled my hands into fists, holding as much sand as I could. Then, I stumbled to my feet, trying to watch over Zeke and keep John and that Taser a manageable distance away from me.

"What do you want from me?" Of course, I knew he didn't want me. He wanted my mother.

"For such a genius, you sure did grow up to be an idiot." He advanced on me. In my nightmares he was a giant. So huge and powerful that I was helpless against his bigger size.

But now that I was an adult, he really wasn't that much bigger than me. And fear left in a burst of rage so great, it threatened to drown me, the emotion rose up and geysered from me in a torrent of sheer fury.

He had stolen that from me. Stolen my childhood. My teen years. My love of water. My grandparents.

"You aren't going to steal anything else from me." The sand ground against my clenched fists.

If I could rip him apart with my bare hands I would do it. He'd taken everything. And now he had the audacity to think he would take Zeke away from me too?

I didn't think so.

He raised his eyebrows. "What are you babbling about?"

Zeke lay unmoving in the surf, his position eerily similar to the night we met and I had dragged him to safety. I had to figure out how to disable Stanley and get Zeke away from the pull of the tide. My heart thundered in my chest, pounding so hard, it boomed against my ribcage.

"Where's your mother?"

"Why'd you kill Grammy and Grampy?" I countered. No way was I giving up Mama. He was going to be pissed when he figured out that we'd lied and that she wasn't meeting us here.

Zeke thought this man was a sleeper. Part of a larger conspiracy to eliminate survivors of World War II who had potentially posed a threat to foreign relations if it were ever revealed they were alive and well and living in the U.S.

"That's not important." He dismissed the most significant night of my life with a flick of his hand.

"Are you serious?" I kept my eye on the stun gun but I was pretty sure he wouldn't use it on me until he found out where my mother was.

"It was just a job," he said.

A preternatural calm descended over me as he casually dismissed my pain, my mother's pain, and the last thirteen years of running, hiding.

"A job."

Frankly, I thought he could sense that I wasn't afraid of him anymore. I was more afraid of losing Zeke. But I processed his unemotional admission. A job. So Zeke had been right.

And somehow John Stanley was wrapped up in Zeke's problems.

"Who hired you?"

He jerked back as if I'd shot him. "What?"

Right here, this was the information that Zeke needed. Who hired John Stanley?

"You heard me."

He tilted his head to the right, his hair unkempt, more than a few days scraggly stubble on his face obscured his chin and heavier cheeks. The years had not been kind to him. He looked…old and slightly defeated. His bushy eyebrows lowered over his angry eyes. "What the hell difference does it make?"

I demanded flatly, "Who was the job for?"

"Classified." He shot back.

"Huh, too bad."

"Why do you care anyway?"

"You're kidding. Right?" I could feel my temper beginning to boil again. "You killed my grandparents!" I shouted.

"They were a threat to national security," he said, absolutely serious.

"Really?" I said derisively. "You never questioned that? My Grampy was an insurance salesman. My Grammy made prize winning strawberry jam for the state fair. They were hardly security threats."

"Enough of this." He ignored my sarcasm. "Where is your mother?"

The fear that had been part of my life for literally years melted away in a moment of extreme clarity. This was always about my mother. "You didn't kill them because of national security. You wanted them away from her."

He flushed. "It was a job."

"They didn't like you." I twisted that knife just a little harder.

"I was never good enough in their eyes," he snarled.

"Because you weren't good enough, *John*." I pulled my memories of those arguments between my mother and grandparents to the forefront, heated whispers and angry accusations. My grandparents had been against their marriage from the start. "You are never going to be as good as my father."

He gave a bark of laughter. "Ha. But who's in the ground and who's standing here?" John jabbed his thumb at his barrel chest. "I'm still standing. Once he was out of the way, I was good enough for her."

My heart stopped.

There was something there. Something in those words that made me want to turn away. Made me want to run.

Because there was a sort of secret glee. As if…he'd had something to do with my father's death.

And then he did it. He shattered what was left of my childhood memories. "Your precious father was no match for me."

"You—"

"Opened the playing field for my seduction."

My knees weakened. "You killed my father?"

He smirked as if pleased he could finally reveal his secret.

And my rage imploded, like well-set C4 designed to decimate a building, all the frustration over everything that had been done to my family, all the heartache we'd endured, the loss we'd suffered coalesced into an incandescent rage.

I threw the sand in his face.

He howled and dropped the Taser.

Then I launched myself at him. My arms swung and my legs kicked at any spot on his body I could reach, I angled my palm and slammed the heel toward his face. I connected with nose and heard the satisfying crunch as the cartilage broke. Blood gushed. "Ouch, you bitch."

He curled his fingers around my shoulders so hard that his fingers dug into the soft tissue on pressure points and rendered my arms useless. I jerked my knee up into his groin, and connected hard with his balls.

He moaned and dropped to his knees, then I jammed my knee into the underside of his jaw. I must have hit the exact right spot because his eyes rolled back in his head and he toppled over onto the sand unconscious.

I needed to restrain him. We'd planned ahead for this. I dug through Zeke's back pocket until I pulled the bungee cord out in triumph.

I shook it at the sky. Luckily John had fallen with his

right arm behind him and I quickly pressed his left arm together with his right. Then I wrapped the thick elastic band tightly around his wrists in a figure eight until there was only enough give to secure the metal hooks.

I hoped his fucking hands fell off.

By the time I finished I was sweating from a combination of fear and thrill of conquering my nemesis. In my mind, John Stanley had been ten feet tall and invincible. But I had taken him down. The adrenaline that fueled my attack on him zoomed through me and my hands shook with the aftermath of the chemical dump.

My brain was working at warp speed. I couldn't even process his confession. He'd killed my father. Targeted my mother.

I watched as the water tickled my toes. Too amped up to freak out. Right now I was superwoman. I could conquer anything.

A bigger wave rolled onto the sand, and kept coming until it covered Zeke's calves. I had to get him away from the water.

"Zeke." I knelt beside him and cupped his cheek in my palm. My knuckles were red and bruised from the attack. I couldn't help but lean down and brush my lips over Zeke's. He was cold, his lips beginning to turn blue. Another wave rolled toward me, but I was more worried about warming him up. I needed him awake so he could help me. I didn't know Lucas Goodman's phone number. It was embedded in Zeke's brain. Every time he'd used his phone he'd erased the history. So I needed Zeke awake to call Lucas and Jamie to come get John.

"Wake up."

I was also shoving some of Stanley's revelations to the

back of my mind. I needed time to process, to accept what he had done.

Then I had to decide if I was going to tell my mother. After all, she'd let this monster into our lives. I wasn't sure I wanted her to live with the guilt.

"I need you to wake up, babe."

I rolled him until I could get my arms underneath his armpits and partially lift him up. The water shushed in and helped me pull Zeke just a little farther away from the encroaching waves.

When the tide tugged on his feet I held strong. With a major inhale, I waited for the next incoming wave, I had to get him out of the path of the water. And I had to do it soon. With each inflow, I pulled him further up the beach.

The sand was cool against the back of my thighs and the breeze from the ocean was scented with brine. Usually that calmed me but I wanted to get Zeke out of danger. With the last tug I lost my balance and fell back on the sand. Zeke lay between my thighs, his torso spread me wide, and his head lolled against my breasts.

The position was similar to the first time we'd ended up on the sand. But then I'd only had an inkling of arousal. Now, even with John Stanley trussed up and unconscious several feet from us, my body tingled with awareness. As if I recognized him on some primordial level, my sex softened, my nipples hardened, and I had the urge to wrap him up in my arms and never let him go.

Cray-cray. I needed to get my head on straight. Zeke didn't need me mooning over him. He needed me to wake him up and get the heck out of here.

And frankly I needed him. I couldn't move John Stanley on my own.

Yet, I couldn't help myself. I lifted Zeke's head into my

lap. The chill of the ocean and his wet clothes seeped into the crotch of my shorts. I brushed the miniscule fuzz of his hair, the buzz cut tickled my palm even as I mourned the loss of his beautiful curls.

The new cut emphasized his high cheekbones and the dark ocean blue of his eyes and gave him a harder, more intense look. While he was out of it, I brushed a light kiss over his lips. His mouth was cool and wet beneath mine. But his breath was warm and even. "Wake up. I need you."

The next wave rolled up to us, slid along my calves and up to the back of my thighs. I held on tightly to him, not about to let the tide pull him back out.

"Back off, ocean. He's mine." I pressed my palm along the side of his face and brushed my thumb over his cheekbone. "Zeke, wake up."

Finally, his lashes fluttered open.

HE MUST BE DREAMING. Sunshine's voice whispered in his ear and her lips were warm and firm against his mouth. He swore she'd just said he was hers.

Damn, he liked that.

But she'd never been that soft with him. As if she were always on guard, always one step out the door, worrying about what could happen, imagining the worst case scenario and then planning for it.

Not to mention he must have just had a superior wipeout since he could feel the cold, wet sand beneath his legs and lower back. But the rest of him was surrounded by her sensual heat and the unique scent of sand and sea and cucumber that was Sunshine.

Zeke's eyes popped open just as she smoothed her palm

over his chest. Sunshine leaned over him, her hair askew, and her eyes concerned. He swore she'd just been kissing him. As he stared up at her, he had that disorientation again. That same feeling that struck him two days ago. That moment of recognition. *Oh there you are.*

A wave washed up and rolled over their legs cresting at his butt and then backing away.

Sunshine.

Shit. The last thing he remembered, they'd been standing on the sand and then he'd been hit with some serious voltage.

She was in trouble. He had to help her.

Zeke pushed up from the sand and nearly knocked his forehead on her chin. "You okay?"

She scrambled to her feet. "I'm fine." She tucked her hands behind her back.

Zeke finally noted her shorts were wet. The waves. She hadn't freaked. "You...the water."

"I know. But right now we need to call Jamie and Lucas so they can get John Stanley to the authorities without outing you." She gestured behind her and finally Zeke saw her nemesis laid out on the sand.

Even though Chen was in custody, Zeke hadn't been cleared. He hadn't heard a word. But he knew that Carson would want to talk to Stanley. "Okay. We follow the plan. Call Jamie and Lucas. John Stanley broke a million rules when he married your mother and then continued to chase after you for the last thirteen years."

"We just have to make sure he stays here and unconscious until they can come and take him away." Sunshine said, "We have to time it right so that you're gone before they get here."

Zeke stared at the man who'd made her life miserable. His gaze shot to hers. "You did this?"

"I did." She had a wide, pleased smile on her face. "But I wasn't able to get any information for you about who hired him."

"It's okay. Two problems down. One more to go." Zeke smiled. "Together we're invincible."

He had the goofiest urge to flex his biceps like an old cartoon character.

Her answering smile was soft, triumphant.

He'd enjoy the feeling of accomplishment later, when he wasn't still so fuzzy from the Taser. But then peripherally he noted the figure easing toward them. And suddenly everything fell into place. He couldn't believe that he hadn't seen the pattern sooner. He was fucked.

"Sunshine," Zeke whispered desperately. "Run."

CHAPTER 38

Zeke wouldn't have ever thought the traitor was someone he knew. Someone he'd put his faith in.

He tried to shove Sunshine away. "Run," he hissed again.

"What?"

"Actually, I'll need her to stay right there with you, Zeke." Assistant Director Armbruster stood ten feet away, his feet and legs spread in a combative stance. "How kind of you to all gather together for me."

Shit, shit, shit.

Sunshine's eyes widened. Her gray gaze reflected the murky sky above as she mouthed, "A.D.A.?"

Zeke dipped his chin but tried to keep his gaze centered on the man responsible for all his problems. And Zeke finally realized, there was no way for him to get out of this intact.

No one was going to believe a disgraced NSA hacker, who had allegedly given a top secret encryption program to a threat to national security, over one of the highest ranking directors in the organization.

"Let her go." He had to try even though he had no leverage and no weapon. It was tucked safely in Sunshine's purse, too far away for either of them to get to it.

"You should have left it alone." Armbruster held a weapon along the side of his leg. "If you'd just quit trying to find Chen we could have let it all go. In your own way it was your OCD that prompted this whole situation."

Sunshine propped her hands on her hips. "So you're the one who gave Susan Chen the encryption program?"

"Yes, my dear. Liam was an exceptional research scientist, but the man could not program to save his life. And keeping both the names and results of the experiment tightly controlled was imperative."

"You failed," she said derisively.

"I'm well aware," Armbruster said. "This has been one long series of problems, but if I eliminate our threat to national security here, and sadly you will be collateral damage, I should be able to clean up the whole mess."

Zeke was turning around all the information in his head. "You were the one who ordered the hits in 1995?" He started at the beginning.

"Yes."

"Why?" Zeke thought about his grandfather, who'd done nothing to harm anyone since he'd arrived in the United States in 1946. He'd put his head down, worked odd jobs, stayed off radar. Why would this man want him dead?

"It wasn't personal," Armbruster replied. "Something you probably didn't know, but my father was one of the code breakers picked up in the initial raid."

Of course, not all Germans were blond-haired and blue eyed, but Armbruster had a particularly Eastern European look. "Funny, you don't look German."

Zeke curled his fingers around Sunshine's hand, and she squeezed hard.

"My father was Russian. Working undercover at the castle. The Russians had infiltrated the German stronghold. They were only hours from taking the castle and getting the American and U.K. encryption codes when apparently TICOM found the castle first."

"What does that have to do with your father?"

"He didn't tell the Americans and Brits he was Russian. He pretended to be a German code breaker. And they bought it. He was relocated to the United States. But in 1995 if the Russians had discovered that their undercover operative had actually been debriefed and had willingly come to the U.S. and was still alive and well and living in the United States, it would have been disastrous for our country."

But that wasn't it. Zeke studied Armbruster. "What else?"

"Well, it's true it would have been disastrous for me personally too. Our entire family would have been handed over to the Russian government as a peace offering. I wasn't about to leave my cushy life in the U.S. for Mother Russia. They aren't as kind to traitors as we are here." He turned his hand over and studied his buffed fingernails.

"So you ordered the deaths that destroyed twelve families."

"But kept America safe." He enunciated quite nicely.

He was so full of shit.

Sunshine clenched her fists by her side. "Do you know how many lives you changed forever?"

"Again, the needs of the many outweigh the needs of the few." Armbruster smiled without an ounce of remorse.

Star Trek? Really?

"Did you know he killed my father?" Sunshine demanded waving her arm at her stepfather.

Shit, just what exactly had Zeke missed while unconscious?

"John?" At that Armbruster faltered. "Well, that was certainly a breach."

Sunshine looked mad enough to spit. "Yet it was okay for him to marry my mother?"

"He was a tad unstable. A replacement for the first sleeper who died of a heart attack. But he did the job he was assigned."

Zeke was still looking for patterns. Looking for sense in a situation that likely made no sense. "What made you choose the 5491 descendants for the experiment? It was you, right?"

"Here's the thing." Armbruster paced around. Sunshine jerked her head at the sand, but Zeke had no idea what she was trying to communicate. "Having all those descendants out there constituted loose threads. You all have very little left in the way of family. If the experiment wasn't a success then there would have been less questions."

And expedient for Armbruster as well. Those loose ends had probably been nagging at him for a long time.

"So you'd known Liam since boarding school."

"Very clever, Zeke." Armbruster said, "Yes. We met at The American School in England. Years ago. We both had a fondness for spy novels and what ifs. Imagine my surprise when Liam told me that he'd created a drug that would enhance our agents' capabilities. We could have had the strongest espionage force in the world."

Armbruster's eyes shone with a fanatical light. He really had believed in the experiment. Zeke couldn't wrap his head around the man's complete disregard for reality and for other human beings. This was the man who was the champion of the field agent.

But instead of yelling at him, Zeke tried to keep Armbruster talking. "But the experiment, the drug, didn't work."

"Liam desperately wanted the drug to work. He'd been looking to adapt the enhancement drug for cancer therapy. He wanted to keep going even after it was clear, from the unfortunate circumstances surrounding Brad Johnson's death, that the drug was not at the stage where we could use it in the field. Or anywhere for that matter."

"But Liam and Susan kept going anyway?"

"So bothersome." Armbruster brushed some sand from his jacket. "The experiment could not continue. But Liam wouldn't listen."

"So *you* shot Liam?"

"He was dying anyway." The cold-hearted statement might have been surprising since Armbruster and Liam had been friends since they were pre-teens. Except for the fact that Armbruster had ordered twelve people killed, collateral damage okay, including his own father. All to preserve his own way of life.

"It really is a shame that you had to keep digging. You're an exceptional employee." Then Armbruster got angry. "What the fuck made you keep going on this anyway? It all happened so long ago."

Zeke grinned at the irony. "That would be you."

"Me?" Armbruster sputtered. "But, you didn't even know it was me."

"Nope. But when you decided to use the 5491 descendants as guinea pigs for Liam's experiment, the drug triggered a higher level of pattern analysis in my brain. Even once I was given the antidote, I knew there was an underlying pattern, and with my OCD I just couldn't let it go."

"Balls," Armbruster muttered. "Well, we'd best get on with this."

Zeke wasn't ready to die yet. But he had no idea how they were going to get out of this. "So were you the one who allowed Oliver Krychef back into the country?"

"Ah, yes, Oliver. I'm hoping he will dispose of Ms. Chen." He grinned. "That will tie up that thread nice and neatly."

"You helped her escape?" Zeke raised his eyebrows.

"Quite right."

So Armbruster didn't know that Carson and Jamie had picked up both Chen and Krychef.

Sunshine fluttered her hands in front of her face. "I don't feel so good."

"Don't worry dear, it won't be for much longer."

She fell into a graceful faint, but as she was falling she shot Zeke a look of pure intent.

He dropped to his knees beside her. "Sunshine!"

Armbruster grumbled. "Just get her up. Story time is over."

While Armbruster's attention was fractured, she shoved the Taser toward Zeke. He could hear it powering up. "God, Sunshine. What's wrong? Are you okay?" he cried melodramatically, hoping his babbling would cover up the noise while the Taser juiced.

"I trust you," she mouthed. "Do it."

Armbruster scrambled over the sand toward them. He held his weapon like he knew how to use it. After all, he'd been a field agent at one point in his life. Zeke, on the other hand, spent most of his time at his computer.

"Get her up," Armbruster commanded as he trained the gun on Zeke.

"I'm surprised you don't have backup with you." Zeke commented as he lifted Sunshine to her feet, carefully keeping the Taser out of view. He shifted her body so that she was slightly behind him because there was an off chance that Armbruster would discharge his weapon when Zeke tased him.

"Let's go," Armbruster commanded gruffly. As soon as he waved the gun, Zeke pressed the button and jammed the Taser against Armbruster's neck.

Armbruster reflexively pulled the trigger. The double action revolver pumped out two bullets. The first one seared past Zeke's bicep. The second went wild.

The burn from the bullet grazing his skin hurt like a son of a bitch. But Zeke ignored it, his mission was to protect Sunshine.

Armbruster had dropped, unfortunately right on top of Sunshine. She hit the sand with an oof.

"Jesus. Are you okay?" Shit, what if he inadvertently caused her to get shot? "You aren't hit are you?"

"I'm fine." Her voice was muffled as Zeke helped her shove Armbruster's dead weight off her. "But we probably need to get him tied up before he regains consciousness."

"What are we going to use to restrain him?"

They'd already used the bungee on her stepfather. She tugged on her gray shirt to straighten it out.

"Aha!" Sunshine chortled.

"What?"

She quickly unhooked her bra and with clumsy moves pulled the straps out the bottom of one sleeve and then the other.

"Impressive." Zeke grinned.

"Ha!" She held up the pale pink elastic and cotton in triumph. Zeke laughed.

"You want to do the honors?" He gestured to Armbruster.

She quickly wrapped his wrists in a figure eight similar to the way she'd restrained her stepfather. Zeke's mouth quirked at her handiwork. "I like that use for your bra a lot better than the other one."

She snickered.

He bent over the man who had caused him and his family, and the rest of the people on the 5491 list great pain and resisted the urge to kick him. "He destroyed dozens of lives, altered our destinies, without a single shred of remorse for the way he fucked with us all."

Sunshine squatted beside Zeke. Her arm curled around his shoulders and her head rested in the crook of his neck as she looked down at the man personally responsible for ravaging her family.

"But not everything bad came from what he did," she said softly.

He didn't know how she could say that.

She trailed her fingers across the back of his neck and his skin tingled at the casual, intimate touch. Maybe she was right. There were definitely some good things that had ultimately come from Armbruster's actions.

"It's all over." The relief that zoomed through Zeke was overlaid with the bite of pain as warm blood ran down his arm. Adrenaline still pumped through him at warp speed, dulling the true pain and making him feel like he could jump tall buildings in a single bound. Or at least he could save the girl. Maybe even keep the girl.

He straightened and held out his uninjured arm.

Sunshine jumped up and gasped. "Oh my Goddess, you're bleeding!"

"It's just a graze." He grinned, ignoring the fact that it hurt like hell and blood was running down his arm.

"So tough?"

He cupped her jaw with his good hand. "You're okay?" He skimmed his hand over her searching for any injuries. Searching for any hurts he could make better.

"I…think so." She shifted her gaze out to the ocean. "Physically anyway."

Zeke curled her into his embrace. Her forehead rested against his jaw as they stared out at the waves. The water rushed up on to the shore. And Sunshine didn't even flinch. The cold seawater flooded around their ankles, and then scurried back out to the vast ocean.

"It's a lot to take in." She let out a gentle sigh of contentment. "A lot to look forward to."

She squeezed his torso.

Zeke bit back a groan as the pain from his wound was starting to make itself known. He'd live, but he was going to hurt like hell for a few days. The water rolled over their feet again. They needed to get out of the cold and make some phone calls. Get this trash cleaned up.

"You're going to be just fine, Sunshine Smith." Zeke held her jaw and pressed four sweet kisses on her lips. He was just about to dive in for one more earth shattering kiss—

"Hands in the air." The sound of multiple weapons being cocked sent a spear of ice through Zeke's heart. Thank God he hadn't told Sunshine how he felt about her.

Shit. This was it. He was going to disappear. Never to be seen again. Unless they could get Armbruster to confess again. Unless he could get someone to believe him over the far more powerful Armbruster.

"It's been a hell of a ride." He groaned and lifted his arms, his palms flat. "I'm cooperating."

"This is crap." Sunshine raised her hands above her shoulders.

"Honey, don't argue with them." Zeke warned her. "You're not in any trouble. They'll let you go once they figure that out."

Zeke was another story.

"I couldn't have said it better, dear."

Zeke turned slowly at his mentor's voice but kept his hands high.

"Uncle Carson!" Sunshine stomped her foot. "Fix this."

"Sunshine, keep your mouth shut. You don't want to bring any of my problems onto you." Zeke was desperate to protect her.

"Forget that." Sunshine said, "You were trying to help me."

Before he could argue with her, Carson said, "At ease, soldiers."

"We have so much to tell you," Sunshine continued. "Zeke didn't do anything wrong."

"I already know." Carson's bald head shone as the sun speared a single ray through the heavy clouds. He made his way toward Zeke and Sunshine.

"Good work, son." Then he pulled something from Zeke's collar.

"You bugged me?"

"Jamie did." Carson frowned. "When she made contact with you in the reptile room at the zoo."

"So you knew all along it was Director Armbruster?"

"No. But I was starting to have my suspicions." Carson

smiled. "Thank you for getting his confession. Pretty sure there's a cell at Guantanamo with his name on it."

The tide rolled toward them. The swell, much larger than the previous ones, ran over their feet but no one moved. Sunshine and Zeke still hadn't been given permission to move.

Then Sunshine yelled, "This is great and all, but he's *bleeding*." She stomped her foot again and the excess water splashed up onto Carson's pants.

Carson said, "You can lower your arms."

Sunshine and Zeke both dropped their arms.

Zeke wanted to groan at the ache but he didn't care about his arm. Joy bubbled through him. He curled his non-injured arm around her waist and yanked her against his body.

She'd just been hit by a small wave and hadn't even noticed.

"Oomph." She muttered against his lips. "Be careful."

"I'll be fine." Zeke kissed her. "Look at where you are."

Sunshine crabbed. "I'd rather a doctor look at your arm."

"I'll be okay." Zeke said, "I'm a survivor."

Sunshine nodded. "Thank you."

He had his freedom back. But suddenly, he didn't want freedom, he wanted something more. And he didn't want her thanks, he wanted her love.

CHAPTER 39

"Sunny!" Stella cried.

Oh my Goddess, my mother was here. "Mama, what are you doing here?"

"We got your message." Mama rushed to me and practically yanked me out of Zeke's arms as she smothered me in a tight embrace.

"You weren't supposed to call in from your new phone." All I could do was be thankful she was late.

"When I didn't hear from you I thought something had happened, so I checked the old number instead."

Blue came up behind my mother, his gaze taking in the cadre of soldiers on the beach, Uncle Carson and Zeke, and the bound bodies of both John Stanley and David Armbruster. He gave a clipped nod to Zeke. "It over?"

"Yes, sir."

"Good work." Blue held out his hand and pumped Zeke's hand vigorously.

Zeke deflected the praise. "It wasn't all me. Sunshine took down Stanley."

"Baby, what happened?"

"I'm sorry, Stella," Carson interrupted. "But you'll have to wait until we've gotten their official statements before Sunshine and Zeke can share their story."

"But—"

"I have to ask you to leave." Carson nodded at Blue. "This is a federal investigation."

Blue brushed a fatherly kiss over my forehead. "Text us when you're done and we'll meet you at the coffee shop in our hotel."

Mama protested for another few seconds, until I distracted her. "Is that a wedding band?"

She blushed, her face radiant. "I guess we have some stories too."

My mother had gotten married. Without me. I waited for the sadness, for the hurt that she didn't need me anymore. But it didn't come. In its place was a giant ray of pure joy. I hugged my mother tightly. "I'm so happy for you."

"Sorry, we didn't wait." Tears shimmered in her eyes.

"Mama. Now neither of us have to wait to start our lives."

WE SAT in the coffee shop just off Ghirardelli Square. I'd called Mama and Blue as soon as I was done giving my statement to Carson. Even though they had the whole confrontation recorded, they wanted my impressions and memories.

My impression: Armbruster was amoral and sociopathic. My memory: complete terror.

But I'd held it together. I'd rescued myself from John Stanley and helped Zeke take down Armbruster.

The adrenaline rush had long since worn off. I was exhausted and just wanted to crash somewhere. But I had to get through this conversation and give my mother the best wedding present in the world. Based on Carson's assurances, John Stanley was going to prison and wouldn't be getting out for a very long time, if ever.

After I gave her that news…I had no idea.

I'd been on the run, restricted for so long that the sudden freedom was terrifying instead of exhilarating. I didn't know what I was going to do with myself.

I blew on my herbal tea, so exhausted I could barely keep my eyes open.

"You okay?" Zeke's hand hovered over mine before he drew it back and thumped it back down on the table.

That was another thing. Ever since his spontaneous embrace on the beach, he hadn't touched me. I had tried to convince him he didn't need to come with me to meet Mama, but Zeke was sticking by my side.

And I wasn't sure what to do with his insistence that he stay. I wanted him to stay. But I wanted him to want to stay, not feel obligated.

I was a mess. "Fine."

Zeke just looked steadily at me.

"Even the cursed men in my family know that when a woman says it's fine, it's absolutely not fine." As if he couldn't bear not to touch me any longer, he pulled me onto his lap. "I think better when I'm touching you."

I'd address that later. Right now I was stuck on only one thing.

"You're cursed?" Mr. Science actually believed in a curse. I couldn't help it. I giggled. "Seriously?"

He rested his forehead on my shoulder curled his arms

around my waist. "I know it's stupid. We're not really cursed."

"But?"

"I am not so good with women."

"Do you want to be?"

"With one in particular, yes." As I sat on his lap, the boom of his heart reverberated against his chest and through my arm and shoulder.

Me. He meant *me*.

My heart thudded in time with Zeke's, both our bodies shaking. My lips lifted tremulously. I had dreamt of having choices for so long. I wasn't about to waste this chance. This choice. I could figure out what I was going to do with my life later. But I knew right now that whatever I did I wanted to do it with Zeke by my side. But still, it was a big step.

Especially for someone as relationship challenged as I was. So I fell back on science. The rules and regulations and laws that had gotten me through life up to this point.

"Ever heard of Hebb's Law?"

"You're talking science right now?" His mouth tipped up. And clearly he wasn't actually thinking about the actual law.

"Yep, Geek Boy."

He laughed hard. His happiness rumbled through him and wrapped around me, filling that dry well with an incandescent joy until I thought it would spill out of me.

"Got it." He brushed a curl of hair from my cheek.

"So what do you think?" My heart thudded painfully against my breastbone.

"I think I love you," he said against my lips.

Oh my Goddess. "I love you too." It was crazy and the least logical moment in my life. But somehow it was true.

His arms tightened around my waist. "Remind me about Hebb's Law."

"Neurons that fire together wire together." I let his heat, his love flow through me and back into him just like the law suggested. "What do you think?"

"Experiments are in order." He proceeded to wire us together.

Carson Black reclined on a lounge chair by the salt water pool at their private bungalow and surveyed the people around him. Not just people, his charges. His responsibilities. They represented his greatest regrets and his greatest accomplishments in all his years in the espionage business. And all the years in his life.

Antoinette perched next to his hip. Gorgeous and glowing in a sexy white bikini. He was so thankful that she'd accepted his need to take care of this group of people when she'd been so young.

Staci sat in the lounge chair next to him. Jordan sat behind her, legs stretched out while Staci rested between his thighs, and their entwined fingers rested gently on the rounded bulge of her very pregnant belly.

The leisurely sweep of Jordan's palm over her shoulder and the casual affection between them was a balm to Carson's soul. After everything they'd been through, they deserved happiness.

"How's work?" She had changed her focus and given up

her work with the CIA. Instead she'd moved into mostly humanitarian work. But she was still teaching.

Her next class was going to focus on Women's Rights and Organizations with a concentration in war torn countries.

"Great." She smiled and looked up at Jordan her eyes glowing. "I've tagged contacts from all over the world to be guest speakers, sharing their personal experiences about the trials and tribulations of living conditions for mothers and children and what they have to do to survive."

Jordan laced his fingers with hers. "Fariya would be thrilled."

Staci's eyes welled with tears. Carson knew she still harbored a great sadness for the woman who'd sacrificed her life so that Staci could live.

Carson tried to redirect the conversation. "You ever going to tell us if it's a boy or a girl?"

Jordan rumbled beside her. "We decided to be surprised about the baby's sex. But after the last sonogram, and another round of blood tests, the doc told us the *bebé* is healthy which is all that matters."

"I'm going to be a grandpa."

Staci laughed and glanced around the patio. "The kid's certainly going to have an eclectic family."

Carson marveled at their contentedness and thanked the stars that Jordan refused to give up on Staci.

Noise from the pool drew their attention.

Zeke had Sunshine perched on his shoulders, her feet tucked under his armpits, and one fist pumped in triumph after they won their game of chicken. And Jamie was sitting on Lucas's shoulders, her fingers gripped his hair as she laughed so hard she was bent over, eyes closed tightly, clearly trusting Lucas to hold on to her. He marveled at how open and relaxed and happy she was.

Sunshine fell back into the water, dipping below the surface, her hair a long black cloud around her body as she floated to the surface before flipping it away from her face. Zeke curved his arm around her shoulders and pressed a kiss to the side of her head.

Zeke pulled her out of the pool with one arm, and she launched into his arms. Sunshine rubbed her palm over his fuzzy head and whispered in his ear.

"Maybe Sunshine can take your class," Carson said as Zeke and Sunshine sauntered over to a lounge chair.

Sunshine had followed Zeke to D.C. Barb had written her letter of recommendation and was acting as her mentor. Sunshine was going to start her first semester at Johns Hopkins in two weeks. They'd found a house that was in between Crypto City and the university and moved in together.

"Sunshine could probably teach my class," Staci quipped.

Sunshine blushed.

"My girl is super smart." Zeke rubbed a towel over his buzzed head.

Sunshine snapped her towel at him. "Keep it up, Geek Boy."

"Watch it, Granola Girl," he snarked but the pure love shining from his eyes belied his teasing words.

Sunshine formed her thumbs and pointer fingers into a heart and flashed the silly symbol at him.

Jamie shoved out of the pool with Lucas right behind her. Not surprisingly, those two were the last to join their little circle. But she was here. And Carson was grateful.

Six months ago he could barely get her to go for coffee.

Remarkably, she and Lucas had stuck. Carson thought it was likely more due to Lucas's stubborn refusal to leave but he could see the warm, soft affection in her eyes when she thought no one was looking. She loved him.

Lucas had moved his business to D.C. and insisted Jamie move in with him. They'd rented Jordan's unit in Alexandria next to Staci's rowhouse.

"Who's up for Mexican?" Jamie asked.

After a chorus of "We're ins," Jamie whispered in Lucas's ear. By the grin on Lucas's face, Carson had a feeling they were going to disappear for a few minutes before they went and got the food. She slithered against his body until they were flush together, not a sliver of sunlight between them.

They were still waiting on Bella and Johnny. And Kat was coming over with her son. But right now, he was content. A feeling of pride and accomplishment swelled over him.

They'd made it.

He threaded his fingers through Antoinette's and lifted her hand to his lips. He brushed a grateful kiss over her knuckles.

She turned her head and smiled at him, her hazel eyes sparkling with the same gratitude. These were his children. Maybe not by birth, but he'd looked out for them, guided them, and tried to mentor them for the past thirteen years. By virtue of his slavish need to follow orders without questioning, he'd inadvertently changed the course of their lives. Of his own life. And then last year, he'd almost lost all of them.

Antoinette's lips curved as if she knew exactly what he was thinking.

"Time for a toast." Antoinette's voice was husky. She

poured champagne into plastic flutes and handed them around to everyone but Staci who got orange juice.

"To Carson," Zeke yelled.

Antoinette murmured, "My hero."

"To the new Assistant Director." Staci raised her paper cup of orange juice.

David Armbruster was awaiting a military tribunal for his role in the deaths that changed their lives. Carson was thankful they'd been successful in discovering Armbruster's treachery and stopping him before he destroyed even more lives.

He glanced around the patio. But they'd made it through, he'd protected his charges and they'd come out on the other side with their own brand of happiness.

The secrets of the past, from World War II through to today, had shaped their futures. His files on those dark days could be closed and stamped cleared.

Carson cheered right along with them.

No more cold secrets. No more hot lies.

They'd all gotten their happy ever after.

WANT to read about Barb's adventures? Dangerous Game is now available!

Thank you for reading Burned! If you like these characters, and the story world, as much as I do, I would appreciate it if you would help others enjoy this book too. Here are some suggestions.

Good: Lend the book to a friend

Better: Recommend the book to your friends

Best: Leave a review at Amazon, BN, Goodreads, Kobo, Apple, Google...basically any place they sell or review eBooks. Every review helps my work get out to other readers and I cannot even express how much it means to me when you let people know you liked my work. Readers have so many choices nowadays and limited dollars to spend. It can be difficult to take a chance on a new author even if the premise sounds appealing. By reviewing books, you give other readers insight into the story world and help them make informed purchases.

Thank you, thank you, thank you for your support!!

p.s. Would you like to know when my next book is available? You can sign up for my new release email list/newsletter at Lisa's Confidants

ACKNOWLEDGMENTS

You'd think with every book written things would get easier, but that isn't always the case. Zeke and Sunshine gave me some fits along the way and took way longer to tell their story than I would have liked. When Zeke first appeared on the page in Blowback I fell in love with this guy, and I was thrilled when it turned out that Sunshine was the perfect girl for him.

Thank you to my editor Megan McKeever for steering me in exactly the right direction and for loving these characters as much as I do.

Huge thank you to Kim Killion and Jennifer at The Killion Group Inc. for cover designs, Facebook banners, formatting, and overall design advice!

Thanks to my super critique partners, Adrienne Bell and LGC Smith, for quick turnaround reads and helping me make the book stronger and our weekly Panera coffee klatch, er, writing dates.

And finally, a gazillion hugs and kisses to Cecilia Gray for our hotel writing marathons with lots and lots of room service.

I've been in love with the same guy for five years.

Unfortunately, he found someone else. At first I was…upset. But once I observed Lucas Goodman with his new friend—yeah, you couldn't really call Jamie Hunt a girl, more like a badass—I knew my chances were over.

Every time I was in their presence, I felt the loss of our relationship keenly. Sexual tension and sheer attraction vibrated between Lucas and Jamie like a nearly visible arc.

They fit. In a way Lucas and I never had.

I've been lucky. I traveled for my job. A lot. I've seen many places in the world. I dined in five-star restaurants and slumbered in five-star hotels. I have my own French-style country villa with a few acres of wine grapes for a backyard.

My job was fascinating. My friends plentiful. My options varied.

And I was bored out of my mind. At thirty-four years old, lately I found I was a little lost. I'd really like someone to share an adventure with me.

That was how I found myself standing in line at the

South Korean Ambassador's residence in Washington, DC on a blind date. Set up by none other than my former lover, Lucas, and his, umm, badass girlfriend, friend, whatever.

At least, I thought it was a date. With Lucas and Jamie I could never tell. It was possible they needed my help on some top-secret super-spy experiment.

Except, who was I kidding? They might involve me if there was some scientific analysis or even a situation that required rudimentary medical knowledge, but I hardly thought my date was going to need me for anything other than, well, a date.

Ken Park, the date, smiled blandly.

He was gorgeous. He had that strong Korean jawline, sculpted cheekbones with smooth and tight skin—that on someone like me would look fake or like I'd had serious work done—and a high forehead.

A thick hank of shiny black hair fell over his right eyebrow in a studied casualness, while the rest of his head was shaved and manscaped to perfection, all clean lines and military-precise sharp edges. I wasn't sure his mental acuity extended past looking good. Like he'd expended all his capacity gelling his hair into those sharp lines, his gaze held a bland vacancy. He seemed far too young for the amount of medals spanning his fairly broad chest.

He was not my type. At all.

I preferred men who looked like men.

A little scruffy and muscular. Yes, that made me shallow. And yeah, I was pretty sure he had some muscles underneath his military uniform—his shoulders were definitely wide, but his ass was smaller than mine.

For some indefinable reason, he rubbed me the wrong way, like a burr in the heel of a running shoe. I was uncomfortable in my skin. Itchy, twitchy. I didn't think he liked me much either.

Except, *except*, I was oddly attracted to him. Mental capacity aside, he emitted pheromones that made my body sit up and beg. My hormones were going haywire. We'd been mostly silent while we waited in the security line.

"So…Ken." What the hell did I say now. "How do you know Ja—" Shit, I almost messed up and said Jamie. "Janine?"

Did I mention that Lucas was dating a spy? He'd never come out and admitted it but I put two and two together and came up with sixty-four. Especially since she mentioned on the phone when she was setting me up that my date knew her as Janine.

His mouth quirked, and I thought maybe there was more under that pretty boy exterior than a sub-par IQ. "We used to date."

Seriously? I was on a date with one of Jamie Hunt's castoffs?

What the hell did I do in a former life to deserve this?

Okay. I needed to let that go. I was determined to relish this experience, if not my date.

Time to focus on the positives. I was going to an embassy party. I'd never been to a diplomatic event and one of the things I'd resolved to do this year was to try new adventures.

My life had become predictable and boring.

He leaned closer, and a shiver cascaded over my spine as he whispered in my ear, "How do you know Janine?" Was it my imagination or did he hesitate over Jamie's cover name?

A strange sort of heat shimmered over my skin as his lips brushed my ear. And a trickle—okay, a flood—of awareness invaded my senses. How could I be attracted to this guy?

"Ah, mutual friend."

He nodded and eased away from me. Suddenly I had the sense that he'd crowded my personal space on purpose, as if he had no intention of being dismissed. Which based on my interpretation of his intelligence didn't seem right.

But whatever I thought I'd seen lurking behind his open gaze disappeared and his face was once again that bland, vacuous mask.

"What brings you to DC?" he asked.

"A conference." Nothing he'd understand based on the way his eyes had glazed when I told him earlier that my specialty was molecular biology. And yet I couldn't shake the idea that he was playing me.

"How nice." But he clearly meant *how boring*.

He might be right on that one.

Ken glanced around, his gaze skimming the security at the entrance. And I couldn't say why, but I thought he was unhappy. "Everything okay?"

"Of course," he answered smoothly. But he was lying through his pretty white smile. His tension was visible in the very relaxed lines of his body. He wasn't happy right now. Somehow I seemed to be the only one who'd picked up on the disparity between his unperturbed posture and his internal tension.

He carefully assessed the guards stationed at the door. His attention lingered on the guard's gun.

"Mmm, don't think so."

He shrugged elegantly, a lift of his shoulder, nothing more. "I thought there would be more guards."

"With guns?"

He inclined his head but his attention was clearly not on me.

I shuddered. "I hate guns."

"They are necessary in a violent world," Ken replied carefully. Almost as if he were reciting a line rather than something he believed. "The Republic of Korea has many enemies."

True. "But what are the odds that those enemies would be here this afternoon?" I said tightly. I mean really. We were in Washington DC. He was military; clearly guns were a way of life for him. Likely he wore one as an extension of his dick rather than an instrument of defense.

A predatory look entered his eyes. "One must always be prepared for war."

Fortunately, I'd never seen the damage a gun could do up close. A ghost of foreboding shivered over my spine. "Give me a nice biological weapon any day."

"Ah, but the potential for disaster is much greater," Ken replied. "I would not have pegged you as quite so bloodthirsty."

Really, he'd actually tried to stereotype *me*?

This date was going downhill fast.

PERFECT. Ken Park mentally rolled his eyes. Who the hell had Jamie stuck him with? Barbara Williams seemed to be a cerebral snob and so absolutely not his type. She'd been so busy making assumptions that she completely missed his ability to do more than form a sentence. Which was irrelevant, and yet he was still pissed. He was tempted to dump her before they got to the receiving line. Unfortunately, he needed her.

Intellectually, Barb was a complete turnoff. Too bad his dick hadn't gotten the message. He thought she was *fine*. She was messing with his concentration and not in a good way.

DC was experiencing an unseasonably warm spring, and Barb had forgone an outer coat. With her coffee-and-cream skin exposed by the shimmering beaded dress, she had the perfect form for his dick to find some excitement.

The drape of her dress revealed the sinuous lines of her back and dipped low, drawing the attention to her absolutely gorgeous rounded ass.

And he needed to get his focus back where it belonged. On this mission. He'd been preparing his whole life for this opportunity. He couldn't blow it now because of a piece of ass, even if it was exquisite.

They finally made it to the entrance. The embassy party, being held at the ambassador's residence rather than the embassy on Massachusetts Avenue, was awfully light on guards. The alternate location was an unusual choice but it was also the reason he had gotten this opportunity tonight.

The lack of security would make his mission easier, fewer people to evade, and yet a subtle unease hovered. Why had Ambassador Choi chosen today to reduce his security staff?

The entrance portico was protected by a temporary canvas popup tent that would shield the entering guests from rain or drone surveillance.

"Invitation, *ju-seyo*," the guard said.

"Ken Park, the Franklin Group, former ROKA, and his companion for the evening." Ken executed a half bow and nod at the security detail and handed the guard the fifty-pound cream invitation engraved with his name and position and the ambassador's seal of The Republic of Korea.

Officially he worked for the lobbyist branch of the Franklin Group, a foreign policy think tank. His familiarity with US politics and South Korean military made him attractive as a lobbyist. After he'd resigned his Korean army commission several years ago, he moved back to the US. The South Koreans believed he was passing them information.

The US knew he was passing information to his birth country. In fact, they facilitated the passing. When he was in the ROK Army he'd passed information to the US.

"*Kamsahamnida.*" The guard welcomed them, and bowed low in the traditional gesture of respect. Ken outranked the soldier by several pay grades.

"Surrender your cell phones, *ju-seyo.*"

Ken had planned ahead for this. "Left them in our vehicle." No way was he letting embassy employees get a look at his cell, even if it was encrypted and the security detail shouldn't have enough time or expertise to break it.

The guard made a note on their invitation.

"Oh," Barb reached for it.

The guard frowned at her.

Jen-jang. Ken could not let her keep that invite. The micro-thin listening patch he'd affixed to the back cost an emperor's fortune. He needed that device to end up inside the ambassador's home office.

That had been the price of the intel he'd acquired for today's mission.

"Is it possible to keep the invitation?" Barb asked. He swore to God, she was practically batting her thick black lashes at the young sentry.

"Sorry, ma'am."

"Oh." She actually seemed disappointed.

"What did you want the invitation for?" Ken held her arm as he led her through the ornate two-story doors and into the foyer of the ambassador's home. Maybe he needed to reassess her. Was it possible she was a plant? He'd trusted Jamie. Perhaps he'd been wrong to do so.

"Memento."

Certainly not of this date, he thought derisively. "For what?"

"Scrapbook," Barb replied dryly. "Surely your mother kept little tokens to remind her of special events."

Yeah. When she was facilitating the escape of her family of five from Gwangju and evading the Korean army, she decided to carry a few party invites in their single suitcase. "She wasn't much for souvenirs."

"Why did Janice recommend me?" Barb blurted out.

"I needed a—" *decoy*, "—date."

She certainly was a stunning decoy. Ken skimmed his appreciative gaze over her assets. The glittering dress with bronze beading accented her lustrous mocha skin. Her short black hair, which he hated on women, feathered against her cheeks and arrowed to a full, luxurious mouth slicked with a shimmering bronze that matched her dress. Her striking deep brown eyes had a slightly exotic tilt and her eyelids sparkled with bronze shadow.

Everything about her screamed *sophistication*.

No one would be paying any attention to him; their focus would be on her. Perfect. Decoy.

Barb snorted, the gesture so absolutely inelegant that he was charmed. That certainly wasn't a scripted response. "I'd think a guy like you could get your own date."

"A guy like me?" He raised one eyebrow, as his mind worked feverishly.

Because clearly she wasn't an asset. And clearly she wasn't a spy. She spoke far too directly for either job. He'd halfway assumed that Jamie would set him up with someone to watch him.

Ken found her directness oddly…refreshing.

"Handsome," she sneered. Looks apparently weren't important to her since she was openly dismissing him. He'd used his pretty-boy face to excellent effect to distract his enemies and adversaries on more than one occasion.

"Muscular."

Now he knew she was lying. He purposely chose suits just a little too big in order to hide the fact that he was very physically fit. His muscles were camouflaged beneath the ill-fitting disguise. It was the Korean way to understate your attributes and conceal your strength from your opponent.

If anything he appeared slightly frail beneath the loose suit.

For whatever bizarre reason, her dismissal and obvious disdain stung.

He wanted to remove his coat, flex his muscles, show her just how muscular he really was, which was anathema to his normal habits. He liked it when people underestimated him.

Barb continued listing his attributes, except her tone indicated she considered them more negatives than positives.

So when she said "Well…." he couldn't resist taunting: "Hung?"

The need to unsettle her, to rattle her, was uncommon and unexpected. Trained operatives couldn't get him to break his cover personality. And she'd done it without even trying.

A flush worked over her face, and her brown eyes sparkled with temper, even as her gaze dropped instinctively to his crotch.

"I was going to say *connected*." Tension made her voice husky.

Now he knew she was thinking about his dick. Which

was far better than her thinking about why she was here with him. She definitely wasn't stupid.

He'd shown his hand by giving in to the desire to let her know that he was more than just a pretty face. Poor strategy on his part. Except he shouldn't need strategy with her, she was nothing more than a simple pawn on this op.

But, oh, was he going to pay Jamie Hunt back for this.

USA Today Bestselling Author Lisa Hughey started writing romance in the fourth grade. That particular story involved a prince and an engagement. Now, she writes about strong heroines who are perfectly capable of rescuing themselves and the heroes who love both their strength and their vulnerability. She pens romances of all types—suspense, paranormal, and contemporary—but at their heart, all her books celebrate the power of love.

She lives in Cape Ann Massachusetts with her fabulously supportive husband and one somewhat grumpy cat.

Beach walks, hiking, and traveling are her favorite ways to pass the time when she isn't plotting new ways to get her characters to fall in love.

Facebook
Instagram
Pinterest
Twitter
Bookbub
www.lisahughey.com
Lisa's Confidants

ALSO BY LISA HUGHEY

Black Cipher Files Romantic Suspense

The Encounter, A Prequel to Blowback

Blowback

Betrayals

Burned

Dangerous Game

**These books are also available in paperback

Black Cipher Files Box Set (includes Blowback, Betrayals, and Burned)

Snow Creek Christmas

Love on Main Street: A Snow Creek Christmas – 7 Author anthology

One Silent Night (from Love on Main Street)

Miracle on Main Street (standalone novella)

Family Stone Romantic Suspense

Stone Cold Heart, (Jess, Family Stone #1)

Carved in Stone (Connor, Family Stone #2)

Heart of Stone (Riley, Family Stone #3)

Still the One (Jack, Family Stone #4)

Jar of Hearts (Keisha & Shane, Family Stone #5)

Queen of Hearts (Shelley, Family Stone #6)

<u>Cold as Stone (John, Family Stone #7)</u>

<u>Family Stone Box Set (Stone Cold Heart, Carved in Stone, Heart of Stone, Still the One, & Jar of Hearts)</u>

<u>The Nostradamus Prophecies</u>

<u>View To A Kill #1</u>

Never Say Never #2

<u>ALIAS</u>

Stalked (ALIAS #1)

Hunted (ALIAS #2)

Vanished (ALIAS #3)

Saved (ALIAS #3.5)

Deceived (ALIAS #4)

<u>Billionaire Breakfast Club</u>

His Semi-Charmed Life (Camp Firefly Falls #11 and Billionaire Breakfast Club #0)

Everything He Wants (Billionaire Breakfast Club #1 The Jock)

Queen of His Daydreams (Camp Firefly Falls #23 and Billionaire Breakfast Club #1.5)

www.ingramcontent.com/pod-product-compliance
Lightning Source LLC
Chambersburg PA
CBHW032204180726
48284CB00001B/185